HAVANA BROWN

HAVANA BROWN

A Joe Erickson Mystery

Lynn-Steven Johanson

LEVEL
BEST BOOKS

First published by Level Best Books 2021

This novel is entirely a work of fiction. The names, characters and incidents portrayed in it are the work of the author's imagination. Any resemblance to actual persons, living or dead, events or localities is entirely coincidental.

Lynn-Steven Johanson asserts the moral right to be identified as the author of this work.

First edition

ISBN: 978-1-953789-58-7

Cover art by Jerry Fess

This book was professionally typeset on Reedsy.
Find out more at reedsy.com

Praise for HAVANA BROWN

"Homicide detective Joe Erickson returns, this time obsessive as ever when he is pitted against a serial killer as methodical as Dexter, and as cold as a winter breeze in Chicago. Fans of thrillers will feel Joe's every frustration and relish his small triumphs, but they won't deny author Lynn-Steven Johanson's talent. Havana Brown has twists and turns, crisp dialog, and introduces readers to a sinister, terrifying, and unforgettable killer." — Gabriel Valjan, Agatha- and Anthony-nominated author of *The Naming Game*

"A gripping, compelling, and fascinating read that pits a ruthless deviant against a dogged and astute detective. A dark, deep, and gritty page-turner." — Lida Sideris, author of a Southern California Mystery series

Chapter One

With his surgical cap in place, he began gloving up. The blue nitrile gloves were pulled onto each hand and over the wrist, and the resultant snap was a sound he had heard over and over again for years. That snap sent an auditory signal to his brain that associated it with the end of the preparation phase and the beginning of surgery.

Picking up the disposable scalpel, he removed the protective blade guard and positioned the scalpel between his first and second fingers and his thumb, the so-called "pencil grip." It was a technique employed by surgeons seeking to make the most accurate cuts.

Placing his left hand on the abdomen for balance, he positioned the number ten blade next to the skin and applied pressure. The scalpel easily broke through the skin exposing the yellow fat layer beneath. A minimal amount of blood appeared as he skillfully moved the scalpel horizontally in a straight line, making what would be a five-inch incision.

Repositioning the blade, he proceeded to make a precise four-inch cut in an acute thirty-degree angle down from the beginning of the horizontal incision. Once complete, he duplicated the incision on the other side. His next step involved lifting the skin and carefully removing any attached tissue underneath. Once completed, he made one final two and one-half inch cut across the bottom connecting the ends of the two vertical incisions. The section of skin had now been excised from the body.

The surgical procedure complete, he picked up the protective guard from the floor next to the brim of his hat and slid it back onto the blade with utmost care, knowing that scalpel cuts were second only to needle sticks as

1

sharps injuries to medical personnel. He couldn't afford a laceration that could expose him to her DNA or leave any trace evidence of his own behind. He had made that mistake once, and fortunately, he was able to clean up the evidence.

Reaching for the zip-top bag he'd brought with him, he lifted the specimen and placed it inside along with the scalpel and zipped it closed, leaving it next to his hat. His work nearly done, he walked to the nearby sink, washed the blood from his nitrile gloves, and dried them on a towel. He returned and pulled a McDonalds take-out bag from his pocket, unfolded it, and dropped the zip-top bag inside. Then he removed his surgeon's cap and placed it into the bag as well.

His final act was lifting her up and placing her onto the bed he had previously prepared by pulling down the sheets and comforter. He straightened her legs, moved her feet together, and placed her dangling arms at her sides. After pulling the bed's sheets and comforter over her nude body, he adjusted her head on the pillow so her lifeless eyes stared at the ceiling. Removing his nitrile gloves, he dropped them into the bag and neatly folded the top over twice. The logo on the bag triggered a memory that caused him to smile, and he softly sang the first few bars of "I'm Lovin' It."

Retrieving his fedora from the floor, he donned it, and with take-out bag in hand, he walked to the door, opened it with his handkerchief covered fingers and, after checking the hallway for potential witnesses, left the apartment complex by way of the stairs and disappeared into the night.

Chapter Two

When Melanie McAdams failed to show up for work on Monday, her co-workers became alarmed. She rarely missed work, always called in if she was sick, and was sitting at her desk each morning before anyone else showed up. After several calls to her cell phone went to voice mail, her supervisor, Patricia Boyle, also became concerned. She traveled to Melanie's apartment on the tree-lined area of North Cleveland Street in the Lincoln Park area and gained entrance to her building. She knocked on her door, but when there was no response, she contacted the building supervisor.

Paul Gonzalez was a short, overweight man in his mid-fifties with a pockmarked face and a jolly disposition. He could not get a response either so he checked the parking garage and found that her car was still there. Patricia explained that she feared Melanie may have experienced some medical emergency. But Gonzalez didn't feel comfortable unlocking her apartment. So, Patricia contacted the police and requested a wellness check.

Two uniformed officers, Edward Fuller and Carlos Saldana, arrived twenty minutes later. After some brief explanations, the four took the elevator up to the fourth floor to McAdams' apartment.

Once they arrived at her door, Saldana knocked but like other attempts, he got no response. Finally, Fuller told Gonzalez to unlock it, and Gonzalez pulled out his key ring, inserted the key, and unlocked the door.

"You'd better stay out here in the hall while we check," ordered Fuller.

Officer Fuller opened the door, and both officers drew their service weapons and entered the apartment. "Chicago P.D., Miss McAdams. Are

3

you here?" called Fuller. But there was no answer. "Chicago P.D., ma'am." An eerie stillness.

"Let's check the rooms," said Fuller who seemed to be in charge.

"Got it," replied Saldana. And the two men began moving to different rooms.

From the bathroom, Fuller yelled, "Clear."

From the kitchen, Saldana yelled, "Clear."

But at the bedroom doorway, Fuller froze. As Saldana was approaching, he turned toward him. "Got somethin'."

"What?"

The two men stepped into the bedroom and saw the pale face of Melanie McAdams. Only her head and neck were visible, the rest of her body covered by the bed's comforter. Fuller moved to the bed and placed three fingers on her neck to check for a pulse.

He looked at his partner and shook his head.

"Shit," muttered Saldana, looking down at her attractive face and assuming it was a drug overdose. "What a waste."

"Better call in the dicks."

The two officers emerged from the apartment with glum expressions. Patricia could read their faces. Saldana walked to the elevator.

"Was she there? Did you find her?" she asked, already anticipating bad news.

"I think we may have. We found the body of a young woman in there."

"Oh, no…" gasped Patricia, melting into tears.

Looking at Gonzalez, Fuller said, "You'd better take her downstairs. Do you have anywhere she can stay? She'll need to stick around for some questions."

"My office. She can stay there."

"Perfect."

Gonzalez put his arm around Patricia. "Come on." And he gently led her down the hall where Saldana was standing, holding the elevator doors open.

Saldana called in a suspicious death which brought in the medical examiner and two detectives, Joe Erickson and his partner, Sam Renaldo.

They had been detectives for over ten years and had been partners for a little over a year. The two men were polar opposites. Joe Erickson was thirty-nine, ruggedly handsome with intense dark brown eyes and dark hair with a few silver hairs beginning to show. At six feet tall, he was lean, like a distance runner. Sam Renaldo was forty-five, five-foot-ten, a little paunchy, and had a Fu Manchu mustache that could use some enhancement. While Joe was intuitive and creative in his assessment of things, Sam tended to diagnose things by facts and figures. They made a good team.

When Joe and Sam arrived, the Cook County Medical Examiner's van was already parked in front of the building. Two Chicago PD cruisers flanked the van. Uniformed officers had already secured the building and put up yellow tape. Joe and Sam made their way to the fourth floor and the apartment. Officer Fuller was manning the door.

"How ya doing, Ed?" asked Sam, more of a greeting than a question. "This some kind of an April Fool's joke?"

"I wish it was."

"How long's the ME been here," inquired Joe.

"Maybe ten minutes."

"Who is it?"

"Solitsky."

"Okay."

"Where's the d.b.?"

"Bedroom."

Kendra Solitsky was a no-nonsense, fifty-two-year-old medical examiner that Joe happened to like. He'd established a good working relationship with her over the years. He also knew her wife, Deborah Thomasino, an attorney with the Cook County State's Attorney's Office. Kendra was a large-boned woman with Eastern European features, reddish-brown hair, and a singular wit.

Joe was about to enter the apartment when Kendra met him as she came out of the door. She was wearing her white Tyvek coveralls and boot covers and carrying her equipment.

"Done already?" asked Joe.

"Don't let anyone in there," she said to Fuller.

"Right."

"Helluva way to start out the month. I'm calling in the evidence techs."

"What's up?" asked Joe.

"Come on. Walk with me."

"So, what do we have here?" asked Sam.

"A dead girl."

"I know that much."

She stopped by the elevator and unzipped her coveralls. "Melanie McAdams, age 32, appears to have died from a stab wound to the heart. Looks like it may have been a narrow blade entering left of the sternum between the third and fourth rib. Death came shortly thereafter. Whoever killed her had some medical training."

"What makes you say that?" asked Joe.

"She was found lying on the bed. The comforter and sheet had been drawn up to her neck. When I pulled them back, I found she was nude, and that's when I found the entrance wound. But when I pulled the comforter all the way back, I found something quite disturbing."

"And that was...?" prodded Sam.

"Let me show you. A picture's worth a thousand words as they say." Kendra pulled out her cell phone, poked at it a few times, and located a photo of the victim. "I don't know who this guy is but... " She held up the screen and showed them the image.

The image made Joe wince, and Sam turn his face away in disgust.

"Jesus Christ!" Sam blurted out.

"Well, I think we can rule Him out," stated Kendra.

"This perp..." began Joe.

"...is one sick son-of-a-bitch," finished Sam.

"I can't argue with that," said Kendra.

"I haven't seen anything like this before, have you?" asked Joe

"No."

"Never," agreed Sam.

"So, now you know why I called in the evidence techs. The moment I saw it, I covered her back up and got out of there."

"So, she wasn't just killed, she was mutilated," said Sam.

"The skin of her suprapubic region down to the urogenital region has been surgically removed post-mortem—"

"Surgically?" asked Joe.

"Rather skillfully, I might add. Whoever wielded the scalpel knew what he was doing."

"Scalpel?"

"Oh, yeah. A knife could never make cuts like those."

"So, we may be looking at what... a doctor, a medic...?"

"Someone in the medical field might be a good start."

"What about time of death?" asked Sam.

"I didn't get that far. The evidence techs will determine that."

The elevator doors opened and Officer Saldana stepped off. "The Boyle woman is downstairs in Gonzalez' office. Two other officers are outside keeping people away from the building entrances."

"Good," said Joe. "Monitor the hallway and make sure none of the residents leave. Tell them this is a crime scene and they have to stay in their apartments so we can interview them."

"Will do. Anything else?"

"Not right now." Saldana stepped away and walked down the hall toward Fuller.

"How soon you think you'll know something, Kendra?"

"Evidence techs will be here for some time. I'll know more when I can do the autopsy. You want to be there for it?"

"I do. Give me a call, you have my number," said Joe.

"I've got your number, all right," she quipped, causing Joe to snort a small chuckle. He pressed the button to the elevator and the doors opened.

"We'd better go interview her boss, " said Sam, as they stepped into the elevator.

"Okay. You do that, and I'll interview the super."

"Stick me with the weepy one."

"Hey, you're the one with all the empathy. You told me that yourself."

"Me and my big mouth."

They rode the elevator down to the ground floor where Kendra went out to her van and waited for the evidence technicians to arrive. They would spend most of the day gathering evidence and examining the body before releasing it to the Medical Examiner.

Joe interviewed Paul Gonzalez but got little helpful information. He described Melanie McAdams as quiet and polite. She had lived in her apartment for about three years, paid her rent on time, and had never complained to him about anything. As far as he was concerned, she was the perfect tenant.

Sam interviewed Patricia Boyle and collected very little information that would prove useful. Ms. Boyle reported Melanie was one of her best analysts. She was very professional, always on time, hardly ever missed work, and was well-liked by her colleagues. She said Melanie had been divorced for about eight years and her ex-husband lived on his family's ranch in Idaho. As far as her personal life, Melanie never talked about it. Boyle suggested speaking with her co-workers. She was good friends with Ann Meyer and suggested Meyer could probably provide some information about her social life.

While Sam was busy with Patricia Boyle, Joe went up the elevator to have a word with one of the two evidence techs who had arrived on the scene. He recognized Art Casey and Jerry Bristow.

"Hey, Joe. Caught this one, did ya?" said Bristow.

"Yeah. You got a time of death yet?"

" According to liver temp, sometime between midnight and two in the morning. But that's only a ballpark figure, you know?"

"Yeah. Thanks. Catch you later." And with that bit of information, Joe went back downstairs and met Sam. They began knocking on doors, but only one of the other tenants on Melanie's floor was at home. According to Gonzalez, they were young working professionals like Melanie and would not be back until after they got off work.

The one tenant who did answer the door was Alvin Cooperman, a tall, thin geeky man of thirty with horn-rimmed glasses and a serious case of unruly, dark hair. He told them he worked from home as a website designer. When asked if they could come in, he reluctantly agreed. The room was beyond neat-as-a-pin clean and smelled of a combination of pine disinfectant and Lysol. Clearly, they were in the apartment of a germaphobe. From his fidgety behavior, it was apparent he was uncomfortable having them there.

"You can sit there," he said, indicating a couch with a slipcover.

Joe and Sam sat down and Cooperman sat in an overstuffed chair across from them.

When asked if he knew Melanie McAdams, he said he didn't know any of his neighbors.

"So, you never bump into any of your neighbors?" asked Joe.

"No."

"How long you lived here?"

"Five, six years, maybe."

"And you've never seen any of the people who live on your floor?" asked Sam.

"Sometimes I see people, but I have no idea who they are. See, I don't especially like being around people, ya know? So, I never talk to them."

"You ever have anybody over? Like friends?"

"I don't have friends. So, no. I never have anybody over."

"What about girlfriends?"

"No."

"No girlfriends?"

"Look at me. Do I look like a good catch to you?"

"Well, I'm not a woman, so I really can't say."

"Take it from me. If you were a woman, you wouldn't be interested. Unless, of course, I had a million dollars, in which case you'd probably fuck my brains out."

"I'm afraid it would take more like three million if I was a woman," remarked Joe. "But I'm the picky type."

"Gee, thanks a lot."

After a few more questions, Sam handed him his card. "I think we're done here. Thank you for your time, Mr. Cooperman. If you do think of anything, please give me a call."

Both Joe and Sam rose from their seats on the couch and stepped to the door which Cooperman immediately opened for them. Before they could turn to say goodbye and offer him a handshake, he closed the door and turned the deadbolt.

"That was productive," Joe said with an incredulous laugh.

"Think he's a suspect? asked Sam with a smile. "What'd you think of all that disinfectant in there?"

"He's got germaphobia. He couldn't bear to touch another person for fear of getting contaminated. There's no way he could cut someone up. Now that we've left, I'll bet he's pulled off that couch's slipcover and begun washing it in a bleach solution."

"What about the other residents?"

"Tell you what, why don't we split this up. I'll go to her workplace and interview Ann Meyer and some of her colleagues. You stay here with the evidence techs and the M.E. Maybe you can knock on doors on the other floors and see if anyone's home. I'll meet you back here."

"Sounds good."

Two hours later, Joe returned. Outside the building, he saw a man standing with some bystanders and grousing about not being able to get back into the building. He was in his late thirties, thick-set, and wearing a tailored suit, tie, and Italian shoes. Joe walked over to him.

Showing his badge, he said, "Can I speak with you a moment? Alone."

Taken somewhat aback by Joe's request, the man complied and followed Joe to a private area of the sidewalk.

"I'm Detective Joe Erickson. And you are?"

"Roger Masterson. I live here. And I can't get into my building."

"I know. It's a crime scene."

"That's what they told me, but they wouldn't give me any details."

"I'm afraid there's been a homicide in your building."

"Homicide?" he said, his voice reduced to almost a whisper. "What happened?"

"A woman was killed."

"Oh, man."

"So, until the evidence technician releases the scene, no one goes in or out. What floor do you live on?"

"Second. It wasn't on my floor, was it?"

"Did you hear anything unusual last night? Strange noises, loud voices, anything out of the ordinary?"

"No, not really."

"Did you happen to notice a stranger inside the building? Anyone you haven't seen previously, between midnight and two o'clock this morning?"

"No, I didn't leave my apartment once I got home. I threw a frozen pizza in the oven, watched a little television. I was tired, so I went to bed at ten."

"Do you happen to know anyone by the name of Melanie McAdams?"

"Yeah. Why?"

"How well do you know her?"

"Just in passing, really. I'd run into her in the lobby or the elevator once in a while. You live here five years, you can't help but see a few of the tenants."

"But you know her name."

"She's good lookin'. You find out their names, you know?"

"Ever ask her out?"

"Well, once. She wasn't interested." He stopped for a moment and looked at Joe. "Are you saying she was the one that was murdered?"

"I didn't say it was her."

"And you didn't say it wasn't."

"Thanks for your time, Mr. Masterson."

Joe began walking away when Masterson asked, "When do you think I can get back to my apartment?"

"When the evidence technicians are finished."

"When's that going to be?"

Joe turned to him and said, "You ever go to a pub after work?"

"Sometimes."

"Might be a good choice today."

"That long, huh?"

"That long."

Joe and Masterson parted company, and Joe made his way to the entrance. He acknowledged the uniform, ducked under the yellow tape, and walked into the lobby hoping to find Sam. He pulled out his cell phone and was about to dial him when the elevator doors opened. Kendra Solitsky pushed forward a gurney with the body of Melanie McAdams wrapped in a white cloth and strapped in place. Sam followed her out of the elevator, and they walked down the hall, stopping when they met Joe.

"She's all mine now," Kendra sighed. "Casey released the body. I'll be doing the autopsy first thing in the morning."

"I'll be there," assured Joe.

"You better be."

"Have I ever stood you up?"

"Come to think of it, you haven't. But there's always a first time. I assume you won't be there," she said eyeing Sam.

"I hate autopsies."

"I know you do. By the way, I sent you two an email. It's a picture of the victim taken from a photo in her apartment. I figured you might find it useful."

"Thanks," replied Joe.

And with that, she wheeled the gurney down the hall and out the door to the Medical Examiner's van.

Joe looked over at Sam. "Did you find anyone at home?"

"Two people. One on the second floor and one on first. The one on first said he didn't know her. And the one on second said she knew her name and he'd run into her in the elevator a few times but that was about it. What about you?"

"Patricia Boyle called and let people at the office know Melanie had died. Her friend, Ann Meyer, was so distraught, she left work and went home. I got her address. She was in no shape to be interviewed, so we can call on her tomorrow. Her co-workers weren't much help."

"Great."

Joe pulled his notepad from the breast pocket of his blazer and referred to it. "Rita Smalley, along with the other five people I spoke with, said she was friendly but reserved, always very professional, and willing to help others. She was really efficient and got a lot of work done. Set an example for new people. But no one seemed to know anything about her outside the office."

"So, she didn't socialize with any of her co-workers?"

"Only an occasional drink after work."

"Great. A mystery woman."

"Hopefully, I'll know more tomorrow when we see her friend."

"Let's hope."

"You have any idea how much longer the team will be working in her apartment?"

"Since they released the body, I'd say they're winding down. Why?"

"I'm hungry."

"Yeah. So am I."

Three hours later, the evidence technicians had completed their work and were loading their equipment and samples into their vehicle. Once their job was done, they released the scene. Uniforms removed the crime scene tape to allow people free access to the building. Melanie McAdams' apartment was sealed and remained off-limits. Joe and Sam spoke briefly with Art Casey who had little to say but would be present at the autopsy tomorrow morning.

They drove back to the West Belmont Avenue Area 3 offices. The building was essentially a large, brown-brick box nearly devoid of windows, and it had functioned as Joe's workplace ever since he was promoted to detective. Housing all the detectives assigned to the 1st, 12th, 18th, 19th, 20th, and 24th Police Districts, Area 3 covered all the northern districts bordering Lake Michigan. Tonight, Joe and Sam would be putting in a little overtime, knocking on doors and seeking any information they could find on Melanie McAdams.

Chapter Three

Early that evening, Joe and Sam, along with Detectives Darius Mitchell and Linda Van Zant from the second shift, returned to Melanie McAdams' apartment complex and began canvassing door to door. The complex had twelve apartments on each of the four floors, and of the forty-four occupants, thirty-eight answered the door. Not a bad percentage. They asked them about Melanie McAdams and showed them her photo emailed by Kendra. The results were disappointing.

Most of the tenants didn't know her. Some said they recognized her and had spoken to her in the elevator or the lobby, but none actually knew her or had any meaningful interactions with her.

"Well, that was two hours with nothing to show for it," complained Sam.

"I wish I had a dollar for every time someone said, 'She kept to herself,'" said Van Zant.

"Or, 'I saw her around but I didn't know her.' I got that numerous times," added Mitchell.

"It's the city. People travel in their own little circles and no one knows their neighbors anymore. Not like it was where I grew up back in Iowa," noted Joe.

"Ah, the good ole days," razzed Sam. He turned to Mitchell and Van Zant, "I guess we're done here. Thanks." The two detectives left and went back to the Area 3 offices.

"Come on, Hawkeye," offered Sam, referring to Joe's Iowa roots. "I'll buy you a drink at Benny's."

Benny's Place was a bar frequented by Chicago's finest. An old establishment that had not been updated in years, it had a kind of neighborhood charm. The old wooden bar ran twenty feet down one side with stools in front and a mirror on the wall behind it. Booths lined one wall while tables and chairs filled the rest of the room.

On this particular evening, the patronage was sparse. When Joe and Sam came through the door, Mike Bridges noticed and waved them over. Mike was a homicide detective and a nineteen-year veteran of the force. He worked out of Detective Area 1, which covered districts adjacent to where Joe and Sam worked out of Area 3. He was a big man who once played linebacker for the University of Illinois. NFL scouts had him in their sights until a career-ending knee injury shattered his dreams of being drafted into the pros. He was sitting with three other cops at a table, all of whom Joe and Sam knew from spending time at the bar.

"Pull up a chair you guys," called Mike. And he scooted his chair over to make room for them. "Getting here kinda late, aren't ya?"

"Been working, not like some of you loafers, " kidded Joe.

"Hey," smiled Vince Murphy, "We got a working-class hero here, boys." Laughter.

"That's me," quipped Joe as he sat down.

Vince Murphy was a uniformed officer in the 18th District. He was a solidly built man around forty with thinning red hair and freckles. A divorced father of three girls, his social life centered around drinking at Benny's and attending Cubs games. At the table next to Vince sat Mitch Williams and Tony Edwards, both detective colleagues of Mike Bridges. Joe and Sam were on good terms with both of them, although Mitch could sometimes rub Joe the wrong way. He was young and cocky and had advanced through the ranks quicker than most because of his wife's political connections. But he was good at his job so most of his colleagues didn't hold it against him. Tony Edwards, on the other hand, had been on the job for a long time and was looking to retire and draw his pension next year. He was more of a listener than a talker, but when he did have something to say, it was worth noting. One of his most unique attributes was his photographic memory, something that often proved useful during investigations.

Lucy, the regular barmaid, came over to the table. "Hey, Sam. Whatcha gonna have?"

"A Bud and a shot of Jack."

She gave Joe a glance. "And Joe? A double scotch on the rocks, right?"

"You got it."

"Comin' right up."

"So, what're you doing working so late?" asked Vince.

"Bangin' on doors," replied Joe.

"Yeah? Shouldn't the second shift guys be handling that?"

"We caught a homicide on North Lincoln today," explained Sam. "Young woman found murdered in her apartment."

"Been trying to find anyone who could give us something to go on. But so far, nothing."

"Got a handle on the perp?" asked Mitch.

"Nada so far," Sam sighed. "She didn't reveal much to other people about her private life, so we've drawn a blank so far. But it's only the first day, so..."

"We're interviewing a close friend of hers from work tomorrow," said Joe. "She was so distraught when she heard the news, she left work and went home. I wasn't able to interview her today."

"Got an MO?" asked Vince.

"This is where it gets weird. The perp used a thin-bladed knife and ran it into her heart. Then he took a scalpel and precisely removed the skin from her genital area."

"For God's sake!" exclaimed Mike.

"That's pretty sick," said Vince who began peeling the label from his bottle of his beer.

"No shit," added Mitch.

"Why would somebody do something like that?" asked Sam.

"I'll tell you why," said Tony, speaking for the first time. "The guy was takin' a trophy."

" What the hell kind of a trophy is that?" questioned Sam.

"Maybe it's the only way he can get some," Mitch said in a boozy, half-

16

hearted attempt to be witty. No one laughed.

"Come on, Mitch." rebuked Joe. "It's not funny! A young woman is dead, and some asshole killed and mutilated her."

"Hey, I was just—"

"Being a jerk." Sam finished his sentence.

"Okay, okay. Ease up. I'm sorry. I should've kept that to myself."

"Yeah, you should of."

"Hey, you need another beer, Mitch?" Vince asked, in an attempt to cool things off. "I'll getcha another beer, okay?"

"No, I need to use the facilities." Mitch slid out of his chair and walked unsteadily back to the restroom.

Joe spoke up. "What the hell is with him, anyway?"

"He has trouble monitoring himself when he drinks too much," said Mike. "Besides, he and his old lady are having some issues, so you might want to cut him some slack. He's not in the best frame of mind right now."

"Sorry to hear that," said Sam.

"That what he gets for marrying a rich bitch," commented Vince.

"You know," said Tony, "the same kind of mutilation happened in the 1st about a year ago. I know because my cousin's a uniform there, and he told me about it. Some perp killed this woman and the mutilation sounds familiar."

"Are you kidding me?" Joe said.

"Shit… " muttered Sam.

"You might wanna check it out."

"Do you suppose there could be others?" Joe wondered.

"I sure as hell hope not. If there is—" began Mike who suddenly stopped and cleared his throat.

The conversation abruptly went silent when they noticed Lucy walking to their table with a tray of drinks.

"Gee, it sure got quiet over here all of a sudden,"

"Vince was talking about you again, Lucy," teased Sam.

"But it was mostly good," added Vince.

"Mostly?" she shot back. She set down Joe's scotch.

"I don't care what he said about you, Lucy," said Joe as he handed her a twenty. "You're a pretty good waitress."

"Thank you, Joe. You're a halfway decent guy, yourself. Be back with your change." Nobody got the best of Lucy when it came to witty repartee. She turned and walked behind the bar and began hitting keys on the cash register. After she left them with their change, they got back onto the subject of the crime.

"Who's your cousin?" Joe asked. "I want to speak with him."

"Jarvis Reed. He and his partner were first on the scene, so he can fill you in on the details. Good guy, works days." Pulling out a pen from his shirt pocket, he tore a page from his notebook, jotted down a phone number, and handed it to Joe. "You can reach him at home after his shift."

"Thanks, Tony."

Three hours and numerous drinks later, Joe, Vince, and Mitch were pretty hammered. Mike, Tony, and Sam had quit drinking an hour before so they would be legal to drive their buddies home. A couple of minutes before midnight they left.

Chapter Four

As Joe drove to the Office of the Cook County Medical Examiner the next morning, he was suffering from a pretty serious hangover, thanks to the significant amount of scotch he'd consumed the previous evening. His inner-self began lecturing him. *Idiot! Thirty-nine years old, and you should know better. These hangovers aren't lasting just one day anymore. They hang on two and three days now. Does that tell you something?*

He pulled his black Camaro into the parking lot. He walked to the imposing light tan building where all the county's dead are taken and autopsied when death is suspected to be a homicide, suicide, accident, or from sudden unexpected natural causes. With thirteen medical examiners on staff and a county of 5.2 million residents, the M.E.'s office was a busy place.

After checking in, he made his way through the corridors leading to Kendra Solitsky's office. As he turned the corner, he saw Art Casey, the evidence technician, a few paces ahead of him. Both obviously were headed for the same place. Art was not the most personable guy but he was a darned good crime scene investigator. He was about fifty, short, pudgy, and bald with a rim of dark hair buzzed close. His fleshy face featured a dimpled chin and a pug nose on which sat a pair of black-rimmed glasses.

Joe caught up to him. "How're you doing, Art?"

"Oh!" Art said in surprise as he turned to his right to see who it was. "Well, if it isn't Detective Erickson."

"Yeah."

"I guess you made it for the autopsy."

"I did."

When they entered Kendra's office, she was already dressed in scrubs and ready to go.

As they gowned up, Joe turned to Art.

"Say, have you run into any other homicides with the same kind of mutilation within the last year or so?"

"No, haven't seen anything like this before."

"Ah. If you do see something in the future, let me know, okay?"

"Of course."

"Did you uncover any unusual evidence at the scene yesterday?"

"She was a neat housekeeper, kept her carpets vacuumed and her floors swept, so we didn't wind up with a year's worth of dust and dirt to analyze. That's a good thing."

They stepped into the operating room for the dead, a facility with state-of-the-art equipment for forensic pathologists to work their magic on human remains.

Kendra and her assistant, Kenny Miller, were finalizing their preparations. Kenny was laying out the M.E.'s tools of the trade next to the autopsy table where Melanie McAdams' body was laid out. As he set down the electric bone saw, Joe winced knowing that this was not a day he would deal well with its high decibel sound. *God's punishment for drinking.*

Joe had witnessed many autopsies, and while they are not pleasant to watch, he could do it because he had learned to detach himself and think of it as a scientific procedure. Sam had trouble with the deconstruction part of it and only attended these post-mortems if it was absolutely necessary for him to do so.

The autopsy lasted two hours, but Joe didn't stick around for the dissection of the tissue samples. He never did. What he did find out from Kendra's examination was that Melanie was a healthy, thirty-two-year-old woman who had never given birth. She had not been raped. Her death was caused by a thin blade that passed between her third and fourth rib and into her heart, just as Kendra had told him earlier. From the angle of the entrance wound, the perpetrator was most likely right-handed.

When it was over, Joe removed his gown and walked out into the corridor. He found the nearest restroom, where he leaned over the sink to get a mouth full of water and swallowed three more Ibuprofen tablets he'd brought with him. They weren't helping much. *Damned hangovers!*

As he left the building, the warmth of the sun felt good on his face. He wished he could go home and sleep, but he needed to interview Ann Meyer. When he called her office, he found she had called in sick, so he drove back to the office and checked in with Sam.

"I didn't learn much we didn't already know. She wasn't raped and the perp was most likely right-handed. The stab wound to the heart was the cause of death."

"Wasn't raped. That surprises me a little. I would have expected that."

"I know. Maybe the guy's dysfunctional."

"Or maybe it's a woman."

"I don't think so. My gut's telling me it's a guy."

"Your gut again?"

"Yeah."

"You sure it isn't acid reflux?"

"Positive."

"If you say so. You get anything from Casey?"

"No. But he did say she was a neat housekeeper so the lab won't have to sift through a lot of extraneous junk. That's all he was willing to say. So, maybe the results will come back from the lab sooner."

"Right."

"Have they notified next of kin?"

"Yeah. Her parents live downstate in Effingham. They're driving up here."

"God," remarked Sam. "What a long, painful trip."

"We need to interview her friend, Ann Meyer. She called in sick today so she should be at home. Ready for a drive?"

They left the office and drove to Wrigleyville, a trendy area in the Lakeview neighborhood, not far from Wrigley Field. Fortunately, the Cubs were playing in San Francisco today so the area was quiet. Meyer lived in an apartment on Addison Street, and Sam found a parking place about a block away. They walked to the red brick apartment building and entered an outer lobby. Joe buzzed Apartment 2C and a male voice answered.

"Yes?"

"Chicago PD. We're here to speak with Ann Meyer."

They were buzzed in, and they took the stairs up to Apartment 2C. Nice place. One of those reclaimed buildings that had been renovated into apartments in the eighties. Joe figured it took some cash to afford to live here. He knocked on the door.

A man with a trimmed mustache and goatee who looked to be in his mid-thirties answered the door. Joe and Sam showed him their IDs. "Chicago PD, I'm Detective Joe Erickson, this is my partner Detective Sam Renaldo. Is Ann Meyer home?"

The man said, "She's here. Come in."

He opened the door and Joe and Sam stepped into the apartment. The living room looked professionally decorated in urban modern decor.

The man spoke, his manner exuding confidence. "I'm Darren Charles, Ann's partner. If you hold on, I'll get her for you."

"No need," came a voice emerging from the hallway. "I'm here." She was wearing a t-shirt, sweatpants, and a pair of flip-flops, and carrying a Lhasa Apso puppy in her arms. She wasn't wearing any makeup and her medium-length blonde hair looked hurriedly brushed back. Her eyes were pink and swollen.

"These two men are detectives from the police department," said Darren. Joe and Sam showed their IDs and introduced themselves.

"I knew someone from the police would be contacting me sooner or later."

"And why's that?" asked Sam.

"I was Melanie McAdams' best friend. Why don't you sit down?" she said, indicating the dining table.

"I'm going to work in the office. Call if you need anything." Darren turned and walked into the hall.

"Thanks, honey," Ann replied. The golden-haired puppy sat in her lap and she stroked it as she talked.

"Darren's an investment banker, and he can work from home. It's been a godsend having him here with me."

"I understand. When was the last time you saw or spoke to Melanie?" asked Joe.

"It was at work last Friday."

"I see. Did she say anything to you on Friday about what she may have planned, who she was going to see on the weekend?"

Ann paused, looked down, and began rubbing the puppy's ear as she tried to maintain her composure. "No. I hardly spoke to her at all. I was really busy because another girl called in sick and I had to cover for her."

Joe could see it wasn't going to take much for Ann to fall apart emotionally, so he tried to pose his questions as delicately as possible. "What can you tell us about Melanie? Everyone we've interviewed has told us she was personable but didn't reveal much about her personal life."

"I was really her only close friend. She had a lot of acquaintances but her friends were few in number. I didn't know any of them."

"How long have you known her?"

"We went to college together at Northwestern. And when I was looking to move from my previous job, she helped get me hired at the firm she works for."

"What can you tell us about her social life?" asked Sam.

"We'd go out to dinner, take in a movie occasionally. She liked foreign films."

"Did she have any particular man in her life? Boyfriend?"

"No. I don't think she ever did."

"Did she happen to be gay?"

"Oh, no. She definitely liked men."

Tears began to well up in her eyes as she began to speak. "Look, she was one of my friends, and I don't want to speak ill of her or anything. But you need to know she had led kind of a...secret life, and I'm afraid that it may have gotten her killed," she sputtered. The puppy looked up at her, seemingly sensing her distress, and it reached up and licked a tear from her cheek.

"Do you need a glass of water or anything?" asked Sam.

"No, I'll be all right." She gently pushed the fluffy pup back down into a seated position, pulled out a handkerchief, and dried her eyes.

"Do either of you recall the movie, *Looking for Mr. Goodbar*, the one with Diane Keaton? From the seventies?"

"Sorry, I'm afraid I haven't seen it," replied Sam.

It was like a light bulb going off in Joe's brain. *What a downer ending that movie had.* "Yeah. I have, but it's been a while. Are you saying she went to bars and picked up men for sex?"

"Uh-huh. It was like she had this second personality. That was her secret life. You'd never know she was like that if you met her. She was always proper and professional about everything. I only knew about it because she confided in me about it one time. I couldn't believe what I was hearing. Needless to say, I was shocked."

"Did you ever go out with her when she…?" Sam trailed off.

"Oh, god, no. I couldn't condone that sort of thing. I told her what she was doing was dangerous, but she shrugged it off. I guess that's how she… satisfied her needs."

"Everyone we've talked to said she kept to herself. Those were their words, 'kept to herself.' Do you know anything else she may have been involved in? Charities? Clubs? Working out at a gym?" probed Joe.

"She never talked about any of those things."

"Do you know any of the bars she may have frequented?"

"No."

"Given what you know about her, would they have been more upscale places?"

"Probably."

"Is there anything else you can tell us about her?" asked Sam.

"Well, her father is a minister."

The interview ended with Ann holding her puppy like a security blanket. They gave her their cards in case she could think of anything that could move the case forward. Joe and Sam walked down the stairs and had just stepped out of the building when they heard a voice behind them.

"Excuse me? Detectives?" They turned and saw Darren Charles walking toward them. He had a serious look on his face.

"Mr. Charles, can we help you?" asked Sam.

"Yes. I didn't want to say anything in front of Ann given what she's going through."

"Is this something about Melanie?"

"Yeah. I overheard what Ann told you about her and her so-called secret life."

"Go on," encouraged Joe as he pulled out his pen and notepad.

"I was in the bar at the Palmer House with one of my clients one evening when I saw Melanie. I'd only met her once, but I recognized her. She didn't see me because we were off in a corner. She sat at the bar and started talking with a guy I know. I could see it was getting pretty friendly and eventually they left together. A few days later I ran into him and asked about the woman I saw him with at the Palmer House. He told me they went back to her place and he got "the screwing of his life" as he put it. When he asked if he could call her, she said she never wanted to see him again. He wasn't ready for that kind of rejection. He got really bent out of shape about it."

"Did he get physical with her?" Joe inquired.

"No, I don't think so. He doesn't strike me as that kind of guy, but you never know."

"How long ago was this?" asked Sam.

"Oh… five, six months ago."

Sam pulled out his notepad and pen. "Do you have the guy's name?"

Darren sighed, "He's going to be pissed that I told you. He's married."

"If it helps find her killer, let him be pissed. We'll be discreet. His wife will never know we questioned him about it," Sam reassured him as he tossed Joe a wink.

"Unless we find out he did it and arrest him. Then his wife may wonder why he's late for dinner," added Joe.

"His name is Dan, Daniel Boggs."

"Address and phone number please?" prodded Sam.

Darren pulled out his cell phone and punched a few keys. "His work phone is 312-555-9121. His home address is 3125 Langston Drive in Evanston.

I'm sure he's not your guy, he's just a dumbass that can't keep his dick in his pants."

Joe and Sam wrote down the information. "How do you know him?" inquired Joe.

"His wife knows Ann. We met at one of her company's functions some years ago. We see them now and then."

"Where's he work?"

"Lakeview Bank and Trust downtown. Something to do with real estate loans."

"A suit," scoffed Sam under his breath. "Thanks." To Sam "suits" were synonymous with white-collar dudes who were too stingy with details and too quick to call their attorneys.

"I ... I hope you get the guy that did this," said Darren.

Joe looked up from his notepad and made eye contact with Darren. "Yeah, so do we."

Darren nodded and looked down at the sidewalk for a few seconds. Then he turned and walked back into the apartment building. Joe's eyes followed him as he walked away.

"What are you thinking?" asked Sam.

"He acts guilty."

"Guilty?"

"Yeah, I get the feeling she screwed him, too."

"What?"

"Maybe not recently, but I'll wager good money she did at some point."

Sam shook his head and smiled. Joe's intuition was a mystery to him, but he was more than often right than wrong.

Joe looked at Sam and said, "I think we should go downtown. I need to look into getting a mortgage."

"You gonna buy a place?"

"Hell, no."

Chapter Five

L akeview Bank and Trust was located on Wacker Drive in the heart of
the Loop. When Joe called and spoke with Daniel Boggs' secretary
to make sure he was available and identified himself as a police
detective, she put him on hold for a few moments. When she came back on
the line, her response was rather curt.

"He's rather busy, today. He'd prefer you make an appointment."

Her voice immediately turned Joe off.

"We're the police. We don't make appointments. We prefer to take people
into custody if they won't talk to us. Now, if that's what he wants, we can
do that."

"Suddenly, she became quite nervous. "No, no. That won't be necessary.
What time would you like to see him?"

"We're on our way downtown as we speak, so how's eleven o'clock?"

"Uh, I think I can move an appointment so he's available at that time," she
said, more than willing to accommodate him. "I'll let him know."

"That would be wonderful. I'll look forward to meeting you. What did
you say your name was?"

"It's Tracey."

"Thank you for your cooperation, Tracey. Goodbye."

Sam looked over at Joe and grinned. "So, she wanted us to make an
appointment?"

"Yeah."

"Jesus. Probably work us in next month, huh?"

"Probably. He's got 'such' a busy schedule."

Traffic was heavy, so it took twenty-five minutes to go the six-and-a-half miles. Entering the large lobby of Lakeview Bank and Trust, they walked to the receptionist's area and said they had an appointment with Daniel Boggs. The receptionist directed them to the sixth floor.

Six-twelve was a corner office. Seated at the receptionist's desk was a professional-looking woman dressed in a charcoal business suit. She was not how Joe imagined her. She looked to be around forty, attractive in a natural way, with blonde hair that fell down to her shoulders, and some tastefully chosen jewelry sans wedding ring. She rose from her chair as they entered and came around the side of her desk.

"Good morning, gentlemen. I'm Tracey, Mr. Boggs' secretary and receptionist."

"Good morning, Tracey," replied Joe, showing his ID. "I'm Detective Joe Erickson. I spoke to you on the phone."

"You certainly did," she acknowledged with a nervous smile.

"Detective Sam Renaldo," said Sam, holding up his ID.

"Gentlemen. If you'll excuse me, I'll tell Mr. Boggs you're here. He's expecting you." She turned and went through a door into an inner office. A moment later, she returned. "You may go in now." And with that, she returned to her desk and sat down.

In the back of his mind, Joe wondered why their presence made Tracey nervous. Her non-verbal communication screamed discomfort. They went through the door, closing it behind them. Daniel Boggs rose to greet them. His six-foot frame filled out an Armani suit and Gucci shoes, and a Stefano Ricci tie hung from his neck. Clearly, this guy made serious bucks.

His office, mostly mahogany and travertine with a touch of brass, exuded richness and warmth. A leather couch and matching chair sat next to a drapery-covered window, and two leather wingback visitor chairs were positioned in front of his desk.

"Come in, come in," he said confidently.

Joe and Sam showed their IDs and introduced themselves.

"I'm a little surprised about your request to see me. What can I do for you?"

"Can we sit down?" asked Sam.

"Oh, sure. Right over here," he said, directing them to the couch and chair by the window.

"We're investigating a homicide," revealed Joe.

"Oh, jeez. Nobody I know, I hope."

"Well, I'm afraid it is."

Boggs looked dumbfounded. Joe broke the silence. "We were told you knew Melanie McAdams."

He didn't speak, but the color disappeared from his face. After a few moments, he was able to get out, "Her?"

"Yeah."

"When?"

"So, you knew her?"

He looked sick. "Uh, sort of. Yeah."

"Could you explain what you mean by "sort of?"

"We met once."

"Under what circumstances?"

"I think I want to speak with my attorney."

"All right," said Sam. "That's your right."

"Does he sound like a suspect to you?" asked Joe.

"He does. Maybe we should place him under arrest."

"What?" asked Boggs.

"Or you could just tell us what happened right here, and if you're innocent, it won't go any further," said Joe.

"If you had nothing to do with it, what do you have to lose?" added Sam.

Silence lengthened as Boggs weighed his options. Beads of flop sweat burst forth on his Just For Men hairline. Seconds later, he inhaled deeply. "All right."

Another pause. "We're waiting," encouraged Joe.

"It's...well, it's embarrassing. Talking about it, I mean. Several months ago, I was at a hotel bar, and she sat down beside me. We started talking, and we hit it off, you know how it is, right? Well, things started heating up, and she asked if I wanted to go back to her place. I asked her, "Why don't we get a room here?" And she said she didn't want to do that. She'd prefer to go to her place."

"And?" pressed Sam.

" You want details?"

"Only a few. We don't want to assume you two were playing chess," clarified Joe.

"Okay. We screwed each other silly. For about two hours. Is that good enough?"

"I think that'll do."

"We heard you wanted to see her again and she told you to get lost. Kinda pissed you off, huh?" Sam contended.

"Where did you hear that?" At that point, Boggs started to get prickly.

"We hear things," replied Joe.

Then Boggs realized who he told about his encounter with Melanie and his face flushed. "That son-of-a-bitch!"

"Hey," warned Joe, "This is a murder investigation, not some parking violation we're talking about here. People are trying to help us and your name came up."

"Where were you two nights ago?" pressed Sam.

"Was that when Melanie was killed?

"Yeah."

"I was in Los Angeles at a conference. I just got back yesterday."

"And you can verify that?"

"What do you want? Names? Phone numbers? My airline tickets? Hotel receipt. I have those in my desk if you want to see them."

"Those will suffice," noted Joe.

Boggs stood up as did Joe and Sam. Boggs walked to his desk, pulled out a drawer, and removed the last two sections of his airline tickets and his hotel receipt. Then he walked back and handed them to Joe.

"I need these back for reimbursement purposes. I hope they prove I was nowhere near Chicago when Melanie was killed."

Joe looked at the tickets and receipt and then at Sam. "Says he was scheduled to land at LAX on Thursday and get back into O'Hare yesterday at 6:15. Hotel receipt matches the dates in question."

"Looks like you have an alibi, Mr. Boggs," stated Sam. "Unless, of course, you flew back to Chicago, killed her, and then flew back to LA."

"Are you kidding me?"

Joe paused, looked at him, and then looked at Sam. "I think he's telling the truth."

Sam looked at Boggs for a couple of seconds. "Then, we won't take up any more of your time, Mr. Boggs."

As they were walking to the door, Joe turned and directed one last question to Boggs. "Any last thing you remember before we leave?"

An indignant Boggs looked at them from in front of his desk and said, "Yeah. She was the best damned fuck I've ever had."

Joe locked eyes with him and let his contempt burn into him. "I'll be sure to tell her father." With that, the two detectives went out the door into the outer office. Upon seeing them, Tracey stood.

"I hope you had a productive visit," she offered, mostly out of protocol.

"Oh, we did," replied Joe. "I hope it wasn't too much of a bother rearranging his schedule. I appreciate your assistance with that."

She gave a little nervous laugh. "Oh, he wasn't pleased." In a low voice she confessed, "He can be 'difficult' sometimes."

"Really?" remarked Sam.

"I hope I didn't lean on you too hard during our phone call. I wasn't having a very good day being stuck in traffic the way we were. I could have been nicer."

"It's okay. I understand."

"Well, if and when I need a mortgage, you'll be the first person I'll call, Tracey."

She didn't know quite how to take that and couldn't figure out if Joe was being sincere or sarcastic. Joe read the look on her face and clarified, "I'm serious. I hope our paths cross again sometime."

"Oh. That…Well, that would be nice," she replied with a glint of hope in her eyes.

And with a nod of his head and a smile, Joe along with Sam left the office.

"What was that about," asked Sam.

"It doesn't hurt to flirt."

"Well, look at you. A poet and you don't know it."

"Besides, she could be an asset if that peckerhead ever enters the picture again. I felt kind of sorry for her. I'll bet he's a real joy to work for."

"He was a piece of work all right," grumbled Sam. "Too bad I couldn't have marched him out of here in cuffs."

Chapter Six

Michael Fleming walked into a spice shop on the Near North Side and breathed in the wonderful aroma that perfumed the air. Fleming was a charming, good-looking man of thirty-five, six feet tall with a full head of dark brown hair that had recently been styled. Looking about as he moved to the counter, his eyes met Ameera Massoud's, an attractive Lebanese woman in her mid-thirties.

"May I help you?" she asked in her native accent.

Shooting her a smile, Fleming said, "I hope so. Do you have alum?"

"Yes, we do. We have it in bulk. How much would you like?"

"Very good. My mother cans a lot of food, and she asked me if I could bring her some alum. She's not on the internet and doesn't have access to it in large amounts. So, I would guess half-a-pound would last her for a while."

"We can get that for you. One moment, please." She went through a door covered with hanging curtains and said something in Arabic. Returning, she smiled at Fleming. "He's getting it for you now."

Fleming noticed she was wearing a wedding band on her left ring finger. "Your husband?" he probed.

"My brother," she corrected him.

"Sorry, I saw your wedding ring so I naturally assumed..."

"No. My husband was killed many years ago in Lebanon. After that, my family and I came to America."

"I see. I'm sorry for your loss."

"Very kind. Thank you."

"You have a nice store. Now I know it's here, I'm going to have to come back," he smiled, turning on the charm.

"I hope you do," she smiled back.

"You mind if I look around?"

"Not at all."

He began walking around the store looking at all of the unique gifts and spices. Powders, leaves, and oils of all kinds, many he had never heard of on the shelves in bottles of all shapes and sizes.

A few moments later, a man in his late twenties pushed through the curtains with a plastic bag full of white powder. He laid it down on the counter and returned through the curtained opening.

"Your brother?" Fleming asked as he read the label marked, "Alum, 8 oz."

"Yes. He doesn't speak much," she noted as she punched keys on the cash register. "With tax, that is ten dollars and seventy-seven cents. Will that be cash or credit?"

"Cash," he replied, and he removed a twenty-dollar bill from a money clip and handed it to her.

"Your change is nine dollars and twenty-three cents. Thank you for coming in, sir."

"You're welcome." Their eyes met and he complimented her, "Like I said, you have a nice store. I'm sure I'll be seeing you again sometime." Then, he turned and left.

Out on the street, he hailed a cab that took him to a frame shop in Lincoln Park. He entered the business he had used numerous times in the past, where he was greeted by a young woman in her early twenties.

"Hi, I'm Jasmine. Can I help you with something?"

His eyes were drawn to the tiny jeweled stud in one of her nostrils. "Is Jason here?"

"He's not in today."

"Oh. I've always dealt with Jason."

"Well, I'm sure I can help you. What are you looking for?"

"Frames."

"Okay.

Fleming pulled a half-sheet of yellow-lined paper from his pocket and handed it to her. On it were written his specifications.

"As you can see, I need two frames made with regular glass, and I want that frame number. Can you help me with this?"

"I should be able to. Come over to the table here, and I'll go find those frames for you."

He sat on a stool next to the table. A few moments later, she returned. "I'm sorry, but that particular frame is out-of-stock."

"What do you mean "out-of-stock?""

"It means the company is no longer making it."

"What?"

"The company is no longer making that model of frame."

"That's not acceptable!" As he spoke, his voice grew increasingly agitated. "I have several of these frames on my wall and I need to match them. What am I supposed to do? Buy all new frames so I can make everything match?"

"Do they have to match? People mix and match frames all the time."

"Yes, they have to match! I can't mix and match these things. They have to be alike. Oh, god! This is terrible."

In an attempt to appease him and calm him down, Jasmine was able to think fast on her feet. Her bachelor's degree in communications was paying off. In a calming voice, she advised, "Look, there are other companies that make aluminum frames very much like what you want. We may be able to come very close to matching the style of that frame. In fact, we may find a company that has a product that matches it exactly."

"Well, I hope so."

"I'll tell you what. Jason will be in tomorrow, and he knows these companies and their products a lot better than I do. I'll speak to him about what you want, and he can look into it for you. Why don't I take your name and phone number–"

Interrupting. "I don't give out my phone number."

She was taken aback by his immediate, abrupt response, and it put her off-balance. She didn't know quite what to say and her involuntary reaction was "Oh."

Realizing what he said had come out rather brusque, he tried to compensate with his charm. After all, she was a likable girl, trying her best to do her job. "Sorry. I mean, you can tell Jason that Michael Fleming came in wanting additional frames. He knows who I am. I've bought numerous frames from him before. That's 'Fleming.' F-L-E-M-I-N-G. Michael. Tell him I'll be in to see him at this time tomorrow. You can give him that paper with the specifications on it if that's okay?"

"Yes, of course. Michael Fleming."

"That's right. My name is on the paper."

"Yes, I see it there. I'll speak to Jason first thing in the morning, Mr. Fleming."

"I'd appreciate it." He paused a moment and looked her in the eyes. "It's... Jasmine, right?"

"Yes, it is."

"Thank you, Jasmine. I hope you'll accept my apology for becoming upset. But this is something that means a lot to me."

"I think I understand. Apology accepted."

"I promise to be on my best behavior tomorrow." He gave her a little smile before he turned and left the building. Once outside, he hailed another cab and rode off into the mid-afternoon traffic.

That evening, Fleming went into his basement and retrieved a plastic gallon container from a storage cabinet. He placed it on a table along with a large wooden spoon, a scale, a bag of non-iodized salt, and the bag of alum. He filled the container with warm water and measured out ten ounces of salt and dumped it in the water. Then he measured out four ounces of alum and dumped it into the water. After adding the soda ash, he began stirring it with the spoon, thoroughly mixing the solution. It would be ready when he needed it.

The following day, he returned to the frame shop at the exact same time as the previous day. When he entered the store, he saw Jasmine who was wearing a black, low-cut top that showed some cleavage. He liked what he saw.

"Hi there," she said with a smile. "You're back."

"Yes. Is Jason here?"

"He is. Let me get him for you." She turned and his eyes followed her as she disappeared into the back of the store. A few moments later, Jason walked out. When he saw Fleming, he flashed a smile.

"Ah, Michael. Jasmine said you were in the store yesterday. She told me what you wanted, and I think I found what you're looking for."

"That would be wonderful."

"Come over to the table and I'll show you what I've found." Jason brought a catalog with him and they both sat on stools at the table. The catalog was opened to a bookmark and an asterisk was placed next to a frame he'd located.

"I found this frame right here. It's a different company but it looks to be very close if not the same as the one you've been getting. I called them, and they're sending enough material for me to build the two frames for you. I should have the material in three days if you'd like to stop in and approve it. I still have a short piece leftover in the back from your previous orders that we can use for comparison."

"That'll be fine. "

Jason ran his fingers through his salt and pepper beard. "Do you know how many more you may need? Will two be enough?"

"I may need more over time. It depends how much my collection grows."

"Must be some collection you have."

"It is," Fleming replied. "It is."

Chapter Seven

A month went by with no leads in the case. Joe and Sam along with their night shift counterparts had canvassed bars showing Melanie McAdams' photo, but no one remembered seeing her on the night of her death. In fact, only two bartenders remembered seeing her at all, and those were vague recollections such as, "Yeah, I kinda remember her." Not much help.

Then on Monday, a call came in about a homicide in Rogers Park, the 24th District, one of the most northern parts of the city. Detectives Jake Crawford and Kevin Dempsey, colleagues of Joe's and Sam's, took the call and arrived on scene. The victim, a white female named Maria Martinez, was found deceased, lying in her bed. The twenty-eight-year-old accountant was last seen alive on Saturday morning.

The medical examiner was Kendra Solitsky, and when she began examining the body, she immediately called Joe Erickson. When he picked up, she was strictly business.

"Joe, this is Kendra."

"Yeah." Before he could get another word out, she let loose the bad news.

"We've got another one."

"Another one? As in…"

"A mutilation homicide. This one is exactly the same as Melanie McAdams."

"Oh, shit." Joe rocked back in his chair. "Where are you?"

"Jarvis Avenue in Rogers Park."

"Nice area. Who caught it?

"Crawford and Dempsey. They just got here."

"They're good. Tell them about the previous case. I'll talk to them when they get back. Thanks for the call."

"I'd say, 'no problem' but I'd be lying. See ya." Then she ended the call.

Joe put down the phone, leaned back in his chair, and let out a long breath. "Oh, man," he said out loud. *Could this be a serial killer? No way it could be a copycat. No details have been released about the previous victim.*

Joe began a computer search of homicides committed in the last two years. Six-hundred-sixty-four last year and seven-hundred eighty-one the year before that. Concentrating on the previous year, he began filtering out types, first eliminating male victims, then Jane Does, followed by women over the age of forty, then removing all deaths by gunshots, and finally all non-white victims.

The final white female victims under the age of forty whose cause of death was other than gunshot wounds were 110. He then eliminated natural causes, drug overdoses, and trauma from accidents, and the number dropped to twenty-six. One by one he began looking into each case to determine cause of death. Seven were knife wounds. Noting the names and the case file numbers, he began the same search for two years previous. Nine deaths appeared in that population from knife wounds. Again, he jotted down names and file numbers.

When he completed his search of the last two years, he began a search of this year. Two hits, both of them in other Bureau Areas. Noting the names and case file numbers, he decided to give a call to a detective acquaintance who worked one of the cases. The homicide took place in the 6th District which was covered by Area 2. Joe remembered what Tony Edwards had told him about a similar homicide in Benny's a while back, and he had failed to follow up on it. Maybe Eddie Collins could shed some light on the death of a thirty-two-year-old woman who was found dead from a knife wound earlier this year. He called but Eddie was not at his desk, so he left a message.

The second hit was in 15th District covered by Area 4. He didn't know any detectives other than Mike Bridges at Area 4, so he decided to call the lead detective on the case, Andrew Macklin. He happened to be at his desk.

"Detective Macklin," he answered with his deep voice.

"This is Detective Joe Erickson out of Area 3."

"Yeah. What can I do for you?"

"I'm checking into a case you investigated earlier this year. A thirty-two-year-old stabbing victim by the name of Tammy Distefano. You recall that case?"

"Uh-huh. That one's still open. Why you asking?"

"You remember the nature of the stab wounds?" asked Joe.

"Yeah. Multiple stab wounds to the back and neck. She was attacked from behind."

Joe's jaw tightened in disappointment. "I see."

"Why you asking?"

"Following up on a series of attacks on women involving stabbing and mutilation. Possible repeat offender. But it sounds like your vic isn't a match."

"Sorry, I couldn't help you."

"Thanks. By the way, you know Mike Bridges?"

"Oh, sure. We go way back."

"Tell him hello for me."

"Yeah, will do."

The conversation ended. Joe continued making notes on case files from the previous two years and noting the names of the detectives who worked the cases. The majority of them took place in districts covered by Areas 1 and 3. Since he worked out of Area 3, he could pull the physical files for cases investigated by their own detectives. He hadn't been one of them or he would have remembered the crimes.

Sam came in, and Joe filled him in on the second homicide, what he was doing now, and what he had found so far. He needed Sam's help in narrowing down the victims that may have been killed and mutilated in the same way. Sam took the victims from two years ago while Joe started looking into the ones from last year. A few were eliminated because an arrest was made and the case was closed. But several remained unsolved.

"How many you have?" asked Joe.

"Three. And you?"

"Four."

"How many you got that were investigated by our guys?"

"Two."

"I got two. Let's go pull the files."

Half an hour later, they were back at their desks with the files on the murdered women. They contained police reports, witness interviews, reports by detectives, autopsy results, crime scene photographs, and extensive notes taken during the investigation.

The Deanna Frost homicide was from two years ago, and as Sam dug through the documentation on the investigation, he looked at one of the crime scene photographs and blurted out, "I'll be damned."

"What?" asked Joe.

"Look," he said as he passed the 8X10 photo to Joe.

"What's the autopsy report say?" asked Joe, his adrenalin beginning to pump.

"Uhhh…It says, 'the tissue of the suprapubic region down to the'—same thing!"

"Son-of-a-bitch!" exclaimed Joe as he hit his fist on his desk. "We've got another one. Who was the lead detective on that one?"

"Frank Edwards. He retired last year."

"Yeah. He and his wife moved to Florida ."

"We could talk to his partner."

"I guess."

"Now what?"

Joe took a few seconds to get hold of himself. "Let's look through these other files. See what we come up with. As they were looking through the next files, Joe suddenly cried out, "BINGO!"

"No shit?"

"Look here," Joe noted, pointing to the autopsy report. "Barbara Graham. Look. Same description. Jesus. That's three with a probable fourth one today.

The phone rang and Joe picked up. "Joe Erickson."

"Eddie Collins. Got your message."

"Thanks for the call back."

'What can I do for you?"

"You remember a homicide earlier this year. Name of Rebecca Woods? C.O.D. knife wound?"

"Yeah. My partner and I investigated that. Never found the perp."

"Was there any genital mutilation?"

"Yeah, there was."

"Did it appear "surgical" in nature?"

"Yeeeaaahhh." After a pause, he spoke. "Why you asking?"

"We caught a case just like that last month, and it looks like we caught another one today."

"Damn 'n shit." Collins reacted, his voice barely above a whisper. "You thinkin' we got us a serial killer?"

"It's pointing in that direction."

"What a sick motherfucker!"

"Keep this under your hat, okay. My partner and I have just started putting this together today. I need a favor."

"What is it?"

"Can you send over photocopies of the file?"

"Yeah, I can do that. I suppose you need 'em yesterday."

"It would help. "

"Gotcha. Well, keep me up-to-date on this."

"I will. Thanks, Eddie." The call ended. Joe looked at Sam.

"Another one, huh?" asked Sam.

"Yeah."

They looked through their last files. Sam's was a woman found under the L-train that was a rape-murder. It didn't match the MO But Joe's was another hit.

"Oh, my god!

"Another one?" sighed Sam.

"Yeah."

"How many does this make?"

"Six that we know of."

"Damn. How could this connection have not been made until now?"

"Different M.E.'s. Different detectives. Nobody noticed the matching MO's until now." Then Joe let out a breath. "Great."

"What have you got?"

"This one was Nicole Morrison. A thirty-four-year-old woman who lived in Lincoln Park. She was a website designer who worked out of her home. Found in her apartment on Monday by–God!–by her mother when she couldn't be reached by phone. Last seen on Saturday afternoon. Death took place sometime late Saturday evening or early Sunday morning."

Looking at Sam, Joe said, " Besides the mutilations, these killings have other things in common, have you noticed?"

"Like?" asked Sam.

"Check the date on the one you found. Was she killed on a Saturday night or Sunday morning?" asked Joe.

Sam looked at the file and the date. "Yeah, as a matter of fact, she was."

"So were the rest of them. Killed on Saturday or Sunday. Something else. They were all killed in their own apartments. What's that tell you?"

"They brought the guy home or let him in for some reason. It wasn't random. They knew him or had met him beforehand."

"Exactly. Let's go through these files in detail and create an MO for this guy."

Chapter Eight

Halfway through the next morning, Joe and Sam had compiled an MO for the perpetrator, something they could write up and present to the Detective Commander, Lieutenant Sal Vincenzo. He was the type of supervisor who wanted everything documented and laid out in front of him. A visual learner. "Show me, don't tell me."

Their compilation so far showed all the victims were white and in their thirties. All had good-paying jobs. Each was found with the same type of post-mortem mutilation caused by a sharp instrument. All were killed with a thin-blade knife wound to the heart, found in their own apartments, and placed in their beds after death. None had been raped. No prints or DNA evidence was found at any of the crime scenes that could lead to a suspect. According to the forensic reports, the only common elements found in each apartment were a few cat hairs. That in and of itself wasn't unusual except none of the victims owned a cat. All the hairs collected were brown in color.

Sam kicked back in his chair and looked at Joe. "You know something? I don't think I've ever seen a brown cat. I've seen every other color. Black, white, orange, gray. But not brown."

Joe thought for a moment. "Come to think of it, neither have I. Looks like I need to do some checking."

Sam said, "I hate cats. Give me a dog any day. They're happy to see you, come when they're called. You call a cat, and they look at you and think, "Screw you!"

Joe laughed. "It's people like you that caused the bubonic plague to spread throughout Europe during the Dark Ages, you know that?"

"Oh, bullshit!"

"Twenty bucks says it's true."

"You're on."

Joe knew he had just snatched twenty bucks from Sam because he was familiar with European history. During the early Dark Ages, there was a superstition that cats were in league with the devil, and for 300 years, Christians chose to exterminate cats. As a result, few predators were left to keep down the rat population, and the fleas on rats kept the plague spreading throughout Europe.

Joe thought about the cat hair evidence and decided to phone the Chicago Humane Society to see if someone there could put him in touch with an expert on cat breeds. He made the call and a young woman identifying herself as "Wendy" answered. He gave her his name and said he had a question about cat breeds.

"Are you looking for a companion?" she asked in a perky voice.

"No, I'm a police detective, and I'm looking for a murderer."

Silence. A long "Ohhhh," finally came out of her mouth.

"I'm calling to inquire about an expert who could assist me."

"So, you think the cat did it?" she answered with a little wise-ass chuckle.

Joe played along, amused by her wit. "We haven't made an arrest yet, but we have this Persian male under surveillance."

Wendy laughed.

"Actually, I need someone who can provide me with information about specific breeds." He explained what he wanted to know and asked if she knew of such an individual.

"Okay. Well, I think I have just the person for you. She's been a judge for cat shows all around the country."

"A judge for cat shows," repeated Joe. He'd never heard of such a thing. He imagined cats on leashes being paraded around the ring like the Westminster Dog Show on television. If people can show dogs, it stands to reason people can show cats as well. This investigation was opening up new worlds.

"Yeah. She probably knows every breed of cat there is or ever was."

"Sounds like the person I'm looking for."

"Hold on a second." Joe could hear her hitting keys on her computer keyboard. A moment later, "Ah! Here we go. Her name is Evelyn Stewart-Bruce. Her phone number is… Wait a minute. How do I know you're with the police?"

Hm. Good thinking, Wendy. "I'll tell you what, let me give you my office's phone number, and you can call, and they will transfer you to my extension. Just ask for Detective Joe Erickson. How's that?"

That seemed to satisfy her, and she agreed to call him back. He hung up and waited, and about a minute later, his phone rang. He picked up and answered, "Detective Erickson."

"You really are a cop!"

"I really am."

"So, I'll bet you'd like that phone number now, huh?"

"I'd appreciate it."

"It's 312-555-0509.

"Thank you, Wendy. And if I decide I want a furry friend, I'll give you a call."

"Okay-ay. I hope you catch your bad guy. You might try baiting him with some catnip," she giggled.

Joe rolled his eyes and hung up. If only it was that easy.

Jake Crawford and Kevin Dempsey were in that morning, and Joe and Sam cornered them about their investigation of the homicide they caught the day before. As it turned out, it fit the MO to a tee. And so far, they had found no witnesses in her Rogers Park apartment complex. The complex had surveillance cameras, but the system had been out of commission for months. The victim, Maria Martinez, was a thirty-three-year-old accountant who worked for a large firm located in the Loop.

Joe and Sam filled them in on the other victims and what they had discovered about the perpetrator's MO.

"So far, his victims have been white. Given your vic's name and the neighborhood, was she Hispanic?" asked Joe?

"No," replied Crawford. "Divorced but still using her husband's name. She was Polish. Don't ask me to pronounce her maiden name."

"It was Lukasiewicz," said Dempsey.

"Keep this on the Q-T," cautioned Sam. "We don't want the press getting hold of this and splashing "serial killer" all over the front page."

"We're still gathering info and haven't even brought this up to Vincenzo yet. We don't need him wondering why we haven't informed him about it," said Joe.

"Don't worry," assured Dempsey. "Nobody's gonna hear anything from us."

Joe, Sam, Dempsey, and Crawford agreed to share any leads they might get and any evidence that might come through forensics. Joe didn't mention the cat hair since he wanted to pursue that angle so he would know more before sharing anything.

A package arrived around eleven o'clock containing the file sent by Eddie Collins. Joe handed it to Sam to look over while he prepared to contact the cat judge. Joe called the number Wendy had given him, fully expecting his call would roll over to voicemail or wind up on an answering machine. To his surprise, a woman's voice with a velvety British accent answered. She identified herself as Evelyn Stewart-Bruce. He explained who he was and what he was seeking without revealing too much. Preferring to meet face-to-face rather than discussing the matter over the phone, she suggested they meet that afternoon at a coffee shop called The Black Dog, not far from the Area 3 offices on West Belmont. Joe was a little surprised she knew the area but quickly agreed. He didn't know what to expect given her voice over the phone. She could be a clone of Margaret Thatcher for all he knew.

In the meantime, Joe worked with Sam on the file they received from Eddie Collins. After adding the information to the data already collected from the other murders, Joe created a spreadsheet for Lt. Vincenzo to review. That way, he could see the list of crimes, the dates of the murders, locations, and evidence that linked them all together. They finished just in time for Joe to leave for his meeting at the Black Dog.

The coffee shop was within walking distance, and he decided to hoof it rather than drive. He remembered his bet with Sam, and did a search on his phone and found a link that discussed the killing of cats and the spread of bubonic plague. He emailed Sam the link. Smile.

Walking through the door to the coffee shop, he looked at his watch. A little early. Glancing about, he decided to order a large cappuccino.

"Whole or skim milk," asked the barista.

"Whole. I'll live dangerously, today."

From behind, the velvety voice he'd heard over the phone commented, "I respect a man who likes to take risks."

Joe turned to see a slender woman nearly his own height, smile, and say, "I'm Evelyn Stewart-Bruce." And she held out her hand.

"Joe Erickson," he said as he shook her hand. "Nice to meet you. How did you know it was me?"

"You have a rather distinctive voice."

"As do you."

"Ironic is it not? Finding ourselves meeting to discuss cats at an establishment called The Black Dog."

"I hadn't thought about it. I guess it is."

After Joe got his cappuccino, and Evelyn her chai tea, they found a table and sat down. Evelyn had a natural air of sophistication without exuding superiority.

She looked across the table. "You said you wanted to know about brown cats. I find that intriguing. May I be so forward as to ask more specifically what this is for?"

"Well, you may regret wanting to know more once I've explained it to you." Evelyn raised one eyebrow in response, but he continued. "Brown cat hairs have turned up at the scene of one of our homicide investigations, and we believe the suspect may have brought those hairs with him into the murder scene since the victim didn't own a cat."

"Dear me," Evelyn murmured with a slight hint of horror on her face.

"And I've never seen a brown cat. Neither has my partner. So, I could use your input."

She picked up her tea and paused. "So, am I correct in assuming the person you are looking for could be a cat owner?"

"Yeah. We have very little evidence in the case, so we need to pursue that angle," answered Joe.

"I see. Well, first of all, do you know if the hairs came from a cat with long hair or a short hair? That would narrow things down a bit."

Joe had not thought of this. He should have asked the pathologist about it before he set up this meeting. Now, he felt unprepared."Sorry, I don't know at this time. I'll have to find out."

"Well, then. If the hairs are from a short-haired variety, you are probably looking at a Burmese or a Havana Brown. Both come in chocolate brown and are quite beautiful, if I may say so. If the hairs are long, then they may have come from a Somali or an American Bobtail. Both have brown hair but are not entirely brown in color, so you could expect other colors mixed in. The same with an Ocicat. They have short hair but have dark brown spots. Again, you could expect other colors in addition to brown."

"I see," acknowledged Joe as he wrote these names down and added descriptions in his notebook.

"Now, I'm speaking about purebred cats, mind you. It's possible that the hairs from your crime scene may have come from an animal of mixed genetic heritage."

"Like one you'd get from a shelter?"

"Indeed."

"And how would I know what breed of cat these hairs came from? How could it be documented?"

"A DNA test, of course."

" A DNA test on cat hairs?"

"Absolutely. Purebred cats are genetically unique. Different breeds can be identified by their DNA. Hairs are also unique. The hairs of a Burmese will be distinctly different from the hairs of a Havana Brown despite the fact they may be both brown in color. They will look quite different under microscopic examination."

Intrigued by this revelation, Joe decided to probe further. "So, let me ask a hypothetical question here. Suppose I have a sample of cat hair from one scene, and I have a sample of cat hair from another scene. Different time, different place. Would it be possible to prove they came from the same cat?"

"A DNA test could prove that. Certainly."

"Well...you've been a wealth of information, uh...may I call you 'Evelyn'?"

"Only if I may call you 'Joe'."

"Please do."

He didn't even think about her being an attractive woman his own age, whether she was available, someone he might want to get to know. This didn't even register when he was in "cop-think," so focused on his work that nothing else mattered.

" Would you know who could conduct such a test? Surely, that's not something our forensic lab could do, is it?"

"I know that the Veterinary Genetics Laboratory at the University of California at Davis does that sort of thing. They could do it for you. Just offhand, I'm not aware of anyone else, although there could be others."

Joe was busy writing all this down. Evelyn took another sip of her tea as she watched him making notes.

"I'm afraid your coffee may be getting cold," she observed, brushing back her ash blonde hair with her fingers.

"My coffee is always getting cold. Drinking cold coffee comes with the territory."

"I suppose one gets used to all sorts of things in your line of work."

"You have no idea."

"Speaking of ideas," she began, "I have one for you. I believe I could do something that would prove beneficial to your investigation."

"Oh? What's that?"

"You let me know what kind of hair samples you have–short hair or long hair–and I will contact people I know who have those breeds of cats here in the city. And I will collect some hair samples for your lab to use for comparison purposes. How does that sound?"

All of a sudden, Joe's eyes lit up. He was very pleased to have someone volunteer to gather such valuable evidence. "You would do that?"

"If it would help you catch a killer, it's the least I could do."

"That is very generous. Thank you." Joe put down his pen, picked up his coffee cup, and took a drink. "Do you mind if I ask you a question?"

"That depends. Shall I take a risk?"

"I respect a woman who likes to take risks," he parroted back, a smile beginning to form in the corner of his mouth. "Do you own at cat?"

Apparently, she was a little surprised by the question. Perhaps, she was expecting something more on the personal level. Joe could read the surprise in her eyes. But she recovered immediately. "As a matter of fact, I am owned by two Russian Blues. Vanya and Sonia. You don't own them, you know; they own you. And what about you?"

"Me? No, I'm afraid I live alone."

"Pity."

Joe and Evelyn spoke for another half-hour and she explained that cat shows were nothing like the dog shows he had seen on television. She invited him to the International Cat Show to be held in the city that October. He told her he would take her up on her offer. Then Joe got a phone call from Sam.He gave her his card and as they left the shop, she promised she would have the hair samples for him in a week.

Joe walked back to the office. He thought about how his lieutenant would respond to a request to have a lab in California conduct DNA tests on cat hairs. He could feel the earth shake already.

Chapter Nine

J oe met Sam who was standing at his desk with the phone to his ear. The look on his face told Joe something was up.

"I was just about to call you. Vincenzo wants to see us ASAP."

That usually spelled trouble. Joe had worked for Vincenzo long enough to know when he wasn't happy about something. He grabbed the spreadsheet along with the accompanying papers from his desk, stuck them in a file folder, and they headed for Vincenzo's office.

Sam tapped on the door and a familiar voice from within said, "Come in." Vincenzo sat behind his desk, his stout, fifty-year-old frame leaning over a stack of paperwork. He took off his reading glasses and tossed them down on the desk.

"So... What have you two been working on that I don't know about?"

"I assume you've heard something?" Joe asked, sounding him out.

"Sit," was his only response. Joe began to explain.

"Well, we weren't going to present this to you until we had all the facts. But Sam and I got it pretty well put together today."

Joe opened the file folder and handed Vincenzo the spreadsheet and the supporting documentation. Then he explained what they had found during the last few days: six murdered women and a perp with the same MO. Vincenzo put on his glasses, read over the spreadsheet, and glanced at the supporting documents. After he finished, he breathed deeply, put the papers down on his desk, and removed his glasses, dangling them from his right hand.

"That's damned good work, you guys. Thanks for fucking up my life!"

Vincenzo was a good man to work for if he liked you and you did your job well. Joe had proven to be one of his best detectives and had a superior close rate. Sam was no slouch, either.

"So, we've got a god damned serial killer operating in our city, and I'd be willing to bet this butcher's killed more than six. I'll run this through ViCAP and see if I turn up anything else." He sighed and wheeled back in his chair. "I'm going to have to report this to the Exec. He's going to want to know how to handle this."

Joe informed him about the cat hair evidence and spoke about obtaining samples for comparison purposes. Vincenzo thought it was a good idea. Then Joe brought up how it was possible to run cat DNA to prove the hairs at the murder scenes came from the same cat.

"You've got to be kidding me! You want our lab to run DNA tests on cat hairs?"

"No, they can't do it," explained Joe. "Only the University of California at Davis can."

This revelation brought Vincenzo out of his chair. "No. No way am I going to suggest something like that. Maybe the D.A. could order those kinds of tests when we catch the perp, but–Jesus H. Christ, Erickson!–California? DNA? Go get your cat hairs. That's a start. And interview all the lead detectives on these cases. Looks like some are ours. See what you can turn up. Now, get out of here, both of you."

They were about to step through the door when Vincenzo ordered, "Tell Dempsey and Crawford to come in here."

Joe breathed a sigh of relief. Vincenzo's reaction to his DNA idea wasn't as bad as he thought it was going to be. At least the earth didn't shake under his feet. It was only a mild tremor. He'd experienced a lot worse working under him in the past.

As Joe and Sam were walking down the hall, Sam said, "You never told me you could run DNA on cat hair. When you find that out?"

"Today. Say, I sent you a message with a link as I was walking to meet the cat lady. Did you get it?"

Sam grumbled, pulled out his wallet, and handed Joe twenty bucks for proving the systematic killing of cats helped spread bubonic plague during the Dark Ages. "All right. You proved your point. Again."

Joe took the twenty. "You shouldn't bet with me. I thought you'd learned that by now."

Sam shoved his wallet back in his pocket and chose not to respond. He changed the subject and said he would find Dempsey and Crawford and tell them Vincenzo wanted to see them.

Joe went to his desk, called the crime lab, and spoke to Art Casey who collected evidence at the Melanie McAdams murder scene. Joe told him they found six similar crimes with the same MO, and they had slipped through the system without anyone sending up any red flags. Art explained that many pathologists perform autopsies. And if no pathologist saw two victims, no connection would have been made. Then Joe informed him about the presence of brown cat hairs at each of the six crime scenes.

"Can you conduct a comparison of hairs found at the crime scene with samples of hairs from different breeds of cats?" asked Joe.

"To narrow down the type of cat, you mean?" asked Art.

"Yes," replied Joe.

"We could only determine a consistency of hair type, not the breed. That would take a more sophisticated test than we can do."

"Can you clarify if the hairs belong to a short-haired or a long-haired cat?"

"I could do that."

"If you could let me know soon, I'd appreciate it. It involves a lead I'm pursuing."

"Tomorrow soon enough?"

"Thanks, Art, I owe you one."

"Yes, you do."

Hopefully, he could let Evelyn know the hair type tomorrow, and if she could get those samples to him quickly like she promised, he would have something to go on. She seemed willing and reliable. He hated waiting but it was a necessary part of his job. Waiting on witnesses, waiting for lab work, waiting for paperwork, waiting for this, waiting for that. Waiting. Maybe he should figure out an alternative plan so if she doesn't come through... He got up from his desk and walked to the coffee machine to get a cup to clear his mind. Too many things rattling around in there.

Back at his desk, Joe pulled up the spreadsheet on his computer. He copied the victims' names along with the names of lead detectives and pasted them into a separate file. From there, he would find contact information for those detectives who didn't work at Area 3. He would have to track down Frank Edwards who had retired to Florida. His partner, Nate Smith, died of a sudden heart attack last year. And he would need to arrange a more extensive interview with Eddie Collins. In addition, they would need to speak with Gary Nelson, who was lead on the Barbara Graham case, and Michelle Cardona, who was lead on the Nicole Morrison case. He didn't know Nelson personally, but he had worked a murder-suicide case with Cardona a couple of years ago. He'd seen Cardona and Nelson on the floor now and then so he knew they still worked out of Area 3.

Sam returned to his desk, and he and Joe agreed to split up the interviews. Since Joe knew Eddie Collins and Michelle Cardona personally, he would interview them. He would also take responsibility for tracking down Frank Edwards. Sam would take Kevin Dempsey as well as Gary Nelson, who he knew in passing.

Joe did some further research on who conducted the autopsies on the victims and found that a different forensic pathologist conducted each one. Given there are fifteen pathologists conducting autopsies at the Cook County Medical Examiner's Office, it was the luck of the draw that no pathologist got a second victim. No wonder no one recognized the pattern of mutilation and sent up a red flag.

Joe's cell phone vibrated and he answered, "Joe Erickson."

"Hi, Joe." It was Joe's dad calling from Marathon, Iowa, the place where his father lived and where Joe grew up. Immediately, Joe became concerned because his dad never called when he was working. In fact, he usually let Joe call him.

"Hi, Dad. Are you okay?"

"Yeah. Yeah, I just wanted to let you know I sold the '57 a few minutes ago."

"You sold your pride and joy?" Carl's pride and joy was a red and white 1957 Chevrolet Bel Air two-door hardtop he had restored to perfection.

"Why did you sell it?"

"It was time. Time for someone else to enjoy it. I don't drive it much anymore, and it's a shame for it to sit in the garage and gather dust."

"I hope you got a good price for it. Perfection shouldn't come cheap."

"Let me tell you, he paid through the nose for it. California guy. Practically had hundred-dollar bills falling out of his pockets," chuckled Carl. "He came with an enclosed trailer and a fancy pickup, and he's hauling it back to the West Coast."

Through his mirth, he sounded tired and his voice was weak. Joe's mother's death from dementia seven years earlier had aged him considerably. And each time Joe came home to visit him, he seemed a little thinner, a little slower, and older than his 75 years.

"You sound tired, Dad. Are you sure you're okay?"

"Yeah, yeah. I'm all right. Just getting old." Carl was the kind of man who wouldn't share anything with his son even if he wasn't all right. He never wanted to worry anyone or cause anyone to question his independence.

"You need me to come home?"

"No. No, I'm fine. I mean, you can come home if you want to. You're always welcome, you know that."

"I got a little concerned, that's all. If you call me, you usually call in the evening rather than during the day, so I thought something was up."

"Oh, I guess seeing the car go down the road a few minutes ago...I needed to talk to somebody, you know. It was like sending you off to college, except I got to see you once in a while. I'll never see the '57 anymore."

"Maybe you should crack a bottle of wine and celebrate. Count your money, again."

"Maybe I should before I take it to the bank. Good thing they know me. All that cash, they might get to thinking I've become a drug kingpin."

Joe felt bad. He needed to be there with his dad but he couldn't get away at the moment. He knew what it was like to sell your favorite ride. A car like that is part of you if you built it from the ground up, twisting every nut and bolt like he and his father had done. He learned car building from his dad while he was growing up, and he hoped he would be able to settle down someday and have a garage of his own to work in. Always dreamed of building a '69 Camaro Pro-Touring car. He had the skills to do it, thanks to his dad. But now, his factory Camaro was his high-performance ride.

"Say, you still thinking about installing a supercharger on your Camaro?"

"Maybe. A guy I know has a shop, but I'm still thinking about it. He's installed them on other cars, so he knows what he's doing."

"Let me know when you do."

"I'll drive out and give you a test ride."

"Yeah, I'm looking forward to it. Well, I suppose I'd better let you go, son. I'm sure you're busy catching bad guys. I'll talk to you later. Take care."

"Love you, Dad!"

"Yeah. Bye."

The call ended. Carl was a traditional guy with a stoic Swedish upbringing. He had trouble saying, "I love you, too" back to his son, but Joe knew he did. The best response he would usually get from him was an awkward reply of "Yeah" or "I know." That was Dad.

Sam came in as the call was ending and overheard Joe's "Love you." Sam said, "Got a lady I don't know about?"

"Talking to my dad," Joe clarified.

Sam laughed.

A little annoyed, Joe said, "Okay, have it your way. It was my new girlfriend. You'd like her, she's gorgeous!"

"Don't bullshit me. It was your dad. You ready to knock off for the day?"

Joe glanced at his watch. Half-an-hour past quitting time. Some days, time flies by and you lose track. Not uncommon with Joe when he was focusing his attention on something. He wasn't a clock-watcher.

"Yeah, I'm ready." Joe logged off his computer and started placing files in his desk drawer.

"Wanna grab a beer?"

"No, not tonight. I have some things I need to do," replied Joe as he stood and put on his sport coat.

"Like seeing your lady friend?"

"Something like that."

Chapter Ten

Michael Fleming was busy at the workbench in his basement. He had ordered a piece of one-eighth inch aluminum sheet stock custom cut to his specifications, a perfect fit for his new aluminum frame. After spraying it with adhesive and attaching black velvet, it was exactly the same design he had used for his other ones, and he had now perfected his framing process.

Satisfied, he placed the glass into the frame, making sure he left no fingerprint smudges. Then he inserted the spacers, slid in the velvet-covered aluminum sheet containing his trophy, and finally placed the foam core board that provided the backing. With care, he finished screwing the last side of the frame in place and attached the hanger. Picking it up, like it was a priceless award, Fleming turned it over. *Perfection!* It would be added to his fourth row.

He walked across the basement to a wall where he moved several books in the bookcase and released a catch. The bookcase moved slightly, and he pushed on one side. The section swiveled ninety degrees revealing a hidden room. He switched on the lights and entered a carpeted room with wood-paneled walls and a leather love seat.

Walking to the wall, he hung his latest frame and then sat in his love seat admiring his new acquisition. The longer he looked, the more it turned him on. Then he began undressing.

* * *

Joe drove to his apartment and parked his car. He had thought about it for some time now and decided he had procrastinated long enough. He walked three blocks to a fitness center he had passed many times. Since his last drinking bout, he swore he would get back into shape and start living a healthier lifestyle. He was sick and tired of hangovers that were lasting two and three days. Something had to give. He had been a track star in high school, and he wanted to get into good physical shape again. He didn't want to wind up like his fellow detective, Nate Smith, who dropped dead of a heart attack at age fifty-eight while attending a White Sox game.

He stopped in front of the place, aptly named, "The Fitness Center." He looked it over for a time, peered at the ghostly outlines of exercise machines through the large tinted glass windows that made up much of the front of the building. Finally, he worked up the gumption to go inside. It was chock full of various types of workout machines, many in use by men and women busy sweating out calories and toning muscles.

As he looked around, he heard a pleasant female voice. "May I help you?"

Joe looked over and made eye contact with her. A quirk of a smile crossed his lips, and a moment later he walked up to the counter where she was standing. She was thirty-something with cocoa-brown skin, large expressive eyes, and short-cropped hair. Tiny beads of sweat graced her hairline.

"As a matter of fact, you may be able to help me. I'm looking to get back into shape after about fifteen years of neglect and abuse."

She looked him over and observed, "You don't look too neglected and abused to me. I think we can help if you are willing to put in the time and effort."

"I'm more than willing to do that. Do you provide trainers? I'll need one."

"We can arrange that. By the way, I'm Anita Moore. I'm one of the trainers here."

A guy had to be blind not to notice her spandex workout togs that revealed a hard body with about zero fat. "I'm Joe Erickson."

"Nice to meet you, Joe." She reached below the counter and produced several printed sheets of paper. She laid them in front of him as she explained what they were.

"If you're interested in joining the Center, complete this form. And this sheet is the rates, and this is the rules, and these are the rest of the shit we have to give prospective members."

Her irreverence made him grin. He took a liking to her right away and thought she might be someone he'd like to work with. Telling her he would "read the shit," he said he would come back in a day or two when he'd completed the forms.

"Yeah, that's what they all say," she said, looking at him square in the eye, sizing him up.

He was aware of what she was doing and what she was thinking and thought it was a good time to test her.

"I'll tell you what. I will definitely return with my membership application and credit card if I can get you as my personal trainer. How's that?"

"Why do you want me?"

"I like your irreverent attitude."

She tried holding back a smile but wasn't quite successful.

"I don't know. I guess I could take on one more," she answered in an affected fatigued voice.

"Great."

"You don't know what you're getting yourself into. I'm going to make you hurt."

"I hope so. 'No pain, no gain' my old track coach always used to drill into us. You working tomorrow?"

"Tomorrow's Saturday. I don't work Saturdays. Try coming back in on Monday."

"Okay. See you then, Anita."

"I'd better... Joe."

He turned and walked out the door holding the handful of papers. He always liked to have chemistry with people he worked with. And he sensed she was someone who could whip him back into shape and make him enjoy the sweat and pain that went along with it.

At thirty-nine years of age, he knew it wasn't going to be as easy as it was when he was younger. But he also knew that he not only had to begin exercising but also had to change his eating habits as well. He would have to learn to cook for himself. He'd been eating in too many restaurants and bars, and his waistline was beginning to show the proverbial middle-age spread.

Chapter Eleven

J oe was up at his usual time Saturday morning. He was an early riser, generally waking at six o'clock and showered, shaved, and dressed by six-thirty. He wasn't the type who could sleep in like some people. Given his schedule, breakfast usually consisted of black coffee and something from McDonald's or some other fast-food establishment. Lunch was whatever he could grab and dinner was normally eaten at a pub or restaurant. Now that he was turning over a new leaf, his habits were going to change. His first task was to stock his kitchen with food. Yeah, but what kind?

He sat, drank a cup of his favorite Italian-roast coffee, and pondered what to do next. The problem wasn't that he didn't know how to cook. He knew the basics like frying eggs, broiling a steak, and microwaving frozen vegetables. But if he was going to eat right, he needed to buy the proper ingredients, and to buy them, he would need to know what he was going to cook and how to prepare it. He didn't have any cookbooks in his apartment so he decided it was time he purchased some.

Pulling out his laptop, he spent an hour searching through the mind-numbing number of choices of cookbooks online. *How the hell do you narrow these down? This isn't going to work.* He needed to find a bookstore where he could thumb through the pages and look at recipes. He searched for bookstores in his area and found one about fifteen minutes away. That ought to work. Checking their website, he found they opened at nine. An hour from now.

He poured another cup of coffee, walked into the living room, and turned on his television. He sat in his recliner and watched CNN reporting a U.S. Senator was resigning after it was discovered he regularly employed illegal immigrants to work on his sugar cane plantation. *Imagine that.* More of the same old stuff. Russia was misbehaving again, the Middle East was in turmoil, the rich were getting richer and the poor were getting poorer.

The news bored him, and he felt antsy. He needed to do something rather than sit around so he finished drinking his coffee and decided to take a walk. His habit was to carry when he was off-duty so he strapped on his holster, retrieved his Glock 17 from a drawer in his kitchen cupboard, threw on a light nylon jacket, and left his apartment.

A blast of warm air hit him in the face when he opened the door. The temperatures today were forecast to reach into the mid-nineties, and they were getting an early start. *Best get a move on.*

Joe's brisk walk brought him to the bookstore in a little over fifteen minutes. He walked down the street a block and crossed over to the next block after spying a coffee shop. He entered the green painted doors and walked to the counter. The well-dressed woman in a business suit stood in front of him. She ordered a coffee that took a paragraph to describe. About the only thing he understood was "goat's milk." *Goat's milk? You've got to be kidding?* After her order was taken, she stepped aside to wait for her candy-ass coffee conglomeration. A young waitress looked at Joe and asked, "What will you have, sir?"

"Medium, regular coffee. Black," he replied, glancing over at the woman who ordered before him. She sighed rather loudly.

"I like coffee with my coffee," he said to her with a slight smile and a shrug. "You get served quicker that way." She gave him an eye roll. *Guess she doesn't like us common folk.* The waitress brought his coffee, and he paid her adding a twenty-five percent tip.

"Thank you, sir," she said appreciatively when she saw the tip.

"That's for calling me 'sir.'" So many younger people have no sense of respect or manners today, and he liked to reward waitstaff who were polite. Stepping away from the counter, he walked past the woman still waiting for her supremo sundae coffee which he assumed she would get after they finished milking the goat.

Spying an empty table in the corner, he walked over and sat down. He checked his calls, and then did a search for "Havana Brown cats." The search revealed a short-haired, medium-sized cat that was chocolate brown in color with vivid green eyes. Originating in England, it was developed through selective breeding.

He then did a search for Burmese cats. The search turned up the fact that Burmese were short-haired cats and came in four colors. The sable variety had hair in a rich brown color, and they had yellow-gold eyes. The breed originated in the United States and was based on one brown cat brought in from Burma. The breed was also developed by selective breeding.

Both of the breeds looked very similar in Joe's eyes, although he was sure Evelyn Stewart-Bruce could point out a multitude of the differences. He looked at the time–ten after nine. The bookstore should be open. Standing, he downed the rest of his coffee and walked through the green doors and out onto the sidewalk. The temperature seemed to have grown warmer in just the short time he was inside the coffee shop.

The lights inside the bookstore were on, and he opened the door and stepped inside. The door activated a bell that clattered. The place had the faint, pleasant scent of potpourri. Apparently, he was the first customer in the store, so he decided to seek out assistance from the proprietor. No one was present behind the counter, but before Joe had taken two steps, a thin, red-haired man appeared from behind a row of books.

"Ah! My first customer of the day. Good morning. I'm Jeffrey. How can I help you?"

"I'm looking for some books on healthy cooking. I guess you could say I am not that experienced in the kitchen, so I'm looking for something basic to get me started."

"Absolutely. How many will you be cooking for?"

"Just me."

"Well then, we have exactly what you're looking for if I may say so. Now, if you'll follow me...."

Joe followed Jeffrey to the middle of the store to an aisle labeled "Cooking."

He pulled out two books with titles on healthy eating for one.

"I would recommend both of these. They don't duplicate each other's recipes, and what one doesn't have, the other one does. They are both excellent. And if you should have company, you simply double the recipe amounts as needed."

"Thank you."

"Oh! And let me get one other book for you to look at as well. I would highly suggest this one if you are a novice in the kitchen. Excuse me for one second." Jeffrey left and came back with another, smaller book.

"If you're not an experienced cook, this one will teach you all about spices and how to use them, ways to cook things like bake, fry, broil, sauté, and so forth. It's positively invaluable if you really wish to cook well. And it's not all that expensive."

"So, you would say that these three books would be a good start?"

"Oh, yes. And I guarantee, if you master these three books, you will be back here for more sophisticated books for your palate in the future."

"Well, we'll see about that. I'll trust you and take these three."

"Wonderful!"

They walked to the counter, and after Jeffrey handed Joe his receipt, he said, "We do offer cooking classes, in case you're interested. We have a lot of fun, and the best part is...we get to eat our projects."

"I'll keep that in mind," Joe replied as he took his plastic bag. "Maybe when I'm past the novice stage." He left the store with his newly acquired books and headed back to his apartment. He had some reading to do before he went to the supermarket.

Once he got back to his apartment, he shed his jacket and placed his Glock in the kitchen drawer. He grabbed a bottle of water from the fridge, sat down in his recliner, and for the next two hours, he paged through his cookbooks looking at recipes and making a list of ingredients. He figured he needed enough for a week's worth of breakfasts and dinners. Lunch he would have to catch whenever he could while he was at work, but he could control the choice of food better.

Feeling that his list was complete, he checked the temperature, Ninety-two. He changed into a short-sleeved, navy-colored shirt he could wear untucked. The tail was long enough to cover his Glock. The supermarket on Clybourn was too far to walk carrying multiple bags of groceries, so he drove his Camaro over to the store. The place was busy on a Saturday afternoon with a lot of women pushing carts around. Seizing a cart, he began a new experience: grocery shopping.

Not knowing where things were located slowed him down. So did thoughts like, *Should I get one or several of these?* But one by one he ticked items off his list. His cart was getting full, and he was getting close to completing his list when he pushed his cart around a corner, and BANG! He collided with another shopper's cart.

She was a very attractive woman whose surprise quickly turned into annoyance. Joe's immediate reaction was to apologize.

"Oh, I'm sorry. You all right?"

She opened her carton of eggs and saw they were not damaged. Looking up, she brushed back her long, dark hair and said, "Apparently."

"I couldn't see you until it was too late. Sorry."

"No harm done," she stated, remaining aloof as she pushed her cart past him.

Joe pushed his cart through the aisle, failing to find what he was looking for. He carefully rounded the corner and entered the next aisle and spotted it. Cans of chopped tomatoes. He pushed his cart near them and squatted down to look at the various brands. As he was comparing two cans, he was knocked over by a shopping cart. The cans went flying as he was knocked off his feet and landed on his knees. Hearing the woman's voice, he knew who it was.

"Oh, no!" She came around the front of her cart as he was picking himself up.

Seeing him, she blurted out, "Oh, my god! I can't believe this. Are you all right?"

Rising to his feet, Joe dusted himself off and assured her, "I'm okay. But you'd better check your eggs."

She looked at him not knowing how to react. Then Joe smiled and it was infectious. She laughed.

"Maybe I should," she smiled. "I apologize." Then she noticed his holster partially sticking out under his disheveled shirt. "I hope you're not going to shoot me, now."

Joe realized his shirt had pulled up and he quickly pulled it down. "Fortunately, I've never had to shoot anyone. People watch TV and think cops shoot people."

"So, you're a cop," she said seeking confirmation.

"Detective. I'm Joe."

"Well, Joe," she said, "I have to be on my way. Perhaps we'll bump into each other again some time."

"Perhaps."

She smiled ever so slightly, started to push her cart forward, and then stopped.

"I would go for the store brand chopped tomatoes if I were you. Just as good and less expensive." And with that, she pushed her cart past him.

He watched her as she pushed her cart up to the checkout lane. *Mm. Those eyes of hers!* He picked up the two cans of tomatoes off the floor and put the brand-name one back. The other one he dropped in his cart and grabbed a second one off the shelf. Wouldn't hurt to have two. At that point, he realized, *Idiot. You didn't even get her name.* He could still walk up and ask her, but that wouldn't be cool. If she was interested, she'd be making the first move. After all, she knew his name and could figure out where he worked.

In another five minutes, he had finished his list and checked out. He'd never purchased this much stuff in his life. And…He had no idea groceries could be this expensive. Damn! How does a family of five or six afford to live, anyway?

With the back seat of his Camaro taken up by sacks, and the passenger seat and trunk full of produce, he drove home. Several trips were required to move all of the groceries from his car into his apartment, and even longer to find places for everything in his kitchen. *This is tiring.*

He was looking forward to cooking his first healthy meal tonight, but he would have to decide which recipe to use. After everything was put away, he sat down in his recliner and started leafing through one of his new cookbooks. He drifted off to sleep and didn't wake up until 7:00. *Damn. No time to cook now. Looks like I'll have to begin tomorrow. Time to stroll down to the bistro.*

Chapter Twelve

Sunday had been a culinary triumph. Joe made a burrito wrap buttered with roasted red pepper hummus filled with two scrambled eggs for breakfast; an apple and cranberry lettuce salad with a balsamic vinaigrette for lunch; and garlic butter linguini with pancetta for dinner. His reaction was, *This is kinda fun, and the results are pretty tasty. I think I can get into this.*

The breakfast merited repeating Monday morning, and he remade the salad for his lunch. His dad, who knew a lot about wine, would have to brief him about appropriate wines to go with the foods he was learning to prepare.

He went into work early feeling pretty good about himself. His plan for this week was to interview Eddie Collins and Michelle Cardona to see if they could provide any insights into the killer of Melanie McAdams and others. But first, he needed to go through appropriate channels to get a forwarding address and phone number for Frank Edwards.

He walked to Vincenzo's office and found him leaning forward on his desk hunched over a cup of coffee and a Danish. He knocked. Vincenzo looked up.

"You're early," he said as wiped his mouth with a napkin.

"So are you," responded Joe.

"What do you want?"

"I need Frank Edwards' new address info in Florida. Can you get it for me?"

"What do you want that for?"

"He was lead detective on one of the serial cases. The Deanna Frost homicide two years ago. He worked it with Nate Smith. I can't ask him." He saw Vincenzo's face sadden. He and Nate had come through the ranks together.

"Yeah, I see your point there. Nate was a good man. I miss him." He paused momentarily. "I'll look into it for you."

"Thanks."

"Say, where you going with this? What's your strategy for the week?"

Joe figured this conversation might take a while so he sat down in one of the chairs in front of Vincenzo's desk.

"Interview all the lead detectives on the homicides we've tied to this guy. See if we can get any leads. I'm taking Frank Edwards, Eddie Collins over in Area 1, and Michelle Cardona here. Sam's doing Gary Nelson and Kevin Dempsey."

"Okay. I'll help keep your schedule light so you two can get this done. Let's hope it leads to something. What about the cat hair angle?"

"I think the cat lady will come through this week. She's a little eccentric so I don't want to push it."

"A cat lady? Eccentric? How can that be?"

Joe chuckled. "Actually, she's not bad."

Vincenzo picked up his coffee mug and took a sip. "Anything else?"

"You turn up anything in ViCAP?"

"No. But only about eight percent of law enforcement agencies report, so there may be more out there that's gone unreported."

"Too bad."

"Yeah. Keep me informed. This might hit the press this week so be prepared. When shit hits the fan, it won't be distributed evenly."

"Gotcha."

Joe got up from his chair and left. Vincenzo was full of those little adages. Joe had become used to them over the years. He had once entertained the thought that Vincenzo spent his spare time collecting and memorizing clever sayings for future use. He still hadn't completely ruled it out.

Sam was at his desk talking on the phone. He had a serious look on his face and was writing in his notebook. Joe felt a knot beginning to form in his gut. Sam hung up the phone and looked at him.

"What is it?"

"Suicide. In Boystown."

Joe was relieved to hear it was a suicide. Not that a suicide could ever be a good thing, mind you. Relief came from knowing their serial killer had not struck again.

They arrived at the apartment building on North Pine Grove Avenue in the 19th District. The four-story red and brown brick building was in a popular, artsy part of the city. Uniforms had already done their jobs and the Medical Examiner's van was on the scene. Calloway, the officer at the door, directed them up to the second floor.

They decided to take the stairs rather than wait for the elevator. When they pushed through the door onto the second floor, they were met by Officer Terry Kennedy. He was about to stop them when they produced their IDs.

"Detectives Erickson and Renaldo," announced Joe.

"Terry Kennedy. Third door on the right."

They walked down the hall to meet another officer manning the door to the apartment. His nameplate read, "Petroff." They identified themselves.

"What have you got?" asked Sam.

Officer Petroff pulled out his notebook. "White male, thirty-eight. Evan Higbee. He's lived here eight years. He was found by a friend who had a key to his apartment. Said Higbee was a computer programmer who worked for a large firm downtown. He left a note."

"Who's the M.E.?" asked Joe. Before Petroff had a chance to answer, he heard a familiar voice from inside the apartment.

"That you, 'Detective Erickson'?"

"That you, 'Dr. Solitsky'?"

"Unfortunately. You can step inside. But don't come any farther than the door."

As they entered the room, Joe could see it was a small, studio apartment with sterile white walls. Framed artwork as well as rugs, pillows, and throws added pops of color.

The body of a man lay on a gray microfiber sofa. Kendra met them at the door dressed in customary white Tyvek coveralls, gloves, and boot covers. "Looks like he chose to o.d. on a bottle of sleeping pills. Empty prescription bottle along with a note was left on the coffee table." She handed Joe the suicide note which was inside a plastic sleeve. "Time of death was between 2:00 and 4:00 am."

Joe read the note. "I'm sorry for the heinous things I have done. I can't live with myself any longer." Joe looked from Kendra to Sam. "Heinous things?"

"You got me," shrugged Kendra.

"Evidence techs on their way?" asked Sam.

"Should be here anytime. It's pretty straightforward the way things look. No signs of foul play. He wrote a note, swallowed the pills, and laid down to die. Shame."

"Yeah," acknowledged Joe. He handed the suicide note to Sam. "Okay, well, if you turn up anything hinky, you'll let me know?"

"You'll be the first to get a call."

Sam handed the note back to Kendra. "We'll let you get back to work."

"I appreciate your thoughtfulness," she replied and returned to her duties.

"Heinous," repeated Joe. "That means like something evil, grisly. Remind you of something?"

"You're not thinking…"

"I don't think we can rule it out."

As Joe and Sam stepped back into the hallway, the elevator door opened and John Gustafson, the evidence tech, emerged carrying his equipment. Gustafson was known as "Big John" to his colleagues because, like the song, "he stood six-foot-six and weighed two-forty-five." Because it was a suicide, he didn't bring an associate to assist in processing the crime scene.

Joe and Sam had worked with Gustafson on several occasions and knew his work methods. Once he got started, he despised interruptions, and God help anyone who disturbed his crime scene. But he was willing to talk after he had completed his investigation.

Joe greeted him. "Good morning, John."

"Joe, Sam," he said, acknowledging them with a nod. He didn't waste any time setting down his equipment, opening a case, and removing a biohazard kit. No time for conversation. He always arrived with a purpose and went straight to work.

Sam spoke to Officer Petroff. "Where's the guy who found the victim?"

"He's outside with my partner. He was pretty shaken up."

Joe and Sam met with Bobby Affannato, the friend who found the body of Evan Higbee. They had known each other since they were in college at DePaul University and had remained friends ever since. Bobby was a freelance journalist and an adjunct professor at Roosevelt University.

"This comes as such a shock. I had no idea he was depressed or had problems. I just can't believe this."

"Did he have any issues with women?" asked Sam.

"What do you mean "issues?""

"Did he like women?"

"He wasn't gay."

"That's not what I'm asking. Some men don't like women. They're misogynists."

"Oh, no. He wasn't like that. He liked women. He didn't have anyone in his life at the moment. At least that I know of. I'm sure he would have told me if he did. Why are you asking?"

"We have to pursue all avenues. So, his suicide came out of the blue, so to speak?"

"Yeah. I don't know. Maybe I was blind to signs I should have picked up on," he sniffed as he pulled a handkerchief from his pocket. "I wish he would have called me. I would have talked to him, gotten him some help." He dabbed his eyes and then blew his nose.

Joe decided to probe into Higbee's background a little farther. "Was he always a computer programmer? Did he ever do anything else? Military or..."

"No. After college, he applied and got a job with the Arius Corporation. He's worked there ever since."

"In his note, he referred to the 'heinous things' he'd done. You saw the note, I assume. Do you have any idea what he could have been referring to?" asked Joe.

"No idea. No idea."

"What about next of kin," asked Sam. "Does he have parents, siblings that you know of?"

"Yeah. His parents are both gone. But he has a sister who lives in Grayslake. Sharon. I don't know her husband's name but he's on the village board up there. I'm sorry. I..."

"It's okay. We can find out who she is."

"Do you know of any hobbies or activities he was engaged in? Anything that could have led to his wanting to take his life?"

"He was a Republican."

That response annoyed Joe, and he let Bobby know it. "Very funny. That's not very helpful."

"I don't see how this is relevant," retorted Bobby.

"Everything is relevant when we investigate an unnatural death. Look, I understand your pain, but if you'll be patient, we're close to being done."

"All right. He went to concerts, out to bars, nice restaurants. He went on dates, he loved movies, he didn't like sports. That's the extent of it. Maybe you should check his computer."

"We will," said Sam. "I think we're done here. If you can think of anything else that would help us, here's my card."

They took Bobby's phone number and address information, and then went knocking on doors on Higbee's floor. They got few answers. Those who did open their doors didn't know him. Others were probably at work. Shortly after noon, the M.E. and evidence tech released the body. Nothing hinky according to Kendra.

After Big John finished up, Joe spoke with him. His preliminary opinion was the same as Kendra's—suicide by overdose.

"I'm particularly interested if you find evidence of cat hairs because it could tie him to other crimes," said Joe. "So, could you give me a call if you either find or fail to find cat hairs?"

"I can do that."

Joe thanked him. He would wait for the autopsy report and the results from the crime lab. If he got a positive call from Big John, that would be a game-changer. If the findings were negative and there were no anomalies, then a report would be filed and the case would likely be closed.

Sam ordered Officer Petroff to seal Evan Higbee's apartment. Joe had the remaining uniforms open up the perimeter and then stand down. Their work was done.

On the way back to the office, Sam was driving. He looked over at Joe and asked, "You like this guy for the serial killer?"

"I don't know. He doesn't appear to own a cat, but those cat hairs could have been picked up elsewhere. A girlfriend's place, a parent's house."

"Right."

"We need to have forensics go over his computer. And I think we need to talk to his employer. If nothing else, I'd still like to know what the heinous thing was that led him to end it all."

"Like carving up women?"

"Maybe."

"It's too easy. To have a guy off himself like this and fall in our laps. We need to follow up. But it's too easy," declared Sam.

"Agreed." Joe paused as he thought about it and decided to change the subject. "I spoke with Vincenzo early this morning. He said he was going to lighten our load so we could continue to pursue this serial case."

"Oh, yeah? I'll believe it when it happens."

"Give him a chance. I'm going to get cracking on setting up interviews with Michelle and Eddie. Vincenzo said he was going to get me Frank Edward's contact information in Florida."

Sam pulled to a stop behind a delivery van stuck in traffic. "Hey, I'm starving. You want to stop and get something to eat?"

"No thanks. I brought something from home."

"From home? What's happening to you?"

Joe was able to speak with Michelle Cardona that afternoon. She was the lead detective on the Nicole Morrison murder that took place in Lincoln

Park two years ago. She remembered the case vividly. Michelle transferred over from Vice, and the first case she caught as lead detective was the Nicole Morrison homicide. The way she described it, it could have been the Melanie McAdams' case. The MO's and the scenes were practically identical.

"We looked into bars and clubs she used to frequent. One person in a club we checked remembered her talking with a guy on the evening before she was killed. But she couldn't give much of a description. Tall, dark, and handsome. Jesus. Maybe it was you."

"Should have put me in a lineup."

She asked why he was inquiring into her unsolved case, and he knew he had to be upfront with her. He wasn't about to concoct a story when the truth was going to come out soon anyway. Besides, he had a gut feeling she could be trusted. So, he told her about the Melanie McAdams murder and the replicated details in the Nicole Morrison murder.

"You've got to be kidding me," she responded in disbelief.

And then he informed her about how he and his partner sifted through unsolved homicides and discovered six with the same MO. He now had conclusive evidence of a serial killer operating in the city.

"How the hell could this have happened? How could these six murders happen and never be linked together?"

Joe explained his theory about how they could have slipped by the system. Bringing her up to speed about where they were in their investigation and what Vincenzo knew, he cautioned her about the need to be discreet regarding what he had told her.

"Only you, Eddie Collins from Area 1, Sam, Vincenzo, and I know about this. Vincenzo has probably talked about this with the Deputy Chief, but so far, nothing has leaked to the press. But from what Vincenzo told me, it sounds like the Department will have some kind of official statement soon."

"They sure as hell won't hear anything from me. If I can help in any way, let me know."

Meeting with Cardona wasn't that helpful from an investigative point of view, but Joe felt he had gained another ally. And if he needed her assistance in this investigation, he was confident she would give it her best.

Late that afternoon Joe received a phone call from Art Casey who informed him the cat hairs found at the scene of the crimes were from a short-haired cat. Joe thanked him for checking and immediately called Evelyn Stewart Bruce. His call went to her voicemail, so he left her a message. He was hopeful she would be able to provide him with samples within a few days.

After work, he went to The Fitness Center and his appointment with Anita. She had him start out with a series of stretches to loosen up before running him through cardio machines and introducing him to machines to work on building upper body strength.

"You know, I don't want to come out of here looking like Arnold Schwarzenegger. You know that, right?"

She laughed. "Don't worry. When I get done with you, you'll be able to outrun the Terminator. Trust me."

He started walking on the treadmill and then worked his way up to jogging. He could not believe what lousy condition he was in. Before long he had to move back to a walking pace again.

He admitted to Anita, "I'm embarrassed. I had no idea I had turned into such a couch potato."

"Most people don't. But just remember this: baby steps. Days will turn into weeks and weeks will turn into months. If you have the discipline to stay with it, you'll be in tip-top shape again. It's a gradual process. If you push too hard, you may injure yourself."

When his session was over, Anita had him stretch again, and she gave him instructions about what to do at home. "You're going to have some discomfort. That's normal. But you'll work your way out of that if you discipline yourself. Drink a lot of water and move around. Take Ibuprofen or Tylenol if you need to. But don't just sit in your recliner."

That last statement took him a little by surprise. "How'd you know I had a recliner?"

She just gave him a look. Did she have ESP or was he that predictable? She didn't answer him. Instead, they confirmed his next workout for the same time day after tomorrow. He would do some brisk walking tomorrow to exercise the muscles he had worked out today.

Baby steps. He remembered back to track practice in high school and the first murderous day when his sadistic coach would run him half to death. When he thought he was going to die. When the inside of his lungs felt like they were on fire. When he questioned why he was doing this. All those sweaty red faces, the gasping, the hard breathing, some guys losing their lunch. But by the time the meets rolled around, he was in shape and winning medals. The memories made him smile. *I can do this again,* he thought. *I can do this.*

Chapter Thirteen

Joe arrived at the office carrying his lunch, a salmon and arugula salad, leftovers from a double batch he made the night before. An envelope with "Joe Erickson" written on it was on his desk. Inside was a handwritten note that read, "Frank Edwards" followed by a phone number. *Thanks, Lieutenant.* He copied the name and number into his phone.

He searched for the Arius Corporation, and almost immediately, the website appeared showing a full-screen color image of a handsome family with the line, "Our People are Number One." Their corporate offices were located on the fortieth floor in a tower on Dearborn. Beneath the address was an 800 number. He called it and was connected with their Human Resources department where an automated message informed him the office didn't open until ten o'clock. Figures.

Knowing that it was probably not too early for a retired detective, he decided to call Frank Edwards in Florida. The phone was answered after the second ring.

"Edwards residence," a pleasant female voice said.

"Good morning. This is Joe Erickson, and I'm a detective with the Chicago Police Department. Could I speak with Frank, please?"

"Sure. Just a minute." He could hear her walking and then raising her voice, "FRANK! THE PHONE'S FOR YOU!" A moment later another phone picked up.

A gruff voice barked, "This is Frank."

"Frank, this is Joe Erickson calling from Chicago PD. Sorry to bother you. Sal Vincenzo gave me your phone number."

Hearing Vincenzo's name caused his attitude to flip from annoyed to jovial. "Hey, how's he doin'?"

"He's fine. Same as always."

"Good to hear." Then he paused momentarily. "Joe Erickson. Yeah. I sorta remember you. Young guy. Yeah. What can I do for you?"

"You remember the Deanna Frost homicide? You were the lead detective on it."

"Like it was yesterday. Jefferson Park. It was the last damned case I worked before I retired. My only regret leaving the force was I never caught the motherfucker that did it."

Joe overheard Frank's wife reprimand him. "Sorry. Sorry honey." Joe could hardly keep from cracking up knowing what a tough guy Edwards was known to be.

Joe went on to explain the links to other murders they had found. He was wondering if he could pick Frank's brain about his investigation.

"I can do you one better. The wife and I are packin' up to fly back to Chicago. Our son is getting married in Oak Park. We'll be there in a few days. We're comin' in a week early so my wife can visit family. If you want to meet up, we can have a sit-down and discuss it over some drinks."

"That would be great, Frank."

They exchanged cell phone numbers, and Frank agreed to call him as soon as they got settled in their hotel. Having Frank Edwards back in Chicago where Joe could interview him face-to-face was a stroke of luck. Now, if he could only corral Eddie Collins, he would have his comparison research set. He gave Eddie a call. No luck. He wasn't answering so Joe left him a message.

Sam rolled in as Joe was finishing up his voice mail to Eddie.

"How did your interview go with Michelle Cardona."

"The interview went fine. But I learned zip. She did say that a witness saw her with a guy in a bar the night before she was killed. She couldn't give a helpful description. What about you?"

"I spoke with Dempsey about the case he's working now. Maria Martinez was kind of a romantic. The candlelight dinner type. Not a party girl like the others. That's where she's different."

"I wonder how she met the killer if she didn't go to bars or nightclubs."

"We're working that angle right now. Hobbies, church, activities, work. So far, we haven't come up with jack."

"She was an accountant downtown, wasn't she?"

"Yeah."

"And Higbee was a programmer downtown, right? Let see… Who'd she work for?" Joe pulled up his spreadsheet. "Uh… the Milligan Group. A large energy conglomerate. Higbee worked for the Arius Corporation. They're a pharmaceutical manufacturer. I don't see a connection."

Joe and Sam worked on potential links until ten o'clock. At that point, they left the office and drove downtown to the Arius Corporation. The traffic in the Loop was heavily congested. Thankfully, there were no accidents. They left their car in a parking garage half a block from the tower and walked the short distance. They took the elevator up to the fortieth floor and entered a richly appointed space. Showing their IDs made the desk attendant visibly nervous. They asked if they could speak with someone in the HR Department.

"And this would be about?"

"One of your employees," responded Joe.

"I see," the attendant replied, as he picked up the phone, asking that the person on the other end come to the front desk right away because "two policemen are here."

In no time at all, a polished, silver-haired man in a blue pinstripe suit walked out and greeted them.

"Good morning. I'm William Jensen. May I help you, gentlemen?"

They showed him their IDs, and Joe explained, "We'd like to ask you a few questions about one of your employees."

"We're not in the habit of discussing our employees, Mr. Erickson."

"Mr. Jensen, we're detectives investigating a homicide. I don't think your employee will care anymore."

Jensen's face lost its color, and he stammered, "Oh, oh, dear. Why don't we go down to my office?"

They followed Jensen to an office with a large window overlooking the Chicago skyline.

"Can I get you anything? Coffee? Soft drink?"

Joe and Sam both declined. Jensen indicated the two wingback leather chairs and sat down behind his desk.

"You say one of our employees has been murdered?"

"Your employee's case is not a murder," said Sam. "It looks to be a suicide." Jensen reacted, "Oh, I thought—"

"Any unnatural death, whether it be murder or suicide, has to be investigated," explained Joe. "So, that's why we're here."

"Who was it?"

"It was one of your computer programmers by the name of Evan Higbee," said Joe.

"Evan Higbee? Well, he's not even employed here anymore," snorted Jensen who sounded insulted that Higbee's name would be associated with their company.

Joe and Sam looked at each other, obviously a little taken aback by this revelation as well as Jensen's reaction.

"Since when?" asked Sam. "His best friend told us he was employed here."

"Since two weeks ago."

"You're a very large company, and you employ many people. How is it you're so familiar with Evan Higbee? Did he work directly for you?"

"No, he did not."

"Then, how do you know about him?" pressed Joe.

"Like I told you before, it's not our policy to speak about our employees. There are confidentiality issues I'm sure you know about—"

"We are trying to find out why he may have taken his life, Mr. Jensen. There's always a reason behind these things. Was he fired? Surely you can tell us that." asked Sam.

Jensen fiddled with a pen on his desk. Joe could sense Jensen was feeling conflicted about speaking about Higbee, so he tried another tactic. "Look, I know you have to protect the company from privacy violations and employee harassment suits. We understand that. But this guy is dead. In his suicide note, he referred to, and I quote, "heinous things I did," unquote. Now, could I assume you may know what he was referring to? Whatever you tell us will not come back to haunt you or your company. We don't talk to the *Tribune* or the *Sun-Times* people. We just want to know the truth here so we can close this case."

"All right. I can tell you some of it, but I can't go into much detail because Legal is still wrestling with what, if anything, to do about it. About six months ago, an audit turned up a "discrepancy" in the system that could not be accounted for. It turns out it had been going on for some time. We hired some experts to figure it out, and after some considerable scrutiny, they found it and traced it to Higbee. He'd been embezzling from the company. I called him in, laid out the facts, and he admitted to it. I had no recourse but to terminate him."

"So, maybe this was the "heinous things" he was referring to," said Sam. "And maybe he didn't want to face prosecution."

"Have you turned this over to the police?" asked Joe.

"No. That's what Legal is wrestling with at the moment. I guess his death will complicate matters even more."

"Were there ever any complaints filed against him in the workplace? By women or anything like that?"

"No, never. He was always a model employee...until this."

After a few more questions, Joe stood indicating their interview was over. He thanked Jensen and reached across the desk and shook his hand. Sam did the same.

"Sorry, we had to have this discussion. The details of his termination will remain between the three of us," Joe assured him. "By the way, we have robbery and cyber-crimes divisions should your Legal Department wish to turn this matter over to the police."

"I appreciate that. At this point, it may be simpler to eat the loss. It wasn't like he stole a million dollars."

As Joe and Sam rode the elevator down to the ground level, Sam said, "That's not the heinous kind of stuff we were looking for, huh?"

"No."

"Two to one says it was a gambling problem."

"You may be right. Say, you interviewed Gary Nelson yet?"

"Tonight. We're getting together at Benny's. You can come along if you want."

"You don't need me there. I'd just cramp your style."

"Sure you would. Admit it. You're just afraid of Nelson."

Joe chuckled. "Yeah, you're right. He scares me. He should scare you, too." Gary Nelson had a reputation among the detectives as being a little on the edge. Some of the detectives referred to him as 'Dirty Gary' behind his back. Joe had never worked with him and figured it was an image Nelson cultivated. Still, you wouldn't want to mess with him.

As they left the building, Joe's cell phone rang. Eddie Collins was returning his call.

"Hey, man. What can I do for you?" asked Eddie.

"I'd like to meet with you and pick your brain about the Rebecca Woods case. We're interviewing all the lead detectives on the six cases we turned up."

"Six!"

"So far."

"Damn 'n shit! Yeah, I can meet with you. When you wanna do it? I'm open all week."

"How about tonight? I'll meet you halfway, someplace in the Loop okay?"

"Yeah, that's cool. Meet me at the bar of the Drake Hotel, say eight o'clock?"

"Going swanky on me, Eddie?"

"Why not? You're picking up the tab." And Eddie ended the call. Typical Eddie.

Joe shook his head muttering an expletive under his breath as he returned his phone to his pocket.

"Something wrong?" Sam asked.

"Every time I see Eddie Collins, it winds up costing me money."

Joe was glad when Eddie moved from the old North Bureau to the Central Bureau of Detectives five years ago. The problem wasn't that Eddie was a lousy detective or anything like that. On the contrary, he was damned good.

But being around him too much used to drive Joe crazy. Eddie had his own style and his own way of doing things. Each time Joe thought of him, the theme to Shaft would automatically pop into his head. And the weird thing about it was—it fit the guy. He was born to play the part.

"I'm meeting Eddie tonight at the Drake Hotel. Hopefully, we'll have something tangible to go on tomorrow morning." Then Joe remembered he had not told Sam about Frank Edwards. "Oh, and Frank Edwards will be back in town in a few days for his son's wedding, so I'll have a chance to talk with him about the Deanna Frost case."

"Kinda destroyed your hopes for an all-expenses-paid trip to Florida, huh?"

Neither man was all that optimistic given the lack of evidence they had found so far. The best clue they had were cat hairs.

That evening Joe drove downtown to the elegant Drake Hotel and parked. He made his way to the famous Coq D'or Bar that opened one day after the repeal of Prohibition in 1933. He saw Eddie sitting at one of the tables with a stunning woman, a good ten years his junior.

"Hey, Joe. Come on over, man. "Lola, honey, this is Joe Erickson. Joe, Lola."

Lola stood and shook Joe's hand. "Nice to meet you, Joe."

"My pleasure."

"Well, I'd better be on my way and leave you two boys to your business." And with a wink, she said to Eddie, "I'll see you up in the room later." Turning, she walked away and disappeared around the corner.

"Where do you come up with these beautiful women, Eddie?"

"Must be my charm, cuz it sure ain't my money."

Over a couple of single malt scotches, Joe brought Eddie up to speed on what they had found and the common links to all six homicides. Eddie remembered the Rebecca Woods case all too well.

"Her apartment was in Morgan Park. You see a woman's body ripped up like that, you can't un-see that shit, you know what I mean? For months, I couldn't touch a woman without seein' that butcher's handiwork in my head." He shuddered. "Man, it messed with my mind somethin' awful."

Joe always knew Eddie as a pretty tough cookie despite his eccentricities, but he didn't know this case would have affected him like that. After spending years in law enforcement, many as a homicide detective, one would think he'd become immune to those feelings. But some cases can get to you, and it was obvious this one did.

Joe needed to get Eddie out of his funk so he could make some progress, so he changed the subject. Maybe focusing on the evidence would do it.

"Four of the girls were partiers and liked to go out to bars and clubs. We think it may be possible they met the killer in one of those places. But Rebecca Woods was not that type. She went to church, sang in the choir, loved to go to movies, and worked in a daycare. Did you find any evidence how she may have met her killer?"

Eddie sighed. "We checked her workplace, her friends, parents, pastor, and we didn't turn up a thing. It was like the guy was some kind of phantom or somethin.'"

"This is the one murder that didn't take place in the northern part of the city. That's the anomaly. Five of the victims lived in the north so the killer must have met these women around where they lived. But this one worked in the central area close to where she lived. How did the killer meet her and strike so far outside his killing zone?"

"She could have traveled up north for some reason. A lot of festivals, plays, restaurants, and shit up there," said Eddie. "They could have met that way, maybe. The case is still open. I could contact two of her friends and ask if they recall anything more about her traveling up there to do stuff."

"Good idea. She wouldn't go alone. Chances are one of her friends would have gone with her if she did."

Eddie agreed to locate and re-interview her parents and friends and get back to Joe. He finished his scotch and excused himself. No doubt he was eager to get up to the room to see his honey. Joe got the tab for their drinks which included two Eddie and his girlfriend drank before Joe got there. He broke into a smile. That was Eddie.

Chapter Fourteen

When Joe came into the office the next morning, Sam met him. "What has our resident chef fixed for himself today?"

"A prawn pasta salad."

"You're turning into a regular Julia Child, you know that?"

Joe tapped his flat belly with both hands. "Yeah, and proud of it." Sam looked down, touched his little paunch, and grunted. Joe's healthy eating along with his workouts with Anita were paying off. He'd dropped ten pounds and lost an inch off his waistline.

"Kevin Dempsey told me Maria Martinez's funeral is today at ten o'clock," said Sam. "I was thinking since Melanie McAdams' services were held so far downstate, maybe we should show up at this one and take a look around. What do you think?"

"Good idea. I assume Dempsey and Crawford will be there, too?"

"Yeah, I figure two more sets of eyes couldn't hurt."

The funeral services were being held at St. Ignatius Catholic Church in Rogers Park. The parish served a multicultural population that made up the area. Joe and Sam arrived about thirty minutes prior to the start of services. A white hearse was out front. Small groups of people were beginning to stream into the church.

Sam and Joe walked up the steps and entered the beautiful church. People were greeting Maria's family, shaking hands, hugging, and passing along condolences. Joe and Sam decided to hang back and observe, trying their best not to stand out. As they were positioning themselves in the back, a handsome man in his mid-thirties walked up to them.

"May I help you, gentlemen?"

"We're here to observe," replied Sam.

"Observe? I'm afraid I—"

Joe cleared his throat and subtly showed him his ID. "We're investigating Ms. Martinez's death. And you are?"

"I'm Michael Fleming, one of the funeral directors. I'll just let you gentlemen remain incognito." Fleming walked away. He knew sooner or later the police would begin checking out the funerals of his victims. But he was convinced there was nothing they had on him that could connect him to any of the murders. He looked to his left and his eye went to his shoulder. Reaching up, he brushed a few cat hairs off his suitcoat.

Joe noticed that Dempsey and Crawford had arrived. They both walked up to commiserate with the family, assuring her parents they were doing everything possible to solve the case. After passing the casket, they walked to the back of the church and took up positions on the opposite side of the aisle.

Joe watched Fleming and another funeral director acting as solemn hosts. He saw Fleming talking to six men he presumed to be pallbearers, apparently instructing them on the duties they would perform.

Of the one-hundred or so people who came to the funeral mass, no one seemed suspicious or out of place to Joe. In some cases, a killer would get off attending the funeral of the person he'd killed. Today didn't look as though any such person was present.

After the priest concluded the mass and the pallbearers carried the casket to the hearse, Joe watched as people left the church. Some of them gave him and Sam puzzling looks, wondering what they were doing there. After the church emptied, Dempsey and Crawford walked over to where Joe and Sam were standing.

"You see anyone suspicious?" asked Dempsey.

Joe shook his head. "No. Everyone looked like they were here to grieve."

"That's what we thought," said Crawford. "I don't think the perp was among the mourners. We're heading back."

"So are we. Joe's lunch is waiting for him."

"We've heard you've turned into a gourmet? Started wearing a chef's hat at home. Any truth to that?" asked Crawford in his smart-assed way.

"Just getting into shape and eating right. Turning over a new leaf. No more junk food. I don't intend to end my life like Nate Smith."

Crawford's attitude immediately changed, and he backed off. Nate had been a good friend and he took his death pretty hard. "Yeah, he was a great guy, but he didn't take good care of himself."

"Come on. Let's go," urged Dempsey. And the two began to leave the church.

Sam turned to Joe. "You sure shut him up."

Joe felt a little sheepish bringing up a sore spot with Crawford. But Crawford was a smartass, and he knew he wasn't going to let up if he didn't put a stop to it.

"Yeah." Joe paused. "Did you notice that funeral director? He had some kind of animal hair on his shoulder."

"No, I didn't. Jesus, Joe. Half of the population of Chicago probably has pet hair on their clothes."

"Yeah. You're probably right."

They returned to the office, and after lunch, Joe received a phone call from Evelyn Stewart-Bruce saying she had collected the cat hair samples for him. He asked where she would like to meet, and she asked if he would like to meet her for dinner. At her place. He could see where this was going. Dinner, wine, and... no, I don't think so. He didn't know anything about her, and he'd seen *Fatal Attraction.*

"I'm so sorry, Evelyn, but I'm afraid I'll have to take a rain check on that dinner. I'm sure I'll be missing out on something special, but I'm working a night assignment for the foreseeable future."

He lied, but he didn't want to get involved with a woman he didn't have feelings for. He was old-fashioned that way. And what's more, he didn't want to seem unkind to someone who went out of her way to assist him with his investigation. She seemed to understand and didn't appear put off by his declining her invitation. So, they agreed to meet that afternoon at the coffee shop where they met the first time.

When Joe walked into the coffee shop, Evelyn was already seated at a table with a cup of tea in front of her. She gave him a smile and a little wave. No customers were at the counter, so he was able to get a quick black coffee before making his way over to Evelyn's table.

"Greetings, Joe," she said. "Not living dangerously today?"

"Hi, Evelyn. No, as a matter of fact, I didn't want to take the time. Black coffee is my preferred drink of choice, anyway."

"I see."

"Nice to see you. I apologize once again for not accepting your kind dinner invitation."

"Oh, that's quite all right. I thought perhaps I scared you off. I should have mentioned my husband is a gourmet cook, and he loves to demonstrate his culinary expertise whenever he can."

Joe felt like an idiot thinking Evelyn's offer was an attempt at seduction. *Yeah, Evelyn, you should have. And just out of curiosity, where's your wedding ring?*

"Like I said, I'll take a rain check. Some other time, I hope."

"Of course."

"And I'm still interested in seeing the cat show this fall."

"Wonderful. I would love to show you around. Evelyn took a sip from her tea. "Speaking of cats…" She reached over to the adjacent chair and retrieved her purse. "I have what I promised you."

She opened her purse and removed two envelopes and placed them on the table. On one was written, "Havana Brown," while on the other was written, "Burmese."

"I was able to contact a couple of breeders. Inside the envelopes, you'll find sealed plastic bags which contain the hair samples. I hope you'll find that satisfactory."

She impressed him with her knowledge of packaging evidence. "I'm certain it will prove more than satisfactory." He picked up the envelopes and placed them in his inside blazer pocket.

"Thank you for your help, Evelyn. I appreciate this very much."

"You're welcome. If I can help you with anything else, just let me know."

Husband or no husband, she conveyed more than a simple offer of assistance. His gut feeling about her had been right. He shouldn't have felt like an idiot after all. *Trust in the force, Joe!*

"I'll keep that in mind," he answered as he rose from the table. "This may lead to the break we've been looking for."

"Must you leave so soon? You haven't finished your coffee," she implored, clearly disappointed.

"I'm afraid so. Forensics is expecting these samples, and I told them I would have them there before the shift change. I'm sorry I can't spend more time with you. Next time?"

"I hope so."

He gave her a smile, grabbed his paper cup of coffee, and split. Maybe it wasn't nice, but he didn't have time for this nonsense. And probably there would not be a next time.

As he walked back to the office, he called Art Casey, the evidence technician from the Melanie McAdams case. He told Art about what he'd found regarding brown cat hairs present in each of the six homicide scenes and that he had samples from two different brown-colored cat breeds. If his theory was correct, they could narrow the breed of cat the hairs came from.

"Can your lab run a comparison of my samples against the ones found at the crime scenes?" asked Joe.

"Certainly. But as you know, the lab is backed up. You might not get an answer for weeks," cautioned Art.

"Art, you're a knowledgeable man with a microscope. You have the expertise to verify if one of these two samples is consistent with the hairs found at one of the crime scenes. Am I right?"

There was a pause. "I'm afraid this perp is going to kill again, and right now we've got nothing to go on. I need a favor. Can you help me out?"

Another pause. "All right. I'll need to do this on my own time. But it won't be official until the lab runs the tests. I can tell you if the hairs you have would be consistent with a particular breed. Call me tomorrow morning, and I can arrange a time for you to bring in the samples."

Joe thanked him, continuing toward his office. If something matched, they would have their first piece of evidence pointing toward the killer. Like Anita said: baby steps.

After work, he met Anita at The Fitness Center, and she gave him a good workout. He could feel he was progressing in just the week he'd been exercising. He was getting his breath back and was feeling better.

"You keep working like this, Joe, and you're gonna to be ready to run in a 5K before long."

"Not my thing," said Joe as he continued pumping his legs on the Airdyne bike. "I'll leave that kind of abuse to you."

"Not my thing, either. That's for the competitor-types. I'm just into looking good and feeling good."

"My goals as well."

"You came in halfway there, and now you're on your way to achieving the other half. You're one of my few clients that seem to have the discipline to make it."

Chapter Fifteen

After delivering the hair samples to Art Casey on Friday, Joe received a phone call the following Monday. Art had finished comparing the samples.

"Well, I was able to come up with an unofficial answer for you, Joe. The hairs from the crime scene are consistent with your sample from a Havana Brown. The other sample from the Burmese didn't have the same characteristics."

"That's good news, Art. I owe you one."

"Who collected these samples for you?"

"A cat show judge by the name of Evelyn Stewart-Bruce. She got the two samples from cat breeders she knew."

"I see. I'll need to document the chain of evidence for the lab. Do you know who the breeders were? Joe could hear him entering notes on his computer.

"No, but I could find out ."

"It's okay. I'll contact you if I need any additional documentation." And with that, he ended the call. Art wasn't big on chit-chat.

Joe had just found the first actual lead in the case. Their path forward now was to seek a person who was in constant contact with at least one Havana Brown cat. He got on the internet and did a search for "Havana Brown cats" and found that they were a rare breed. That was a stroke of luck when it came to tracking down owners in the Chicago area.

He continued eating his lunch. One thing about cooking well: it wasn't cheap. His grocery bill each week was significant, but it was being compensated for by staying out of the bars at night. That's an expense that used to eat into his budget, too.

Sam wasn't back from lunch yet when Joe's phone rang. Vincenzo was asking to see him. Good. He had some news he wanted to give him. A woman was seated in front of Vincenzo's desk.

"Joe, I want you to meet Destiny Alexander. She's a criminal profiler, formerly with the FBI's Behavior Analysis Unit. She's been brought in to assist with the case you're working on. Destiny, this is Joe Erickson, one of our best detectives."

"Actually, we've met," said Destiny.

"You have?"

"Yeah," smiled Joe. "We bumped into each other in a supermarket."

They shook hands and Joe took a seat next to her. Then Joe said, "Say, I got a break on the cat hair thing."

"Yeah?" All of a sudden, Vincenzo was all ears.

"The hairs from one of the crime scenes were a preliminary match to a hair sample I provided from a purebred Havana Brown cat. Havana Browns are a rare breed. Whoever the perp is either owns one or is in close proximity to one."

Vincenzo then asked, "One crime scene?"

"Yeah. The Melanie McAdams scene. The crime lab can run the sample against the hairs found at all the crime scenes to determine if they're consistent, but it's going to take time. Art Casey, one of the crime scene techs, ran an unofficial check for me as a favor. We won't get the official results from the lab for weeks."

"You're going to have to fill me in," said Destiny.

"He will," assured Vincenzo. He looked at Joe. "What do you and Sam have on your docket tomorrow?"

"Nothing I can't clear. Why?"

"First thing in the morning, I want you two to bring Ms. Alexander up to speed on what you've found about these cases. She's going to be putting together a profile on this guy. It should help us narrow down who we should be looking for."

Joe glanced at Destiny and then back at Vincenzo. "We can do that."

Vincenzo concluded their meeting by saying, "Okay then. Do you need anything else from me?"

"Nothing that I can think of."

"Good. See you tomorrow then."

Joe accompanied Destiny down the hall toward his desk to introduce her to Sam, who had returned from lunch. Joe introduced him to Destiny and gave him the particulars about her job. Neither of them had worked with a criminal profiler before and her answers to their questions were enlightening and her knowledge impressed them.

Joe spent the remainder of that afternoon copying documents from the six homicides to create a binder of information for Destiny to work from to create her profile. He despised this kind of busy work that any secretary could do. But a secretary wasn't capable of discerning what was important and what was irrelevant from the files. So, it was up to him and Sam to make those determinations.

The next morning when Joe got to work, Destiny was already there. He was on his way to the refrigerator with his lunch in hand when he saw her at his desk, removing things from her briefcase. Her hair was pulled back, and she was dressed in khaki slacks and an ivory blouse. Simple yet effective. As he walked over toward her, she looked up.

"You're here even earlier than me. Is this the norm for you?"

"Pretty much. I like to get a feel for the place I'm working in." She glanced at the plastic sack dangling from his hand. "Your lunch?"

"It is, as a matter of fact."

"I heard you were a bit of a gourmet."

This made Joe chuckle. "And just who did you hear that from, if I may ask?"

"Oh, I never reveal my sources. But out of curiosity, what little gem did you prepare for yourself today, if you don't mind telling me?"

Joe thought she was going to be another one who was going to harass him about his new cooking and eating habits. Wonderful! Just what he needed.

"First Sam, and now you. Well, I don't mind telling you. You'll probably see me eating it, anyway. It's an asparagus and salmon salad with a balsamic vinaigrette."

She thought that sounded pretty good, like something she would order at an upscale restaurant. "Sounds yummy. Except for the salmon."

"Don't tell me you're a vegan."

"Vegetarian. But I have been known to fall off the wagon once in a while."

"It's good to know you're not perfect. I have a hard time with perfect people. Now, if you'll excuse me, I'd better get this into the fridge."

Joe walked to the refrigerator and deposited his lunch. When he went back to his desk, he pulled out the binder he'd created for Destiny the day before. She opened it and saw it was neatly categorized by each homicide, which contained copies of photos, autopsy reports, and other relevant information. The introduction was a summary that Joe had created and given to Lt. Vincenzo.

Joe could see her visibly react to the first crime scene photo of Deanna Frost. But she maintained her professional composure as she leafed through the binder.

After glancing over it, she looked at Joe. "Did you put this together?"

"The binder, you mean?"

"No. The discovery of the series of murders tied to one individual."

"Yeah." He explained that he and Sam caught the Melanie McAdams case. And when there was a second murder with the same mutilation, he started researching past cases, and that's how he discovered the six homicides with the same MO.

Destiny was favorably impressed by the thought, ingenuity, and time that went into Joe's research. She was told by Vincenzo he had one of the highest solve rates of any detective on the homicide squad. Now, she could understand why. He possessed an intellectual curiosity that would drive him to go the extra mile. She admired that in a cop. In addition to that, she couldn't help but notice he was easy on the eyes. The thought made her smile. Joe picked up on it.

"Something about this amuses you?"

That caught her off guard. *Damn! This is embarrassing.* "No, I was just thinking of something that reminded me of someone at the FBI. Sorry. You had to be there."

Fortunately for her, Sam rolled in and saved the day. "Good morning," he said as he picked up his rather disgusting cup that was desperately in need of washing and transferred coffee from the paper cup he carried in most mornings from Dunkin' Donuts. "You want some coffee? I have an extra cup in my desk." He saw her reaction. "It's clean–or at least it was last month."

"No thanks, I had a coffee already this morning. Is there a room where we can work?"

They adjourned to a conference room. Joe told her that he was going to interview Frank Edwards tomorrow since Frank was flying into Chicago today. Destiny asked if she could be part of the interview.

"I'll ask him and see if it's all right. I don't want to show up with someone he isn't expecting."

"You mean a woman?"

"Someone he doesn't know. We've never worked together, but he knows who I am. Vincenzo told me Frank's an old-school kinda guy, comfortable around people he knows. Just being considerate, that's all." Actually, Joe didn't know how Frank would feel talking about the case with an attractive young woman sitting across from him. She could be a distraction.

"Fair enough," said Destiny.

Beginning mid-morning, each of the lead detectives on five of the six cases, Gary Nelson, Michelle Cardona, Eddie Collins, Kevin Dempsey, as well as Joe were interviewed. Destiny took notes and asked insightful questions of each detective. By the end of the day, Joe and Sam had their notepads full of additional information to add to the dossier they were building on the case. They were also mentally fatigued, but Destiny didn't show it if she was.

"So, do you think this gives you enough to build a profile?" asked Sam.

"Oh, yeah. All of your detectives have given me a lot to go on." Looking at Joe, she said, "What you've compiled here is excellent. Thanks."

"How long does this process normally take you?" asked Joe. "I haven't worked with a profiler before so this is new to me."

"I should have a profile for you in a week to ten days. When it's done, I'll give you a presentation as well as a written report. I'll call when I have the profile ready to go."

Joe handed her his card and urged her to call him if she needed anything else. She thanked them and left the building. Sam looked at Joe and said, "You think this profiling thing is going to help?"

"I don't know. I'm keeping an open mind."

Chapter Sixteen

After Joe had worked out with Anita that evening, he was in the middle of making pasta with chorizo and spinach when his phone rang. Frank Edwards was calling.

"Hey, Frank," answered Joe.

"How you doin', Joe?"

"You have a good flight?"

"Not bad. Jeez, I think it's hotter up here than it is down there, to tell the truth. Anyway, I thought I'd better give you a call. We're pretty much settled in here. We're staying at the Carleton in Oak Park. When you wanna meet?"

"What's good for you?"

"How's tomorrow, say two o'clock?"

Joe thought he'd better breach the subject of Destiny's request to accompany him on the interview. "Yeah, that works. Say, I have a colleague, a criminal profiler that would like to tag along. Would it be all right with you if she sat in?"

"Criminal profiler, huh? Yeah, I suppose that'd be okay."

"I'll warn you, she's attractive. Could be a distraction."

"Distraction," Frank laughed. "What's she gonna do, wear a mini-skirt, show some cleavage?" He laughed some more.

"I believe you'll find her very professional. I'll call you when we pull into the parking lot."

"Okay. Talk with you then." He ended the call.

Joe knew he would have to contact Destiny about the meeting, but he decided to eat dinner first. No hurry. And besides, he was in the middle of cooking and didn't want a phone conversation to interrupt his concentration. Scorched food was not pleasant.

After dumping the steaming penne pasta into a colander, he opened a bottle of Beaujolais and poured himself a glass. He drank it as he stirred the onion, mushroom, artichoke, sundried tomato, and chorizo mixture that had been simmering in the pan. He added the spinach and cooked it until it wilted and then moved the mixture from the pan into a bowl. Ready at last.

The aroma alone had been whetting his appetite, and he was eager to dig in. He liked it very much, and his choice of wine, which he researched on the internet, was a nice complement to the spicy chorizo. Now, the challenge became avoiding the temptation to pig out and go for seconds. He needed the remainder for his lunch the next day.

After cleaning the kitchen, he dialed Destiny. His call went to voice mail, so he left her a message about the meeting tomorrow and asked her to call him back. He poured himself a second glass of Beaujolais and adjourned to his recliner where he kicked off his shoes and turned on the television. Nothing on the networks he wanted to see, so he pulled up a dark mystery series from Finland he'd been watching on Netflix.

That second glass of wine was a mistake, and his cellphone jolted him awake an hour later.

"Joe Erickson," he answered, not bothering to look to see who the caller was.

"Are you drunk?"

Embarrassed, he realized it was Destiny. "No. No, just waking up."

Suppressing a laugh, she began rubbing it in. "Jeez, Joe. It's only eight-fifteen. How old are you, anyway?"

"Never mix a workout, a good meal, and a second glass of wine with a recliner. It's a dangerous combination."

"So, I take it you like living in the danger zone."

Is she flirting with me or does she give everyone a hard time? That's kind of ballsy. She doesn't know me all that well. "Sometimes. As long as it's in my recliner."

She snort-laughed and then asked, "You said in your message you had a meeting set with Frank Edwards?"

"Yeah, tomorrow afternoon at two o'clock in Oak Park. Carleton Hotel. You still want to go?"

"Yes, I do."

The next day Destiny met Joe at the Area 3 office at one o'clock, and they walked down to the parking lot to Joe's Camaro. Taught from his early teen years to observe proper decorum when escorting a young lady, he opened the door for her. It didn't go unnoticed.

"Pretty fancy cars detectives are driving these days."

"It's my personal car," explained Joe after he slid into the driver's seat and buckled up. "It's not regulation but I didn't want to drive one of the crappy fleet vehicles out to Oak Park. Besides, my car needs to stretch its legs with some highway miles. I figured you wouldn't report me."

"You take a lot for granted."

"Occasionally," he said as he turned the key and the black Camaro's V8 rumbled to life.

Joe drove to the Eisenhower Expressway for the eleven-mile trip to Oak Park. It should have taken about twenty minutes, but given traffic, it was hard to gauge the time. Barring any bottlenecks or accidents, they would arrive early.

Destiny brought up something Joe mentioned on the phone the previous night.

"You said last night you worked out. You go to the gym?"

"Yeah, I decided it was time to get back into shape, so I got a membership at a fitness center and hired a personal trainer."

"How's that been working for you?"

"I'm getting there. I dropped ten pounds and I've been cooking for myself rather than going out all the time. I'm rather enjoying that." Joe looked over at her. "What about you? What do you do to keep in shape?"

"I do yoga. Been practicing for years. "

They continued talking about fitness and food. About four miles from Oak Park, traffic slowed to a crawl.

"Great," muttered Joe. "I wonder how long this is going to hold us up."

"Good thing you built in extra time."

"There's an exit for Highway 50 up ahead. If we're still crawling by the time we get there, we can take that exit. It will take us north to Highway 64 which will take us west into Oak Park."

"How do you know that?"

Looking over at her, he smiled. "I used to date a girl from Oak Park."

"Ohhhh. So, what happened?"

"It turned out we weren't compatible. I'm an Aquarius and she's a control freak."

Destiny chuckled, "I see. Well, it's good you found out, I guess. Huh?"

"Yeah."

Traffic was still moving at twenty miles per hour when they reached the exit for Highway 50. So, Joe turned off the expressway onto the exit and drove to Highway 64 and took it into Oak Park. They arrived at the Carleton in downtown Oak Park fifteen minutes ahead of time. Joe parked the Camaro in a space near the back of the hotel, and as they walked to the entrance, he placed a call to Frank Edwards who answered on the second ring.

"Hey-ya, Joe," answered Frank.

"We're a little early. Is that okay?"

"Hell, yes. I'll meet you in the lobby. See you in a couple."

They entered the lobby of the historic hotel and waited near the fireplace. Moments later, Frank appeared. Frank gave a little smile and walked over.

They made introductions and shook hands. Frank suggested they talk in the grill since it wasn't busy at 2:00 pm. After they sat down, a waiter was right there ready to take their order.

Frank didn't wait for ladies first. "Double Crown on the rocks."

No wonder he wanted to meet in here, thought Joe.

"Club soda with a twist for me," said Destiny.

"And for you, sir?"

"Coffee, black," replied Joe. He saw Frank give him a look. "We're both on duty, and I'm driving."

Frank said, "My wife's already drivin' me nuts over this wedding thing, and we just got here. Her family, my family, they're all over the place upstairs yakkin' away. I love my family, don't get me wrong. But the best thing about them is they live far away."

Joe chuckled. Destiny smiled. "Being the only child of an only child, I guess I can't relate very well to that," Joe replied.

"You don't have family?" Frank asked.

"Just my dad. My mom's family was rather small. I have a distant cousin in California that I haven't seen for over twenty years. That's it."

Changing the subject, Frank asked, "Okay, so what do you wanna know about the Deanna Frost case?"

"Tell us what you remember, let's start there," Joe urged.

"The case I couldn't solve. If Nate was still alive, maybe he would have cracked it. He was a bulldog, never gave up on a case. Nate had great instincts, you know?"

"Yeah. There are guys like that." Destiny gave Joe a look, knowing from her discussions with Vincenzo that Joe was one of those guys.

"She didn't show up for work and didn't call in so her boss got concerned and called the police. The uniforms found her and Nate and I got the call. She was lying in bed covered by a blanket, head on the pillow. Nude underneath. When the M.E. started to examine the body, he found the surgery that had been done to her."

Frank looked at Joe and confided, "I've seen a lot of bad stuff over the years, but that... that's the one memory I wish I could blot out."

Frank looked away and let out a breath. His eyes stared off blankly as if he was seeing that image in his mind. He took a deep breath and exhaled.

Destiny decided to step in and asked, "Would you mind if I asked you a question?"

Looking at her seemed to take him from the strange mood into which he'd drifted. "Uh, yeah. Go ahead."

"Tell us what you found out about the victim. Did you get any leads on where she may have met her assailant?"

"She was in her late twenties, typical young, unmarried, career woman.

According to her friends, she liked to barhop, especially ones with live music, attend arts events. She didn't have a steady boyfriend but would connect with a guy once in a while. She wasn't into any long-term relationships. We were able to trace her movements on the Friday night before she was killed. She was at an outdoor concert in Grant Park, and her friend said she was talking to a lot of guys." Frank chuckled as he remembered, "One of them was a real 'babe magnet' as she put it."

"Wait a minute. That wasn't in the report," said Joe.

"What? The babe magnet thing? Didn't think it was worth noting. She was interacting with a lot of people."

"Did she describe him?" asked Destiny.

"Well, barely. I checked my notes to jog my memory on the case. She said he was medium height with dark hair. How's that? Probably describes over half the men in Grant Park."

"What's your take on that?" asked Joe.

"Hard to tell," Frank shrugged. "Coulda been a regular guy in jeans and a t-shirt who had nothing to do with her death. Or, it coulda been the perp. Who knows? With all the people in Grant Park at that concert, there's no way we could track down anybody that was there. Surveillance footage was useless."

"This is actually helpful."

"Helpful? How so? I haven't given you jack to go on."

"You confirmed something for us. A witness from one of the other murders saw the vic in a bar talking with quote: 'a really good-looking guy with dark hair' the night before she died. Sound familiar?"

"The bar have a surveillance camera?" asked Frank.

"No, unfortunately. And there was only one witness that had any memory of the vic and the guy, and she couldn't provide specifics beyond what I mentioned. Right now, it's the only thing we have to go on."

Destiny looked at both Frank and Joe. "You know what? If this perpetrator's a handsome guy with loads of personal charm, he's one of the most dangerous men in the city. He can masquerade as a girl's romantic dream, and he can compel her to bring him home to her apartment. And once he's there, the predator's alone with his prey."

Frank spotted the waiter coming with their drinks. "Just in time."

The waiter set the drinks in front of them and walked away. Frank took a healthy sip from his whiskey and set it down. Then he looked at Joe who was sipping his coffee and said, "You know, with all the security cameras around these days, it's a wonder this guy hasn't been caught on video somewhere."

"The lobby of Melanie McAdams apartment didn't have a security camera. One was due to be installed the next month the super told us. What about your case?"

"Nothing. Not even on adjacent buildings. It's like the guy scouted these places beforehand and knew there were no cameras or other people around who could get a close look at him. Not possible, of course."

Destiny spoke up. "No. No. Don't rule that out. What if it wasn't the first time he met them? Maybe he encountered his victims previously. That way, he could find out their addresses, and do some reconnoitering to see if he could pull off another killing?"

"He waits for a second date?"

"Or a casual meeting followed by…a hookup, date, or whatever. Anything that gets him into their apartments."

"People need to know about this guy before he strikes again," warned Frank.

"Yeah, the department's working on a press release as we speak. At least, that's what I've been told. Then the guy will probably go underground and make our job catching him more difficult."

"Got any more clues as to his identity or is this all you've got?"

Joe didn't want to mention the cat hair evidence. "We have a little more, but it's slim pickins."

"That's all we ever got." Frank tipped his drink and finished it, and rather than setting it back down on the table, he looked down into the glass as if he was studying the ice cubes. "We never got that lucky break."

"We're going to need one."

Frank looked up at Destiny and smiled. "Maybe you'll be the lucky charm that helps break this case."

"Let's hope my profile will."

Deciding they'd gotten as much information as they could from Frank Edwards, Joe changed the subject to living in Florida. He bought Frank another double Royal Crown whiskey, and they chatted for another fifteen minutes before parting company with best wishes on the upcoming nuptials.

On their return drive to Chicago, Destiny asked, "What did you mean by the "slim pickins" reference? He explained the Havana Brown cat hair evidence to her and the possibility of DNA testing.

"You discovered that, too?" *Not only good-looking but very resourceful. No wonder Vincenzo said he was one of his best detectives.*

"Yeah. It was one of those things that I found present in each crime scene, and none of the victims owned a cat. I did a little research and found all the hairs were brown, a rare color for a cat." And he went on to explain how he got the samples and how the comparisons were made.

"So, now you're looking for a handsome, dark-haired man who owns a Havana Brown cat. I'd say you've done a good job narrowing down your suspects." *I wonder if he has a girlfriend. Probably does.*

Chapter Seventeen

By the time Joe dropped Destiny at her car, it was quitting time. He enjoyed her company and found her very bright and insightful, not to mention attractive. He contemplated asking her out, but he wasn't so sure she would accept since she was working with him. Mixing work with one's personal life could have serious repercussions, even though she was only temporarily on the job. *Ehh, a woman like her probably has a significant other anyway.*

He changed into his workout clothes and walked to The Fitness Center. He spied Anita working with another client, so he began warming up by going through his stretching routine. By the time he finished, he felt limber and ready to begin running. A woman got off a treadmill, so he grabbed it and began by walking. Gradually, he increased to a jogging pace.

About five minutes into his twenty-minute jog, Anita walked over.

"How you doin', Joe?" She always had a little attitude in her voice. That was one of the things Joe liked about her.

"Pretty good."

"I don't know about the 'pretty' part. Sounds a little arrogant if you ask me. But you seem to be doing okay. How long have you been doing twenty minutes on the treadmill?"

"A couple of weeks."

"Try upping that to twenty-five. Your goal should be thirty."

"Just when I stop hurting, you want me to feel pain again."

"You got that right," she laughed. "When I get done with you, you're gonna be in the best shape of your life."

"I'd better be, it's costing me enough."

"I don't think I like you anymore." She started to walk away and then turned, "Let me know when you're done and we'll work on some weight training."

Joe pushed his jogging to twenty-five minutes, and he could feel the additional burn in his legs. And he knew he would feel it even more tomorrow.

Anita had planned some upper body workouts on the weight machines. She gave him a light workout on each and told him what each one would do and what to expect as they moved forward.

Joe felt good as he walked home. After a shower, he threw on a pair of jeans and a t-shirt and sat down at the table. Looking through his cookbooks for dishes he wanted to prepare for next week, he wrote out a list of ingredients he would need. Then he got into his car and drove to the supermarket.

Once inside, he began filling his cart and checking things off his list. Standing in the spice aisle looking for smoked paprika, he felt a shopping cart hit him from behind. Not hard, but a substantial bump.

"Oh, I'm sorry," came a woman's voice from behind him.

Annoyed, he turned, and to his surprise, there was Destiny with a mischievous look on her face. "You're not sorry," Joe replied with a laugh.

"You're right, I'm not."

"If I was paranoid, I would think you were stalking me. But since I'm not, I would assume we both shop at odd hours."

"Whenever I have free time. It's hard telling when that might be."

Glancing in her cart, he saw it contained mostly fresh fruit and vegetables. "You always shop here?"

"Usually. It's not far from where I live."

"Same here." He didn't want to broach the subject, but he knew if he didn't, he would kick himself later. *What the hell, take a chance.* "Do you have any plans for Friday night?" *There, I said it.*

"Uh, no. Why?"

"How about dinner? You pick the place."

"Oh, that sounds like the kind of invitation I like. Well now. Do you like vegetarian food?"

"There are very few things I don't like, as a matter of fact. I'm open to trying anything."

"Great! There's a wonderful place on Logan Square we can go. They have excellent food. It's small and they don't take reservations, so would it be okay with you if we ate early? Say, six o'clock? Sometimes it's hard to get in between seven and nine."

"Sounds good. Six o'clock it is."

"Perfect. I'll meet you there." She gave him the address and the name of the restaurant. He'd driven past it before so he knew where it was.

"Happy shopping," she said as she pushed her cart past him and up the aisle.

He watched her until she disappeared around the corner. He continued shopping, picking up the rest of his groceries, and then checked out. He felt pleased with himself. He asked and she accepted. He always hated asking a woman out for the first time. No matter how confident and experienced a guy may be, there is always anxiety about the possibility of rejection.

At that point, he started thinking. *Evidently, there isn't a significant other in the picture at the moment.* Then he started wondering why. *With her looks and at her age, shouldn't there be? Maybe she's career-minded. Maybe she's divorced. Maybe there's something wrong with her. Ah, stop thinking like a detective, Joe. You idiot!*

After arriving home and putting his groceries away, he made dinner. The steamed mussels were so good, he could not resist a second helping. He would have to grab lunch somewhere tomorrow since there was nothing left to take to work.

* * *

That same evening, Michael Fleming worked in his basement assembling another picture frame. The glass, the black velvet backing, and the aluminum frame matched the others that hung on the wall of his secret room. Before hanging it, he added a small nametag, centering it at the bottom of the glass. Like all the others, it was labeled with the victim's first name. The aluminum plate read, "Maria."

He unlocked the bookcase, and a section swung open revealing his secret room. Walking up to the wall, he hung this newest addition. This was the eighteenth frame in all. Stepping back, he admired his acquisitions in much the same way an art collector would admire his Salvador Dali prints. But Michael Fleming's collection was far from works of art.

He sat down on the leather love seat. As his eyes moved from one frame to the next, his thoughts were interrupted when a chocolate brown cat jumped onto the arm of the love seat and let out a loud, "meow."

Startled out of his fantasy, he looked at the cat and crooned, "Fidel! How did you get down here? Did Daddy leave the door ajar again?" The Havana Brown cat purred and head-butted his arm. "Oh, do you want some love?" Fleming reached down and began rubbing Fidel's ear, and Fidel responded by closing his green eyes and stretching his head upward, a cat's body language for "Oh my god, yes!"

Fleming talked to his cat as if he was carrying on a conversation with a child. Picking him up and placing him in his lap, he pointed at the wall and said, "See? Look there. Daddy has a new one. That makes eighteen. How about that?" As he stroked his back, Fidel looked up at him and gave a soft meow. "You want more? Well, we can't rush this sort of thing. All in good time."

Fidel chirped as if he understood and then started to squirm. "No, I can't put you down. Come on, let's get you back upstairs where you belong, young man."

He stood up with Fidel under his arm. And after flicking the light switch off and pushing the bookcase closed, he climbed the stairs to the main floor. Fleming settled into his couch and spent the next two hours re-watching a DVD of Brian DePalma's *Dressed to Kill*. He loved that film.

Chapter Eighteen

On Friday, Lt. Vincenzo called Detectives Erickson, Collins, Dempsey, Nelson, Renaldo, and Cardona into his office. They gathered and waited for Vincenzo to arrive, talking amongst themselves. They assumed there was some news he wished to give them on the case. They didn't have to wait long.

Vincenzo entered and walked behind his desk. "Today, there's a press conference scheduled at eleven o'clock where the Superintendent of Police and members of the mayor's office will have an announcement about a string of homicides linked to one particular individual who is presently unknown. After their statements, they will take questions. They've established a hotline for people who may have tips and information ."

Vincenzo took a drink from his coffee mug. "In addition, I met with the Deputy Chief and the 1st Deputy Superintendent about the apparent serial killings. After looking over the evidence, they've decided to establish a task force with the objective of apprehending this perpetrator. Since the majority of the victims came from the Area 3, he wants the task force to work out of Area 3. That's why you're here. Because each of you investigated one of the homicides and already have knowledge of one of the cases, you six now make up the Serial Killer Task Force. Sam, you're the exception. I want you to stand in for Frank Edwards on the Deanna Frost case. I'm going to head up the task force myself. You'll be reporting to me. Any questions?"

The announcement took them by surprise, and for a few moments, they were all left speechless. They had no inkling from Vincenzo this was coming down.

"Yeah. I've got one," piped up Cardona. "Where do you want us to start?"

"Go back and review your case. Re-interview all the people you saw the first time around to see if they have any new information. They might remember something they didn't provide previously. Go over the case with a fine-tooth comb. Then share your findings with each other. Whoever this guy is, he hasn't committed the perfect crime. Not this many times."

"What about our regular duties?" asked Nelson.

"Until this guy is found or the task force is disbanded, your regular duties with your Areas are suspended. You work exclusively for the task force."

Eddie Collins took a couple of steps forward. "What do we have to go on? I mean, anything turn up from the more recent homicides?"

"Thanks to some good work by Erickson here, we now know that the perp either owns or is in regular contact with a Havana Brown cat." Most everyone had deer-in-the-headlights looks. Vincenzo noticed and clarified.

"That's a rare breed of domestic cat. Chocolate brown, short-haired variety. Hairs consistent with a Havana Brown have been found at each of the crime scenes, and none of the victims owned a cat. That's about all we have to go on other than what's in your reports. We have a criminal profiler putting together a profile on the perp. As soon as she's completed her work, we'll meet and she'll present her findings. She told me it should be sometime early next week."

"Who's going to be taking phone calls from the public once the newspapers print the story?" asked Joe.

"To begin with, all of you are," replied Vincenzo. A communal groan came from them all. "Look, I know you're going to get flooded with a lot of calls when this story first hits. That's typical, but you may get that one lead from a caller that could break this case wide open. An 800-line has been set up, and it's already been connected to your phones. Eddie, I'll show you to your desk once we're done here. IT is setting up your computer as we speak. Any other questions?" The room was silent. "Email me if you do. Come on," he said to Collins, "I'll show you where you're going to work."

Vincenzo walked out the door with Collins in tow. Cardona, Dempsey, Nelson, Joe, and Sam stood in silence, looking at each other. Finally,

Cardona looked at Joe.

"Did you volunteer me for this thing?

"I had nothing to do with it," Joe stated. "Like he said, he chose those of us who were leads on previous the cases."

"Except me," grumbled Sam. "I have to learn Edwards' case from scratch.

"Fresh eyes, Sam," said Joe.

Sam was not appeased by Joe's suggestion. "Easy for you to say."

"I don't mind serving on this task force. I'm not going to like the pressure they're going to put on us to solve this thing," Cardona pointed out. "People are going to expect results."

"And so is the mayor's office," added Nelson. "You know what they're like."

"I can't wait for all the 'helpful' phone calls we're going to get," complained Dempsey. "Should be fun once the nut cases start calling."

"We'll do our best. What more can they ask?" replied Joe. And at that point, an idea popped into his head. "If you'll excuse me, I need to make a phone call before I get overwhelmed."

He walked to his desk, picked up the phone, and called Evelyn Stewart-Bruce. She picked up on the third ring.

"Hello, Joe," she answered. "I didn't expect to hear from you."

"Well, I had a follow-up question after our last conversation."

"Of course."

"Would you have any idea how many breeders of Havana Browns there are in the Chicago area?"

"Oh, dear. That would be hard to say. Professional breeders, there are two that I know of. But there is always the possibility that someone obtained a pair and began breeding kittens in an indiscriminate manner."

"So, if I wanted a kitten, I would most likely need to go through a reputable breeder."

"Someone who has a reputation for showing the breed, yes."

"And they would keep records of all the clients who purchased kittens?"

"Oh, yes. They would keep meticulous records on who purchased a kitten, on what date, their address information, etc."

"And would they be willing to share that information in a police investigation?"

"I doubt that very much. That would be considered an invasion of privacy and could damage their reputation. I would think you would have to subpoena their records to get what you were looking for."

"I was afraid of that."

"Besides, you could be looking at hundreds of clients. Four or five kittens per litter, two litters per year, cats can have litters for five or so years. That would be what? Fifty clients over a five-year period. That would be simply one female with one breeder. And who's to say the kitten was purchased in Chicago?"

"I see what you mean."

"Why are you asking?"

"Watch the special news conference at eleven o'clock this morning. That's all I can say. Thank you, Evelyn. You've been a great help. Again."

"You're welcome to contact me anytime, Joe. You know that."

He ended the call. He could hear the invitation still in her voice. *Damn, is her husband impotent or something?*

At eleven o'clock, they all stood around a television in the conference room and watched the news conference. High muckety-mucks from the mayor's office along with the Superintendent of Police read statements to the press and then took questions. As expected, they didn't reveal much other than the fact that six homicides over the past twenty-four months had been linked to a single perpetrator. All the victims were single women ranging in age from twenty-five to thirty-four. Each one was found in her own home. The suspect is thought to be a dark-haired white male, medium height and build. They released no other details about the crimes.

Requests were made for people with any information to call the police hotline number. The toll-free number was given out and run across the bottom of the screen several times during the news conference. Phones started ringing shortly thereafter.

"Here we go," said Joe. And he walked to his desk and picked up the phone. "Detective Erickson." And so went the rest of his day. He had to order lunch from a nearby deli since he didn't take time to leave his desk.

Joe took notes, logging in each call. For the most part, they weren't helpful. They ranged from, "My neighbor is creepy" to "Why didn't the police do something about this sooner?" By the end of the day, he had nothing solid in terms of leads nor any caller with credible information. However, he did gain one thing: a splitting headache.

He reached into his desk and shook three Ibuprofen tablets into his hand and washed them down with cold coffee. By quitting time, the throbbing in his head had lessoned to a mild ache. So much for day one. Going home would do a lot in terms of relieving the stress that caused his headache. As he was walking to his car he remembered. His date with Destiny tonight. *Shit! Of all nights to be stressed out.* Maybe a good workout was what he needed to sweat this crap out of his system.

At The Fitness Center, he was stretching when Anita came up to him. "How'd your day go, copper?"

"Lousy. I have a headache from taking hotline calls all day."

"Oh, I heard about that. So, you're a part of the investigation, huh?"

"Yeah."

"Maybe I can help. Sit up." And she kneeled behind him. "Now cross your legs and let your arms hang loose in front of you. I'm going to release the tension you've built up today. All you have to do is close your eyes and relax."

For the next few minutes, she massaged his temples and the base of his neck.

When she finished, she said, "Okay, slowly open your eyes. How do you feel?"

Joe opened his eyes and realized his face was completely relaxed and the pain in his head was gone. "That's amazing! Where did you learn that?"

"Swedish Massage Institute. My job in a previous life."

He swung his body around toward her. "Thank you."

"You're welcome. Now, finish your stretches and go home. No strenuous exercising today. Come back Monday when you're feeling better. And about those phone calls. Take a break now and then and go for a short walk.

It'll relieve the stress. And go easy on the caffeine."

"Will do." She gave him a pat on the shoulder, rose, and left to assist other clients. He finished his stretching exercises and then walked home, grateful that he wouldn't be experiencing a headache during his dinner with Destiny. *That Anita, she's something.*

Chapter Nineteen

At home, Joe showered, shaved, and got dressed. He couldn't remember how long it had been since he had dinner with a female acquaintance, a date, if you will, and he was feeling a little nervous. He thought about drinking a glass of wine but worried he might doze off in his recliner. So, he decided to skip the wine and relax for an hour. Turning on the television, he watched CNN's coverage of the earthquake in South America and the story of the U.S. congressman who collapsed during a Congressional hearing. Exhaustion, they said.

Joe took a cab to the restaurant on Logan Square and met Destiny walking to the door at five minutes before six. Apparently, the "five minutes before is on time" was a rule of thumb for both of them.

"I couldn't have timed this better," said Joe.

"I guess not. A good omen, maybe," she smiled.

They entered the diner and were escorted to their seats. The small, intimate space had a friendly and relaxed atmosphere. The aromas that wafted through the air were wonderful. Shortly after being seated, their waitress greeted them and handed them menus.

"Good evening," she said. "I'm Gloria and I'll be your waitress. May I get you something to drink?"

Joe asked for a glass of red wine, specifying Merlot if they had it. Destiny ordered a glass of Pinot Grigio. After looking over the menu, Joe had a few questions.

"I'm a virgin when it comes to eating vegetarian cuisine. You're going to have to help me out here."

"Be glad to."

"What are seitan and tempeh? I've never heard of either one."

Destiny explained they were meat substitutes, one made from wheat gluten, the other from soy protein.

"Seitan tastes like chicken and tempeh has a flavor leaning toward mushrooms." She went on to explain how each was made and how they were used in vegetarian cooking. Joe absorbed everything she said.

"I hope I didn't turn you off to the menu."

"No. No, I'm willing to try anything once."

The wine arrived, and Joe asked, "You have a handle on the profile?"

"Oh, yeah."

"I checked out your credentials when I found we'd be working together. Very impressive. Masters in Forensic Psychology from Georgetown, several years with the FBI's Behavior Analysis Unit. I hope you don't mind."

"I assumed you found my website and reviewed my career. I would have expected nothing less from a good detective."

What made you want to go into private work?"

"I'm not going to knock working at the FBI. I enjoyed my time there, and it taught me a great deal. And the people you get to work with are top-notch. But I was getting a little burned out. And I saw an opportunity and decided to set up my own consulting practice."

"Big gamble leaving a secure job with a great future. Ever regret doing it?"

"Not really. It was a little slow at first, but I made enough contacts over the years that I got great references. And my name was recognizable to certain people. Besides, my parting with the agency was amicable. I still have a lot of friends there. What about you?"

"I grew up in Marathon, Iowa, population three hundred-some people. My dad still lives there. I got a bachelor's degree in law enforcement, became a cop, and then a detective. And I don't have a website."

"Short and sweet."

"Not that much to say. I'm actually a rather boring guy."

"Except you're working to stay in shape, you like good food, you've been a gearhead all your life, and you've never been married."

Joe was surprised she knew all that about him. "How did you know all that?"

"I like to check out who I'm going to be working with, too," she smiled. "Don't worry, I didn't use my contacts at the FBI in case you're wondering."

"So, what else did you find out about me?" he asked, taking a sip of wine.

"You have the best solve-rate of any detective in Area 3. And Vincenzo thinks you can be a pain in the ass sometimes," she smiled in an amused sort of way.

Joe chuckled. "My methods are sometimes...unorthodox, shall I say?"

Her eyes locked onto his. "Nothing wrong with thinking outside the box. Especially if it gets you results."

The waitress interrupted the moment and took their dinner order.

Trying to rekindle their conversation, Destiny confided, "To tell you the truth, I try to think outside the box as well. I employ specific investigative methods I learned at the FBI. But I also like to keep current on new theories like those that have evolved out of England and Australia. The way I see it, it's good to consider alternative ways of thinking when I'm developing a profile."

"And how's your profile coming on our perp?"

"It's finished, and I'm presenting on Monday. But let's not talk shop, okay?"

"If you like."

"What do you do to have fun?"

"I don't have fun."

Destiny laughed. "Of course, you do. Everyone has fun. What do you like to do when you're not being Mr. Detective?"

"You really want to know?"

"Yeah."

"Several things, but right now, cooking has my attention."

"Cooking," she repeated as if he might have said "pole dancing."

"I know, you probably think that's a weird thing for a guy like me to be interested in."

"No, not at all."

"It's become a new interest for me. I've found I really like preparing good food and trying new recipes.

Destiny paused and asked with a subtle, provocative smile, "Are you good at it?"

"Well, I haven't burned down the kitchen, yet."

She laughed, nearly choking on her wine.

"Actually, I'm pretty good, if I do say so myself. I plan on taking some cooking classes once I've gained a little more confidence in the kitchen. I would hate to look like a rank amateur among the more experienced students."

"I think it's great you like to cook."

"Really?"

"Of course. I mean, I assumed you did after seeing you in the supermarket with the kind of groceries you had in your cart. A lot of single guys only cook well enough to survive, and they hate it. You've embraced it."

"I like good, healthy food. Preparing it's fun. It relaxes me."

"That's a fascinating side of you I didn't expect."

Their conversation flowed so easily, so effortlessly that time seemed to fly by until their dinner arrived. Blackened tofu salads to begin with and later, avocado tostadas for Destiny and enchiladas for Joe. He was impressed by the skillful combination of ingredients and the rich, savory taste of both the salad and the enchiladas. *I may have to learn to cook some vegetarian dishes in the future.*

They talked for half an hour after they finished their dinner. Being with Destiny was easy and fun. And those eyes! They communicated more than just a casual interest. He picked up the tab and they left the diner. Still early, Joe wanted to spend more time with her.

"You want to take a walk?"

"Love to." Mm. Just what he wanted to hear.

The sidewalks were busy. The area was popular with a lot of restaurants and bars catering to many differing tastes. They walked and talked for half an hour, eventually winding up back on North Milwaukee. Joe stopped in front of a retro-inspired neighborhood bar he knew.

"You want to go inside? They have an open-air patio in back where we could sit."

"Sounds nice."

They entered the bar and Joe ordered a beer for him and a Pinot Grigio for Destiny. They walked back to the patio and sat down at an open table. The cooler evening air felt good. They started talking, and before they knew it, it was midnight.

"Holy cow! Look at the time," Joe said, looking at his watch. "Did you know it was midnight?"

"No," said Destiny. "You want to go?"

"Do you?"

"To tell you the truth, I'm beginning to fade."

The place was louder and more crowded than it was when they came in. Joe tipped the bartender, and they made their way out the door.

"Can I get you a taxi?"

"That would be nice."

He hailed a cab, handed the driver a twenty, and opened the door.

"Lovely evening. Thanks. We should do this again."

"I hope so," Destiny replied, and she planted a light kiss on his cheek.

"Good night." He made eye contact with her and winked. Then, he shut the door and watched the taxi drive away.

Ohhhh, boy! he thought and walked back into the bar.

Chapter Twenty

The next day was Saturday, and about lunchtime, Joe had an urge to call Destiny, but he thought better of it. He didn't want to come on too strong or needy. So, he decided to send her a text instead.

Enjoyed your company last evening. It was fun!

About an hour later, Destiny responded. *I thought you didn't have fun.*

He texted her back. *Last night I did. You must have had something to do with it.*

Nice. I had fun, too.

Great! Looking forward to the next time.

When will that be?

Anytime you like.

Really?

I have a lot of time on my hands. I lead a boring life.

Boring! Ha! What are you doing tonight?

Nothing.

Call me later. Five-ish?

Okay.

At two o'clock, Joe's phone rang. Sam was calling to ask Joe to come to the 24th District. A woman came into the police station to report she saw a man with Maria Martinez the night before she died.

Joe drove up north to Rogers Park. He was hoping that this could be the break they needed. Dempsey and Crawford, the investigating detectives, had traced her movements during the last week of her life and had come up empty. Today, Dempsey was out of town, and Crawford was down with the flu, so Sam and Joe were called in to interview the woman. Sam was already there when Joe arrived. They were escorted to an interview room where they met Gabriela Torres, a young woman in her late twenties. She clicked off her cell phone as they came into the room.

"Gabriela?" asked Joe.

"Yes, but you can call me Gabby," she replied as she stood up.

"I'm Detective Joe Erickson, and this is my partner, Sam Renaldo."

"¿Cómo estás?," asked Sam.

She smiled. "Bien, gracias," she replied.

"Have a seat, Gabby," said Joe. "You came in because you saw someone with Maria Martinez, is that correct?"

"Yes."

"Tell us about it.

"Well, it was the Friday before she was killed. And we were both in this Hispanic bar on North Clarke Street. I don't go out to bars that often, but on that night, I decided to go out with one of my girlfriends. Well, she talked me into it."

"How did you know Maria Martinez?" asked Sam.

"I didn't really know her personally. I just knew her from church. Knew who she was because we both went to St. Ignatius, and we worked together on a couple of projects there."

"I see. Go on," urged Sam.

"Well, my friend, Araceli, and I were in the bar, and I noticed Maria was in there talking to this guy. And after a few minutes, they got into this argument and she left."

"Was it a heated argument?" asked Joe.

"Oh, yeah. She was pretty mad. So was he."

"Did he leave, too?" asked Sam?

"No, he stayed in the bar and started talking to other girls."

"Do you remember what time this was?" asked Joe.

"It was early. Maybe ten-thirty. Something like that."

"And how long did you stay?"

"We met a couple of guys and we left about midnight or so. Went to a party a few blocks away."

"Was he still in the bar at the time you left?"

"I wasn't paying any attention. My thoughts were elsewhere. You know... " she said, her face turning pink from embarrassment.

"Yeah," smiled Joe, "I understand. Can you describe him?"

"Uh-huh. He was not too tall, maybe five-foot-nine, thin, dark hair combed back, good-looking, soul patch, and a tattoo of a spider web on the back of his neck."

"Would you recognize him if you saw him again?" asked Sam.

"Oh, sure. Like I said, he was nice looking."

Joe and Sam continued to question Gabby for another ten minutes. Then, they took her contact information and thanked her for coming in. Outside, Sam hailed a taxi for her.

"We'll have to stake out that bar so we can bring that guy in," said Sam.

"Yeah, and I'll stick out like a sore thumb in a Hispanic bar. But you won't. Maybe you and Cardona could go in. You could pass as a couple."

"She'll love that."

"It's the best lead we've got so far."

"You mean the only lead we've got so far."

Joe looked at his watch. "Four-thirty. I've got to go."

"Got a date?"

"Maybe."

"Ha! When you gonna cook for me?"

"When you grow some taste buds. See you tomorrow."

Joe drove back to his place and made it there a little after five. He called Destiny and his call went to voicemail.

He didn't feel hungry yet, so he poured himself a glass of Pinot Noir and sat down in his recliner. He started thinking about the lead they received and how serial killers do everything they can to keep under the radar. They're exceptionally clever. An argument with a woman in a bar is exactly what one of these creatures would want to avoid. The more he thought about it, the more he began having doubts. *A dime to a dollar this isn't our perp. Probably an ex-boyfriend or some abusive drunk who thinks he's god's gift to women.*

The phone rang and it was Destiny. She apologized for missing his call but didn't explain why. He explained the news about Gabriela Torres coming forward with a lead.

"That's great. Congratulations!"

"Yeah."

"You don't sound very excited about it."

Then he went on to give her details about the interview and how the suspect didn't feel right to him.

"I know what you mean. But you can't rule him out. There are always anomalies."

"I realize that. I'm not ruling him out. I hope it's him. But my gut's telling me different.

"You always trust your gut?"

"Most of the time. And most of the time, it's right."

"You'll find out when you bring him in and start an investigation. We'll see if he fits the profile."

"Yeah. I'll be anxious to see it."

"Tomorrow." She paused and then asked, "What are you doing tonight?"

"Vegetating at home."

"You want to vegetate with another person?"

"What did you have in mind?"

"You like movies?"

"Of course."

"What about foreign films?"

"I don't mind reading subtitles. Why? Do you have one in mind?"

"Well, yeah. They're showing Patrice Leconte's film, *Man on a Train*, tonight at Loyola, and I happened to have scored two tickets. Do you know it?"

"No."

"It's great! I thought maybe we could get a bite somewhere and then go see it."

"You know of any suitable restaurants in Rogers Park?"

"You like Japanese?"

Now, this immediately appealed to Joe. "Absolutely. I love sushi."

"There's a place on Devon Avenue."

"What time's the film start?"

"Eight."

"Oh, that means I should pick you up fairly soon."

"I'm ready anytime you are." She gave Joe her address which was not far from his apartment. Fifteen minutes later, they were on their way north to Rogers Park.

What they were doing didn't matter. Just being with Destiny gave him a sense of euphoria he hadn't felt for a long time. Conversation was so easy despite the fact he wasn't a conversationalist by nature. He could sense she felt the same way about him.

The food at the restaurant was very good, and so was the film. If only the people he dealt with were as civilized as the two men in the film. He drove her home, and they spent an hour talking in the car outside her apartment. Seemed like ten minutes. A nice kiss goodnight capped the evening. As he drove away, he wished he could sneak into her dreams and cuddle with her all night long.

Chapter Twenty-One

At ten o'clock Monday morning, Lieutenant Vincenzo and the task force detectives gathered in one of the conference rooms. Destiny had set up for her presentation and interfaced her laptop with a large overhead television screen. The screen saver showed the Illinois' state seal.

Joe was eager to obtain her profile information and a little frustrated that Destiny hadn't given him a preview during their time together. But he respected her discipline to separate personal from professional.

Joe, Sam, and detectives Dempsey, Cardona, and Nelson, along with Lieutenant Vincenzo stood around holding notepads.

Vincenzo asked, "Is everyone here?" Then he noticed someone was missing. "Where's Collins?" he barked.

"Right here," said Eddie, walking through the door holding a tall Starbucks cup.

"Okay, we're all here. If everyone will take a seat."

Vincenzo walked to the front of the room and stood next to Destiny. Looking out over his detectives, he began his introduction.

"Some of you may have met Destiny Alexander, but if you haven't, Destiny is a criminal profiler who has been brought in to assist us with this case. A former FBI agent and a member of their Behavior Analysis Unit, she now works as a freelance consultant out of Chicago. Her work has contributed to many criminal investigations around the country. She's completed a profile on our perpetrator. She's here today to give us insight into who this person is." He looked at her, nodded, and said, "Destiny, it's all yours."

As Vincenzo took the nearest chair, Destiny began. "Thank you, Lieutenant, and good morning to each of you. I'd like to relate a caveat I always share before I begin my presentation. I'd like you to keep in mind that a profile is not what Hollywood portrays on television shows. Simply put, a criminal profile provides an outline to help focus the investigation. It's not definitive. The next thing I ask is for you to hold your questions until the presentation is over. I'll be glad to entertain any questions you may have at that time."

"Are there any questions before I begin?" She looked around the room and saw there were no hands.

"Okay, then," and she began by touching her laptop and bringing up a new image on the screen: 'Lust Killer.'

"The person we're seeking can be described as a lust killer. By that, I mean a person who is sexually aroused by the act of killing. A lust killer's motive usually begins sometime during puberty when fantasies become associated with things ranging from body parts to underwear, and then grow increasingly deviant. At some later date, he spots a chance to act upon his fantasies, and that's when he commits a murder. Jack the Ripper is a good example of a lust killer. He appeared to enjoy killing and mutilating his victims. Psychologists have developed numerous theories, but they can't agree on the cause of these aberrant behaviors."

Reaching for her laptop, she pressed a key and the screen changed to 'Types of Offenders.'

"For those of you not familiar with serial killer types, there are essentially two: organized and disorganized offenders. The organized offender plans his murders and displays control at the scene of the crime. The disorganized offender, on the other hand, acts spontaneously and chooses his victims at random or from people he knows. His crimes scenes are often messy and involve overkill. The perpetrator in your case is a man exhibiting characteristics of an organized offender. He plans and chooses his targets ahead of time, possibly stalking them to determine their suitability as a victim. He will often wait until he feels the time is right to strike."

She touched her laptop again and photographs of John Wayne Gacy and

Ted Bundy appeared on the television screen.

"You've no doubt heard of John Wayne Gacy and Ted Bundy. Both of them were examples of organized offenders. Both were also sexual sadists who tortured their victims. But there is no evidence that this perpetrator has tortured his victims before killing them."

Once again, she touched her laptop, and a 'List of Characteristics' appeared. The detectives' faces went to their notepads, and they began recording the information.

"We are dealing with a white male between the ages of thirty and forty. He has above-average intelligence and is a college graduate. He probably works as a professional or has experience in a medical-related field because of his knowledge of anatomy. He would appear normal to anyone who meets him. More than likely, he is not married but appears attractive and charismatic to the opposite sex. He would drive a newer car and live in a decent neighborhood. These offenders lead what's referred to as 'two-faced lives'. A Jekyll and Hyde existence, if you will. They will choose the time and place to wear whichever one of these faces. He functions in a job primarily during the day and commits these offenses at night."

"Based on his known victims, he has been targeting women between the ages of twenty-five and thirty-five. All have been attractive with dark hair and nice figures."

"His signature is using a thin-bladed knife to penetrate the heart of his victims, and then removing the skin of the genital region with surgical precision. Then he places the victims in their beds and covers them as if he is tucking them in for the night. This strange dichotomy of violence and tenderness defies explanation. The skin acts as a trophy that he preserves in one way or another. By keeping it, he is able to prolong the fantasy of the kill. While between crimes, he can view a trophy and relive the killing of a particular victim over again in his mind. But these fantasies never end, and he is always in the process of targeting the next victim."

"It's hard to say why he takes such grotesque trophies. The act of taking them could provide some kind of sexual satisfaction. Or he may have some sexual dysfunction and cannot perform with a woman. He may have suffered humiliation for it, and he is acting out his anger toward women. One can speculate about this, but there is really no way of knowing for sure."

"The lack of any forensic evidence other than a few cat hairs shows that he is well- versed about police work and forensics. He may be trained or at least well-read on the subject and carefully prepares in order to leave no evidence behind."

"One thing you can count on: he is extremely intelligent, and he will continue killing until he is stopped." She looked around the room. The silence was palpable. "This concludes my presentation. I will now take questions."

Michelle Cardona's hand went up and she said, "I have a question. You said this perp is charismatic, attractive to the opposite sex. What do you base that on?"

Destiny answered, "First of all, statistics from other cases similar to this one. Women are commonly attracted to good-looking men with a certain degree of magnetism. They can be good boys or bad boys, it works both ways. Second, if you examine their photographs, all the victims were very striking in appearance. If they invited a man to their apartment for sex, odds are he would fit these characteristics."

"You mentioned 'his knowledge of anatomy.' What did you mean by that?" asked Gary Nelson.

"That's a reference to his placement of the knife, the weapon used to kill each of the victims. The entry wound in each case was between the ribs where the knife would go directly into the heart. He would have to possess the knowledge to know where to plunge the knife and at what angle to penetrate the heart to achieve an almost immediate death."

Joe spoke up next. "Do you think it's odd that he doesn't rape them?" he asked. "He has opportunity, but he chooses to kill rather than assault them. I find that strange."

"I agree that it's atypical," Destiny replied. "That's why there may be something sexual associated with the mutilation. But I'm not a psychiatrist, so I can't provide a clinical opinion about this." She looked at him. "It's only a gut feeling."

Joe got her little joke but suppressed a smile. The questions and answers continued for another half-hour. When the session drew down to a close, Destiny produced copies of her written profile and passed them out to each member of the team.

"Could this guy have some kind of sexual fetish?" asked Eddie.

"It would be atypical since fetishes involve sexual excitement with body parts that are not sexual. Feet are most common. But rather than fetishism, there is another common paraphilia called 'piquerism' which involves sexual arousal by stabbing with a sharp instrument. I don't think we can rule that out. I have made a reference to that in my written profile." She looked around the room and didn't see any more hands, so she continued.

"I've given you a verbal summary of my profile. What I'm giving you now is a more comprehensive written profile that contains my research, statistics, charts, citations, and other data. I didn't want you distracted with it during my presentation. If you have questions after reading through it, you can email me, and I'll get back to you."

At that point, the session ended with a few concluding remarks from Lieutenant Vincenzo.

"I don't need to remind you this is confidential information. It must not be seen or fall into the hands of anyone who could make this public. It could make our jobs a lot more difficult."

Heads around the room nodded in agreement as members of the team leafed through the profile.

"All right, you're dismissed," ordered Vincenzo. The sound of chair legs scraped against the floor as the detectives pushed back from the table and rose to leave. The Lieutenant stepped to Destiny who was disconnecting her computer .

"Thank you for your good work on this," he said, reaching out to shake her hand. "I'm impressed, and I don't impress too easily."

She shook his hand. "You're welcome, and don't hesitate contacting me if you need to. I hope you keep me apprised on your investigation."

"I will." And he turned and left the room. That left Destiny alone with Joe who was still seated at the table looking through her profile.

"So, who's going to keep you in the loop on this case?"

"You are. At least, I hope you are."

"Think you can be trusted?"

"What do you think?"

"I think I need to vet you first."

"Oh? And just what's that going to consist of?"

"I'll let you know once I've cleared you." And he turned and left the room without giving her time to respond.

Chapter Twenty-Two

A May 23rd memorial service was held at the funeral home with only about three dozen people in attendance. The deceased, Karen Welch, was a woman who had died of pancreatic cancer at the age of fifty-two. A pewter urn with her name, birth, and death dates etched onto it held her cremains. Displayed on a small table artfully decorated with flowers, it was next to a framed photograph of the deceased, a smiling woman no one would suspect had a terminal disease.

Her two daughters, Kirsten and Kylie, both in their late twenties, greeted people who came to pay their final respects. They were the only surviving relatives since their mother had no living parents or siblings, and her ex-husband had not been in their lives for many years. Neither of the daughters was married, but Kylie had a fiancé deployed overseas in the army. He had been unable to return to the States at this time. Kylie had taken a leave of absence from her job two months ago and had moved from Kansas City to Chicago to help Kirsten when their mother could no longer care for herself.

The service was non-denominational. Their mother was not a regular churchgoer. But Kirsten urged her to speak with a member of the clergy since she thought her mother could find a sense of peace in her final days. She suggested a minister from the Unitarian church she attended, and her mother had been talking with him for the past several months. He agreed to conduct the service today.

The funeral director in charge was Michael Fleming, who found himself attracted to Kirsten. She was just his style—tall, slender, and attractive with long dark hair. She had no idea he had already begun stalking her.

Fleming had been the one who helped the girls with arrangements for their mother's cremation as well as the memorial service. Turning on his sincerity and charm, he succeeded in gaining their trust and consoling them in their grief. He was good at saying all the right words. In addition to his professionalism, he impressed Kylie with his good looks and charisma.

The memorial service was short, followed by a ride to the cemetery for a short internment ceremony. Once the rites concluded, Fleming approached Kylie and Kirsten and said, "If there's anything I can do for either of you, please let me know. Feel free to call. Again, I'm very sorry for your loss." He shook their hands and they thanked him for his kindness.

As Kylie drove away from the cemetery, she said to Kirsten, "Did you notice he wasn't wearing a ring?"

"Who?"

"Michael Fleming, the funeral director."

"No, I didn't. Why?"

"Jeez, Kirsten. You're so obtuse!"

"What are you talking about?"

"Michael Fleming. You should check him out," said Kylie, looking over at Kirsten to check her reaction.

Kirsten sighed. "You're sick, Kylie."

"Oh, come on. I would if I wasn't involved with Jason. He's hot."

"He's probably got a girlfriend. Or a boyfriend."

"I saw the way he was looking at you. No way he's gay."

"I don't want to talk about it."

"You didn't find him attractive?"

"Of course, I did. I'm not blind."

"Well... Just saying. Men in his line of work make really good money, you know?"

"I know that," said Kirsten.

"So?"

"Now's not the time."

"Okay." Kylie paused and drove on without speaking. A couple miles later she broke the silence. "You want to go to Mom's place? I've got two bottles of wine. We could order take-out. What do you say?"

"Okay. Chinese?"

"Sounds good."

While the Welch sisters were commiserating at their mother's apartment that evening, full of kung pao chicken and buzzed on wine, Michael Fleming was scouting Kirsten's place of residence. She lived in an apartment complex on Karlov Avenue in Kilbourn Park, a neighborhood in Northwest Chicago.

Fleming parked his Lexus three blocks away. As he got out, he put on a dark brown fedora to help disguise his face and walked briskly past the apartment building. He looked for security cameras near the doors and spotted one. Then he turned the corner and saw another security camera over a second entrance. No doubt the interior of the complex had cameras as well. He now knew what he was up against. He would have to improvise.

Walking back to his Lexus, he removed his hat and slid into the driver's seat. Tossing the fedora onto the back seat, he started the car and headed for home, fantasizing the whole time about what he wanted to do to Kirsten Welch.

Suddenly, a car pulled out in front of him from a side street, and he reacted instinctively, slamming hard on his brakes. Getting jolted out of his fantasy made him angry.

"Idiot asshole," he snarled at the driver he almost crashed into. She was oblivious to the fact that she'd almost been t-boned since she was too involved in her cellphone conversation to notice his vehicle. *It's only a matter of time until I pump you full of embalming fluid, bitch!* Rivulets of sweat ran down his forehead. He reached up with his forearm and wiped the sweat away as an impatient driver behind him honked, urging him to go.

Once home, he opened the front door and was greeted by his cat, that lithesome Havana Brown.

"Hi, Fidel! How you doing, boy?" he said with the kind of affection he showered on no human being. "Did you have a good day, buddy?"

Fidel chirped back and rubbed up against Fleming's leg, leaving a few hairs on his pants. Fleming tossed his suitcoat on a chair, and removed his tie, laying it on top of his coat. Then the two of them walked into the kitchen where Fidel watched Fleming put a frozen lasagna in the oven. Fidel leaped up onto one of the stools and demanded more attention which Fleming was happy to provide.

Rubbing Fidel's cheek, he said, "You're a good boy, aren't you?" Fidel was enjoying the stroking, turning his head and closing his eyes as Fleming's fingers passed across his whiskers and cheek. "I've found another one, you know that?" Fleming paused. The only sound was Fidel's purring.

"Kirsten's a pretty girl. She'll make a fine addition. A fine addition." He checked the level in Fidel's automated food dispenser and added water to his fancy feline water fountain. Heading down into his basement and opening the door to his secret room, he began looking at his wall. Thinking about Kirsten excited him, and his mind drifted to what she would look like without her clothes and what her expression would be when he plunged the knife into her heart. *Would she look more like Rebecca? Or Nicole? Or maybe Deanna?* He couldn't wait to find out.

Chapter Twenty-Three

O n Saturday, Joe returned to the bookstore where he'd purchased his cookbooks. He wanted to cook for Destiny and needed to get a couple of vegetarian cookbooks so he could prepare a meal she could eat. That, and he wanted to impress her with his culinary skills.

He was making his way back to the cooking section when he met Jeffrey, the salesperson who had assisted him on his first visit.

"Hello," Joe said, greeting him.

"Ohhhh! I remember you," replied Jeffrey. "Cookbooks, right?"

"You have a good memory."

"I do. And how did they work out for you?"

"Very well, thanks. They were good choices."

"I figured you might be back. What can I do for you today?"

"I'm looking for some vegetarian cookbooks. I have a girlfriend who's a vegetarian. And I need to learn to prepare some things for her."

"Oh," said Jeffrey. "Of course. We have some excellent choices. Let me show you." Jeffrey pulled a book from the shelf.

"This is a classic. I would start with this one," he said, handing it to Joe. Then he pulled another and held it up. "I have this book myself and really like it. Use it all the time. Practically worn it out."

"It's that good, huh?"

"Take my word, for it. To tell you the truth, I'm not a onehundred per-cent vegetarian. I eat fish occasionally. But these recipes are for dishes you'll find in a lot of vegetarian restaurants."

"That's a pretty good recommendation. I'll take both."

"I guarantee your girlfriend will not be disappointed."

That evening he was pulling the finished lasagna out of the oven when his phone rang. It was Destiny.

"Hi," he answered.

"Hi. What are you up to?"

"I was just pulling something out of the oven.

"Oh, yeah. What have you cooked for yourself tonight?"

He didn't know whether he should lie or tell her the truth. But he figured he would see what her reaction would be to his foray into vegetarian cuisine. "Butternut squash and spinach lasagna."

"Oh, you dog! You cooked vegetarian without telling me?"

"It was a test run. To see if I could do it successfully."

"And did you?"

"Apparently so."

"Are you into sharing?"

"Of course. Come on over if you want."

"Of course, I want." He gave her his address. "See you in a few."

Joe hustled to spruce up the kitchen, set the table, and uncork the wine. He was as nervous as a kid getting ready for his high school prom. He poured himself a glass of wine.

"Mm," he muttered. *A good Merlot.* He walked into the living room and sat in his recliner to enjoy the wine and wait for the doorbell. Ten minutes later, it rang, and he buzzed her in. Moments later, he heard a knock.

There stood Destiny looking terrific in faded black jeans and a silver blouse over a black tank top. "Come in," he said.

"Oo, it smells wonderful."

"Would you like a glass of Merlot?"

"Please."

Pulling a chair out for her, he seated her at the table and sat across from her.

"Well, this is a pleasant surprise. I was planning to ask you over once I made sure I could successfully prepare this. I cooked it, but I don't know if it tastes good. So, I guess you're now my test subject."

"If it tastes anything like it smells, I think you succeeded. This wine is very good."

"It is. My dad recommended this winery. He's become a wine connoisseur over the years. He's known to pass along a tip now and then."

"Nice."

"I suppose we'd better eat before it gets cold." Joe placed a salad on the table, along with a bottle of his own balsamic vinaigrette. Then he dished up the lasagna. He watched Destiny's reaction after taking a bite. Her eyes lit up.

"Oh, Joe. This is divine."

"Yeah?"

"Oh, yeah," she smiled and took another bite.

He sampled it and had to agree. For a dish with no meat, it was pretty tasty. He remembered Jeffrey's words: "Your girlfriend will not be disappointed." He was right. *Thanks, Jeffrey.*

They finished their dinner, filled their glasses with the last of the Merlot, went into the living room and sat on the couch.

"I really appreciate you learning to cook vegetarian just for me. That's sweet of you. And taking time to practice in order to get it right. I'm impressed."

"Well, I didn't want to invite you to dinner and serve you some colossal failure, you know. How to ruin a date in one bite."

"It would've been all right."

"No, it wouldn't. You deserve my best effort."

"Really?"

"Yeah. My best—"

Joe's sentence was interrupted when Destiny leaned in and kissed him. The more they kissed, the more passionate and frenetic they got. Finally, Joe stood and pulled Destiny up and said, "Come on."

He led her into the bedroom where they literally tore each other's clothes off. Buttons popped off, elastic ripped, and shoes flew.

Afterward, they lay next to each other, breathing heavily.

"Oh, my god, Joe," she breathed. "That was amazing."

"The lasagna or the wine?"

Slapping his arm, she said, "This, dummy!"

Rolling his head to meet hers, he smiled and said, "I know." He leaned over and kissed her. "So, you ready to do it again?"

Destiny's eyes got big. "You're kidding, right?"

"Yeah. I'm kidding." He reached over and interlaced his fingers with hers. "This could lead to something, you know that?"

"Uh-huh."

"And you're okay with that?"

"Yeah, I'm okay with that."

"Good. So am I."

When the afterglow passed, they showered, and Joe handed Destiny a spare robe. He cracked open another bottle of Merlot, and they snuggled together in the living room, drinking and watching *Casablanca* on TCM.

As the credits ran, Joe held up his glass to Destiny and spoke Bogart's words, "Here's lookin' at you, kid."

Destiny clinked his glass and responded, "What do you see?"

"A beautiful woman I'd never let fly away."

"I like that."

"Yeah?"

"Oh, yeah. I want to get to know everything about you."

"You might not like everything you find."

"Let me be the judge of that."

They finished their wine and fell asleep in each other's arms. Joe awoke at midnight and picked her up, and carried her into the bedroom where he laid her on the bed. Pulling the comforter up, he slipped in beside her.He closed his eyes and sleep came soon after.

The next morning, they awoke, made love again, and curled up in bed until late morning. They rose, showered, and the two of them improvised breakfast with what Joe had in his refrigerator. Vegetarian omelets, toast, and coffee.

After breakfast, Joe asked, "So, what are we going to do, today?"

" There's a Renoir exhibit at the Art Institute. How's that sound? Or is that too artsy for you?"

"Of the Impressionists, I like Renoir the best. I especially like his paintings of people dancing."

"I'm impressed you know your Renoir."

"I've spent a lot of time at the Art Institute during my off-hours. I have a great appreciation for art."

Destiny kissed him. "I am going to have to get to know you better."

Joe kissed her back. "I hope so."

"So, the Art Institute it is."

Joe's cell phone. His dad's area code. Suddenly, he felt chills.

"Hello."

A woman's voice responded. "Is this Joe Erickson?"

Oh, shit! "Yes. Is something wrong?" Destiny could tell by the concern in Joe's voice that something was seriously wrong.

"This is Linda Jackson. I'm a nurse at Spencer Hospital."

Joe interrupted, "Is my dad okay?"

"Your father is stable. But he's had a heart attack."

"How serious?"

"We don't know the extent of the damage yet. He's sedated and being monitored in our intensive care unit."

"When did it happen?" asked Joe.

"Early this morning. EMT's brought him to the hospital at eight-thirty."

"I see."

"Is there anyone else we should contact?"

"No. I'm on my way. I want you to keep me posted with any updates, okay?"

"Yes, of course."

"I should be there in about seven hours."

The call ended, and he looked at Destiny. "My dad's had a heart attack. They don't know how serious yet. I've gotta go."

"Don't worry about anything here. I'll clean up and take care of your apartment."

"Thanks," he said opening a drawer and pulling out a key. "Here's a spare key to let you lock up." He dashed into the bedroom, grabbed his duffel bag, and threw clothes into it along with his travel kit. Five minutes later, Joe came out of the bedroom carrying his duffel.

"I'm so sorry this had to happen," he said, wrapping his free arm around Destiny.

"Don't apologize. Life happens. I'll take care of things here. You want me to call Lieutenant Vincenzo for you?"

"No, I'll call him. But thanks. You're the best."

"Uh-uh. You are." She kissed him. "Drive carefully. I want you back in one piece."

Joe smiled. "Count on it." And he turned and went out the door.

Chapter Twenty-Four

Joe fired up his Camaro and took the Kennedy Expressway, Chicago's name for a section of Interstate 90, out of the city. He had recently topped off the fuel tank so he would not have to stop for gas until he was most of the way there.

The seven-hour trip gave him time to think. Time to think about what had happened to his dad. How bad was his attack? How much damage had the attack done to his heart? Would he pull through? Not knowing was driving him crazy, and he forced himself to think about other things.

And then there was Destiny and where their relationship might lead. If anywhere. He'd been in a couple of relationships that didn't work out. In the end, it was his job that drove them apart. Neither of the women could get used to the odd hours and the unexpected interruptions that typified the life of a police detective. One ended amicably, the other badly. And he didn't want to go through the emotional devastation again. Each one took a lot of recovery time and each one left scars. Maybe because Destiny was in the law enforcement field herself, things would be different. She might understand. She was beautiful, intelligent, passionate, and he liked being with her. Maybe fate stepped in and brought the right one into his life.

When thinking about Destiny got to be too much, he began concentrating on the case he was working. He assumed there would be another victim but hoped it wouldn't happen while he was away. The issue wasn't that he didn't trust Sam and his other colleagues to investigate the crime. They were good. But being out of the loop and unable to visually take in the crime scene would be a problem for him. He needed to be there. *Damnit,*

Dad. Why now? Then he considered how unfair that thought was. *Sorry.*

Traffic was light. As he cruised across Illinois, he began thinking about the killer. During her profile presentation, in reference to his question about something sexual associated with the mutilation, Destiny mentioned she could not comment because she was not a psychiatrist. Joe still couldn't get a grip on why the killer did not rape his victims before killing them. How could someone get sexual gratification out of committing murder rather than having intercourse? He didn't know any psychiatrists. However, he did know a clinical psychologist who had provided insights for Joe in the past. Maybe he could help answer some of these questions. He dialed Dr. Jerry Markham's number.

A woman's voice answered, "Markham residence."

"Hi. Could I speak with Jerry, please?"

"Just a minute." He could hear her call his name and then a barely detectable answer in the background. "He's busy at the moment. Can I—"

Joe butted in. "No, he's not. Tell him it's Joe Erickson."

She sighed, covered the mouthpiece and he heard her say something resembling his name.

A moment later, a man's voice came over the phone. "For god's sake. Don't you know it's Sunday?"

"Yeah, I know. How are you doing?"

"Up until a minute ago, pretty well."

"I'm sorry I caught you in flagrante delicto–"

That raised a big laugh from Jerry. "In my dreams! What do you want, Erickson?"

"Your expert clinical opinion on something."

"It's going to cost you."

"Put it on my tab. I'm working a case. What would motivate a killer to remove part of a female victim's genital area but not rape her?"

"Jesus. Are you working the serial killer case?"

"I can't say. But I'd appreciate it if you didn't remember I asked the question."

"Okay. Well, it could be a number of things. But I remember a clinical case we studied when I was getting my Ph.D. A young man could not perform with a woman. He wasn't gay. It went back to his childhood and issues of abuse that grew out of some traumatic sexual events with his mother. Violence and incest. I don't remember the exact details. Anyway, it shamed him to the point that it prevented him from achieving an erection for intercourse. He was a teenager, and all the anxiety and anger caused him to explode. And he wound up killing and mutilating his mother when he was fifteen."

"Holy shit! How long ago was this?"

"Twenty years ago, I suppose."

"So, he'd be about thirty-five now?"

"Probably. If twenty and fifteen still equal thirty-five. But with my kid's new math, you can't be sure anymore."

"What kind of mutilation?"

"He slashed off her groin area, as I remember."

"Can you find out who this guy was?"

"I doubt it. Juvenile records are always sealed. You know that."

"Do you know where this happened?"

"Nah. They don't release any identifying information when we study these cases." He chuckled, "My guess would be dueling banjos country. But that's probably unfair to all the guys who marry their cousins."

"If he could not get it up for intercourse, could he get sexual gratification from mutilating his victims? Could carving them up be a substitute for intercourse?"

"Possibly. A sick mind is capable of a lot of perverse things. The very thought of mutilating someone could cause him to get an erection, just like the thought of sex does for a normal man. Hell, he might even achieve orgasm while carving them up."

"Jesus."

"You'd be surprised the depths of depravity some people can sink to."

"Thanks, Jerry. I owe you big time."

"Yeah. That's what you said the last time. Now fuck off, Erickson. The

Cubs are on TV and at the moment, they're winning."

After his call with Jerry, Joe's mind was whirling with thoughts of a possible lead on the serial killer. Is this the same kid all grown up and acting out to achieve sexual gratification? Killing his victims is one thing, but why is he mutilating them and taking trophies? How sick is that? Maybe the questions won't be answered until he's apprehended.

At Rockford, he exited onto U.S. Highway 20, an expressway that would take him across Iowa, and his thoughts once again focused on his dad. Joe had been speaking with him every other week and his dad hadn't mentioned he was having issues of any kind. But he'd noticed some things about his attitude. Dad sold his '57 Chevy, and that was a surprise. He had many years left to enjoy owning and driving it, and it wasn't like him to give it up like he did. Maybe he sensed something.

His dad was seventy-five years old, and that wasn't that old by today's standards, but Joe had recognized he wasn't as vigorous as he used to be. His mom's dementia and subsequent death had aged him. Living alone, cooking for himself, going to restaurants, he probably wasn't eating the way he should, either. All sorts of things were running through Joe's mind. He was hoping for an update from the hospital but so far there were no calls. Maybe that was a good sign.

At Ft. Dodge, he exited the expressway and stopped for gas, hit the restroom, and got himself a large coffee. He'd been driving five-and-a-half hours and had another hour-and-a-half to go before he reached the hospital. Before long he would pick up Highway 71 that would take him north to Spencer. He felt like calling Lieutenant Vincenzo, to let him know of his situation, but on second thought he would call him at work first thing in the morning. Vincenzo didn't like to be bothered at home, even though this was a legitimate reason.

The last ninety minutes seemed to take forever. When he reached Spencer, he drove directly to the hospital, where he was directed to the ICU.

"Excuse me," he said to a nurse in the hall.

"May I help you?"

"Yes. I'm Joe Erickson. I just rolled in from Chicago. Linda Jackson called

147

me about my father who suffered a heart attack this morning. He's a patient here."

"Of course. I'm Laura Windsor. If you'll follow me, I'll get Dr. Shayne for you."

Nurse Windsor led him into an empty waiting room. Pulling out his cellphone, he checked it for messages. One from Destiny: "Let me know as soon as you arrive." A heart emoji followed. He texted her back: "Arrived. Waiting to hear. Will let you know."

As he was dumping emails into the trash, a tall, middle-aged man wearing scrubs entered the room.

"Are you Joe Erickson?" he asked.

Rising from his seat, Joe said, "I am."

He shook Joe's hand and said, "I'm Doctor Shayne. I've been treating your father."

"Pleased to meet you, doctor. How is he?"

"He's had a major coronary event. We ran tests and found one artery completely blocked and another ninety percent blocked, so we had to do two angioplasty procedures to open up the arteries. Then two stents were inserted to keep the arteries open. Both procedures were successful. But there's been some damage.

"How much?"

"We won't know that for a while yet. We'll be running further blood tests and an EKG tomorrow to determine the extent of the damage."

"Why wasn't I called. I asked to be called to be updated on his condition. I'm his only next of kin."

"Well...He wouldn't allow us to. He was adamant about that. He was told you were on your way and he said he didn't want to worry you while you were driving."

"Sounds like him. Is it possible to see him?"

"Sure. We gave him something to sleep, so if you wish to speak with him, you'll have to wait until morning. If all goes well, we may be moving him out of ICU and into a private room sometime tomorrow. Do you have any questions?"

"Not right now."

"Joe followed him to the ICU. " You have five minutes. You'll have more time tomorrow."

"Thanks, Doctor."

Joe entered the room. His dad was hooked to an elaborate arrangement of wires and hoses, and the electronics hummed and beeped. Looking at his dad's face, he saw a fragile, vulnerable man, pale and lacking the healthy color he had always had. Reaching out his hand, he placed it on his dad's hand. He felt the once-strong hand that had brandished tools with such skill and caressed his mother's hair when she no longer recognized him. Tears came to his eyes, and Joe was never one to cry easily. *Come on, Dad. You've got to get better. You can do it.* He bowed his head and said a prayer. Then, he opened his eyes and looked into his face.

"Time to go," came a quiet voice from a few feet away. He looked over and saw it was the duty nurse. "Your five minutes is up," she said in a polite but firm tone.

"Yeah, I guess it is," Joe replied with the hint of a smile. She gave a pleasant smile back. And he turned, walked through the doors, and took the stairs down to the first floor, leaving the building. After sitting in his car for a few minutes, he called Destiny and explained the situation to her. She was empathetic and comforting.

"You'll feel better when he's awake and you can talk with him," she said. "Seeing him in the ICU like that had to have been disconcerting for you."

"Yeah."

"Where're you staying?"

"Dad's house. I figured I could check and see if he needed any work done before he got home. And people in town will want to know how he's doing. Small towns are like that."

"Okay. Will you call me tomorrow and let me know how he's doing?"

"Of course."

"Good. Now, you'd better go somewhere and get dinner."

"It's supper around here."

"Feed yourself, Joe. You can't sustain yourself on coffee."

"How did you know that?"

"I just know. Surely there's a place that has good food."

"On a Sunday? Fat chance."

"Guess the Magic Chef might have to find a grocery store, huh?"

"Might have to."

"Good night, my dear."

That made Joe smile. "Good night."

Still early evening, Joe decided to call Sam, tell him his situation, and let him know what he learned from Jerry Markham.

"I'll look into the killing and mutilation crime," said Sam. "But it's going to be slow not knowing the year and the location."

"It may not be our guy, but it sounds too close not to check out."

"Right."

"I don't know when I'll get back. I'm calling Vincenzo first thing in the morning. I'll stay in touch. Talk to you later."

"I'm thinking of you, man."

"Thanks."

Joe started his car and did the unthinkable. He drove to the south end of town, stopped at McDonald's, and wolfed down a Big Mac.

Joe arrived at his dad's well-kept bungalow in Marathon half an hour later. He recognized the smell of the house that had become so familiar over the years. He opened the refrigerator. Practically empty except for a container of milk and a couple bottles of white wine. *For god's sake! Doesn't he cook for himself?*

The cupboards were almost as bare as the refrigerator. A large box of Shredded Wheat and a few cans of soup. He would have to check to see if his dad was getting Meals on Wheels.

Joe looked about. By nature, his dad was a neat person. No dirty dishes were in the sink, the bed was made, the newspaper and magazines were placed on the coffee table, and there were no empty glasses or bottles lying around. He dropped off his duffel bag in the spare bedroom and returned to the kitchen. Taking a wine glass from the rack, he re-opened a half-full bottle of Cabernet Sauvignon and poured himself a healthy amount. No sense letting good wine go bad.

Looking out the window, he saw Dad's neighbor's light was on. Maude Nyberg was an eighty-year-old widow and knew everything that went on in town. She would want to know two things: who was in Carl Erickson's house and how was he was doing. Joe grabbed the phone book and took his glass into the living room. He looked up Maude's number and called her. She knew him, of course, since she and her late husband had lived in their house for fifty years. She told Joe she had been talking with Carl in his garage when he clutched his chest and sat down complaining of chest pains. She called 9-1-1, and he was rushed to the hospital. Joe thanked her. She was pleased that he had come home. He told her about his dad's condition and promised to keep her updated. He knew she would keep most of the town apprised of his condition as well.

The wine was good, and he went back for a second glass. Turning on the television, he found a black and white movie from the forties with Peter Lorre and Sidney Greenstreet playing on one of the cable channels. He didn't know the title, but it kept him interested until the combination of the wine and the drive acted as a sedative. He awoke at midnight and went into the bedroom to sleep the rest of the night.

Chapter Twenty-Five

Waking at five, Joe dressed in jogging clothes and went for a run. He needed to clear his head before traveling to Spencer to see his dad. Running also gave him time to think about what Jerry Markham had told him about the kid who mutilated his mother and whether the similarities had any connection to the case he was working. He needed to let Vincenzo know what he'd discovered. Maybe they could track down the guy, and if nothing else, eliminate him as a suspect.

The streets were pretty quiet at five in the morning. The town was beginning to wake up and lights were on in a few houses. Joe finished his run at five-thirty and walked another five minutes to cool down. He was used to running on a treadmill at the gym, but running on the street and breathing fresh air felt good. He may have to start doing that when he returned to Chicago.

After showering and getting dressed, he had time to kill so he decided to drive to Spencer and find a place to eat breakfast. The café in Marathon had closed years ago, and there was no place to eat and no place to buy groceries anymore. Even the bank and the post office had closed. Only the tavern and the grain elevator remained in what was once a bustling little town in 1960. Progress.

Driving to Spencer took half an hour, and Joe pulled his Camaro into the parking lot of a mom-and-pop diner. The place was small with a counter lined with stools and a row of booths along the wall. Through a window in the back, one could see the kitchen and the cook busily preparing food. The place was quite busy, a sign that they must serve good food. Joe sat down at the counter and a hefty, gray-haired waitress in her late fifties laid a menu in front of him, along with a glass of water.

"Would you like coffee?"

"I would, thanks." He looked at the menu.

"The specials today are on the board," she said indicating the blackboard on the wall behind her "I'll give you a minute."

Joe looked at the three specials–half the prices he would pay in Chicago. So, when she came back, he ordered the "Early Bird Special," which consisted of two eggs, two strips of bacon, two sausage links, choice of potatoes, and toast.

"I'll have my eggs scrambled, hash browns, and wheat toast."

She wrote down his order and thanked him. Starting to turn, she stopped and looked at Joe. "Have I seen you in here before?"

"No, I'm from Illinois. Just here for a short time."

"I grew up in Illinois. Where you from?"

"Chicago. And you?"

"Bushnell. Bet you've never heard of it."

"Of course, I have," teased Joe. "Everyone's heard of Bushnell."

"I think I feel my leg getting pulled. Be back in a bit."

Joe looked around. The patrons were a cross-section of the community. Uniforms, casual attire, t-shirts, and business suits. Everyone mixing with one another without regard to class or station in life. Much different from the big city. Something refreshing in that.

Joe was in the middle of checking his email when the waitress slid a plate in front of him.

"Here you go. Is there anything else I can get you?"

"This looks fine. What did you say your name was?"

"I didn't. It's Gladys. My husband and I own this place. Have for thirty years."

"It's a nice place. I'll probably be back."

"I hope so." And then she moved on to wait on other customers. When he was nearly finished, Gladys came by and left the check.

"What brings you to Spencer, if you don't mind me being snoopy?"

"My dad's in the hospital. Heart attack. They may be moving him out of ICU today."

"Oh, my," she replied with genuine concern. "I'm sorry to hear that. I hope he's going to be okay."

"Yeah, so do I."

When Joe finished, he left a tip and stepped to the cash register. Gladys checked him out. As she gave him his change she said, "We hope to see you again. Uh…What did you say your name was?" Joe smiled at her choice of words.

"I didn't. It's Joe."

"Well, good luck with everything, Joe." He thanked her, and as he walked to his car, he realized he should call Vincenzo.

He slid into the seat and dialed Vincenzo's number.

"Vincenzo."

"It's Joe Erickson. I have an emergency. My dad's had a serious heart attack. I'm in Iowa, and I need a few days."

"How bad?"

"I'm going to find out this morning. They opened up two blocked arteries and put in stents, but they'd given him something to sleep so I didn't get to talk to him when I got here."

"Take as much time as you need. Keep me posted."

"One more thing. I may have stumbled onto a potential lead. Could you follow up?"

"Of course. Whatcha got?"

"I got bored driving to Iowa and started thinking about the case. So, I called Jerry Markham, you know the clinical psych acquaintance of mine?"

"Yeah."

"I had a question about our perp. Anyway, during our conversation, he told me about a clinical case he studied in grad school. It involved a teenager who was sexually abused by his mother. And he wound up murdering her and slashing off her groin area with a knife. Today, this kid would now be the age of the individual Destiny cited in the profile."

"You got Markham's phone number?"

"Yeah. I know this is a long shot, and juvie records are sealed..."

"Does he know where this wonderful event took place?"

"No, nothing that would violate privacy laws. You know how it is."

"Yeah. I'll put somebody on this. We can search newspaper accounts. Might turn up something that way."

"Great. I'll text you Markham's number."

"Good work, Joe. Hope this leads somewhere. And Joe...I'll keep your dad in my prayers."

"Thanks, Lieutenant. Talk to you soon."

Vincenzo, for all his toughness and his drill sergeant demeanor, wasn't without a soft side. He knew the pain of losing a father, and he could empathize with Joe's situation.

At the hospital, Joe went up to ICU and stopped at the nurses' station. The nurse on duty told him his father was currently stable and would not need to be transferred to another larger, more specialized hospital for further treatment.

"He was rather cranky this morning when we woke him up."

"That's probably a good sign."

"You can have a seat in the waiting room, and I'll let you know when you can see him."

"Fine." More waiting. He texted Jerry Markham's phone number to Vincenzo. To keep occupied, he looked through a couple of magazines, the subject matter he had no interest in. He stood up to walk over and turn on the television when, the nurse opened the door and said, "Your uncle is here."

Joe thought, *What the hell? I don't have an uncle!*

In walked a tall, string bean of a man, a retired farmer named Russell Montgomery. Joe couldn't help but smile at his dad's best friend's subterfuge. He rose, and shook his hand saying, "Good to see you, Uncle Monte."

"Well, I had to say I was your dad's brother or the damned nurses wouldn't let me see him."

"I know. Rules suck."

"They sure as heck do."

Joe finally had someone to pass the time with, and after an hour had gone by, the nurse came in and told him the doctor would like to speak with him. Joe followed her out of the room and down the hall to a consultation room where Doctor Shayne was looking over a chart.

"It's Joe, right?"

"Yes."

"Let me get straight to the point. We ran an EKG this morning and found that the damage to your father's heart is moderate. It's affected about twenty percent of the heart muscle in the area of the blocked arteries."

"What's that mean exactly?" asked Joe.

"What it means is twenty percent of his heart no longer functions. Now, that's not catastrophic. People can live relatively normal lives with just eighty percent of their heart working. But he's going to require medication and monitoring to make sure he maintains this level of performance."

"Could he lose more heart function due to his attack?"

"If he doesn't take care of himself, yes. And it's possible that his age could be a determining factor in causing additional deterioration over time."

"Where do we go from here, doctor? How long before you think he can be released from the hospital?"

"If there are no complications, three days. We're moving him out of ICU later this morning. He'll be in a private room. He's awake. You and your uncle can go see him for a short time if you want—one at a time."

A few minutes later, Joe walked through the ICU doors and up to his father's bed.

"Hi, Dad."

Carl turned his head toward Joe. "Oh, hi." His voice was weak and didn't have the resonance it usually did. "Sorry you have to see me like this."

"It's okay. I'm just glad you're going to be all right."

"Yeah. The doctor said I might be able to go home in a couple of days."

"That's what he told me."

"Good."

"Uncle Monte's here."

"Uncle?"

"Yeah."

Carl managed a short laugh. "He always was a good liar. I sure as hell wouldn't want that jasper for a brother."

"But he's a pretty good friend."

"He is that."

"They don't want me to spend much time in here. They're moving you to a private room later this morning, so I'll see you then. I'll leave so Monte can see you."

"All right. Tell my "older" brother he can come in."

Joe saw that his dad hadn't lost his sense of humor, another good sign. He left and told Monte that Carl was waiting to see him. He asked Monte to call him when they moved Dad to a private room. He didn't want to hang around the hospital waiting room for hours even though he knew Monte would. What was there to do in Spencer, Iowa? He found plenty to do when he was a kid, but now that he was an adult, he didn't know anyone, and the town was no longer recognizable from what it was twenty years ago.

An idea struck him as he was leaving the ICU. He went into the waiting room but found he no longer had it to himself. Two people were in there now, fully engaged watching FOX News, so he walked out to his car to get some privacy.

Sliding into the driver's seat, he called Destiny. She answered right away, and he updated her on his dad's condition. He had chosen not to tell her about the tip he'd received from Jerry Markham–too much information for one night. He was saving that bit of news for today. But after mulling it over, he realized she might have resources the police department didn't have. After telling her about the teenager's savage mutilation murder of his mother, he asked her opinion.

"He'd be the right age, now, wouldn't he? And if he never received the kind of intense psychological therapy necessary, I'd be looking at him as a person of interest."

"But how would we find out who he is? Juvie records are sealed, and Jerry said there were no details about who he was or where it happened. Vincenzo mentioned putting someone onto searching newspapers for articles about the crime."

"I may be able to help. I still have friends at the Bureau. Let me make a call and see if someone can find the information for you."

"So, you didn't burn all your bridges when you left?"

"Let's just say I only scorched a couple of old ones."

"Thanks."

He knew she'd come through. Sometimes you had to utilize what resources were available to you. He wasn't really using her, was he?

"Call me tonight?"

"Promise."

Joe's mind was spinning. He was torn between thinking about the case, the new lead, his dad, Destiny, and it was beginning to drive him crazy. Everything was getting intense, and he had to do something to relax. So, he decided to drive north and spend some time at Lake Okoboji. He had not been to the resort area for many years. The sight of the blue water coupled with the warmth of the Iowa sunshine could provide a few hours of distraction from all the things bouncing around in his head.

Joe drove to Arnold's Park and found a place to park his car. He walked down to the lake and sat at the shore. Such a peaceful place with only the faint sounds of speedboats skimming over the water. He wasn't there ten minutes when his cell phone rang. Destiny was calling.

"Hi."

"You're not going to believe this. I called my friend at the Bureau, and it wasn't fifteen minutes before she called me back. This kid was an FBI case."

"You're kidding?"

"No. The Bureau got involved because he fled across the state line after he committed the crime. The murder took place in Greene County, Pennsylvania, and he fled into Ohio. That's where he was apprehended. His name was David Eugene Burton."

"David Eugene Burton."

"That's right. You can probably find information about the crime by searching the Waynesburg, Pennsylvania, newspaper."

"Wow, that's a helpful coincidence, huh? I'm going to call Vincenzo and let him know what you found. This should save a lot of time."

"Okay, talk with you later."

Well, so much for a peaceful distraction. Joe called Vincenzo who was in a meeting. This couldn't wait so he called Sam and told him what he'd found out.

"What are you talking about? What about a kid and a murder?"

"When Vincenzo gets back in the office, tell him you got a phone call from me. Tell him the kid's name is David Eugene Burton. And the murder happened in Greene County, Pennsylvania. He'll know what it means. He can call me if he needs to."

"Okay. David Eugene Burton. Greene County, Pennsylvania. Got it."

Joe took a deep breath and blew it out. Then he laid back in the grass, looked up at the clear blue sky, and closed his eyes. He concentrated on his breathing and relaxing his body. After twenty minutes, he sat up and decided to walk around. Before he had a chance to explore much of the park area renovations, his phone rang. The call was from Monte.

"Hello, Monte."

"Yeah, they moved your dad, and he's in his room now. You wanted me to call you."

"Thanks. I'll be there in about half an hour."

"Okey-dokey."

Joe drove back to the hospital. He found his dad sleeping and Monte sitting by his side.

"He nodded off a few minutes ago. The nurse said it's good for him to sleep."

"How's he feeling?"

"I'm feeling okay," said Carl, opening his eyes. "Just a little weak is all."

"Good."

Monte stood up and stretched. "I'll leave you two alone for a while."

Carl looked up at Joe. "It's always good to see you, Joe. I'm sorry you had to come back under these circumstances."

"It's okay, Dad. I wanted to see if you were going to be all right."

"The doctor told me I should make a complete recovery and lead a normal life if I behave myself."

"I'm glad to hear it."

"I appreciate you being here, but you don't have to stick around. There's nothing you can do except waste your time waiting for them to release me."

"I know that. I want to make sure you get out of the hospital and back home with no issues."

"Monte will give me a ride home. And you know Maude. She'll be bringing me three meals a day whether I want them or not."

"Maybe you should let her. Your cupboards look pretty bare. What have you been eating, anyway?"

"I eat. I've been taking good care of myself. I was about to go to the store when this happened."

"You want me to pick up some stuff for you?"

"No, you don't know what I like. Besides, Monte and I go out to eat a few times a week, go chase women over in Pocahontas. Come on. I know how to boil water. You shouldn't worry about me."

At that point, a young nurse entered with some medication. "Mr. Erickson," she said in a sweet voice. "It's time for some medication."

"I'll be back a little later, Dad."

Joe left the hospital, went to the supermarket, and bought two-hundred dollars' worth of groceries for his dad's refrigerator and cupboards. Easy things that he could microwave and fix without a lot of fuss. Things that had a long shelf life. Then he drove back to Marathon. After he unloaded the car and put all the groceries away, he walked next door and told Maude about his dad's condition. She was pleased he would be home soon.

"Don't you worry about your dad. I'll make sure he's well taken care of. He's gonna be sick and tired of me lookin' in on him."

"People are going to start talking."

"Let 'em. We could use a little scandal in this town."

After sitting with his dad at the hospital that afternoon, Joe returned to his dad's house and called Destiny.

"When do you think your dad will be able to come home?"

"I spoke to the doctor this afternoon, and he said they plan to release him tomorrow. A day earlier than they originally thought."

"They don't keep patients in the hospital very long anymore. They feel it's better for them to recuperate at home. Does he have people to come in and help out with things?"

"Oh, yeah."

"I miss you," she said.

"I'll be back soon. Promise."

Chapter Twenty-Six

Since Carl was being released from Spencer Hospital at 11:00 am, Joe drove up earlier that morning to be present when his dad received instructions from Doctor Shayne. Shortly before noon, a nurse pushed Carl out to Joe's car in a wheelchair. Joe looked over at his dad and said, "What do you want to do?"

"Go home, of course."

"We could stop and get some lunch somewhere."

"Nope. I want to go home."

"Home it is." And before long, the black Camaro was cruising down Highway 71 toward Marathon. Half an hour later, they pulled into the driveway. Maude came out of her house and gave Carl a hug.

"You scared the bejesus out me, you know that, Carl? Don't you be doing that anymore!"

"I scared the bejesus out of myself. I won't be pulling any more of those shenanigans for a while, at least."

"I should hope not. Well, I'll let you get settled. I'll bring you over some of my oatmeal cookies after bit."

Joe and Carl went into the house.

"I got you some groceries, and I signed you up for Meals on Wheels."

"What did you do that for?"

"Because you'll get a meal delivered every day, Monday through Friday, so you won't have to cook for yourself all the time. You should have been getting Meals on Wheels years ago."

"Those are for old people!"

"Well, like it or not, you qualify. They start arriving tomorrow."

"All right."

"And the groceries I got you are either frozen or things that go on the shelf. You can fix most everything in the microwave in a matter of minutes. You can follow instructions, can't you?"

"I restored two cars, didn't I?"

Carl sat down in his favorite chair, a comfortable recliner.

"I suppose you're busy working on murder cases back there," Carl said.

"We're investigating a bad situation right now. We have a serial killer at large who's been preying on young women, and we don't have much to go on. I think I may have stumbled on to something, but I won't know until I get back."

"Then, you'd better get back there. It sounds like you're needed."

"I am, but you come first. My lieutenant told me to take as much time as I want."

"You don't need to baby me, Joe. I have Monte who'll look in on me, and Maude who'll feed me. She'll make me fat if I let her. And I'm more than capable of driving myself to Sioux Rapids to the doctor for checkups."

"I know that, Dad."

"Besides, if you stay here another few days, we'll just sit around and stare at each other."

Joe felt conflicted. His dad was right, but he didn't want to leave him so soon after he was released from the hospital. In all probability, they would wind up spending most of the day watching television. He would want to go have coffee with his buddies in the morning, but he would prefer to go with Monte, anyway.

"So, what you're telling me is you don't want me here?"

"Yeah. Get your ass home, kid!"

They both chuckled. Joe agreed he would leave the next day.

Joe went next door and spoke to Maude who was busy baking oatmeal cookies. The smell was wonderful.

He handed her his card with his cell phone number written on it and asked if she would keep an eye on his dad while he was recovering.

"Well, of course, I'll look after him. We've looked after each other ever since your mom passed away. He and my Fred were friends for over half their lives, you know that."

Joe didn't expect anything less from Maude. She was the best of small-town folk.

Twenty minutes later, as Joe left Maude's house, he saw Monte's car in the driveway. Dad's best buddy had dropped by to spend some time with him, so Joe went into the bedroom to leave the two friends to talk.

He called Destiny first but his call went to voicemail. Then he called Sam who picked up.

"Hey, stranger," greeted Sam.

"Hey, yourself."

"How's your dad doing?"

"Better. He came home today, and I'll be traveling back to the city tomorrow."

"Good to hear."

"Have you been able to make any progress tracking down David Eugene Burton?"

"Yes and no. He was deemed mentally unfit for trial and remanded to a mental health facility. He was treated and held there until he was eighteen when his attorney petitioned the court that he was now mentally fit and was no longer a threat to society. The court agreed and he was released."

"Then what?"

"This is where everything goes foggy. His mother owned a parcel of land, and since he was the sole heir, he inherited her estate which was valued around a hundred-fifty-thousand dollars."

"Are you kidding me?"

"No. He sold the land, and after taxes, he had the money transferred to an account in the Cayman Islands. After that, he disappeared. We can't find any trace of him. At least, so far. We're still looking."

"All right. I'll see you tomorrow."

"Got it."

Joe's dad and Monte were in the living room talking away. Joe handed

Monte his card. " I'm heading home tomorrow, so if you need me, here's the number. I'm going to run over to Laurens now and pick up something for supper. "You want to stay, Monte?

"No, no. That's fine. You should enjoy your last supper together." Then he caught himself and laughed. "Well, I didn't mean it like that!"

"The hell you didn't," said Carl, rubbing it in. "Want a glass of wine?"

"Thought you'd never ask," Monte replied.

"Stay put, I'll get it," said Joe. "Merlot?"

"Works for me," said Monte.

When Joe returned with the food he'd picked up in Laurens, Monte had left, and his dad was napping in the recliner. Too much excitement for the first day out of the hospital. He decided to call Destiny again and this time she picked up.

"Hi. How are things?"

"Good enough that I'll be coming home tomorrow."

"Great. You'll call me when you get in?"

"Well, of course. You think I wouldn't?"

He repeated the news that Sam had relayed about David Eugene Burton and Destiny let out a sigh. Silence.

"What are you thinking?"

"I have no way of knowing his I.Q., but he would have received a good education in the medical facility he was sentenced to. And if he's smart, which it sounds like he is, he would know how to disappear. He could be anywhere."

"Including Chicago."

"Right."

"I wonder if we could obtain a photo of him so we could have one of our forensic artists age it so we could see what he might look like today."

"Great idea, Joe."

"I'll look into that when I get back."

After dinner, Joe and his dad watched TV. At nine o'clock, his dad said, "I think it's time for me to go to bed. See you in the morning."

"I jog in the morning, so I'll be up and around early. If you hear something, just ignore it."

"Okay. Good night."

"Good night, Dad."

The next morning Joe was up at 5:00 am and out the door in his jogging clothes a few minutes later. As he ran, he began thinking about what he would do if he was David Eugene Burton. His past would follow him wherever he went. Joe suspected he fell off the radar because he was probably using an alias. But if Burton was highly intelligent, he might have gone a step further and created an entirely new identity.

In the digital age, creating a new identity is not as easy as it used to be. Years ago, if some guy wanted to disappear, he needed to find an infant near his own age who died shortly after birth, preferably the child of a single, unmarried mother. That way, the child would be practically anonymous since no family would remember the birth. With that information, he could apply for a certified birth certificate. Then he could assume a new name, obtain a driver's license, a social security number, a passport, and be on his way to becoming someone else. Not anymore. But if he did it in a foreign country, one that wasn't as sophisticated as the US, it would be much easier. He immediately wondered if Burton had spent time abroad.

He finished his jog, clocking about two miles. Back at the house, he was greeted by the smell of coffee, and he found his dad standing over the stove scrambling eggs.

"You're up early."

"Early? I get up at this time every day. Thought I'd cook you breakfast since you're leaving this morning. I wanted to show you I can handle myself around the kitchen."

"Thanks, Dad."

"Well, don't just stand there. Sit down ."

Carl and Joe enjoyed their breakfast and spoke of things going on around town. Joe reminded him that he needed to exercise, and the community center gym would be a good place for him to walk, especially when the weather was bad. Carl promised he would follow his doctor's orders and take his medication. Knowing his dad, Joe was a little skeptical.

After breakfast, Joe showered, dressed, packed up his belongings, and tossed them into the trunk of the car. He sent Destiny a short text at 7:00 am: "On my way!" Then, he walked back into the kitchen.

"Well, I guess I'm leaving."

"Don't worry about me. I'll be fine."

They gave each other a hug. "I love you, Dad."

"I know. Now, go back and catch that murdering son-of-a-bitch!"

That elicited a smile from Joe. "I'll do my best."

Leaving was emotional for him, and he blinked back a tear as he buckled in and fired up his Camaro. He glanced to his left and saw his dad's face in the kitchen window. He gave him a wave and Carl waved back. Then he backed out onto the street and drove out of town toward the highway that would take him back to the Windy City.

Chapter Twenty-Seven

Shortly after 2:30 pm, Joe arrived at his apartment. He made two phone calls, one to his dad to let him know he'd made it home, and the other to Destiny. Dad's answering machine picked up, so he left a message. He would try calling him later. However, Destiny answered.

"Hi there, traveler."

"I'm back."

"I'm glad. Did you just arrive?"

"A few minutes ago, yeah."

"Tired?"

"Oh, a little fatigued from driving that long. But not so much."

"You want to come over?"

"Are you offering to open your inner sanctum?"

"Will you walk into my parlor, said a spider to a fly."

Joe laughed. "What time?"

"How about now? I have a nice bottle of Pinot Noir that's been begging me to pop its cork."

"Well, if that's the case, I'll be there in a few."

Joe had never been to Destiny's apartment. The place was a more upscale complex than the one he lived in. But after a high-profile job with the FBI, she could probably afford it.

"So good to see you. I've missed you," she said when she opened the door.

"I've missed you, too."

When he stepped through the door, he was taken aback. Her living room resembled something out of a magazine. A large area rug graced the oak floor between a matching couch and love seat, pillows in all the right colors were perfectly placed. Original paintings hung from the walls, and bronze sculptures and lamps sat on brass and glass tables. But despite the opulent furnishings, it was warm and inviting.

"Wow! Do you actually use this room or just look at it?"

Destiny laughed, "Of course I use it."

"It's beautiful. What do you call this style?"

"It's contemporary, something I happen to like. I wish I could say I did all this myself, but I have a decorator friend, and she designed it for me and helped pick the pieces."

"She's got some talent. This makes my place look like..."

"A typical bachelor's pad?"

"You're being kind."

"There's nothing wrong with your place. Totally functional. That's what most men want, isn't it?"

"More or less."

"But there's nothing on your walls. I could help you out with that sometime if you want."

"That's okay. I have a classic poster of Farrah Fawcett I could put up..."

Destiny laughed. "Come on. How about that glass of wine?"

In her kitchen was an uncorked bottle of Pinot Noir. She poured a glass for him and one for herself. Then she reached out and they clinked glasses.

"To your dad's health."

"Thank you. Much appreciated."

She picked up the bottle and they walked back to the living room and sat on the couch.

They talked about Joe's dad, the discovery Joe made about the case, and as they did so, they finished the bottle of wine. One thing led to another and they wound up in bed. Joe's fatigue from driving coupled with the wine, and the exertion from lovemaking caused him to doze off. Destiny looked over at him, watching him breathe. She smiled and kissed him.

Michael Fleming had plans for the evening, too. Nefarious plans. He had it all worked out. He was going to drive up to Kilbourn Park and kill Kirsten Welch. He wanted her from the moment he'd laid eyes on her when she and her sister had contacted his employer to handle their mother's funeral arrangements. He would gain entrance to her apartment, telling her she needed to sign a paper. Once in, he would slip his knife in her heart, exactly like he did to all the others.

Fleming drove to Kilbourn Park and found a parking place on West Cornelia Avenue three blocks away, where he knew there were no surveillance cameras. He used his burner phone to call her land line to make sure she was home.

"Hello."

"Hi. It's Michael Fleming from the Wesley-Donner Funeral Home."

"Oh, yes."

"I have a paper I need you to sign, and I happen to be in your neighborhood on other business. I was wondering if it would be convenient for me to stop by and have you sign it. I know it's Sunday, but it would save you a trip to the funeral home."

"That's very thoughtful."

"I could come back some other time if you have company. I wouldn't want to inconvenience you."

"No, I'm here alone. I'll ring you up when you get here."

"Thank you. I'll be there in a few minutes. Good-bye."

Fleming smiled. She was alone—just what he wanted to hear. His hand reached to his belt and he felt the knife in place under his windbreaker. Ready. Taking a deep breath, he picked up his briefcase and began walking the three blocks to meet with Kirsten Welch.

The apartment complex's security camera was sure to capture his image, but with his fedora pulled down and his sunglasses on, he made sure the rest of his face was indistinguishable by using a handkerchief to feign blowing his nose as he passed by. Once inside, he covered his finger with the handkerchief when he pushed the button for Kirsten's apartment. After being buzzed in, he used the stairs rather than the elevator, to reach the third floor.

Seeing no security cameras and no one in the hall, Fleming removed his sunglasses and walked to her door. His adrenalin was flowing as he rang her doorbell. When the door opened, his jaw dropped. Standing before him was not who he expected to see. Rather than Kirsten, it was her sister, Kylie. She was wearing a t-shirt and no bra which left little to the imagination. Short shorts and barefoot.

"I take it you were expecting Kirsten?"

"Uh…as a matter of fact…" He was totally thrown off his game plan. *Now what to do?* he thought, beginning to panic. *I didn't bring any fucking paper to sign.* Beads of sweat formed at his hairline.

"Come in. I can sign your paper just as easily as Kirsten, can't I?"

"Of course. It doesn't really make any difference, I guess." He laid his briefcase on the kitchen table.

"Where's your sister?"

"Indiana on business." Kylie had found Fleming attractive and desirable when she had dealings with him at the funeral home. "He's hot," she had told her sister. And not having sex for several months, she was feeling a little randy and thought boffing a great-looking guy like Fleming might be a fun way to spend a Sunday afternoon. She didn't have anything better to do. Besides, her boyfriend would never find out about this one little indiscretion, anyway.

"Why don't you take off your jacket and stay awhile."

"I may just do that." And as he turned around to face her, his arm came up and his hand plunged the knife between her ribs and into her heart.

"You were going to give me a little something, weren't you Momma?" said Fleming. "Well, I'm here to collect."

The final look in her eyes was one of horror as she looked into his face. Then she exhaled, her head flopped back, and she became dead weight.

Fleming laid her on the tile floor. She had quit breathing but he checked her pulse. She was dead. He removed the knife, pulled off her T-shirt and shorts, and saw she was wearing no panties. *I see what you were up to*, he thought. *Surprise, surprise!* Opening his briefcase, he prepared for surgery.

HAVANA BROWN

Once his work was over, he carried Kylie's body into the bedroom, placed her in bed, and covered her as he had done with all his other victims. He proceeded to clean up any traces of blood and washed his instruments and gloved hands in the kitchen sink. Then he packed everything into his briefcase. On went the sunglasses and fedora.

As he was about to reach for the doorknob to make his escape, he heard a key in the lock. *Oh, no! What to do?* He couldn't kill her, too. It could lead authorities back to the funeral home. He ducked behind the door. And as Kirsten came into the room, he swung with all his might and smacked her in the jaw with his fist. A direct hit. She let out a cry and collapsed onto the floor. His hand hurt like hell. He reached down and pulled her into the room. Then he fled down the stairs.

He left the building and walked away for several blocks. Spotting an older commercial building, he entered and ducked into a restroom where he removed his fedora, sunglasses, and windbreaker and placed them in his briefcase. Then he took a circuitous route to his car that included busy North Pulaski Road.

Once inside his car, he started shaking. He'd never come this close to getting caught before. The more he thought about it, the more upset he became. He had to get home. He could see the car in front and the car in the rear had him parked in pretty tight. He backed up, moved forward, backed up again, then began to pull out. As he did, his front bumper hit the rear bumper of the car in front of him. *Son-of-a-bitch! I've got to get out of here.* So, he pulled out into the street and drove off.

But someone had seen him. Suzy Wright was walking her dog and saw what happened. A good citizen, she took down Fleming's license plate number and the plate number of the car that he hit. When she got home, she reported the incident to the police.

When Fleming got home, he drove his car into the garage, then took his briefcase down to the basement. He was upset but he had make preparations. He couldn't wait until tomorrow. When he went back upstairs. Fidel ran up to him, let out a meow, and brushed up against his legs.

"Hey, Fidel," Fleming said with tenderness. "Did you miss me?" He knelt down and petted his chocolate brown companion. "Daddy had a close call today."

After giving attention to his cat, Fleming made himself a tall gin gimlet. Afterward, he walked into his living room where he sat down with Fidel at his side. When he had finished his gimlet, he got up and made himself another in hopes of calming down. Normally, he had nerves of steel, or at least he thought he did. But what happened today had wounded his resolve and shaken his confidence. He wondered what the next time would be like given today's debacle.

Chapter Twenty-Eight

J oe awakened around six o'clock that evening to the jarring sound of the ringtone coming from his cell phone. He saw the call was from Sam.

"Hey," answered Joe.

"I know you're in Iowa, but I thought you'd want to know—"

"I'm not in Iowa," interrupted Joe. "I just got back."

"Ah. Well, there's been another murder. I'm on the scene right now."

"Okay, I want to be there. What's the address?"

"Kilbourn Park. 3300 block of Karlov Avenue. And Joe, this time we have a witness."

"On my way."

Destiny, who was working on her laptop at the kitchen table, heard Joe's animated voice and came into the bedroom.

"What's going on?"

"There's been another murder. Sam is on the scene."

"I'll turn on the shower and get you a towel."

Destiny was waiting for him in the kitchen. Unable to sleep, she had showered and dressed while Joe was sleeping.

"It's a good thing you slept. You may have a late night."

"Sorry to run out on you like this. Love you," he said. "I'll call."

"You'd better. I love you, too."

Omigod! He said it. And it came from out of the blue. Omigod! He said it and so did I. He loves me.

As Joe drove to the Kilbourn Park address, his mind was not on Sam and the murder but what had just taken place in Destiny's apartment. He told Destiny he loved her, and it just slipped out unconsciously. Somehow, he said what he had been thinking and feeling. He'd been afraid to admit it, not knowing how she would react. Now he knew she felt the same way. Wow! Their relationship had just taken a big step forward.

When Joe turned onto Karlov Avenue, his mind switched to cop-think. Police cruisers were parked in front of the address and the ME's van had already arrived. He walked up to the officer on the scene, showed him his ID, and entered the building. Another officer directed him to the third floor. Taking the stairs, he found Sam talking with the officer stationed outside the open door to an apartment.

"I got here as soon as I could."

"It's our guy, again. Same MO. Kendra's in there along with the evidence techs."

"When did it happen?"

"Two hours ago. It appears the sister of the victim came home and caught the perp inside the apartment. He coldcocked her and knocked her unconscious as soon as she stepped through the door."

"She get a look at him?"

"No, just a dark figure, peripheral vision. When she came to, she looked for her sister who was staying with her. Found her all right—in the bedroom, under the blankets, dead. Well, she went into hysterics, started screaming. A neighbor called police. By the time we got here, she'd gone into shock and had to be hospitalized. What little we know we got from the first uniforms on the scene. We may be able to get more from her once she's been treated and can talk with us."

"Who's we?"

"While you were gone, I've been working with Cardona. She's interviewing others in the building right now."

"If he rendered her unconscious, why didn't he kill her, too? Two for one."

"Good question. He had opportunity. Time, maybe?"

"Yeah. I dunno. He's meticulous. She disrupted his plans. Maybe it caused him to panic and run."

"Could be.

"The apartment complex has surveillance cameras. Somebody collecting the video?"

"We're working on it."

"What about surveillance video around the area?"

"Working on that, too."

"You talk with Kendra?"

At that moment, Kendra Solitsky came to the door. She lowered her mask and asked, "Did I hear my name taken in vain?"

"Only once," Sam said.

Kendra chuckled. "That's disappointing. What do you want to know, guys?"

"Same type of mutilation?" asked Joe.

"Same as the others. Knife wound to the heart appears to be the cause of death. Same surgical mutilation. When are you going to catch this disgrace to the human race?"

"This time we got ourselves a witness and we swabbed for DNA on her face," said Sam.

"I heard. I hope she can give you something good. Well, I'd better get back in there and do my job. That's why they pay me that outrageously high salary. Talk to you later." Kendra turned and walked back into the apartment.

The stairway door opened and Vincenzo stepped into the hallway. He didn't expect to see Joe on the scene.

"So, you're back I see," By the look on his face, he was annoyed about something. "How's your old man?"

"Pretty good given he had a major heart attack. But he wanted me to get back home. He has people to look after him."

"Good. We can use you." He looked at Sam and said, "So, this animal struck again, huh?"

"Yeah, but we have a witness and possibly some evidence this time." Sam ran through the same explanation he gave to Joe. Vincenzo was not pleased.

"So, we probably don't have a viable witness after all, and we might accidentally have some DNA, is that where we're at?"

"That's the way it looks at the moment, Lieutenant."

Vincenzo let out a deep sigh. "All right. Keep me informed. He turned, and Joe and Sam watched as he walked away cursing under his breath.

"She still might recall something by tomorrow. All the traumatic stress may be repressing her memory," said Sam.

"Yeah."

"You back at work tomorrow?"

"I'll be in. Look, I'm taking off. You and Cardona have this handled?"

"Yeah."

Joe left and went back to his car. He called Destiny and let her know he was finished at the scene.

"You hungry?"

"As a matter of fact..."

"Come back to my place. I'll have supper ready for you."

"Supper, huh?"

"That's what you call it in your neck of the woods, right?"

"It is."

"See you in a bit."

When Destiny opened the door to her apartment, Joe could smell the captivating aroma of her cooking.

"Wine?"

"Please."

She poured from the bottle of Pinot Noir she had opened. She handed Joe a glass and raised hers. "To love."

Joe looked into her blue eyes and repeated, "To love."

They made themselves comfortable on the couch and he told her what he learned at the scene. The living witness was bothering him.

"Why do you suppose this guy decided to knock the witness unconscious when he could have killed her, too? It doesn't make sense to me."

"I can only speculate. It may be possible he was preying on a specific person, and he had no interest in another target. Another possibility is each one of the women knew him. And by killing both, the suspect pool would shrink significantly. Or…he simply panicked. It's hard to tell."

Destiny poured Joe another glass of wine, then changed the subject.

"Did you mean what you said before you left earlier?"

"That I love you? Yeah, I meant it. I would have said it earlier but didn't know how you'd react. I didn't want to screw things up between us."

"I was afraid of the same thing. I was hoping you'd say it first so I could tell you."

Joe paused, looking into Destiny's eyes. "So, where do we go from here?"

Chapter Twenty-Nine

When Joe got into work the next morning, he walked down to Vincenzo's office. His door was open and Joe poked his head inside.

"You got a minute?"

"Come on in."

"I was wondering if my inquiry on David Eugene Burton turned up anything yet."

Vincenzo reached for a folder on his desk and handed it to Joe. "Yeah, it did. He's dead. It was a promising lead, but it turns out he was killed eight years ago in a car accident near San Diego. It's all in there."

Joe grimaced. "Shit! I thought for sure we had a line on our guy."

"So did I. It wouldn't be the first time a lead went up in flames. Maybe we can get something from our witness today. I'm having Cardona interview her. I think maybe a woman talking with her might be less stressful, you know? I'm hoping the ME and the evidence techs can turn up something. There's a priority on evidence retrieval on this one."

"I'll do some digging, Lieutenant."

"Yeah. Well, use a big shovel."

Joe left Vincenzo's office with the Burton file and walked back to his desk. He started reading through the information about Burton's death: photocopies of the death certificate, the accident report, photographs from the scene, and newspaper stories. He noticed there was no autopsy report. Cause of death was listed as blunt force trauma to the head. The accident report stated he was not wearing a seat belt and was thrown through the windshield. In cases like this, autopsies were not always necessary. Joe made note of the name of the funeral home listed on the death certificate. He was going to follow up with some questions he had about the final disposition of the remains. *I guess there's no need for a forensic artist to age a known photograph of David Eugene Burton now.*

It would be several hours before he could make a call to California, so Joe met with Sam, Crawford, and Dempsey, to review surveillance footage from the apartment complex and the surrounding neighborhood. With Kirsten's arrival at her apartment placed at approximately 4:30 pm, they narrowed suspects to an individual with the fedora who entered the building at 4:13 pm. Apparently, the suspect must have been known to the victim or someone in the building who buzzed him in.

They reviewed footage all morning and were able to trace his movements to a commercial building on Addison. He entered the building at 4:47 pm and never came out.

"How can that be?" asked Dempsey. "What did he do? Stay overnight?"

"Maybe he has an office in there," said Crawford.

"No, I don't think so," countered Joe. "He's too smart to lead us to his office."

"This guy has to screw up some time," stated Crawford.

"It's worth checking out," said Dempsey.

"Do it," said Sam. "Have a photo made and see if anyone can identify him based on the clothing he's wearing and his physical description. We might get lucky."

Dempsey and Crawford got up and left. Joe looked at Sam and said, "Stop the video. Ask yourself: If you just killed someone, and you were getting away on foot, why would you go in that building?"

Sam thought for a minute, and then his eyes lit up. "To change clothes. Alter my identity so if I was picked up on a surveillance camera…"

Joe finished his sentence, "I'd be just another pedestrian."

"Call Dempsey and Crawford and have them search the restrooms. See if he discarded a hat and a windbreaker. Hopefully, the custodians haven't emptied the trash yet." Sam called Crawford and they agreed to search the restroom trash receptacles for the clothing items.

"He's gonna be carrying something. Something to transport his stuff, right?" said Sam.

"So, let's watch for people coming out of the building carrying a bag, a briefcase, anything at all," suggested Joe.

"Got it."

They began watching the surveillance video of people leaving the building after the suspect entered. Ten minutes later, a man exited carrying a plastic bag.

"Look!" said Sam. "A guy with a large plastic bag. Look big enough for a briefcase to fit in?"

"Yeah."

"Ten minutes after he entered. About the right amount of time to find a restroom, change clothes, and leave the building."

The man who was carrying the plastic bag was dressed in a polo shirt, baseball cap, and sunglasses. They tried to follow him on surveillance video that officers had retrieved from neighboring businesses but lost him on North Pulaski Road amidst the foot traffic around the shops and bars.

Crawford and Dempsey returned empty-handed. They were none too happy having to search through restroom trash most of the morning. The inside of the building did not have any surveillance cameras and they drew a blank on any witnesses.

"I suppose we could have all the restrooms doors and toilet seats printed," said Dempsey, his sarcastic voice reflecting his annoyance.

"You know how many prints those doors have?" asked Joe. "Besides, this guy's too smart to leave any prints. He knew how to disappear in the crowd of people on Pulaski and disguise himself to make his escape. We're up against someone very clever."

"We need to have uniforms check any businesses along North Pulaski between Addison and Newport for outside surveillance footage," said Sam. "Somebody might have recorded an image of this guy."

"I'll put in the request," said Crawford.

That afternoon, Joe looked through police reports for any citations that might have been written in the area: parking tickets, traffic infractions, drug-related offenses, or other reported police matters. One, in particular, caught his eye. Three blocks from the crime scene, on West Cornelia Avenue, there was a hit-and-run incident reported by a passerby. He wrote down the information noting the vehicle involved was a Lexus owned by a Michael John Fleming. *Michael Fleming? Where have I heard that name before?* He would need to check that out.

* * *

On Monday morning, Michael Fleming was at work, when a uniformed officer appeared at his door.

"Mr. Fleming? Michael Fleming?"

Fleming looked up in surprise.

"Yes. What can I do for you, Officer?"

"I'm Officer Otis Johnson, Mr. Fleming. We had a report of a hit-and-run involving your vehicle yesterday afternoon in the vicinity of West Cornelia Avenue. Were you driving in that area yesterday?"

Omigod, someone saw me hit that fucking car! "Yes, I was parked on West Cornelia for a while."

"Do you remember hitting a car in that location?"

"No."

"Well, there was a witness that said you did."

"I don't think that's possible. I have my car here today. You're welcome to take a look." He knew the damage was only paint-related and he could talk his way out of a citation.

In the employee parking area, Officer Johnson walked around the Lexus and looked at the front bumper, where he found a paint scrape.

"What's this here?"

"Omigod," exclaimed Fleming, feigning surprise.

Officer Johnson squatted down and examined the damage, rubbing his finger across the scrape. "This is gray paint on your bumper, and the car that was hit was gray in color," he said, looking up at Fleming. "And there was white paint left on the other car's rear bumper."

"Well, if I did that pulling out of my parking place, I'm sorry. I certainly didn't feel any bump. I would have stopped and left a note if I had."

"It looks pretty minor," said Officer Johnson, rising to a standing position.

"I can't believe I did that. If you'll give me the car owner's information, I'll contact my insurance company and let them know about it. I'm not the kind of person who would leave the scene of an accident."

"The damage is minor on her vehicle as well. I spoke to her about it, and she just wants it fixed." He reached into his pocket, pulled out his notepad, and tore out a page. Handing it to Fleming, he said, "This is her name, VIN number of the vehicle, and the phone number of her insurance agent. I suggest you call. I won't cite you for leaving the scene if you take care of this."

"I certainly will. This is quite embarrassing. Thank you, Officer."

"You have a nice day," replied Officer Johnson who turned and walked back through the funeral home and out to his cruiser.

Fleming breathed a huge sigh of relief. He dodged a bullet but realized he might not be out of the woods. His accident would still place him in the vicinity of the murder, and he would need to establish a reason for being there. Walking back to his office, he made a call to his insurance agent about the accident. He would have to get an estimate for getting his own car repaired.

Sweat soaked his shirt. He removed his suit coat and thought about an alibi. One he could provide to give a reasonable explanation why he was in the area. Hopefully, he wouldn't need one.

His schedule was slow today. No embalming required and no funerals on the calendar. He would speak with Herb Wesley, his boss, and see if he could take the rest of the day off. He wanted to return to North Pulaski Road to find a bar or restaurant where he could say he was during the time of the killing. He would need to find one with no surveillance cameras if that was possible. In any case, he would become a regular patron for the next month so he would be remembered.

When Fleming left work, he drove to North Pulaski Road and found a parking place on West Eddy Street. He walked two blocks to Pulaski and began checking out bars. He found one, The M&H Lounge, a small intimate bar and grill that didn't seem to have surveillance cameras inside.

Numerous patrons were drinking and having lunch. Fleming sat down on a stool at the bar and was greeted by the bartender, a woman in her fifties.

"What can I get you?" she asked in a low, smoker's voice.

"I'll start with the Goose Island you have on tap."

"Coming up."

He looked around and saw two waitresses serving customers. He paid for the pint and moved to one of the tables. A couple minutes later, a young woman approached his table.

"Hi," she smiled. "Would you like to see a menu?"

"I would."

She handed him a laminated sheet. "I'll be back in a couple of minutes."

He looked over the fare. Typical pub food—mostly deep-fried stuff with a few choices cooked on the grill. He needed to make an impression so she would remember him if—and the question was *if*—she was working yesterday. He would have to find out. Laying down his menu, he looked up and caught the waitress's eye.

"Did you make up your mind?"

"How are the portabella mushrooms?"

"Oh, they're very good. I love them."

"That's a pretty good recommendation. I'll have those with a side order of ranch dressing."

"Got it."

"I think you maybe waited on me yesterday, too," he said, testing the waters.

"I may have. We were really busy with the Cubs playing and all."

"Yeah, it gets a little crazy when they win, doesn't it? I'm sorry, what's your name again?"

"Sophia. People call me Sophie."

"Sophie! That's right. I'm terrible with names."

"I'm not so good with names, either."

"I'm Michael, in case you don't remember."

"Michael. Got it. I'll be back with your order, Michael." And she turned and walked away. He was pleased with himself. She'd remember him now if someone asked.

* * *

Joe made a call to the McGregor-Beaulieu Mortuary in San Diego which handled the burial of David Eugene Burton. The secretary connected him to James McGregor, one of the owners.

"Yes, detective. How can I be of service?" he asked in a deep, smooth voice.

Joe explained he had the death certificate for David Eugene Burton and that it listed the McGregor-Beaulieu Mortuary as the recipient of the remains.

"Could you tell me the details regarding the disposition of the remains?" asked Joe. "It came up in one of our investigations and we'd like to clarify the issue."

"I believe I can assist you with that. Let me pull that up on my computer."

"Yes, I have a vague recollection of this one, actually. It was a rather strange case. We attempted to contact the next of kin but we were unable to do so. However, an anonymous individual paid for cremation with instructions for internment at Memorial Park Cemetery. The payment came in form of a postal money order."

"Do you recall the condition of the body?"

"Well, there were considerable facial injuries, so it would have taken significant cosmetic reconstruction had it been a traditional funeral."

"I see," replied Joe. "So, if I wanted to verify the deceased was really David Eugene Burton, it would now be impossible."

"It would appear so," said McGregor. "Is there a question as to the identity of Mr. Burton?

"No. Just a question to satisfy my curiosity, that's all. Thank you for your time, Mr. McGregor. You've been most helpful."

Joe hung up the phone. David Burton was ashes, and so was Joe's lead. He would have to pursue other lines of investigation, starting with what Michael Fleming was doing three blocks away from the murder site.

He got on the Secretary of State's Driver database and ran a search for Michael John Fleming. An image popped up almost immediately. *Hm. Good-looking guy.* Five-foot-eleven, one-hundred seventy-five pounds, brown eyes, thirty-four years old. Looking at the address, Joe saw he lived in the West Ridge neighborhood. *Nice area.* He checked the Auto Registration database. *Drives a Lexus. He might have money.* Somehow, Fleming looked vaguely familiar. But for the life of him, Joe couldn't figure out where he'd seen him. *Screw it!* He printed a copy of the license and placed it in a file for future reference. He and Sam would check him out tomorrow.

Chapter Thirty

The next day, Joe and Sam drove to Michael Fleming's West Bryn Mawr Avenue address in the West Ridge neighborhood on the Northside of the city. The one-story brick home with a single-car garage looked well-maintained but with minimal landscaping.

They got out of their car and walked up to the door. Sam rang the doorbell a couple of times but there was no response.

"Young guy, he's probably at work," said Sam.

"Yeah. Let's see if any of his neighbors are at home. Maybe one of them can tell us something." Sam took the house to the left and Joe the one to the right. Joe rang the doorbell, and a wizened woman in her eighties answered the door. Joe showed her his ID.

"Good morning, ma'am. I'm Detective Joe Erickson of the Chicago Police Department."

Before he could finish, her arms shot up into the air. "I didn't do it."

Oh, great. I've encountered a comedian! Joe thought. "Didn't do what?"

"Soliciting," she answered with a sparkle in her eye.

Joe laughed. "Lucky for you, I don't work Vice. I'm here to ask if you know your neighbor, Michael Fleming?"

As she lowered her arms, her demeanor became serious. "Nothing's happened to him, I hope."

"No, ma'am. We just want to ask him a few questions, that's all."

"Well, that's good. He's a nice young man. I would hate to have anything happen to him."

"Do you know where he works?"

"Michael's an undertaker."

"I see. Do you know which funeral home he works for?"

"Oh, dear. I knew you were going to ask me that. Uh...it's W-something, I think."

"W-something."

"Yes...like Western-something. Two names. This old memory isn't what it once was."

"That's all right. I believe we can figure it out. Has he lived here long?"

"Oh, three years I suppose."

"Nice young man, you say."

"Yes, always personable when I see him. But he pretty much keeps to himself."

"Well, thank you for your time, ma'am. And stay off those street corners."

"A girl's gotta make a living!"

Sam met Joe back at the car.

"Did you get anything?"

"His elderly neighbor said he works for a funeral home. She said the name of it sounds like Western-something."

"Close. Wesley-Donner Funeral Home. It's on West Lawrence Avenue."

"Great. Let's go."

Joe and Sam drove to West Lawrence Avenue which was not far from Fleming's address. The storefront mortuary featured a steel and canvas portico covering the entrance. They opened the door and stepped inside.

They were greeted by a thin, middle-aged man. "Good morning, gentlemen."

Joe flashed his ID. "I'm Detective Joe Erickson, and this is my partner, Detective Sam Renaldo.

"Oh, dear. Is something wrong?"

"No. We're here to speak with Michael Fleming. Is he here?"

"May I ask what this is about?"

"No. Is he here?"

His manner turned cold. "He is. If you'll follow me."

The attendant walked them through a door and down a corridor to an office with an open door. Fleming was seated behind the desk, clicking away on his keyboard.

"Michael?" the man said, getting his attention.

"Yes, Allan?"

"There are two police detectives here to see you."

Fleming was expecting them sooner or later, and he was prepared. He rose and began putting on his suitcoat. "Send them in." He rounded his desk and greeted them at the door.

Joe and Sam showed their IDs and introduced themselves. Fleming shook hands with them and said, "Have a seat. To what do I owe the pleasure?"

"Your vehicle was involved in a fender-bender on West Cornelia Avenue Sunday afternoon," stated Sam, seeking confirmation.

"I wouldn't call it a fender-bender, exactly," said Fleming. "You see, as I was pulling out of a parking place, my front bumper brushed against the rear bumper of the car in front of me. I left a little paint on the bumper. I didn't even know I did it."

"We don't care about the paint you left on the other vehicle's bumper. We're investigating a homicide that happened three blocks away. Maybe you heard about it?"

"No, as a matter of fact, I didn't."

"Well, we'd like to know what you were doing in the area during this time," asked Sam. "You don't live in that area."

"I was watching the Cubs play at the M&H Lounge on Pulaski."

"You couldn't do that at home?"

"I live alone, Detective. I need to get out and socialize occasionally. Be around people."

"So, did you go there with anyone?"

"No, I went by myself."

"Can anyone verify you were there?" asked Joe.

"It was pretty busy. But maybe the waitress could. Her name is Sophie, I think. Yeah, Sophie. She might remember me. I was drinking Goose Island."

"How long did you stay?" asked Sam.

"I left sometime after the game was over. Don't remember the exact time.

Cubs won," smiled Fleming.

"I heard. Unfortunately, I was a little busy at the time."

Joe was looking at Fleming's charcoal gray suit and saw some stray animal hairs on the sleeve and shoulder. Then it dawned on him where he'd seen him before—Maria Martinez's funeral service. He was one of the funeral directors at the church. He also wondered if Fleming owned a cat. He could point out the hairs and ask, but that could tip his hand if the guy was guilty. Cat hairs were the only tangible evidence they had up to this point. He saw a scotch tape dispenser on Fleming's desk and thought of something.

Joe pulled out his notebook, flipped it open, and purposely tore a page. "Shit," he said. "Sorry. Uh...Could I bother you for a piece of scotch tape?"

"Here," replied Fleming, and he turned the dispenser toward Joe. Reaching for the tape, Joe tore off a two-inch strip, held his notebook beneath the edge of the desk, and mimed putting it on the page. While Sam and Fleming conversed, Joe wrapped it around his finger.

Joe looked over at Sam and said, "You have any more questions for Mr. Fleming?"

"No, I think we've established his whereabouts." Joe stood up and Sam followed while Fleming walked around the side of his desk.

"I'm sorry we had to bother you, but we have to check out every possible lead," said Joe.

"You wouldn't be doing your job if you didn't," replied Fleming. He shook hands with Sam, and then with Joe.

Then Joe said, "You have something on your shoulder." And he reached up and removed the small piece of paper he had palmed after tearing it from his notebook. At the same time, he used the scotch tape on his finger to pick up a sample of hairs from Fleming's suit.

Fleming looked at him oddly. "Here you go," said Joe, and he deposited the small piece of paper into Fleming's hand. "I couldn't let you walk around with this on your dark suit."

"He's a neat freak," said Sam, rolling his eyes and playing along. "You should have to work with him. Thanks for your time. We'll show ourselves out."

When Joe and Sam got to their car Joe pulled a small evidence bag from his pocket and placed the scotch tape containing the hairs inside and sealed it up.

"What was that about?" asked Sam.

"He had animal hair on his clothes. I want to make sure it isn't brown cat hair as in Havana Brown cat hair."

"Ahh. Cleverly done, partner. I never knew you had sticky fingers."

"Only when necessary. We saw this guy before—at Maria Martinez's funeral. He was one of the funeral directors—he came up to us and asked us who we were, remember?"

"Oh, yeah. A little attitude if I recall."

"Uh-huh. Let's go. I want to run this to the crime lab and see if Art Casey will do a rush comparison on these hairs.

"It's not admissible, you know."

"I know that. You know that. That's why I don't want it to go through official channels. But...I want to know if we've got another piece of the puzzle. Morticians are skilled with a scalpel, right? And they would know the location of internal organs. He would know exactly where to place a knife so it would penetrate the heart. He was in the vicinity of the last murder, and two to one says those hairs belong to a cat. Sound like a suspect to you?"

"Best we've got so far."

"This afternoon we can check his alibi at the M&H Lounge."

"Why don't we check his alibi there after work?" Sly smile.

"Sounds like a plan."

They drove to the crime lab and Joe asked to see Art Casey. A few minutes later Art walked out, and when he saw Joe and Sam he said, "I suppose you're needing another favor."

"Yeah, I do."

"This makes how many?"

"I thought you were keeping count."

"Yeah, right. What do you need?"

Joe pulled the evidence bag from his jacket and handed it to Art. "I need to know if this is cat hair, and if it is, does it match the brown cat hair found at the murder scenes."

"Okay."

"And Art?"

"Yeah."

"Keep this off the books."

"Someday you're going to get my nuts in a wringer, you know that?"

"Just tell us yes or no and then destroy it. That's all we need to know. It could be key evidence in pointing us to a suspect."

"But you had to break the rules to get it, right?"

"Only bent them a little."

Art let out a deep breath. "All right. I suppose you need it yesterday like you always do."

"It would be much appreciated."

"Yeah. I'll call you later today. You're gonna owe me a house by the time I retire!" Art turned and walked back into the lab.

Joe looked at Sam, and they both chuckled. "He's probably right," said Sam.

"I'll get him a bottle of George Dickel Number 8, his favorite whiskey. That should smooth things over. You want to grab a bite at the M&H Lounge? They open at eleven. We could kill two birds."

Sam looked at his watch. "Yeah. Should be time for lunch by the time we get there. You actually going to eat pub food rather than your fancy gourmet stuff?"

"I'm not a purist. I can make exceptions."

Sam and Joe drove to North Pulaski Road and found a parking place a block from the M&H Lounge. They found the place was busy with lunch clientele, but they spotted a vacant table near the sidewall and grabbed it. They had barely placed butts in seats before a waitress was there with menus.

"Can I get you guys something to drink?"

"Water with lemon for me," said Joe.

"Ice tea," said Sam.

"Sweet?"

"You are."

"I meant the tea," she responded with a smile.

"Oh. Plain will do."

She left to get their drinks and Joe asked, "How old do you think she is?"

"I don't know. Twenty-four, five."

"And you're what...forty-two."

"So. I don't discriminate. I'm an equal opportunity flirter. What can I say?"

"She might be the girl we need to talk with so don't piss her off."

"Me?"

"Yeah, you."

They looked at their menus and a few minutes later the waitress came back with their drinks.

"Have you made up your minds?"

"Could I ask you a question first?" asked Joe.

"Sure."

"Is your name Sophie?"

She looked at Joe strangely. "Yeah. Why?"

Not wanting to draw attention to the fact they were cops, Joe pulled his ID and covertly showed it to her at the edge of the table.

"I'm Detective Joe Erickson and he's my partner, Detective Sam Renaldo. We need a little information from you. It won't take long."

"Okay, I guess..."

Joe pulled out his cell phone and pulled up the driver's license photo of Michael Fleming. "Can you tell us if this man was in here on Sunday afternoon?" He showed it to her.

"Oh. That's Michael."

"So, you remember him?"

"Uh-huh. Kinda hunky."

"Yeah. Was he in here Sunday?"

"I think so. Well, I think maybe he was. We were really busy so it was hard to remember everybody that was in here, ya know?"

"You think maybe he was?" asked Sam.

"Well, you see. He was in here yesterday and I waited on him. And we talked a little about the Cubs game in here the day before—we weren't so busy yesterday—and he told me he thought I was the one that waited on him."

"Do you specifically remember waiting on him? Like what he ordered or drank or talked about?" asked Sam.

"No, not exactly. I was run ragged that day. We were packed. He was probably here but I can't say for sure. He ordered Goose Island yesterday. But...sorry. Is he in trouble?"

"We can't comment on an investigation," replied Sam. "But a word to the wise: I would advise against accepting a date with him."

Her eyes widened. "Ohhh. Thanks for the heads-up."

"That's quite all right. We won't keep you any longer. I guess you can take our orders now," said Joe.

After they ordered, Joe said, "You know what he was doing don't you?"

"Yeah. Looks like he was trying to establish an alibi. Either that or he was here in a crowded bar and she doesn't remember. Reasonable doubt."

"Too many coincidences. And I don't like coincidences. I think we need to do a thorough background check on this dude."

"Agreed."

After they finished lunch, they returned to the office and began a workup on Michael John Fleming.

About 3:15, Joe received a call from Art Casey.

"Your hairs are a match."

"Thanks, Art.

"I want a ranch-style house with a full basement and a double garage. Just so you know."

After work, Joe went to The Fitness Center for a workout with Anita. Jogging while in Iowa kept him in shape aerobically, but he lost a lot of his muscle tone. Now, he had to go through the discomfort of getting it back.

"What's the matter, Joe?" she asked. "You wimping out on me?"

"Lost my edge while I was out of town. Now everything hurts."

"Awww." She patted him on the shoulder. "Toughen up! Drink a lot of water and take some Ibuprofen. You need to make sure you're hydrated. Your muscles will be back in shape in another week."

Easy for you to say, Joe thought.

"When you come in tomorrow, we'll give your arms and legs a rest and concentrate on stretching and aerobics."

"Thanks, Anita. You're not half as mean as they say you are."

"You watch yourself, white boy!" she said with her typical tongue-in-cheek humor.

Chapter Thirty-One

The next morning, Joe began researching the life of Michael John Fleming. He was not active on social media which surprised him. A good-looking, unmarried guy with no Facebook, Twitter, or Instagram accounts seemed odd. And he found no activity on dating or match sites. Was he a loner or was there some other reason for him to be anti-social?

He had learned that Fleming was thirty-four years old, born August 21st in San Francisco to James Fleming and Phyllis Jacobs Fleming. His father, an airline pilot, died in a plane crash when Fleming was nine years old. His mother never remarried. She worked as an executive secretary for a law firm in San Francisco until her death from cancer when Fleming was twenty years old.

Fleming's mother set up a trust fund for him, and he received a considerable amount of money from it once he reached the age of twenty-five. At age twenty-two, he graduated from San Francisco State University with a bachelor's degree in business administration. He worked at several entry-level positions until he was twenty-five. Once he gained access to his trust fund, he spent a year traveling abroad: Europe, Asia, Australia. At twenty-six, he enrolled in a community college in Arizona where, two years later, he received an associate's degree in Mortuary Science. He moved to Florida and worked for the Preston Funeral Home and Crematory in Miami. Three years later he got a job with the Wesley-Donner Funeral Home in Chicago. Seemed unremarkable except for his trust fund. Joe would need a court order to obtain his bank statements and income tax records, and that wasn't going to happen. Fleming had no arrest record and no motor vehicle citations. Clean as a whistle.

Looking at Destiny's profile again, Joe compared it to Fleming: a white male between thirty and forty, above-average intelligence, a college graduate, works as a professional, has experience in a medical-related field. Appears normal, probably not married, attractive, and charismatic to the opposite sex. Drives a newer car, lives in a decent neighborhood.

Christ! That's Fleming to a tee! But he wanted to talk with Destiny before going any further.

He checked in with Sam who had been on the phone.

"What are smiling about?" asked Joe.

"I was calling all the veterinarians in the area trying to find out if wonder boy had a cat. Bingo. I struck gold with a place on North Clark. I asked if they knew Michael Fleming. The receptionist confirmed he was a client and I told her he referred me. I was able to finesse her into telling me he owns—get this—a purebred Havana Brown."

"Nice work. You buying her dinner?"

"I didn't have to go that far. Besides, she sounded like she was my mother's age. What did you find out?"

"He fits the profile exactly. I want to contact the Miami police and see if they can do a search–see if they have any homicides matching our MO."

"Miami?"

"Yeah. He was living there for three years before he moved up here. I'm thinking he might have been practicing on women down there before he made the move to Chicago."

"We need to talk with Vincenzo and the rest of the task force. Let them know what we're on to," said Sam.

"Before we do, let me run this past Destiny to see what she has to say."

"Good idea."

Joe called Destiny and she picked up.

"You're calling from your work phone. Is this a business call?"

"Yeah. You got a minute?"

"For you, I got a few. What's up?"

"We got a person of interest. I was wondering if I could run his file past you and see what you think. He matches your profile so I wanted to get your opinion before I let Vincenzo know about it."

"Sure. I'm not busy this afternoon. Is that soon enough?"

"Perfect. Mind if Sam tags along?"

"Not at all. He'll help keep this strictly business."

"Yeah, right. Where would you like to meet?"

"You said there's a coffee shop near your office, right?

"Yeah, The Black Dog. You want to meet there?"

"Sure. Say three o'clock?"

"It's a date. I'll fax you the file I've put together, so you'll have a chance to look it over."

"Great. See you later."

Joe told Sam of the meeting and then faxed Destiny everything he had on Michael Fleming. Next, he searched the internet for the Miami Department of Police and got the contact information for Hector Rojas, Head of the Criminal Investigation Division. He wanted to have things laid out so Vincenzo could make the call to a comparable supervisor. That way they might be more inclined to conduct a search than if the request came from a detective like himself.

Likewise, he searched the Mesa and Phoenix Police Departments' Criminal Divisions for contact information since Fleming attended Mortuary School in their areas. Once again, he got names and phone numbers for Vincenzo.

They had already conducted a search of the perpetrator's MO in ViCAP, and there were no hits. Since the majority of police departments don't participate, getting a hit is often a matter of luck.

A few minutes before three o'clock, Joe and Sam walked down to The Black Dog to meet with Destiny. She was already there and, after picking up their coffee orders they joined her in a booth.

"Hello, Detectives," greeted Destiny over her latte and a file she had brought with her.

"Hi," said Joe, "I see you got my fax. What do you think?"

"You were right. He fits the profile in virtually every way."

"But?" added Sam.

"I worry a little about perfect fits. Now, don't get me wrong, I think he is worth pursuing as a suspect. But very few suspects fit a profile this closely. There are always some variations."

"Maybe you've just nailed it this time," suggested Joe.

"Maybe. But a profile is a guide, not a portrait. Keep that in mind. He could very well fit the profile like a glove and not be your perp."

"I thought you'd be more positive about this suspect," said Sam, sounding disappointed.

"Don't get the wrong idea, Sam. I think he's a viable suspect, and if I were a detective, I'd certainly want to know more about him. I did a little digging on him after I got your fax and came up with another photo. From his days as a student at San Francisco State." She pulled a photocopy from her folder and handed it to Joe.

"The quality isn't the best, but you can see he wore glasses back then. From his Illinois driver's license photo, he doesn't now. Looks like he must have slimmed down a little, too."

"Fifteen years can change a person. Given how he looks, how he dresses, he strikes me as rather vain."

"Except for the hair on his clothes," said Sam.

"Then we wouldn't have evidence."

"Excuse me, did I miss something?" asked Destiny.

"Yeah, you did," said Sam, and he went on to explain Joe's surreptitious way of appropriating a sample of hair from Fleming's suit coat.

"Well, that was clever of you. You're lucky you weren't caught," Destiny admonished. "What would you have done if he had noticed?"

"It was a risk I was willing to take. And now we know the hairs from his coat are a match to the same type of hairs from the murder scenes."

"This is big," added Sam. "When you add all this stuff together, he looks better and better."

"You know this is all circumstantial," said Destiny. "But keep searching. There's bound to be something more incriminating that's going to pop up.

If not for this guy, someone else. A guy like this has to have made some mistakes at some point. If you keep digging, you'll find them."

"I'm a patient man," said Joe. "And I don't give up."

They finished their coffees. Destiny drove back to her apartment while Joe and Sam hoofed it back to the office.

"You seeing her," asked Sam.

"Yeah. How'd you know?"

"You two have a vibe between you."

"A vibe?"

"Yeah."

"What the hell's a vibe?"

"I dunno. You can't really explain it. It's something you sense."

"Oh. So, what do you sense?"

"You're a lucky bastard!"

Chapter Thirty-Two

After dinner, Joe sent Vincenzo an email letting him know that he and Sam may have a promising lead in the case. He got an email back with a typically short Vincenzo answer: Taskforce meeting Monday morning. 10:00 sharp!

At ten o'clock Monday morning, members of the task force gathered in the conference room. Michelle Cardona, Eddie Collins, Gary Nelson, Kevin Dempsey, Sam, and Joe were mulling about. Vincenzo had popped for donuts, and there was coffee.

Vincenzo got the meeting started. First, he asked Cardona to report on her interview with Kirsten Welch.

"She was still hospitalized when I interviewed her. She was emotionally stable and agreed to speak with me. She'd been X-rayed earlier, and they found she had a fractured jaw."

"Jesus," muttered Vincenzo.

"Sadly, she didn't give me much more than we already knew. She unlocked the door to her apartment, and when she came into the apartment, she caught a fleeting glimpse in her peripheral vision, a dark image. The next thing she remembers is waking up on the floor with an aching jaw."

"Could she give any details about the dark image?" Sam asked.

"No. She only got a glimpse for a fraction of a second. She was hit almost simultaneously when she stepped through the door. Peripheral vision doesn't provide a lot of detail."

"Did you ask her about any other sensory things like smell?" asked Eddie.

"I did. She doesn't remember anything out of the ordinary."

Dempsey stopped rolling his pen around his fingers and asked, "If he was caught in the act, why didn't he kill the sister? For all intents and purposes, she was a dead duck. He could have had his way with her, too."

"Good question," said Cardona.

"Maybe he panicked and wasn't thinking straight—just wanted to get out of there," said Sam.

"Or maybe he wanted to be somewhere in case he needed an alibi," suggested Joe.

"An alibi?" questioned Nelson.

"Sure," replied Joe, "in case he needed to account for his whereabouts at the time."

Vincenzo refocused the topic of conversation. Speculating wasn't getting them anywhere, so he turned to Joe and Sam.

"Okay, Joe and Sam think they have a promising lead. Let's hear what you've got."

Joe and Sam presented their information on Michael John Fleming, starting with his background, his employment as a funeral director, his proximity to the most recent murder, his flimsy alibi, and the cat hair comparisons.

"That's all circumstantial," said Dempsey.

"I know," said Sam, "but it's a start. We'd like to dig further."

"Does anyone else have any persons of interest right now?" asked Vincenzo.

No one was forthcoming. Finally, Eddie spoke up. "Looks like we should either rule him out or take him down."

"We're gonna need something incriminating on this guy," said Vincenzo. "He could've picked up those cat hairs taking his parakeet to the vet for all we know. Hell, my mother-in-law has a Maine Coon, and I come home covered with hair every time I go there to visit."

Joe pulled papers from a folder and handed them to Vincenzo. "Lieutenant, since Fleming went to school in the Mesa-Phoenix area and worked in Miami as a mortician before moving to Chicago, I went ahead and got contact information for the criminal bureaus in each of those cities. I was thinking you could call and see if they could conduct searches. I think those department heads would likely respond to your request more so than to mine."

"You're probably right about that. I'll get on it today. So, you're thinking there might be a trail of dead women we can follow?"

"It's possible."

"Does this guy fit the profile?" asked Eddie.

"Actually, Destiny thinks he's too good a fit."

"How the hell can he be too good?"

"She said there are usually some deviations. With Fleming, there aren't any."

"Okay," said Vincenzo. "Let's do some more research before we bring him in for questioning. I need to see some results. I'm the one whose ass is on the line here, and I don't want it handed to me by my superiors. Got that?"

They all agreed, and Vincenzo dismissed the meeting and walked out of the room. Joe walked over to Cardona who was refilling her coffee cup.

"Did you feel you established a good relationship with Kirsten Welch?"

"Yeah, I think so."

"Do you think you could find out from her when her sister's funeral will be and what funeral home is handling the arrangements?"

"Why would you like to know that?" she asked.

"I'd like to attend the service. Especially if the Wesley-Donner Funeral Home is in charge.

"Ah," she remarked. "That wouldn't be where your person of interest works, would it?"

"It would."

"I can find out for you. Maybe I'll attend myself. I think she would appreciate it."

"I'm sure she would."

Joe went back to his desk and pulled up the Wesley-Donner Funeral Home's website to see if any obituary information had been posted. Nothing for a Kylie Welch. Out of curiosity, he scrolled through the obituaries and came across another obituary six weeks ago with the name "Karen Welch."

He clicked and began reading. Then his jaw dropped. The fifty-two-year-old woman was survived by two daughters, Kirsten and Kylie. *Holy shit!*

"SAM!" he yelled. "Come here and look at this!

Sam leaped from his chair and was behind Joe's computer in an instant. "What is it?"

"Read this obituary from six weeks ago."

Sam began reading. "You've got to be shitting me. Fleming probably handled their mother's arrangements for them."

"Yeah. It's no wonder she would have let him into the apartment. She knew him."

Joe put up his fist and Sam bumped it with his. What a way to start out the day. He sent an email with the screenshot and the link to Vincenzo and cc'd the other task force members.

"You think he meets his victims through his work?" asked Sam. "You know, family members of deceased relatives?"

"Rather ghoulish, don't you think?"

"What he does to women is what's ghoulish."

"Let's check it out."

Only the funeral service for Maria Martinez was through the Wesley-Donner Funeral Home. In searching for the victims' names, none of them turned up in other obituaries as surviving relatives.

"I guess we struck out there," said Sam.

"Not necessarily. He could have met them as friends of the family who wouldn't have been listed in the obit."

"True, and if that's the case, we'll have a hell of a time piecing it together."

"Or maybe he's an opportunist, you know? Meets them in bars, restaurants, museums, god-knows-where. He's a handsome guy, a chick magnet. He could see the type of woman he likes and use his charm and good looks to start a conversation. She finds him attractive and so begins the dance of death."

He walked over to Michelle Cardona, who was speaking with Gary Nelson. Gary didn't seem too pleased and once he saw Joe walking toward them, he broke off the conversation and turned away.

"Hey, Michelle. I hope I didn't interrupt something important."

"As a matter of fact, I'm glad you did. He can be a prick, sometimes."

"I've never worked with Nelson."

"You'd probably get along fine. You're a man. What do you need?"

"Have you spoken to Kirsten yet?"

"No, I was going to do that tomorrow."

"Good," said Joe, relieved she hadn't seen Kirsten yet. "If she says the service will be at the Wesley-Donner Funeral Home, figure out a reason to ask if Michael Fleming is the funeral home representative she's dealing with. He may have been the one who assisted with their mother's services six weeks ago."

"You're kidding. Wow…Well, yeah, I can slip that into the conversation. No problem."

"Thanks, Michelle."

Joe walked back to his desk and sent Destiny a text. *What are you doing tonight?*

A few minutes later he got a text back saying, *Spending the night at your house.*

Chapter Thirty-Three

Early that same evening, Michael Fleming was at work in his basement preparing a new solution.

He slipped on a plastic apron, rubber gloves, and eye protection he had stolen from work. Measuring out small amounts of soda ash, alum, and pickling salt, he poured them into a gallon container, added hot water, and stirred the contents until they were thoroughly mixed. Then he poured two gallons of hot water into a small tub, measured several cups of the chemicals he had just mixed, and added them to the tub. He would need to keep stirring it several times a day with a wood spoon and continuing to add more chemicals over the next three days.

Later would come the next phase of the process, something he had performed numerous times. By now, it was as familiar as mixing a gimlet.

In about ten days, he would be adding another frame to his wall. He got off on reliving his kills, and he would fantasize about how he slipped in the knife so he could re-experience the sexual stimulation he got from it, and then visualize them dying all over again. Feeling them go limp in his arms, seeing their eyes roll back in their heads and, sensing their breathing cease was exhilarating.

He removed his apron and hung it up. Off came his rubber gloves and his eye protection which he stowed on a shelf. Walking to the other end of his basement, he opened the entrance into his secret room, turned on the light, and sat down on his love seat. He looked at his wall trying to decide which killing to relive this evening. After a moment, his eyes fixed on Juanita from Mesa.

CHAPTER THIRTY-THREE

* * *

The next Saturday, Destiny woke up Joe at 7:00 am, and said softly in his ear, "Joe. Joe, you need to wake up."

"Why, what time is it?" he asked.

"It's seven o'clock."

He rolled over and put his arms around her as if it was an invitation for some morning frolicking."

"Don't get any ideas. I have something planned for us today, and we need to get up."

"Planned? What is it?"

"It's a surprise, now get up. I'll get the shower going."

Destiny rolled out of bed and walked into the bathroom where she turned on the shower. Then, she returned to the bedroom, grabbed Joe by the hand, and pulled him up.

"Come on. Get in the shower. I'll wash your back for you."

"Well, how can I turn down that invitation?" And he jumped out of bed, gave her a playful slap on the rear, and chased her into the bathroom, both of them laughing like teenagers.

After they had dressed, Destiny said, "You need to pack an overnight bag. Casual stuff."

"Where are we going?"

"You'll find out. Your car have a full tank of gas?"

"Nearly."

"You have a GPS device?"

"It's built into the car."

"Great. Let's eat some breakfast, and then we can be on our way."

"And you're not going to give me any clues about where we're going?"

"I told you, it's a surprise. It wouldn't be a surprise if I let you guess, now would it?"

Destiny made veggie omelets and Joe made a pot of his favorite Italian-roast coffee. He poured the remainder of the pot into two travel mugs for the trip.

Joe checked his phone and saw that he received a text from Cardona letting him know the funeral service for Kylie Welch was scheduled for Tuesday at 10:00 am at the Wesley-Donner Funeral Home.

Grabbing his overnight bag from the bedroom, he met Destiny by the door.

"Ready?" he asked.

"Ready."

After locking up the apartment, they tossed their bags in the Camaro's trunk and buckled their seat belts. Joe started the engine, brought up the GPS, and looked over at Destiny.

"Okay. Where to?"

"Oglesby."

"Oglesby?" asked Joe in surprise. Where's that??

"About an hour and twenty minutes away."

"What's in Oglesby?"

"You'll see. It's a chance for you to get away from it all and stop thinking about work for a change."

The GPS directed Joe out of Chicago west, and an hour and a half later as they arrived in Oglesby, Joe saw a sign for Starved Rock State Park. Destiny directed him into the park and to the Starved Rock Lodge, a huge log hotel and conference center.

"So, this is the surprise?"

"Part of it."

They checked in, and they were directed to a rustic log cabin. Joe was a bit overwhelmed by the place and the accommodations: historic log cabins built in the 1930s in the middle of a pine forest. So restful.

"Don't get too comfy," said Destiny. "We have a couple's massage in fifteen minutes."

"A couple's massage?"

"What? You've never had a massage before?"

"No, actually. I haven't."

"You're going to love it. I promise. You're in for a treat."

"Look, I don't have to get naked for some guy named Chaz, do I?"

"You are so bad! No, that's not how it works. You've watched too many movies. Trust me, it will be an experience you'll want to repeat."

Afterward, Joe's body felt like a rubber band. He couldn't believe how much his muscles had relaxed and how much easier it was to breathe.

"I told you it would be something you'd like, huh?"

"You get these often?"

"About every three weeks. More often if I need one. It complements my yoga and martial arts workouts."

"You're trained in martial arts, too? You never told me that."

"Need to know basis."

"I'm going to feel a lot safer walking you home at night."

"Come on, let's go for a walk and then have lunch at the lodge. I've got something special planned for this afternoon."

"Another surprise?"

"Yeah, I think you're going to like this, too."

They walked the trails for over an hour, enjoying the beautiful landscape. The views brought back memories of growing up in Northwest Iowa and the wooded areas around Sioux Rapids and Linn Grove. But those places never had canyons and waterfalls like this park did. Joe felt like he was on a different planet, compared to Chicago.

While they were eating lunch in the lodge restaurant, Joe got a call from Vincenzo.

"I know you're not on call this weekend, but I wanted to give you a heads-up on something."

"Yeah?"

"Our first known victim, Deanna Frost. There was a trace of DNA taken from the body that we re-ran through the system. It was a very small amount."

"Okay, so what did you get?"

"You're not gonna believe this. It was a hit on David Eugene Burton."

Joe was stunned. "How can that be? He's dead."

"I know."

"What's the probability of another person having the same DNA?"

"Four million to one."

"Those aren't especially good odds, Lieutenant."

"I realize that. But I thought you should know about it. Something to think about. Talk to you Monday."

Joe ended the conversation. Destiny read the look on his face and knew something from work disturbed him.

"What is it?"

"There's a remote possibility that David Burton isn't dead."

"I thought he was killed and cremated."

"So did I. DNA. The probability is four million to one, but still…"

"Get it out of your head. This will contaminate your weekend if you let it. Come on. Let's go."

"Get in the car and drive. I'll direct you."

When they parked, they were outside Oglesby where Destiny arranged for them to go white water rafting on the Vermillion River.

"Ever been white water rafting?"

"Nope. Have you?"

"Several times. Once on the Colorado River. It was so freakin' scary I wet myself. But it didn't matter. I was soaked to the bone when we were done, anyway. This ought to be fun."

"If you say so."

"You trusted me about the massage, and wasn't I right?"

"Yeah."

"You'll find this a real blast."

And a blast it was. Beginning at 1:30 pm, the five-member crew navigated the nine miles of river and fourteen rapids in three and a half hours. By the end, they were wet and tired from all the paddling. Joe had to hand it to Destiny. She knew how to plan a special day.

After getting back to their cabin, they showered and dressed for dinner. The restaurant, known for excellent food, lived up to its reputation.

Back at the cabin, Joe pulled Destiny close and said, "Thank you for this. It was wonderful."

"You deserved it. You work too hard."

"I know. I've never had anyone show me how to relax and enjoy myself."

"Until now."

"One of the reasons I love you."

"And I love you, too."

And they wound up sleeping very well that night.

The next morning, they put their belongings in the car and walked to the lodge for breakfast. Destiny noticed Joe seemed in a particularly pensive mood.

"What's the matter? You seem like you're bothered by something."

"It's that phone call I got from Vincenzo. It's been haunting me. I know you want me to avoid thinking about work this weekend, but this thing is getting to me."

"Can you do anything about it right now? Other than think about it?"

"No, not really."

"You said the probability is four million to one. That means the probability is three people in this state could have the same DNA markers. And eighty-two people in the country could match. I know you don't believe in coincidences. Neither do I. But let it go until tomorrow, okay? Don't let it ruin this wonderful weekend."

He knew she was right. Stewing about it now wouldn't do any good and it would only throw cold water on everything Destiny had planned for him.

"You're right. I need to pack it away until Monday. So, what do you have planned today?"

"Home, and then you'll see."

"I don't know if I can take any more surprises."

"Just one more, then I'm done."

"This has got to be costing you a fortune. I'm almost embarrassed—"

"Hush! I can afford it. And besides, nothing is too good for you."

After breakfast, they checked out and drove the hour and a half back to Chicago and to Destiny's apartment. She invited Joe in saying there was some time before the final phase of her "Joe's Weekend." Once inside, she handed him an envelope.

"What's this?"

"Open it."

He saw two tickets for today's Chicago Cubs-Los Angeles Dodgers game. But they weren't just any tickets. They were tickets to a suite.

"Are you kidding me? Suite seats? How did you manage that?"

"It helps to know someone who knows someone."

"This is going to be amazing!" he exclaimed, his hands tingling. "Here, you'd better hold on to these." He handed them to her and gave her a hug.

"A good way to top off the weekend?"

"Second only to spending it with you! You've been way too good to me."

"Hungry?"

"As a matter of fact..."

"I made something before we left and put it in the freezer. I thought we could eat and then catch an Uber to Wrigley."

"Sounds good."

Watching the game from a suite could spoil a person in no time. Joe had been to Wrigley Field with friends to watch the Cubs play quite a few times over the years. But never in luxury. Despite the fact the Cubs ultimately lost 3-2, this was one game he would always remember.

Chapter Thirty-Four

Monday morning rolled around as Monday mornings tend to do, and Joe went to work even earlier than usual. He was attempting to get back in the groove and wrap his head around the job he had mostly forgotten about for the past two days. However, having those two days off freshened his outlook and sharpened his mind.

He was sitting there staring at his computer screen, lost in thought, when he felt a hand on his shoulder. He turned and saw Vincenzo behind him.

"Hey," said Joe. "I didn't know you were there."

"Lost in space, huh?"

"Yeah. I guess I was."

Vincenzo pulled up a chair and sat down next to Joe. He usually didn't have these little one-on-ones with his detectives, but since Joe always came in early, he would occasionally make an exception.

"Lieutenant, I'm having a real issue with the DNA possibly implicating David Burton. All the documentation from California confirms he's dead. I don't get it."

"Neither do I. I'm not dismissing it, but it doesn't make any sense to me either. How the hell can DNA from a dead man show up on a dead woman's body? Was it planted to throw us off or what?"

"That would be damned clever. But how would somebody get hold of it?"

"Beats the hell out of me."

"One possibility, I guess. Makes more sense than him still being alive."

"I made calls to the heads of criminal investigations in Miami, Mesa, and Phoenix, and they're willing to research their unsolved homicides to see if they have any corresponding MO's."

"That's good news."

"Yeah. And I gave them your name and contact information so they can report back to you. It's a detective to detective thing, so you should hear from each of them sometime this week. I wanted to give you a heads-up. Let me know as soon as you hear back."

"Hopefully, we'll get a hit on a comparable MO in one of those places."

"Hopefully, is right. If this Michael Fleming is our guy, we need some evidence. Right now, we don't have jack shit. If we get a hit in either place, I think we can bring him in for questioning."

"Okay."

"I don't need to tell you I'm getting a lot of heat from upstairs on this. We have to solve this thing. We can't afford to let another killing happen, you know what I mean?"

"Yeah. Cardona and I are going to the memorial service for Kylie Welch this morning at ten. It's at the same funeral home that arranged her mother's funeral."

"Good idea." Vincenzo rose from his chair and stretched his shoulders.

"Thanks, Lieutenant."

Vincenzo nodded and walked back toward his office. This investigation was taking its toll on him. The bounce and energy were missing from his stride and his face was drawn. He looked like he could use some sleep, too.

Joe and Cardona drove to the funeral home and parked in the visitors lot. Not many cars for ten minutes prior to services. There were about thirty people inside, most of them young, around the ages of Kirsten and Kylie.

A pewter urn held Kylie's cremains. It was displayed on a small table, adorned with flowers and a framed color photograph of a smiling Kylie, a beautiful young woman whose life was snuffed out by a psychotic killer.

Next to the urn display was an easel with a bulletin board covered with photos of Kylie as a child, mostly with her sister and her mother. In several photos was a handsome young man, obviously a romantic interest in her life.

Glancing about, Joe caught sight of Margaret Kummeyer, a reporter for the Chicago Tribune. *Oh, great! What's she doing here?* He tried to alert Cardona, but before he could, his eyes met Margaret's, and he knew she would want to speak with him. He elbowed Cardona.

"Michelle. Look to your two o'clock and who do you see?"

"Oh, Christ! What's she want?" Michelle said under her breath.

"Let me handle her. I've dealt with her before."

"Be my guest."

First in the receiving line was Kylie's sister, Kirsten. She was constantly dabbing at her eyes.

Next to Kirsten stood a man in his mid-twenties in an army dress uniform, who introduced himself as Sergeant Jason Maxwell, Kylie's fiancé. Next to him were Jason's parents, and Jason's younger brother. A handsome family. Joe and Cardona introduced themselves, offered their condolences and assurances that the police were doing everything in their power to apprehend the person responsible.

Joe had been eyeing Michael Fleming who was standing with the minister at the edge of the gathering. The minister stepped forward and introduced himself.

"Good morning, everyone. Good morning. I'm the Reverend Jacob Tower of the Universal Unitarian Church, and if you'll each find a seat, our service will begin shortly."

Joe and Cardona found chairs in the rear and sat down. Reverend Tower's service was short, about thirty-five minutes. But it was a sensitive, heartfelt rendering of a life taken too soon replete with a message of hope and peace for friends and family. Obviously, Reverend Tower had performed such services many times before, and he was good at his job. Kylie's friends, some of whom had traveled from Kansas City, were invited to speak. They recounted what a generous, fun-loving person she was. Her fiancé attempted to read a prepared message about what she meant to him, but he couldn't get through it, so his younger brother stepped forward and finished reading it for him. There were few dry eyes.

After the service when people were mingling, Joe approached Kirsten and introduced himself again. "It was a nice service. I wish I could have known your sister given all the nice things people said about her. She sounded like a wonderful person."

"Thank you," Kirsten replied through a jaw wired shut. "I appreciate you and Detective Cardona being here today."

"I'm sorry to hear your mother passed away not long ago. I imagine the staff here at Wesley-Donner were a big help since they were here for your mother's passing, too."

"They were."

"Did Michael Fleming assist you this time, too?"

"Oh, he did. He was so kind and understanding. I don't know what I would have done without him."

Warning lights went off in Joe's mind. "That's good," he told her. *What to do?*

Kirsten let out a little chuckle that Joe noticed.

"What is it?"

She looked a little embarrassed. "Maybe I shouldn't say this, but…after my Mom's memorial service, Kylie said I should check him out. She thought he was hot."

Then an idea popped into Joe's head. "That might not be such a good idea. He's been married and divorced, and he's got a domestic battery charge on his rap sheet. Don't say anything to anyone, that's confidential information."

Kirsten's eyes got big. "Oh, my god," she gasped. "And he seems like such a nice guy."

"Well, in my line of work, I've found that some men have a dark side, Kirsten. You've heard of Jekyll and Hyde? Consider yourself forewarned." He paused to let it sink in. "I'm sorry for your loss. But let me tell you something. You don't get over something like this. What you do is learn to deal with it. Time will be your best friend." He handed her his card. "We have victims counseling available. Call me if you think it would be beneficial, and I can refer you."

"Thank you," she said. "I appreciate that."

Joe gave her a little smile and walked away to join Cardona, confident in the fact he'd squashed any notion she might have had about getting closer to Michael Fleming. *Sometimes it's necessary to lie.*

Before he reached Cardona, he felt an arm slip under his. It was Margaret Kummeyer, guiding him over to a vacant corner. What she lacked in stature, she made up for with her dauntless manner and persistence.

"I need to speak with you, Joe."

"Why are you here, Margaret? There's no story here."

"Then why are you here?"

Joe looked and tried to catch Cardona's eye but couldn't. "I'm here to comfort the bereaved sister and represent the Chicago Police Department."

"Oh, cut the bullshit! Why are you really here?"

"All right. On the chance we may pick up some random clue for our investigation. At the present time, we have diddley-shit, to be honest with you. But don't print that."

"Okay. Now, can I ask you a question?"

"You know I can't comment on an ongoing investigation."

"Is it true the killer has been cutting off his victim's 'lady parts' after he kills them?"

Holy shit! Where did she get that? went through Joe's mind at warp speed. "I can't confirm or deny something like that."

Her brown eyes lit up behind her black-rimmed glasses. "He has, hasn't he?"

"Look, Margaret. I don't know where you got that information, but if you print it, you'll never get another tip or confirmation from me as long as you live. You got that?"

"Jesus, Joe."

"I've been a pretty good source for you over the years. Don't blow it with this."

Margaret was taken aback. After a pause, she said, "It's that important it stays out of the media?"

"Yeah. It's that important, Margaret."

After a moment, she agreed. He could see she wasn't happy to give up a lead like this. To appease her, Joe offered a trade. "Look, if you sit on this, I'll promise you'll get the scoop once we catch this guy. Deal?"

"Deal."

"By the way. Tell your source that if I find out who he is, I'm going to kick his ass!"

She smiled. "See you around, Detective."

On the ride back to the office, Cardona asked, "What was that little tête-à-tête you were having with Margaret Kummeyer over in the corner?"

"She knows about the mutilations, in detail."

"What?"

"Evidently, somebody leaked the details to her."

"She going to print it?"

"No."

"How can you be so sure?"

"I threatened to shut her off if she printed it. She values me as a source more so than printing those details. Knowing her, I'm pretty sure she'll sit on it."

"Sounds like you have Margaret wrapped around your little finger."

"No one has Margaret wrapped around anything."

"It's good you quashed it. I wonder who the jerk was that leaked it to her."

"I don't know, but I better not find out who he is."

Chapter Thirty-Five

On Wednesday afternoon, Joe got a phone call from Detective Felicia Alvarez from the Mesa Arizona Police Department's Criminal Investigations Division. She was tasked with researching all the unsolved homicides during the years Michael Fleming was getting his degree in Mortuary Science in Mesa.

"Detective Erickson?"

"Yes. You can call me Joe."

"Very well, Joe. I'm Felicia. Your Lieutenant told my Commander Burke that you were looking for unsolved homicides with MO's with genital mutilations, is that correct?"

"That's correct, yes."

"Well, we don't have any unsolved homicides that match your MO. Now, I'm not saying that two of our unsolved cases couldn't have been matches. But there is no way to tell."

"How's that?"

"Both women were determined to fit the age range, but by the time they were found in the desert, their remains were skeletal. It doesn't take much time for a body to decompose given the climate and scavengers that roam the desert."

"Were the two individuals identified?"

"They were. In one case, the dental records were matched to a missing person's report, and in another, we had her DNA on file."

"What about cause of death? Could that be determined?"

"In one case, there was a mark made by a sharp object, probably a knife, on the left side of the sternum between the third and fourth rib. In the other, there was a similar mark on the top of the fourth rib half-an-inch from the left side of the sternum."

"Really?" And what do you make of that?"

"We believe the cause of death was a stab wound."

"To the heart?"

"Possibly."

"How far apart in time did these homicides take place?"

"From the point each woman was reported missing, eight months."

"Would it be possible for you to send us copies of the murder books on each of your victims? Our case has some disturbing things in common."

"I'll speak with my commander about it, and he can get back with your Lieutenant. Would that work?"

"That would be great. Thank you, Felicia. Your help in this matter is much appreciated."

"No problem, Joe. I just sent you an email with my contact information. If you need anything else, let me know."

Joe noticed he had a voicemail. He hoped it was from the Miami Police Department, but instead, it was from his cat lady, Evelyn Stewart-Bruce. *What does she want? Dinner, drinks, and a banana basket for dessert?* Then he rebuked himself and figured he'd better return her call. She picked up on the second ring.

"It's Joe Erickson, returning your call."

"Ah, Joe."

"What can I do for you?"

"Actually, it's more like what I can do for you. You remember we discussed DNA testing and the University of California at Davis as the only research laboratory capable of doing such work?"

"Yes."

"Out of curiosity, I contacted the director, Doctor Alec Davies. He's from England, as I am. As we chatted, I discovered we both grew up in Sussex. Small world!"

"Nice connection."

"Sorry to bore you with trivialities. But it allowed me to steer our conversation toward the possibility of running a DNA test on hair samples from your crime scene, and he said he would be happy to do it for you at no charge if you just send him the samples."

"Really!"

"Really, indeed. It would be mitochondrial in nature if there is no hair root, you know. But it would provide some degree of a match for you."

"That would certainly help. How did you manage such a thing?"

"Sometimes charm has a way of, shall I say, helping one realize a goal."

"Thank you. Thank you, Evelyn. I'll run that past my lieutenant and get back with you."

"I shall look forward to your call, Joe."

When Joe hung up, he chuckled. *Oh, that woman!* She'd done him a huge favor. Cultivating sources paid off. He hoped she wouldn't expect too much in return.

The feline DNA reminded him of the DNA found from David Burton on the body of Deanna Frost. He couldn't get it out of his mind. If it was planted by someone trying to mess with them, how did they get their hands on it? And why wasn't it planted on any of the other victims? Was a sample of Burton's blood stored somewhere? Prison maybe? Why would someone want to frame a dead man? None of this made sense.

What made more sense was that David Burton was still alive. But how could that be? Joe had read everything about him. He was extremely intelligent. Would he have been capable of staging his own death? Maybe. People had done it, but it was a lot harder now than it was years ago. It wasn't so easy in our digital age. But someone really smart could figure out a way.

It would've taken a lot of planning, but could he have found another man who was his own age and physical type, even a look-a-like, staged the car accident, disfigured the face just enough to make identification difficult, and then cremated the evidence? Then he could assume the man's identity.

That's crazy, Joe, he thought. *That's one of those bullshit plots for a television series.* He could never watch cop shows on TV because of how inaccurate and ridiculous they often were. If he presented that theory, Vincenzo would chew his ass so bad, he'd have to shit standing up. *Okay, back to square one.*

Joe called the crime lab to speak with Art Casey.

"The DNA recovered from the body of Deanna Frost two years ago. It was recently run again, and it flagged a person in the system. Odds were four million to one on this guy. Could you tell me how much DNA was recovered from the body and where?"

"I can check for you. Thanks for the bottle of George Dickel, by the way. I assume that came from you. It's not every day I find a bottle of my favorite booze on my doorstep."

"Yeah, a little show of appreciation for all the help you've given me."

"I'll get back to you."

As soon as Joe hung up the phone, it rang.

"Homicide. Detective Erickson."

"This is Detective Tyler Dalton from the Miami Police Department.The head of our Homicide Unit gave me your contact information and said to give you a call about unsolved cases for young women who went missing for the dates your lieutenant gave him. I did the research for you, and I came up with four unsolved cases."

"I see," said Joe. "Do you have any bodies with matching MO's?"

"We recovered one body, but there was no mutilation involved. The other three women's bodies have never been recovered if they are deceased. That's not uncommon around here, unfortunately."

"Why is that?"

"Alligators."

"Alligators?"

"Yeah. They'll eat a human body and leave very little. We've found if criminals want to dispose of a body, they'll take it to an out-of-the-way place infested with alligators and dump it. They'll devour the evidence."

"Jeez. That's gruesome."

"It is. Sometimes some unfortunate fisherman will find the leftovers, a head, or the remains of a torso. It's not a pretty sight."

"I don't envy you that kind of work. We don't have that problem up here."

"Be thankful."

"Thank you for checking, Detective Dalton."

"Sorry we couldn't help you."

It was time to call it quits for the day. Joe drove to his apartment, changed into his workout clothes, and walked to The Fitness Center. Anita really put him through his paces. By the time he finished, his lungs hurt, and he was beat.

After dinner, Joe poured himself another glass of wine and called his dad. He hadn't spoken to him for almost a week. He seemed to be recovering after his heart attack, but Joe was concerned about Carl's attitude which wasn't as upbeat as it usually was.

From the tone of his voice, Joe knew something was wrong. His dad sounded depressed, and that wasn't like him.

"What's wrong, Dad?"

He paused, and then he said, "Uh…we buried Monte today."

The news hit Joe square in the gut. He was silent for several seconds not knowing what to say. Monte was in his late seventies but always so youthful for his age. How could that be?

"My god, Dad. What happened?"

"He went to sleep and never woke up. A massive stroke, the coroner thinks," said Carl, his voice sounding tired and weak.

"Oh, Dad, I'm so sorry. You should have called me. I would have driven up for the services."

"I knew you were busy, and there was nothing you could have done, anyway. So, I thought I'd tell you the next time you called. I didn't want to trouble you."

"It wouldn't have been any trouble."

Joe felt terrible. He needed to be in Marathon to comfort his dad at a time like this. Monte was his dad's best friend. They did everything together. Monte and his wife, Florence, were like fixtures in their home when he was growing up. When Florence died, Carl and his wife were there for Monte, and it was Monte that helped Carl deal with the dementia and eventual death of Joe's mother. He was the brother Carl never had. Joe feared Monte's

223

death would not bode well for his dad's health. Now, he would have no one to pal around with, and he would feel lonely and isolated.

"Why don't you think about spending a few weeks with me? It would be good for you to get away. Take your mind off things. Besides, I'm sure Destiny would love to meet you."

"The girl you told me about?"

"Yeah."

"I don't think the city and I would get along very well. I could get raped and killed up there."

Now there's a little bit of that sarcastic wit coming through. "I don't think you'll have to worry about that, Dad."

"Thanks for the offer, but I'd rather stay right here. I'll be fine. I'll just have to get used to chasing those wild women on my own from now on." His chuckle was tinged with sadness.

"Well, if you catch one, call me and I'll give you some guidance."

That made Carl laugh. "I might need it. Look, Joe, I'd love to talk to you some more, but I'm practically falling asleep here. It's been a long, tiring day, you know. I need to get to bed. Give me a call in a few days, okay?"

"I will, Dad. And I'm so sorry about Monte. Love you."

"Love you, too," said Carl. Now that was a switch. He never said that. What's going on with him?

Chapter Thirty-Six

J oe had a restless night. His father and the case weighed heavily on his mind. Rather than toss and turn for a couple of hours waiting for the alarm to go off, he got up at four o'clock, threw on his workout clothes, and went for a jog.

By the time he returned to his apartment, he felt alert. His mind was fresh and his thinking sharp. *Maybe I should do this every day...but not quite this early.*

He wanted to call Destiny last night, but he was in a funk. Better to wait a day when he had a little more emotional perspective.

As he drove to the office, he thought about what Vincenzo's reaction to the calls he received from Miami and Mesa would be. Such scant evidence would preclude them from bringing Fleming in for questioning. They couldn't seem to get anything on this guy. Joe didn't like Fleming, but he couldn't let his feelings toward the man cloud his judgment. But if Fleming was the serial killer, the task force would have to come up with some creative ideas and some compelling evidence to prove it.

"So, you haven't heard from Phoenix yet?" Vincenzo asked.

"Not yet."

"Those two bodies in Mesa. What do you think?"

"Suspicious but inconclusive. There's no way we'll ever know. My gut tells me it was him, but..."

"Coincidences. I hate 'em."

"Yeah."

"You know, not bringing him in might not be such a bad thing when you think about it. If we don't question him, then he doesn't know we have him on our radar."

"He knows, Lieutenant. When we talked with him at the funeral home, I could tell he knew we were thinking of him as a person of interest. It didn't faze him, though. Arrogant prick was playing with us. You could read it in his body language."

"Those arrogant types, they think they're invincible. Let him think he's too clever to get caught. So, where do we go from here? I'm all ears."

"I think we should surveil him. Tail him and see where he goes, what he does, and who he sees."

"I can't afford those kinds of resources."

"I'm talking about one guy, me. Let me try it and see where it leads. All these killings have happened on weekends. I'll watch him Friday through Sunday."

"Like I said, I can't afford to pay you all that overtime."

"Look, I'll do it on my own. If I don't turn up anything, then I've just wasted my time."

"I can't approve of this. You know that," said Vincenzo. "But...I guess I have no control over what you do on your own time."

"Got it."

After Vincenzo left, Sam walked over to Joe's desk with an extra cup of coffee.

"You look like you could use some good coffee."

"Hey. Thanks for that. How's your part of the investigation going?"

"Witnesses interviewed by Frank Edwards and Nate Smith haven't provided any new information. At least the ones I can locate. There's two that have left town, and I'm working on locating them. So far, I haven't found new addresses."

"That picture of Fleming we got from his driver's license photo. Did anyone recognize him based on that?"

"Not one could ID him. It's been two years. That doesn't help."

"What do you make of the DNA report on your case coming back with a hit on David Eugene Burton? You saw that, right?"

"Oh, yeah. How the hell can that be? That's what I'd like to know."

"I've been thinking about that and it's been driving me crazy. According to the State of California and the funeral director that handled the disposition of the body, he's been dead eight years."

"Then, how did his DNA get on Deanna Frost's body two years ago?"

"What was it Sherlock Holmes once said? 'When you have eliminated the impossible, whatever remains, however improbable, must be the truth.'"

"Okay."

"So, he's either still alive or someone else has the same DNA, like a brother he supposedly doesn't have."

"Okay, if he's dead, how could someone get his DNA? He was cremated. So, could someone have access to one of his blood samples? From when he was incarcerated?"

"Possibly. But why would someone want to have a sample of his DNA? What good would it do them? And why would someone want to plant it on a murder victim?" asked Joe.

"To throw us off. To make us scratch our heads. Like we're doing right now."

"Then why didn't the perp plant DNA on all of his victims and make us think a dead man is committing these crimes from the grave?"

Could DNA be transferred from an item to the victim? I mean, could the perp own something of Burton's and happen to have rubbed it or touched it against Dianna Frost and left DNA on her body? The DNA was degraded, right?"

"Contaminated. It was mixed with Frost's blood," corrected Joe. "Art Casey is looking into how much DNA was actually collected."

"There's another possibility."

"Yeah?"

"There's a one in four million chance it's Burton's DNA, right? So, that leaves…"

"Thirty-nine other people in the country that could match," said Joe, remembering Destiny's figures.

"Damn, you're good," said Sam. "I didn't know you were a math whiz."

"I'm not. Just have a good memory."

Sam was as bothered by it as Joe and he wasn't going to let it go.

"This is going to sound crazy, but…do you think Burton…"

Joe finished his sentence. "…could still be alive?"

"Yeah."

"I've considered it, but the more I've thought about him faking his own death, the more it sounds like the plot of a bad TV show."

"I know, but I don't think we should dismiss the possibility, do you?"

"No, I'm not dismissing it. But it's not high on my list, either. At least not until we find more corroborating evidence."

Shortly after 11:30, Joe received a phone call from Sergeant Cecilia Beckett who identified herself the Head of the Homicide Unit's Resource Squad at the Phoenix Police Department.

"Sergeant Beckett. Thank you for calling."

"We have a Cold Case Squad within the Homicide Unit here. And I did some checking on cold cases from the dates your Lieutenant Vincenzo provided to our Homicide Lieutenant. Unfortunately, we don't have any MO's that match yours. I'm sorry. You have a serial killer up there, right? How many victims so far?"

"Six we can prove in the last two years."

"Suspects?"

"A person of interest. So far, no evidence."

"Well, Detective, I hope you get this guy. ."

"Thanks, Sergeant."

Joe sent Vincenzo an email with an update from the Phoenix PD. Another dead end. He would not be pleased.

Joe sat back in his chair and sipped his coffee. *Maybe Michael Fleming didn't kill any women while he was studying to be a mortician. Maybe that was because he was learning to practice with a scalpel. Or maybe during his second year, he decided to take a practicum in homicidal-mania and tested his skills on the two women found in the desert.*

Then another thought occurred to him. He went over to Sam's desk."I have an idea. It may be off-the-wall, but…"

228

"I'm listening."

"Check the Pennsylvania and neighboring state records and see if David Burton's mother ever gave birth to another child. See if he has a brother."

"There's no record of him having a brother. Only a sister that died in infancy. You know that."

"I'm talking about an earlier birth, a child his mother might have had when she was a teenager and put up for adoption."

"Jesus...You think..."

"I don't know. But it could explain a few things."

Chapter Thirty-Seven

Late Friday morning, Sam rushed over to Joe's desk waving a few papers and acting like he just won the lottery. He was almost giddy with excitement.

"Joe! You're not gonna believe this!"

"What is it?"

"Burton's old lady got knocked up and had a kid when she was fifteen years old! Here's a screenshot of the birth certificate."

"Nice work, Sam." He scanned the certificate, then looked up. It says 'Father: unknown.' So, she either didn't know who the father was, or she didn't want to say who he was."

"Yeah. Maybe not unusual with teen births. That would make this kid four years older than David Burton. You know, they could have the same father. It's possible."

"It is. That could explain the DNA match."

"We need to find out who this guy is and where he's at."

"Let's talk to Vincenzo and see if he can look into it. If this kid was adopted, getting access to the adoption records will take a court order."

Interesting angle all right, Joe thought. But he still wasn't convinced...yet. And he wasn't willing to stop pursuing Michael Fleming because of it. His gut was telling him he was on the right track with Fleming.

Joe and Sam discussed their finding with Vincenzo, and he was pleased they'd discovered this link. He told them he would contact his superiors and get the ball rolling on the adoption angle. And if they needed to open up the adoption records, he'd obtain a court order. But since the records were in Pennsylvania, he knew there would be red tape, and red tape meant time. And time was what they didn't have.

At four o'clock, Joe swung by the Wesley-Donner Funeral Home and saw that Fleming's Lexus was still parked in the staff lot. Joe parked his Camaro where he could watch Fleming's white Lexus. At 4:35, Fleming got into his car. Joe followed at a distance.

Joe knew this would not be an easy tail, given the time of day and the heavy traffic. He followed Fleming for eight blocks to a liquor store. A few minutes later, Fleming left the store carrying a sack. Fleming then drove north, apparently traveling toward his home in West Ridge. Joe followed, trying to keep a sharp eye on the Lexus and the traffic. The closer he got to the West Ridge area, the more the traffic thinned, and he began to hang back.

As Fleming turned onto West Bryn Mawr Avenue, Joe drove farther, made a U-turn, and parked his car a block and a half away from Fleming's house. The position gave him a good view of Fleming's garage and driveway.

Stakeouts are dull. You have to be alert to the smallest thing that might happen. If you have a partner, at least you have a second set of eyes and someone to talk to, but the process ranks right up there with watching dust collect. With no partner, a stakeout is worse.

At 6:00 pm, Joe reached into his cooler and grabbed a ham and swiss sandwich and a can of Red Bull. With no activity as 7:00 passed, he began thinking maybe Fleming was going to spend the evening at home. Then at 8:30, a gray Honda Accord pulled up in front of Fleming's house and honked. Fleming came out, got in, and the car took off.

Uber! Joe began following the Honda as it drove south into the Lincoln Park area. He was able to keep track of the car until it stopped in front of a bar and grill on North Lincoln Avenue where Joe watched Fleming get out and walk in the door. Joe was able to park two blocks away.

Upon entering the bar, Joe could see it was a busy night, and the place was packed. A band was setting up in the back. He spotted Fleming, maneuvering his way through the crowd toward the band. Joe eased his way to the bar and ordered a Guinness, then eased his way to a dark corner.

Fleming appeared to be looking for someone. As he maneuvered through the crowd of people, Joe turned his back so Fleming wouldn't see his face. And as he did so, he accidentally bumped into a woman who was standing next to him holding a full pint of beer. The beer sloshed over the side of her glass and onto her hand and wrist.

"Oh!"

"I'm sorry. Here," Joe said as he offered her his handkerchief.

"It's all right."

"Here. Let me hold your beer so you can wipe off your hand. The least I can do."

She hesitated and then handed Joe her glass. Taking his handkerchief, she dried her hand and wrist. Exchanging his handkerchief for her beer, she remarked, "Gee, and I thought chivalry was dead.

Looking into her green eyes, he said, "It's too bad people aren't taught manners anymore."

"Mm." She paused, sizing Joe up. "I'm Jo."

"Now, that's interesting."

" Why is that so interesting?"

"So am I."

"You're Jo, too?

"Joe with an E."

"What if I said I don't believe you?"

"What if I said I don't care if you believe me or not?"

Jo laughed, and he knew by the way she looked at him that this could be leading somewhere he didn't need it to go. He took a drink from his can of Guinness and glanced over at the bar. *Shit!* Fleming just made him. Now he had to make Fleming think this was some kind of coincidence.

"This is my first time here. You come here often?"

"Once in a while. I don't go out every weekend. Too expensive...and too many jerks. And now, with that serial killer they've talked about on the news, too scary."

"It is. Women have to be very careful until we catch this guy." As soon as he said it, he knew he'd screwed up. *Damnit!*

"We?" Jo asked with suspicion.

"Yeah, 'we', as in Chicago PD." And he pulled back his jacket to reveal his shield. "I'm a homicide detective."

Jo's eyes widened. "Are you kidding me?"

"No."

"Wow...Wow."

" Joe took another drink and glanced toward the bar. Fleming was no longer there.

"Are you on duty or something? I see you glancing around as we've been talking."

"Hold on just a second," Joe said as he looked over her shoulder and checked for Fleming. He didn't see him anywhere in the crowd so he figured he'd left the bar. So, he decided to tell her. "Sorry about that. I normally work on days. But I'm here because I want to check out a person of interest in a case I'm working on, and I followed him in here tonight. That's the main reason I'm here."

"Oh," said Jo, more than a hint of disappointment in her voice. "So, you're not really interested in me."

"No, that's not true, but it's a little hard to balance two things at the same time, Jo. Listen, I hadn't planned on meeting someone like you tonight. Bumping into you was...serendipity."

"You're just saying that."

"Look at me. Come on, look at me. I'm serious. You're a nice person, and I'm glad I met you. But I'm already involved with someone so..."

"Just my luck."

"Hey, don't feel bad."

"You're one of the first nice guys I've run into in some time. Most of the guys I meet want to take you back to their place for a one-nighter. I even had one guy insist on going back to my place of all things."

Suddenly lightning flashed, and Joe said, "What did this guy look like?"

"Why?"

"Indulge me, okay?"

"About thirty-five, dark hair, medium height, really good looking. He's in here tonight."

Holy shit! "What was his name, do you remember?"

"Yeah, it was Michael."

"Do you remember anything else?"

"I remember him being really nice and kind of sexy, but there was something kinda creepy about him underneath all of that. I can't put my finger on it. It was more of a feeling, you know what I mean?"

"So, what did you say to him?"

"Fuck off, buddy. You're not coming in my house!"

"Jo, you might have just saved your own life."

Her jaw dropped when he said it, and she gasped. "Are you trying to tell me that he might be the...."

"Like I said. He's a person of interest. Keep this to yourself because only you and the detectives at Chicago PD know this."

"Oh my god...."

"Let me give you a word of advice. I've seen first-hand what this killer does to women. Until we catch him, don't try hooking up with anyone in a bar, okay? I would hate to see your pretty face on a slab at the morgue."

"Thanks, Joe. I think I need to go home now."

"You want me to get you a cab?"

"That would be wonderful. I won't forget this."

"In case I need to get hold of you. What's your last name?"

"It's MacDonald. Jolene MacDonald."

They left the bar, and Joe flagged down a cab and paid the cabbie to take her home. He made a note of her name and caught her School Street address when she gave it to the driver. Joe thought to himself as the cab pulled away: *You are one lucky lady.*

Joe had no idea where Fleming was. He could have gone anywhere. As Joe walked the two blocks to his car, he had the strange feeling he was being watched. At one point, he turned back, retracing his steps for a block to make sure he wasn't being followed. As he rounded a corner, he ducked into a doorway and waited. And waited. Ten minutes went by and there was no sign of Fleming.

Figuring he had waited long enough, he walked to his car. Since it was still early, he called Destiny.

"I thought you were on surveillance tonight."

"I was, but I lost him."

"You lost him?"

"He made me when I was talking with one of his near-victims."

"You're kidding?"

"I wish I was."

"Wow. Was she pretty?"

"She was the hottest woman I've ever seen."

"Really. Why don't you come over and tell me about it?"

"I thought you were visiting your mom."

"Just got home. I'll crack a bottle of Pinot Noir..."

"Joe laughed. "You know how to entice a guy."

"Well, that's what's on the menu. Wine and enticement. I can guarantee the wine. The enticement, well..."

"See you in a few."

Joe turned the key and the Camaro rumbled to life. He pulled out the parking spot and onto the street. As he did, Michael Fleming stepped from the shadows and watched him drive away.

Chapter Thirty-Eight

After spending Saturday with Destiny, Joe prepared to surveil Michael Fleming that evening. Once again, he parked his Camaro one-and-a-half blocks away from Fleming's home on West Bryn Mawr Avenue. He decided he should alert the homeowners in case they got curious about a black car parked in front of their house.

Joe walked to the front door and rang the bell. A middle-aged man answered the door and Joe showed him his ID and introduced himself.

"Why don't you step inside ?" said the man.

"There's a man living on the next block who's a person of interest in a case I'm working on."

"Oh, really. What's he suspected of?"

"At this point, he's not a suspect," explained Joe. "So, that means he'll either become a suspect or he won't. But my point is: I didn't want you wondering why some strange guy is sitting in a car outside your house for hours at a time."

"I understand. We would find that a little disconcerting, to tell you the truth. My wife, especially. She'd call the police sooner or later."

"Well, that's what I wanted to avoid. It wouldn't be good to draw attention to the fact I was there. So, I wanted to alert you to my presence."

"What if one of my neighbors asks about you? I have a rather nosy one next door," he said, indicating left with his head.

"Tell the person I'm a police detective on surveillance, and I should be left alone."

"Okay, then...that's what I'll do if it comes up. I don't suppose you could you tell me what this guy may have done?"

"I can't talk about a case. He may have done nothing at all."

"I see. Well, hopefully, he isn't that serial killer I've heard about."

"Hopefully not. Well, thank you, uh…"

"They call me Finn, short for Phineas. Named after my grandfather. Finn Hogan."

He reached out and shook Joe's hand.

"Nice to meet you, Finn," said Joe, handing Finn one of his cards. "In case you need to get hold of me for any reason."

Finn took the card and led Joe to the door. "Oh, and if you need to take a leak, ring the bell. Always willing to help out the police."

"Only if I get desperate," Joe said as he went out the door.

Joe prepared for another long surveillance. Peeling off his coat, he sat there in his t-shirt and jeans. With the windows rolled down, he could get the benefit of a slight breeze which made sitting there a little more bearable. Plugging earbuds into his cellphone, he dialed in some music.

Several hours went by with no activity. At 8:40, a red Ford Taurus pulled up next to Fleming's house. *Another Uber ride?* A moment later, Fleming left his house and got in.

Following the Taurus took Joe all the way down into the Loop to a popular bar in the Theatre District, a place sure to be packed on a Saturday night. Joe parked in a garage a block away. When he walked into the bar, he saw Fleming working his way to the back.

Joe attracted the attention of the bartender. Showing his ID, he said, "Do you have a surveillance system?"

"We do. Let me get my boss." And he went in the back room. Not long after, he came out with a woman in her late thirties and pointed to Joe.

"May I help you?"

"Yeah, I'm Detective Joe Erickson with Chicago PD, and I was wondering if there was someplace where I could observe your crowd without being seen. You have a customer I'm interested in, and I'd rather he didn't know I was here."

"Is he dangerous?"

"Possibly, but I can't prove it."

"I don't need dangerous people in here. Go through that door on your right and I'll meet you on the other side."

She led him to a second-floor room with four monitors mounted on the wall. "You can watch from here."

Joe sat down and began looking for Fleming who he spotted talking to two women. *He doesn't waste any time.*

When one of the women walked away, Fleming was left with the one with long, dark hair. Joe couldn't hear what they were saying but he could read their body language. She was inviting; her gestures suggesting she liked him; smiling and laughing, indicating his charm was working. Fleming was stalking his prey, and unbeknownst to her, she was inviting a predator into her personal space.

When a booth opened up, they grabbed it. They polished off a couple more drinks, and Joe realized this mating dance could continue for the next hour. Fleming was good. Really good. Joe knew he had to stop him. He couldn't let this girl take Fleming home. Then he saw his chance. She picked up her purse and appeared to head to the restroom. When she came out, he stuck his ID in her face.

"Detective Joe Erickson, Chicago PD. You're sitting with Michael Fleming, correct?"

"Uh...Yeah."

"We have him under surveillance, and it would be best if you would leave immediately."

"I don't understand..."

"Ma'am, for your safety, you need to leave immediately." Joe pulled back his coat and showed his service weapon. "I'm not kidding. He's dangerous."

She gasped. "All right."

Joe guided her out.

"Do you need a taxi?" Joe asked.

"I can get one on the corner."

"Stay away from him, if you ever see him again. He has a long rap sheet for domestic violence."

"Omigod!" she cried as she turned and walked quickly up the street.

Joe went back to watch the security monitors. Fleming was still sitting in the booth but appeared to be annoyed that the woman was taking so long. Finally, he called over a waitress and asked her something. She came back and evidently told him the restroom was empty. He responded angrily, by hammering the table with his fist and throwing down some cash. But he didn't leave. He looked around the bar as if he was searching for someone. Was it the girl? Then, it occurred to Joe. *Maybe, he's looking for me. Maybe he's thinking I'm here and screwing with him.* Joe watched as Fleming walked through the bar and even made a sweep of the men's restroom. Thorough. Then he left the bar in a huff.

Joe sat there for a few minutes in case Fleming decided to return. When he didn't, Joe went downstairs and thanked Nancy for the use of their security system.

"Did you see what you needed to see?"

"And then some. Chicago PD thanks you for your cooperation."

"Great. Glad I could help."

"I think I'll mosey out to the bar and treat myself to a beer."

"The first one's on the house."

"You don't need to do that."

"First rule of being in a bar: don't piss off the manager."

Joe cracked a smile. "Gotcha. First one's on you."

* * *

Sunday proved fruitless. Joe watched Fleming's house from 4:00 until 10:00 pm. Since there was no movement, Joe decided to pack it in. Evidently, Fleming was staying home, something Joe wished he could have done.

Chapter Thirty-Nine

By Tuesday, they got a court order to gain access to the adoption records for David Eugene Burton's brother. On Thursday, Vincenzo called a meeting of the task force to provide details.

"I think it's possible we may have a breakthrough thanks to some creative thinking by two members of our task force. A search was done, that discovered David Eugene Burton's mother had a child out of wedlock when she was a teenager. That could account for the DNA found on Deanna Frost's body that matched the already deceased David Burton. The child was a boy who was adopted by Ronald and Miriam Winslow of Indianapolis, Indiana. Terence Ronald Winslow attended one of the top public high schools in Indianapolis, and immediately after graduation, enlisted in the United States Army and served four years as a medic. After receiving an honorable discharge, he enrolled in a technical school where he became a laboratory technician."

He married an Illinois girl, moved to Joliet, and went to work for a medical laboratory. A few years later, they got divorced, but he continues to live in Joliet. Now that's only forty miles away, so he would have easy access to and from the city."

"And as a medic, this dude would know how to handle a scalpel," added Eddie.

"You going to bring him in?" asked Cardona.

"I've asked the Joliet PD to take him into custody, and I need to send a couple of you down there to question him. Any volunteers?"

"I'll do it," piped up Cardona.

"So, will I," added Sam.

"Okay, good."

"Maybe this eliminates Michael Fleming, huh?" suggested Dempsey, looking at Joe.

"Anything's possible," replied Joe, but he wasn't about to eliminate Fleming. At least, not yet.

"Well then," said Vincenzo. "I'll call the Chief down there and tell them you're paying them a visit today. Take a DNA kit with you and see if Winslow will volunteer a DNA sample."

"Got it," confirmed Cardona.

"All right, you're dismissed. Joe, I want to speak with you for a minute."

After everyone filed out, Vincenzo asked, "Did you happen to stake out Fleming this weekend like you said you were going to?

"Yeah, I followed him to two bars, Friday and Saturday."

Joe told him what happened each night.

"Keep doing what you're doing until I tell you to stop. You've got the best instincts of anybody in the department. And the more I hear about Fleming, the less I like him. But this damned DNA thing...how do we explain that other than Burton's brother?"

"I don't know. DNA doesn't lie." Joe paused a moment. "Maybe I'm wrong about Fleming. But my gut tells me otherwise."

"Let's wait and see what happens with Burton's brother."

Joe walked back over to Sam's desk.

"I'll bet Winslow has no idea he had a brother who killed his mother and was locked away for it," said Joe.

"I don't think I'll spring that on him as a way to get acquainted."

"Good idea."

"I thought you'd be keen on doing this."

"I've got some other things going on that are taking up my time today. You're more than up to it."

Well, it'll be interesting, I'll say that. See you later, man," said Sam, and he left with his briefcase locked and loaded.

Joe's phone rang. Art Casey was calling.

"I have that information you asked for."

"Great. What did you find out?"

"The DNA was present on a single swab taken from the victim's navel. The amount was a trace and it was mixed with a trace sample of the victim's own blood. My guess is that the area was swabbed despite the fact no blood evidence was visibly present."

"How do you account for no visible evidence being there?"

"This is just speculation on my part, mind you, but it could be transfer, microscopic spray, or…"

"Cleaning up a smear of blood from a nicked finger?"

"Possibly. With the folds of the navel, the area could easily retain trace evidence."

"I see. So, let's say the perpetrator cut himself, left a tiny bit of blood in the navel, and then he cleaned it up. Could trace DNA remain?"

"Absolutely."

"Thank you, Art. I think I owe you another bottle of George Dickel."

"Don't think I haven't forgotten about the house," he said and hung up.

Joe sent an email update to Vincenzo about his conversation with Art Casey and his theory about the DNA evidence.

When Sam and Cardona returned from Joliet, they made a beeline for Vincenzo's office. A few minutes later, Sam was back at his desk ready to fill Joe in on their questioning of Winslow.

"It wasn't much of an interrogation," said Sam. "He wasn't very cooperative after we explained why we were there and what the circumstances were."

"What did he say when he found out he had a brother?"

"Said he wasn't surprised since he knew he was adopted."

"How did he react when you told him he had a teenage brother who murdered his mother?"

"Now, that surprised him, and it took him a while to process that. But once he had, he said, "Well, you can pick your friends, but you can't pick your family, huh?"

"Jeez," chuckled Joe.

"Yeah."

"Was he forthcoming about anything?"

"A few things. He said he never drives into Chicago because he hates the traffic. He'd never heard of Deanna Frost."

"Of course."

"I asked if he could provide an alibi for the date of the murder and he said, "How the hell am I supposed to remember what I was doing a year ago?"

"So, did he have any qualms about giving a DNA sample?"

"He refused. At that point, he wanted to talk to a lawyer. But we got the soda can he was drinking out of, so we got his DNA anyway. The thing that struck me most was his harassment of Cardona throughout the interview."

"What do you mean?"

"I mean, this guy is a piece of work. He asked her if she colored her hair, if she had a significant other, if she had breast implants, shit like that. God! By the time we were done, Cardona was livid."

"I imagine. Did he mess with you, too?"

"No, just her."

"I wonder if he hates women or just took a disliking to Cardona."

"I don't know if he was acting out because he was pissed for being held for questioning or if he dislikes women in authority. Both maybe."

"So, what do you think?" asked Joe. "Could he be our guy?"

"It was hard to get a read on him. I guess we'll have to wait and see what the DNA says."

"Yeah. Maybe Cardona will get the last laugh, huh?"

* * *

Friday evening, Joe was parked on West Bryn Mawr in his usual place, surveilling Michael Fleming's home. But tonight, instead of an Uber driver, the garage door opened at 6:20 pm, and Fleming backed his white Lexus out of the garage and drove away.

Joe gave him a block then tailed him, keeping a safe distance. He wondered why Fleming had deviated from using an Uber on weekends. Something was up and it didn't take long to get an answer.

Fleming turned into the parking lot of the Wesley-Donner Funeral Home. Joe drove past and parked on a side street where he had a good view. After a few minutes, a pearl white Cadillac hearse pulled out and drove away. Joe figured Fleming was on call and had to transport a body back to the funeral home. He followed the hearse to Methodist Hospital, where the hearse pulled in at the rear of the building.

Joe drove back to his apartment, figuring that in addition to collecting a body, there was a good chance that paperwork and embalming could occupy Fleming for the remainder of the evening.

* * *

On Saturday, Fleming took an Uber to an Irish pub on North Lincoln Avenue. When Joe came through the door, he walked to the bar and ordered a drink. He caught the attention of a grizzle-bearded, heavy-set man tending bar and ordered a Guinness that they had on tap. As he waited for his pint to arrive, he looked for Michael Fleming but didn't see him. But he did see the woman he had warned away from Fleming the previous week. She stood near a corner table in an animated conversation with a woman Joe recognized as the friend she was with last week. *Oh, shit,* he thought. *What are the odds?* He walked over to them.

"Hello, again."

"Oh!" she said. "It's you."

"It is. What a coincidence the 'four' of us are here tonight."

"The four of us?" she asked.

"Michael is here, too. I saw him come in here earlier. I thought I should give you a heads up before you ran into him."

"Oh, no," she said. "Just my luck…It's Joe, right?"

"Yeah."

"This is my friend, Cassandra."

"Nice to meet you, Cassandra," said Joe, shaking her hand. "You were with…I'm sorry but I didn't get your name last week."

"Allison."

"You were with Allison last week, too, weren't you?"

"I was until she ran off all of a sudden. She called me from a cab saying she was going home and would explain later."

"Yeah."

"Are you still–"

Suddenly from out of nowhere, Michael Fleming appeared, and he was pissed. He stepped between Allison and Cassandra and directed his ire toward Joe.

"What the hell are you doing here?" he asked, butting himself into their three-way conversation.

Allison gasped, and Cassandra stepped to the side to get out of his personal space.

"I'm here to enjoy myself on a Saturday night," said Joe calmly. "You have a problem with that?"

"Are you following me?"

"Why would I be following you?"

"This is the second time I've run into you in a bar. What's the chance of that?"

"If you come into my neighborhood, I'd say the chances are reasonably good you might run into me somewhere. I live around here."

"And how do you know Allison? Were you in the bar with us last week?"

"Did you see me there?"

Fleming focused on Allison. "And why did you suddenly disappear? Did he say something to you?"

"You don't have to answer him, Allison." Joe's eyes met Fleming's. "I suggest you move on, mister."

"You'll regret this," warned Fleming.

"Are you threatening a police officer?"

Fleming's eyes burned into Joe's for a couple of seconds, and then he walked out of the bar, seething with anger.

"Wow," said Allison. "I thought you two were going to punch each other out."

"He's a coward," replied Joe. "He only picks on women."

"For a cool-looking guy, he sure is creepy," noted Cassandra.

"He's that all right. And then some."

Before Allison and Cassandra split, Joe took down their names and contact information in case he needed witnesses to what had transpired tonight or Allison's testimony about Fleming's attempted seduction.

* * *

Michael Fleming drove straight home. His anger had morphed into a strong resentment of Joe Erickson. Once inside, he was greeted by Fidel, and the cat's presence had a calming effect on him.

"There you are," he said. "Did you just wake up?"

Fidel swished his long tail, looked up at him, and let out a plaintive meow. Fleming reached down and gave him a couple of head-to-tail strokes. "You're a good boy, aren't you?"

Fleming walked into the kitchen and made himself a tall gin gimlet and returned to the living room to sit in the dark. Fidel jumped in his lap and demanded attention.

"What are we going to do with that cop, Fidel? He's a stalker. I don't like him messing with us. He needs to be taught a lesson, doesn't he? Maybe it's time we get to know this cop a little better, you think?"

Chapter Forty

The results of Terence Winslow's DNA test came back from the lab on Monday, and Vincenzo called a meeting of the task force.

"I hope he's a match," said Cardona. "Because I want to be the one to arrest that obnoxious pig!"

"I'm sure that can be arranged," said Nelson. "Can I watch?"

"Gladly," snapped Cardona.

"I heard about it. You shouldn't let him get under your skin like that," said Eddie. "He was getting off on your reaction."

"Yeah, well you didn't have to listen to his sexist comments for an hour."

Vincenzo walked into the room and everyone sat down. He was hard to read, so it was not immediately apparent if the news was good or bad.

"I just got the results of Terence Winslow's DNA test, which was compared to the DNA profile taken from the body of Deanna Frost. I regret to inform everyone that our hope of a breakthrough just went down the shitter."

A collective groan went up. Cardona looked like she'd explode.

"Close but no cigar as they say," Vincenzo continued. "The DNA results showed a close match, indicating same mother and father, but enough differences to conclude the samples are from brothers. So, it looks like we're back to having no suspects and only a person of interest. Keep digging, folks. We've got to do better."

When Vincenzo left the room everyone sat in silence until Sam said, "So, Cardona, when you gonna let Winslow know he's not a suspect?"

"Up yours, Renaldo," she snarled. And with that, the detectives' stifled laughter could no longer be suppressed, as an angry Cardona stomped out.

"She's gonna crucify you, man," said Eddie.

Sam looked at Eddie. "I'll apologize to her later."

"You damned well better," said Joe. "She never forgets, you know."

When Joe got back to his desk, he found a package on his chair from the Mesa Police Department. Inside were copies of the files Detective Alvarez agreed to send him on the two murdered women whose remains were found in the desert.

Joe read through the two files and looked at living photographs of the two women. He realized they were both of a similar type as the Chicago victims. Marilyn Harris was twenty-eight and worked as a secretary for a construction company while Katrina Romero was thirty and worked as a pre-school teacher.

Both had suggestions of knife wounds on a rib and sternum just as Detective Alvarez had said. But as Joe read farther along in Katrina Romero's autopsy report, he suddenly stopped. Alvarez had failed to mention that the pathologist who performed the autopsy noted a thin, shallow mark a quarter of an inch long, made by an object with a sharp edge, on the superior pubic ramus of the pelvis. *Superior pubic ramus? What the hell is that?* He decided to call Kendra Solitsky for clarification.

"Well, the superior pubic ramus is a part of the pubic bone which forms a portion of the obturator foramen," Kendra began.

"In English, Kendra."

"Sorry. It's part of the pubic bone. It goes across the front of your body and attaches to your pelvis on each side".

"Okay." A pause followed.

"You're touching yourself, aren't you?"

"Found it."

"Oh, god!"

"I have an autopsy report from a homicide in Mesa, Arizona, that may be related to our case. Skeletal remains found in the desert. The pathologist noted a thin, shallow mark a quarter of an inch long, made by an object with a sharp edge, on the superior pubic ramus area of the pelvis. My question is, could it have been made by our killer wielding a scalpel ?"

"Without seeing the actual mark, I can't say for sure, but I can tell you that it's in the right area. And if he cut too deep, a scalpel could leave a mark on the bone."

"That's what I needed to know."

"So, you think this could be the work of the perp up here?"

"It's possible."

"There was a knife mark on this woman's sternum, and it's theorized she died from a knife wound. Our person of interest was getting a degree in mortuary science there at the time."

"Interesting. He would have been learning to use a scalpel."

"And there was a similar victim killed eight months later. A cut mark on a rib near the heart, another desert decomposition."

"It looks like your person of interest has been leaving a trail of bodies."

"Yeah, and we haven't been able to prove it."

After the call, Joe took the file down to Vincenzo's office. He knocked on the door, and Vincenzo said, "Come on in. I was just going to call you."

Joe handed the Mesa files to Vincenzo and explained what he learned fromKendra.

"Good work. Bit by bit, the evidence is mounting on this guy. But everything we're getting is circumstantial. We need something conclusive."

"I know, Lieutenant. I'm working on it."

"The reason I was going to call you in here is…Michael Fleming filed a harassment complaint against you."

"What? That's bullshit!"

"Have you leaned on him or done anything to make him feel intimidated?"

"No. I didn't even talk to him until Saturday night when he tried to intimidate me. And I have two witnesses to prove it."

"He doesn't like you watching him. It cramps his style."

"Yeah. He was pretty pissed off when he confronted me in the bar. He accused me of following him and chasing his young lady away."

"You been using your personal car to tail him?"

"Uh-huh."

"Ditch it. He's seeing black cars everywhere, and he's thinking you're behind every tree, building, and lamppost. Start using unmarked cars instead. And you may want to alter the way you conduct your surveillance, so he thinks he's won. Then, he might get careless."

"Understood."

"Don't worry about the harassment complaint. He doesn't have a leg to stand on. We have a right to surveil a person of interest."

"Thanks, Lieutenant."

"Now, get out of here. I've got work to do."

Joe went to the motor pool and arranged to use a light gray Dodge Challenger for surveillance during the coming weekend. Fleming must have recognized his black Camaro. The next week, he would switch cars.

After work, Joe went home, changed into his workout clothes, and jogged to The Fitness Center. He'd been working out religiously for several months, and he was now in tip-top shape. Except for the days he was in Iowa, he'd never missed a session with Anita. She'd become more than a physical trainer; she was a friend.

Unbeknownst to Joe, Michael Fleming watched them through a pair of binoculars from a block away. Fleming had taken a week's vacation from work and begun spying on Joe, waiting for his black Camaro to leave the Area 3 parking lot. Fleming had rented a car so his white Lexus wouldn't be recognized, and he followed Joe to his apartment building and then to The Fitness Center. He wanted to know everything about Joe Erickson.

Chapter Forty-One

On Tuesday at 5:15 pm, Fleming watched Joe came home from work. Shortly after, Joe came outside again and jogged down the street.

Twenty minutes later, Joe returned to his apartment. Shortly before 7:00, Fleming watched Joe leave his apartment, again, get into his car, and drive away. Fleming followed him eight blocks to an apartment complex. Ten minutes later, Joe emerged holding hands with a stunningly attractive woman. Her slender body and long dark hair were Fleming's style.

He followed them to one of the city's finest Italian restaurants on West Madison Street. He had to hand it to Erickson. He has good taste. Fleming entered a pizza place across the street, sat down next to the window, and ordered a pizza and beer. For the next hour, he waited for Erickson and the woman to come out.

After an hour, they left the restaurant. Fleming followed the Camaro to the woman's apartment. It was 8:30, and Fleming kept his vigil until midnight. *Guess he's staying the night. Better enjoy it while you can, buddy.* He went home and decided to concentrate his efforts on Erickson's woman.

* * *

On Wednesday, Fleming staked out the woman's apartment. Wearing workout clothes, she finally left her apartment at 2:20 pm when an Uber ride showed up and took her to a martial arts center on Halsted Street. Fleming saw her go inside. After an hour, she left. Assuming she was returning home, Fleming decided to check out the center.

"Do you have beginning self-defense classes for women? I noticed the woman who just left–the one in the blue workout clothes."

"Oh, that was Destiny. She's no beginner," said the woman behind the counter.

"Oh, really?"

"She already has a black belt in Jiu-Jitsu, and she's taking advanced training in Muay Thai."

Fleming was not pleased to hear this. "Wow. I'll bet she can handle herself in a situation."

"Like the man said, 'I pity the fool'," she said, laughing. "But to answer your question, yes. We have self-defense classes for women and men." She handed him a sheet with information.

"Well, thank you. I'll have my girlfriend look it over and get back to you." He gave her a smile and left the building cursing under his breath. He really wanted to punish Erickson by making this Destiny-chick his next victim. But he couldn't take the chance she'd defend herself and beat the shit out of him.

Fleming drove to the M&H Lounge on North Pulaski Road. He'd previously used it as an alibi, but he had grown to like the place. He had little to eat all day and needed something substantial in his belly before he began watching Erickson.

* * *

Late that afternoon, Joe went to The Fitness Center. Fleming watched him from half a block away. An hour later, Joe and a black woman stepped outside. Before Joe left, he patted her on the back before jogging away. Her eyes followed him for a few seconds before she turned and went back inside. *Hm. Pretty friendly there* thought Fleming. *Maybe more than just a trainer.*

On Friday, July 1st, knowing Joe would be watching his house. Fleming programmed various lights in his house to go on and off at certain times and left the television on so it would look as though he was home. He knew

The Fitness Center closed at 8:00 pm, so that was when he planned to make his move.

At 7:55, Fleming walked into The Fitness Center wearing a fedora and horn-rimmed glasses. He knew that this woman locked up when the place closed. When he walked in, the Center was empty. Anita was standing at the desk, and when she saw him, she said, "We're about to close. You'll have to come back tomorrow."

"Oh, sorry," he said, turning on the charm. "I was told I could pick up a membership form. You wouldn't happen to have one handy, would you?"

"Uhh, yeah. I do," she said, and she reached down behind the counter for the form.

As she did, Fleming moved to the end of the counter and slid his knife out of its sheath. In less than ten minutes, Anita was dead, mutilated, and Fleming was out the back door. He drove to the rental car agency and turned in his car. Then he called a taxi on his burner phone and had it drop him at Navy Pier where he dumped the fedora, shirt, and pants he wore over his other clothes. He changed glasses, put on a White Sox cap, and glued on a false mustache. Then he hailed a cab which took him from Navy Pier to an address within three blocks of his house. When he got home, the first thing he did was remove the false mustache and flush it down the toilet. He changed his shirt and then opened the garage door and pushed his garbage can out to the street for pick-up on Monday morning. It was a few days early, but knowing Joe was watching him, it established he was at home. After going back inside, he burned the White Sox cap and shirt in his fireplace. He would dispose of the scalpel and gloves at work. Fleming had recorded television shows he could watch to establish an alibi.

Quite pleased with himself over his retaliation for Detective Erickson's meddling in his affairs, Fleming made himself a pitcher of gin gimlets to celebrate and sat down with Fidel to catch up on some television.

* * *

When Anita didn't come home, Jada Robinson, her partner, tried calling her cellphone, but her calls went to voice mail. Concerned about her welfare, Jada called the police and a unit was dispatched to The Fitness Center. The officers entered through the unlocked front door and found Anita's mutilated body. They called in detectives who alerted Vincenzo as head of the task force. He, in turn, called in Joe and Sam to follow up.

Joe was sitting in the gray Challenger surveilling Fleming when he got the call. Upon hearing the address, he felt his heart miss a beat. His forehead broke out in a sweat.

When he got to the scene, three police cruisers and two unmarked cars were already there. He held out his ID as he ducked under the yellow crime scene tape. An officer at the door took his name and badge number, and he entered the place he knew all too well. Sam was already there along with two detectives from the night shift, Felix Rojas and Dennis Franklin.

"Where's the body?" asked Joe.

"Back here," said Sam, guiding Joe behind a wall.

Joe took one look at Anita's mutilated body lying on the floor and gasped. He felt nauseated and had to turn away, his voice colored by the shock of seeing his friend.

"Oh, no. No..."

Sam looked at him and saw Joe had turned pale. "You know her?"

"Yeah. She's my physical trainer...and a friend."

"Jesus, I'm sorry, Joe. Maybe you should go outside and get some air."

"Yeah."

"Come on, I'll go with you." Sam placed an arm around Joe's shoulder and led him outside. The night was cooling down, and they leaned against the fender of one of the cruisers and talked.

"This was my fault," said Joe.

"What do you mean?"

"This is the killer's way of punishing me."

"Michael Fleming?"

"You know it."

"I thought you were watching him tonight."

"I was. I don't know how he did it. It seemed like he was home all night.

The lights were turning on and off. His car never left the garage. No Ubers, taxis. But somehow that son-of-a-bitch just sent me a message."

"We'll have to let forensics do its work and see if anything turns up."

"It won't. He's too clever."

"It's too bad The Fitness Center doesn't have video surveillance inside."

"I know. It should have."

"We'll be checking cameras on neighboring buildings tomorrow. Maybe we'll get something."

"Not likely. He had that figured out already."

"Joe, why don't you go home. It's not good for you to be here. We've got it covered."

Joe looked at Sam. "You're probably right. I feel like I'm going to be sick. See you on Monday." Joe walked to his car, leaned over the front fender, and vomited. He hadn't been bothered by a crime scene since his first days as a rookie, but this one got to him. He grabbed a Red Bull from his console, took a mouthful, gargled with it, and spit. As Joe sat in his car getting himself together, Sam called Destiny and explained what had happened.

"I think he could use some company tonight, someone to talk to."

"I'll see to it. Thanks for calling, Sam."

Destiny arrived at Joe's shortly after he got home. She brought a bottle of Pinot Noir with the hope that a glass or two would loosen him up so he would be willing to talk about his feelings. Like many men, Joe held a lot inside.

He buzzed her in, and when he opened the door she simply said, "I heard."

Tears welled up in his eyes. "It was my fault. He wanted to hurt me and used her to do it. Thank god it wasn't you." And he hugged her.

"If he would've tried anything with me, I would've killed him. Saved everyone a trial."

Joe let her go and chuckled sadly, "Yeah, you probably would have."

"You better believe I would have," she said, holding up the bottle of wine.

"Mm, Pinot Noir. Are you trying to seduce me, Mrs. Robinson?"

"I simply want to get you to talk."

"You'd have better luck seducing me."

"I know. But you need to talk about it."

"Oh."

"Then we'll see about the other part."

Chapter Forty-Two

Joe and Destiny spent all day Saturday together at Joe's apartment. They talked, cooked lunch together, drank wine, and ordered in Chinese for dinner. Destiny coaxed Joe to open up and talk about more things than he had ever spoken about to another person in his life. Releasing those pent-up feelings gave him a sense of serenity he needed right now, and she gained an intimate understanding of the man she loved.

Vincenzo called at 10:00 to offer his condolences and to ask for details regarding his surveillance of Fleming earlier that evening.

"I don't know how he fooled me like he did, Lieutenant. But he's devious enough to do it and make it seem like he was at home the whole time."

"I believe you. He's good at covering his tracks, you've got to give him that. I've got Sam surveilling him tonight and tomorrow night. I want you taking it easy this weekend."

"Thanks. He just made a score. I doubt he'll be out prowling around."

"In case he does, we're on him. We're having a task force meeting Monday morning at ten. Just wanted you to know before I send out the email."

"Good."

"We were working on collecting any video from the area today so maybe we'll have something by then."

If Vincenzo wasn't absolutely convinced about Fleming's involvement previously, he was now. After his call, an idea popped into Joe's head and he decided to discuss it with Destiny.

"I need to keep watch on Fleming's activities, but he knows me and will recognize me if I'm anywhere close to him. I was thinking of a disguise of some kind so I don't look like me. Any ideas how I can do that?"

"Hmmm. Let me think."

"I'm not talking *Mission Impossible*."

"That's fiction, not reality. That kind of stuff would never look real up close. But you can change your appearance a lot with a wig, facial hair, and glasses."

"That's doable."

"But it has to be quality stuff. You can spot a cheap wig a mile away."

"Okay, but where would I go to get good quality stuff?"

She thought for a moment and said, "I volunteer usher at a theatre on Dearborn. I could call the house manager and see if he could put me in touch with their costume department. Someone there would surely know of a professional makeup artist in town."

"It would be great if you could do that. This is out of my league."

Destiny began pressing keys on her phone, looking up something. "I thought so. There's a performance tonight, so I can call John and speak with him before they open the house."

That evening, Destiny called John Matthias, the theatre's house manager, and wanted to know if someone on staff could put her in touch with a professional makeup artist in the city. She was expecting him to say he would check with the costume people, but instead, he said, "Oh, I know somebody. Hold on. We give him comp tickets once in a while for work he does for us."

He tapped some keys on his computer. "Yeah. His name is Wally Kozlov. He's a very talented guy, but he takes a little getting-used-to."

"Oh. How's that?" asked Destiny.

"He's rather bohemian. Lives in a warehouse by himself and makes a living manufacturing body parts for horror film freaks and Halloween. You know, severed heads, arms, hands, those sorts of things. But he really knows his stuff."

"I see."

"And whenever a film shoots in town, they hire him as an assistant make-up artist."

John gave Destiny Wally's phone and address. "Tell him I sent you. He'll be cool with that. He keeps strange hours–works between noon and midnight every day. And I need to warn you–he doesn't have much of a filter. He says what he thinks."

"Okay."

"When are you ushering for us, again?"

"Next weekend. I'm looking forward to seeing another O'Neill play."

"This one's great. I'll look forward to seeing you."

After the call ended, Destiny looked at Joe. "Well, I've got someone for you, but I think I'd like to tag along if you don't mind." She smiled. "He makes body parts for a living."

Joe paused. "So, you think I might need backup?"

She laughed. "No, I want to meet this guy. Here. Call him." She handed him the notepad with the phone number.

"Now?" Joe looked at his watch. "It's twenty after eight on a Saturday night."

"John said he works from noon to midnight seven days a week. Just tell him that John Matthias gave you his number. He'll be cool with that."

Joe was somewhat reluctant to call, but he dialed the number and a man answered.

"Yeah?"

"Is this Wally Kozlov?"

"Who wants to know?"

"John Matthias gave me your number, and…"

Suddenly, the voice on the other end warmed up. "Oh, yeah. How is John?"

"He's fine."

"That's good. What do you want?"

"My name's Joe Erickson, and I'm a detective investigating the serial murders and–

"Holy shit! I didn't have anything to do with those."

"That's not why I'm calling. I'm in need of some disguise for surveillance purposes, and John said you could help me out."

"Oh! Is that it? Ah, no problem. Come on over. I can fix you up with anything you want."

"When?"

"How about now?"

"Now?"

"Why not?"

"I can't now."

"Tomorrow, then."

"Okay. Uh…What time?"

"Any time after 12:30. I don't get up until noon. John give you my address?"

"Yeah."

"Fine. Ring and I'll buzz you up." Then Wally abruptly hung up.

Joe laughed. "That was some phone call."

"John warned me he doesn't have a filter. He says whatever he thinks."

"It looks like we have a date with Wally Kozlov at a time of our choosing after 12:30 tomorrow. Are you up for it?"

"Oh, yeah. Sounds like an adventure."

At 1:00 pm Sunday, Joe and Destiny rang the bell on the door of a warehouse building in Greektown. A terse voice came over the speaker.

"Yeah?"

"It's Joe Erickson."

"Take the stairs to the second floor." His answer was followed by a buzz that unlocked the door.

Joe and Destiny climbed the steel and concrete stairs to the second floor. The building had the faint odor of chemicals and dust. A thin man in his early forties with his hair pulled back into a ponytail met them in the hallway.

"I take it you're Joe. Who's she?"

"This is my partner, Destiny Alexander. She's a criminal profiler."

"Oh. Well, whatever. Follow me." He turned and they followed him down the hall to a green door. Resembling a macabre setting for a horror classic, the place had realistic body parts hanging from the ceiling and grotesque heads and gruesome torsos sitting on shelves.

"You like my office?"

"I haven't seen one quite like it," said Joe. "You ever get any weird requests?"

"I had this TV personality from LA ask me to make him a seven-inch penis once. I'll have to tell you the story sometime."

Destiny looked at Joe and smiled.

"But, you're here for a disguise. You're clean-shaven so I can give you a mustache, a goatee, a wig, and I've got a lot of glasses to choose from. Go sit in that barber chair over there by the mirrors."

Wally left and went through some curtains.

A minute later, Wally was back with some boxes. He opened one and removed a wig about the same dark brown color as Joe's hair.

" You don't want to deviate much from your own natural color or it won't look right. I mean, if I put a blonde wig on you, you'd look like the co-star of a drag show."

Wally slipped the wig on Joe's head and adjusted it. Then, he took a brush and began styling it. "This is mostly human hair, so it looks natural. And it has a part that has skin showing through. It's longer than your own hair. You might have to use some hairspray to hold it in place."

Wally reached in another box and removed a pair of men's aviator-style glasses. He gave them to Joe and said, "Here, put these on. They have clear lenses. Now turn and take a look in the mirror."

Joe turned and looked at his reflection. His appearance had changed significantly. But Wally wasn't done. He reached into still another box and removed a clear plastic case that contained a dark mustache along with a small bottle of amber liquid. He laid the mustache on the table, removed the cap and brush from the bottle, and began lightly brushing the back of the mustache.

"This is spirit gum. You use it to stick the mustache on."

When he was done, he attached it to Joe's lip.

"Now, look at yourself in the mirror. Think you would be recognized looking like this?"

"I don't think so. Especially if I dress differently."

"I can add a goatee, too, if you want."

"I think this is good."

"You have to remove the spirit gum with acetone and clean the back of the mustache with acetone as well. It's a pain in the ass to be honest. Like I said, it's better if you can grow your own."

"I can. Ten days and I'll have a good one."

"Mm. I can't wait," said Destiny, smiling.

"Partner, huh," laughed Wally.

Joe ignored him and asked, "How do I hold this wig on?

"I'll give you some special tape to use for the front and back."

"Now, I was thinking of a second disguise, clothes that a homeless guy would wear."

"I got just the thing." And Wally once again disappeared and returned with a long, dark gray trench coat that was threadbare and worn, and a dark blue stocking cap. "Try these on."

Joe removed the wig and put on the cap and the coat, then looked at himself in the mirror. "Perfect."

"Tell you what. Go to a Goodwill or Salvation Army store and get yourself baggy pants, a sweatshirt, an old pair of tennis shoes, and gloves you can cut the fingers out of. You'll look the part."

With the wig back in place, Wally gave it a bit of a trim, showed Joe how to use the toupee tape, and remove and clean the mustache with acetone. When asked how much they owed him for all the materials, he said, "Catch this guy, and you don't owe me anything. Just bring the wig and moustache back when you're done."

Joe thanked him and handed Wally his card saying if he ever needed Joe's help, to call him.

"Sure you don't need a bloody arm or a severed head? How about a seven-inch penis?"

"Already got one," said Destiny, indicating Joe with her eyes. That sent Wally into gales of laughter.

When they got out onto the street, Destiny said, "You see why I wanted to come along? You can't get entertainment like that on television."

"You can say that again."

Chapter Forty-Three

B efore Monday morning's meeting of the task force, detectives assembled in the conference room discussing the latest murder. Sam and Joe weren't in the room yet because they were consulting with Lieutenant Vincenzo. Most of the detectives didn't know much beyond what they had heard on the news and emails they had exchanged, but it was rumored that Joe was somehow tied to the victim.

Promptly at 10:00 am, Joe, Sam, and Vincenzo walked into the room. Vincenzo plugged in a laptop.

He began by saying, "You probably already heard there was another murder Friday evening. This one hit close to home. The victim was Joe's physical trainer and friend. Her name was Anita Moore." Vincenzo pushed a key on his laptop, and a photo of smiling Anita inside The Fitness Center appeared on the screen.

"Anita Moore was a thirty-six-year-old African-American woman who was employed as an assistant manager at The Fitness Center of Chicago for the past eleven years." He keyed the laptop again, and Anita's body appeared. Joe looked away.

"The mutilation of Anita Moore is consistent with all the other victims of our killer. However, in this case, there are two significant differences. First, it did not take place in the victim's residence. We think the reason for that is the victim didn't live alone like the others. She lived with a partner. Secondly, all the other victims fit a particular physical type: white, long dark hair, and medium height. Anita Moore was African-American, had short hair, and was five-foot-two."

"Now, Joe believes this was an attempt at intimidation, and the killer used the attack on his friend to send him a message. He'd been surveilling our person of interest and had a confrontation with him in a bar and grill nine days ago. At the time of the murder, Joe was surveilling his house, and it appeared Michael Fleming was home. Lights were being turned on and off, and there was no indication he had left or returned to his residence via Uber or taxi. Shortly before Joe got the call about the homicide, Fleming opened his garage door and pushed his garbage can to the curb for pick-up on Monday. For all intents and purposes, Joe appears to be his alibi for the time of the murder."

"Are we barking up the wrong tree with this guy?" asked Dempsey.

"No," Joe piped up. "There's something about Michael Fleming that doesn't add up."

"Then, why can't we find anything on him?"

Joe's temper simmered. "Because I think Fleming is one of the smartest criminals we've ever come up against. He plans to the nth degree. He figures out where surveillance cameras are, changes clothes to alter his appearance, and knows how to establish an alibi when he needs one."

"I agree," concurred Vincenzo. "When I look at all the circumstantial evidence we have, all the coincidences, the two bodies from Arizona...he's our best bet right now."

"What about the DNA on Deanna Frost's body?" asked Cardona. "If it wasn't David Burton's brother, who the hell was it ?"

"I don't know," said Vincenzo. "That's got me stumped."

Joe got to thinking and decided to throw caution to the wind and bring up his theory. The worst that could happen would be to get ridiculed for it.

"I mentioned this to Sam a few days ago. Sherlock Holmes said, 'When you have eliminated the impossible, whatever remains, however improbable, must be the truth.' So...What if David Burton is still alive?"

The detectives reacted with surprise. Then Vincenzo, in a move that surprised even Joe, said, "Go on. Let's hear it."

"David Burton was brilliant. He had a very high I.Q. He could have planned a way to fake his own death and done it so that no one would have ever suspected. Then, he could take on the identity of another person. And if it was a person with little or no family, he could get away with it. Sounds improbable, I know, but not impossible for someone with a brilliant criminal mind."

Everyone in the room was silent as they digested the idea. Vincenzo was the first to speak. "That would explain the DNA on Deanna Frost's body."

Joe continued. "What if he killed Deanna Frost, and in the process, accidentally nicked himself with the scalpel and left a drop of blood. The pathologist told me the swab with the DNA was taken from her navel. If he left a drop of blood, he probably tried to clean it up but didn't succeed in getting every trace out of the folds ."

After a few moments, Eddie Collins spoke up. "Then, why are we chasing Michael Fleming if David Burton is still alive?"

"Good question," said Nelson.

"What if Michael Fleming is actually David Burton?" asked Joe.

"Isn't that a stretch?" asked Cardona. "I mean, Michael Fleming has been a funeral director in Chicago for what?"

"Three years."

"The only way to know for sure is to get his DNA or his fingerprints," said Dempsey. "And we're not going to be able to get a court order for that. We don't have probable cause."

"He goes to bars and tries to hustle women. I might be able to get the glass he drank out of when he leaves," said Joe. "That could prove the identity issue."

"And link him to the murder," said Vincenzo.

"And don't forget his cat," said Joe. "We can still test his cat's DNA, too."

"What's this about cat DNA?" asked Eddie.

Joe went on to explain how cat hairs were found at all the murder scenes, and that none of the victims owned a cat. Then he explained how he noticed Fleming's suit had animal hair on it and how he obtained a sample, sent it to forensics, and that they confirmed the same type.

"And I found out from a vet's office that Fleming owns that breed of cat," said Sam.

"And you're telling me somebody can do a DNA test on cat hair?" asked Eddie.

"Yeah, a lab at the University of California at Davis can," said Joe.

Vincenzo popped up, "I'm not putting in a requisition for a god damned DNA test on cat hair!"

Joe realized he had pushed Vincenzo's Pissed-Off Button. "The head of the lab said he'd do it for us free of charge. I checked," said Joe, trying to calm Vincenzo.

"Free?" asked Vincenzo.

"Yeah, he said he wanted to help out, given the situation."

"We'll need a sample from his cat then, not his suit."

Vincenzo keyed the computer again and a photo appeared of a man wearing a fedora, glasses, and a windbreaker. He was carrying a Barnes & Noble plastic bag.

"All right. Moving on. This is our perp prior to entering The Fitness Center. The picture is the best one we have from surveillance cameras. The hat and windbreaker are similar to the ones worn by the perp leaving the scene of the Kylie Welch murder. We think he left by the back door. We don't have any video of anyone matching the description after this time, so it's assumed he changed his appearance before he made his getaway and then blended into foot traffic. We've looked at the video, and we haven't seen anyone carrying a bag like the one he entered with."

"Like I said," Joe added. "He had this planned, and he executed it flawlessly. And all the time I was watching his house, watching lights turn on and off. I thought he was home."

"You can program your lights to do that," said Nelson.

"And a taxi service could have dropped him off four blocks away, and he could have walked to his house and entered through a window or a back door. You wouldn't have known," said Sam.

"We checked the dumpsters in the area for hats and windbreaker, found nothing," said Vincenzo. "So, he either figured out a way to carry the stuff with him or stash it somewhere and come back for it. Or cleverly dispose of it."

After splitting duties for the investigation which included checking taxi services and dropping off fares in the area, the meeting broke up. Joe planned to conduct more research on Michael Fleming's background. Later in the day, he went to a Salvation Army store and bought items Wally Kozlov suggested. He found a baggy pair of old suit pants, a faded blue sweatshirt two sizes too large, a pair of black knit gloves he could cut the fingers out of, and a pair of black tennis shoes in his size. His homeless-man costume was now complete. After he aged it with dirt and grime, and it would be ready to wear.

He then looked through the clothes for something that would work for his new mustachioed image. He found a black leather blazer that was a good fit and gave him enough room for his Glock. He found a black and grey checked shirt that went with it. Each worked with jeans. Not an outfit he would choose to wear, but it would work well for his alter-ego. He'd test it Friday evening if Fleming decided to go out hustling.

Joe decided to surveil Fleming every night. He figured Fleming anticipated being watched on weekends, and Joe assumed he might change tactics and start prowling during the week. He exchanged the gray Challenger for a blue Impala this week and set up different surveillance locations.

On Friday night, Joe followed Fleming's Uber to a bar on North Sheffield Avenue. Joe walked into the bar wearing his new disguise. He saw Fleming roaming around trolling for women. As Joe headed for the bar to order a drink, he noticed two women come in. One was Fleming's style: mid-twenties, tall, long, dark hair just past the shoulder. The other one was about the same age but short and blonde. Fleming immediately walked over and started talking to them. Shortly before midnight, Fleming left.

Joe then went up to the two women, showing his police ID.

"Ladies, the man you were speaking with tonight is under surveillance by the police at the present time. And I would advise you to have nothing to do with him from now on."

"You're kidding," said the brunette."

"Are you serious?" asked her friend.

"Deadly serious." He handed each one of them his card. "Did you give him your phone numbers or addresses?

"No, we didn't," both women said.

"Good. But he may be able to find you if he knows your names. Should he try to contact you or come to your apartment, you need to call me immediately no matter what time of day or night, okay?"

"Omigod," responded the brunette. "He didn't seem like the dangerous type."

"He was a really, like charming guy," said the blonde.

"He invited us to this bar in the Lincoln Square neighborhood tomorrow night. Said it would be a fun time."

"Do *not* go there. I can't emphasize that enough. And don't come back to this bar again for a while. If you see him somewhere else, don't mention that I talked to you. I'm going to continue to watch him, and I don't want my cover blown. Do you have a car here?"

"No, we called an Uber a few minutes ago"

"Great. Well, goodnight ladies. And take care." Joe watched as the two women got into their Uber, satisfied he had prevented another possible murder.

* * *

Joe spent Saturday with Destiny. He wondered if Michael Fleming was watching them.

At 4:30, Joe was set up watching Fleming's house from a corner a block and a half away. Like clockwork, an Uber showed up at 8:00. Joe followed it to a bar and grill on North Lincoln Avenue.

When Joe walked into the bar, he looked around for Fleming but didn't see him. He nursed a beer for forty-five minutes and was about to order another when Fleming walked up to the bar between him and another man, and said, "Bartender!" Joe didn't see him but recognized his voice. Fleming didn't notice him. When the bartender walked over, Fleming handed him his glass, and said, "Here you go, sir. Have a good evening." Then he went out the door. Joe watched him get into his Uber and drive away.

Chapter Forty-Four

On Monday, Joe got a call from Maude, his dad's next-door neighbor.

"I hope you don't think I'm meddling, but your father took a fall yesterday. I went over to see him this morning, and he had quite a shiner on his left eye. He said he tripped over a throw rug and hit his face against the coffee table."

"Oh, jeez! Did he seem all right otherwise?"

"Yes. But I've noticed he doesn't get out like he used to. You know how he used to go down to the Community Center?"

"Yeah."

"He doesn't do that anymore. He just sits around the house all the time. I bring him a treat now and then, and we talk. But he doesn't seem like the same old Carl since Monte died."

"Sounds like he's depressed. Does he go to church?"

"That's about the only time he leaves the house. I'm worried about him."

"I'll give him a call. It's been a week since I've talked with him. I've been so busy up here, I've been negligent about calling. And he seldom calls me, of course."

"Oh, I know how he is. I'll keep an eye on him for you."

"Thanks, Maude. You're still my sweetheart."

Maude laughed. "Well, of course I am. You take care, now."

Joe wondered if his dad really tripped over a throw rug like he said or if it could have been something else. A TIA, maybe? Or minor heart attack. Joe called his dad.

"I suppose Maude called you, huh?"

"She was concerned about you, Dad."

"Meddlesome old bitty!"

"No, she's not. I told her to keep an eye on you for me, and that's what she was doing. She told me you have quite the shiner."

"Yeah. Well, I wouldn't except for the damned blood thinner I have to take. Makes it look worse than it is. I bump my hand the tiniest bit, and I get a purple bruise the size of Rhode Island. The damned stuff is..."

"Necessary," Joe filled in the blank. "How did it happen?"

"I think I tripped over the throw rug."

"You think? You mean, you don't know?"

"Well, I hit my head and I knocked myself out for a few seconds, so I don't remember exactly."

"You're sure it was a few seconds?"

"Yeah, I think so. Family Freud was still on."

Joe knew his dad liked to watch reruns of Family Feud, but the channel played one show after the other, so he could have laid there unconscious for half an hour or more and the show would still be playing.

"Did you happened to look at the clock?"

"No, I didn't. I got up and went into the kitchen and got some ice and held it to my face for a while."

"I think you should call the doctor, just to be on the safe side."

"Why? I tripped. Big deal."

"You don't know that. You're taking a blood thinner. A blow to the head could have serious consequences. You could have passed out from some other condition. You need to have it checked out."

"I'm fine, now. I feel fine. I might look like I went ten with Sugar Ray Robinson. But I'm fine."

Stubborn old fart! "All right. I can't make you do what's right. But if you start to feel funny or find yourself on the floor again, you'd better do something about it. I'm serious. Don't make me come home from Chicago and haul you to the doctor."

"I won't. I can take care of myself."

"And I'll be checking in a little more often. I should have been calling you more often anyway."

"It's always good talking to you, Joe. Call whenever you want."

Joe was frustrated by Carl's stubborn refusal to go to the doctor. That was nothing new. But Joe noticed a change in his dad's voice. It had lost some of its rich timber and gained a breathier quality. Maybe it was due in part to age, but the change seemed more pronounced during the last few times they'd spoken. He feared his dad was going downhill.

Sam walked over to Joe's desk to tell him they'd located a cab driver who dropped off a fare on West Hollywood Avenue in the vicinity of Fleming's address on the evening of Anita Moore's murder. Dempsey and Collins were checking into it.

"We may finally have something."

"Yeah, let's hope so. But Fleming doesn't make mistakes like that."

"There's a first time for everything, Joe."

When Dempsey and Collins returned, they met in the conference room with the other members of the task force. Collins took the lead.

"The cab driver, Jemal Chaudri, a Pakistani immigrant, said he picked up a male passenger at Navy Pier at approximately 8:30 pm and drove him to an address on West Hollywood Avenue, arriving sometime around 9:00 pm. The address is three blocks from Fleming's house. The driver described the passenger as white, middle-aged with dark hair, wire-rim glasses, mustache, wearing a White Sox baseball cap. That's all he could remember. And he said the guy didn't speak English, only spoke Spanish ."

"Said he was a good tipper, too," added Dempsey.

"That's it?" asked Vincenzo.

"Pretty much."

"The description doesn't sound much like Fleming," said Cardona.

"Unless he was disguising himself," countered Joe. "Which is what I would do."

"All right," said Vincenzo. "Let's get a composite sketch drawn up and have uniforms canvas the area. See if anyone lives in the vicinity that matches the description. Eddie, you want to get the cab driver in here and match

272

him up with a forensic artist?"

"Sure, Lieutenant."

Vincenzo stood up. "Back to work."

When Joe and Sam reached their desks, Joe said, "You know what I think? He took a taxi to Navy Pier. That's where he changed identities. I'd be willing to bet he was under-dressed and peeled off his outer shirt and pants, tossed the hat, and pulled out another. Then he changed glasses and put on a fake mustache. He could have made the change in a couple of minutes. From there he could have picked up a taxi for the ride to his neighborhood."

"That would take some serious planning."

"It's why he hasn't been caught."

* * *

Surveillance cameras at Navy Pier captured images of a man fitting the description of the suspect entering the area but no footage of him leaving. However, they found footage of a man with a mustache wearing a t-shirt and a White Sox baseball cap leaving Navy Pier a few minutes later. No footage was found of that person entering the area at any time. Joe's theory appeared to be accurate.

The composite sketch of the man described by the taxi driver lacked specifics since he couldn't give any details about the man's face other than he had a mustache and wore wire-rimmed glasses. The sketch artist had to improvise Latino features. The drawing looked rather generic but at least gave the police something to show residents.

Canvasing the neighborhood resulted in nothing. Uniforms going door to door reported no one fitting the description living in the area, and no one saw anyone resembling the composite sketch. If it was Fleming, he made it home. If it wasn't, the person could have walked several blocks, called another cab, and rode to yet another location to cover his tracks.

Wednesday evening, Fleming drove to the funeral home . Another death call. Joe followed him to a nursing home.Thursday evening, Fleming stayed home. No activity other than the lights going out at 11:35 pm.

* * *

Friday night was true to form. An Uber picked up Fleming and took him to a bar on North Sheffield Avenue, a place Fleming had visited before. As soon as Joe entered, he went over to the bar and ordered a drink. Joe drank two-thirds of his beer over a period of fifteen minutes when he finally saw Fleming out of the corner of his eye. He was standing at the end of the bar. In the long mirror behind the bar, Joe could see Fleming's reflection, and he appeared to be giving Joe a close look. *Wonderful!* Joe decided to down the rest of his beer and make a trip to the restroom.

Joe was in one of the stalls when someone pounded on the door.

"I know who you are, you son-of-a-bitch!" yelled Fleming. "Now, come out of there and stop trying to hide!"

Joe swung open the door and landed a right cross on Fleming's chin which dropped him like a sack of potatoes. Joe jumped on top of him pushing his face into the tile floor. He growled in a throaty voice, "I don't know who you're after asshole, but it's not me!"

Then Joe got up, left the stunned Fleming lying in spittle on the floor, and walked out of the bar. He had to admit, flattening Fleming was very satisfying. As Joe watched, a blue Kia pulled up in front of the bar and Fleming slid inside. Joe followed the Kia within two blocks of Fleming's house. Fleming crawled out of the Kia and went inside his home. *Sleep tight, Michael. Better ice that jaw first!*

* * *

On Saturday, Joe called Wally Kozlov.

"Joe Erickson! Nice to hear from you again! What can I do for you?"

"Well, for one, I want to return the wig and mustache. Didn't need the mustache. And second, I need a different wig. I can't use this one anymore."

Joe went on to explain what happened in the restroom.

"You punched him out! I love it!" Wally said, laughing. "Yeah, come on over and I'll fix you up."

Joe called Destiny and asked if she wanted to go with him. "Are you kidding? Of course, I do."

When they reached Wally's shop, he said,

"Nice mustache you got there. Can you grow a goatee?"

"Yeah, that wouldn't be a problem."

"Then do it. I got a different kind of wig in back. Let me get it." Wally went into his backroom and came out with a curly wig and glasses. He put the wig on Joe's head and fiddled with it. "There, what do you think?"

Destiny said, "Now, that's different."

"One more thing," said Wally.

Joe put on a pair of John Lennon-style wire-rimmed glasses. Quite a different look than the aviators.

"Wow," said Joe.

"You look like an English Lit professor I had in college," Destiny said.

"Okay. So, you think this will work?"

"Yeah, it'll work."

Chapter Forty-Five

Michael Fleming was fuming! His frustration grew as he thought about all the wasted weekends, the perfect targets he'd met, the plans that never made it past stage one. Was he losing his charm, his charisma? Not hardly. Those women responded like all his women did–flirting, touching, laughing at his little jokes.

Something was wrong. He'd never had such bad luck. The formula had always, always worked: find the perfect girl, flirt, make her feel special, leave her wanting more, set up a rendezvous, and lure her into his trap.

The more he thought about it, the angrier he got. Was it bad luck or was it something else? Like that god damned cop? Everything had gone without a hitch until Erickson showed up. But how could he know? Or even suspect?

He thought he'd seen Erickson in a couple of bars before he confronted him that one time. Was he crazy thinking Erickson was showing up at all these places and foiling his plans?

He kicked himself for being an idiot, so paranoid he followed some guy into the restroom convinced it was the cop. Jesus! He'd never been attacked and humiliated by anyone like that before. His jaw was still sore from the punch that laid him out. He'd make it a point never to go to that bar again for fear of running into the guy.

Fleming still suspected Erickson was watching him. To prove his suspicions were true, he cruised by Erickson's apartment each day after work to check and see if his black Camaro was in the building's parking lot. Finding it there, he drove home, satisfied he was no longer being surveilled.

Fleming sat on the leather couch in his secret room admiring his wall, fantasizing about previous kills. As he went from photo to photo, he could remember every single one in precise detail. Those memories were a such turn-on, but memories and fantasies were not what he needed.

Like a junkie, Fleming craved his next fix. That friend of Erickson's didn't count. That was payback. Besides, she wasn't his type, and he would never have her framed and hanging on his wall.

If he couldn't succeed with women in a bar, he would have to look elsewhere. He'd been unable to find a suitable woman attending a funeral. Someone like Kirsten Welch. He would have preferred her over her sister, but in the end, Kylie was an acceptable alternative. But it would probably not be wise to use the funeral home again since the police already knew he was connected to the Welch case through the funeral of the girl's mother.

Fleming went upstairs and made himself a tall gin gimlet. Fidel was waiting for him in the kitchen, swishing his tail back and forth in anticipation of a treat. Fleming reached in the cupboard and shook a cat treat into his hand, holding it out to Fidel. The cat stretched up Fleming's leg and meowed

"There you go, boy," Fleming said. "Did you earn it today? Good boy. Yes, you're a good boy, aren't you? Daddy loves Fidel, doesn't he?"

Picking up the newspaper, he began to read, coming across a news article about a big prostitution bust. That sparked an idea.

"Well, look at this, Fidel. The police busted a bunch of hookers. What do you think about that?"

Fidel looked up at him and gave a long, drawn-out meow.

"You know, you might have something there."

Chapter Forty-Six

Weeks went by and August slipped into September. Fleming left his house only on weekday evenings if he got a death call and had to go pick up a body. Otherwise, he stayed home. Fridays and Saturdays, he was on the prowl in bars around town, keeping his hunting grounds in the northern part of the city.

During the same time, Joe interceded on behalf of two women and thwarted Fleming's attempts to prey upon them. He sent them on their way, both never wanting to see Fleming again. Joe was sure that Fleming was becoming increasingly frustrated over the abrupt disappearance of women he thought he had won over. Thankfully, he had not encountered any of these women a second time. Joe didn't need one of them fessing up to Fleming a cop told her he was under surveillance for domestic abuse allegations.

Joe had become adept at changing his appearance, choosing different clothing, wearing different glasses, alternating between a goatee and a full beard. He was lucky to have whiskers that grew fast. The wig Wally prepared for him was perfect.

But, the continuing investigation began taking its toll on Joe. Most of his surveillance was not sanctioned. Although Vincenzo knew about his surveillance of Fleming on weekends, he was not aware Joe was doing it weeknights, too. Winding down became a problem when he returned home, and he would find himself sitting in his recliner just staring off into space. He battled insomnia, and when he slept, nightmares woke him up. He was having sudden flashbacks to The Fitness Center and Anita's body.

Joe was pushing himself beyond what anyone was capable of. He was doing his best to stay in shape. But the lack of sleep, the stress of surveillance, and the psychological pressure were taking their toll. Destiny tried to intervene one Saturday when they were alone together.

"Joe, you can't go on like this. You don't look good."

"I don't?"

"Have you looked at yourself in the mirror?"

"What do you mean?"

"The dark circles under your eyes. And you've become moody and pessimistic lately.

We used to do things together. Laugh and have fun. It's like you've lost interest in everything."

"Oh..." he tried to shrug off.

"And we haven't made love in two weeks."

"I'm sorry. I get home, and I'm tired but I can't seem to sleep. I drink a glass of wine, and I doze off, but I wake up an hour later. It's..."

"I know you have a lot on your plate worrying about your dad, and then there's Anita's death...I've noticed you've been grinding your teeth at night. You never used to do that. And those chronic muscle aches in your neck. It's all stress-related, Joe. You can't go on like this."

"Stop it, okay?" Joe barked. "Just stop!"

Destiny was taken aback by his outburst. She was trying to help him, but she certainly didn't expect him to suddenly fly off the handle.

"I'm sorry. I'm just trying to help."

"Well, don't!"

Silence. Destiny didn't know if she should continue or not. If she said something else, would it make matters worse? Finally, she decided to speak.

"I love you."

"I know. And I love you, too. But you don't seem to get it. I have to catch Fleming before he kills again. I...I owe it to Anita. And to all the other women he's butchered."

Destiny was determined to make her point whether Joe liked it or not. "But Anita wouldn't want you to self-destruct doing it, would she?"

Joe didn't have an answer.

"Can't others in the department help?"

"There's no money for overtime. And the detectives on nights have regular investigations to work on. The task force works specifically on this serial murder and nothing else. But they work during the day unless they're called out to another murder scene."

"Well, things can't go on the way they are now. You can't let this become an obsession. It's a job, Joe. Not a personal crusade."

Then Joe looked up at Destiny and saw the concern in her eyes. Those beautiful blue eyes were seeing through him. Letting out a breath, he said, "Don't worry about me, okay?"

"But I do," Destiny replied, and she kissed him. "I do."

* * *

For the next three weeks, Joe tailed Fleming every weeknight and to bars on Fridays and Saturdays. Then on a Thursday during the last week of September, Fleming's garage door opened, and his Lexus backed out onto the street. Joe figured Fleming had received another death call from the funeral home. He followed the white Lexus, but tonight the Wesley-Donner Funeral Home was not Fleming's destination. *What he up to?* thought Joe as he followed him to an area of the city where prostitutes plied their trade.

Fleming drove past a group of women standing on the sidewalk ready to walk up to a customer's car and negotiate a deal for sex. As he drove farther down and into the next block, he noticed a girl standing alone. She had long, dark hair, net stockings, a short leather skirt, and four-inch heels. She looked young, and Fleming's Lexus slowed as he gave her a close look.

Joe looked her over, too, as he passed by. She matched the physical characteristics of Fleming's victims. Joe turned up the next street and drove into the alley. He put on his homeless-man disguise and began walking toward the block where the young hooker was standing. He waited in the alcove of a building, and a few minutes later watched Fleming approach the girl on foot. He was carrying a small sack that looked like something from a fast-food restaurant. They spoke for a few minutes, apparently negotiating a price. After Fleming handed her some money, they disappeared into a nearby alley.

Once they were out of sight, Joe moved toward the alley. He hoped to catch Fleming with the girl and seize incriminating tools like a scalpel and a knife. He was delayed when a semi-trailer truck rolled slowly past. He made his way down the dark alley as silently as he could, until he saw an image near a dumpster. He flipped on his flashlight and saw Fleming leaning over the body of the girl, pulling down her underwear.

Seeing a homeless man, Fleming growled, "Get out of here!"

With his other hand, Joe pulled his Glock 17 and commanded, "Police! Drop the knife or I'll blow your fucking head off!"

Fleming's eyes widened, and Joe expected, even hoped, he would make an aggressive move or try to attack him so he would have an excuse to blow him away. But to his surprise, Fleming complied, and Joe heard the knife hit the concrete.

"On your knees, hands on your head!"

Again, Fleming complied, and Joe cuffed him and used his foot to push him down to the ground. As he lay on his belly, Joe warned, "You even twitch, and I'll shoot your ass." He squatted and put two fingers to the girl's neck. She was dead, a blood spot near her heart reminiscent of all the other victims. Rising, he moved the flashlight lower and saw a scalpel, zip-top bag, and a pair of blue nitrile gloves next to her thigh. He moved the flashlight up once more and saw her red manicured nails and her young face, not the look of a neglected and malnourished street kid.

Joe shined his flashlight on Fleming's face, and when he did, Fleming looked up at him with an arrogant, perverted smile. That was a mistake. Joe wiped the smile away with a hard kick to the face.

"That's for Anita, you son-of-a-bitch!" Then Joe patted Fleming down. He placed him under arrest, read him his rights, and dragged him by the collar to the mouth of the alley where he made several calls. First, he called in a homicide to dispatch, followed by a call to Vincenzo to let him know that he had caught Fleming in the act of murdering a prostitute. Then he called Margaret Kummeyer, the reporter because he promised her earlier, she would get the scoop when the arrest was made. Once the police showed up to take over the investigation, he called Destiny to let her know he'd caught the serial killer, but he was remorseful he hadn't acted fast enough to save the young girl.

"I should have gone in there sooner. If I had, she might still be alive."

"Joe, you can't blame yourself. There may have been nothing you could have done to save her."

"I don't know, but I could have charged in there. I could have…"

"When you're done, come over. I'll wait up for you, okay?"

"Okay. But it might be really late."

"It doesn't matter. I'll be up."

Joe answered questions for the uniforms. They called in the detectives from Area 1 who took over. Lieutenant Vincenzo showed up at the scene.

After Joe filled him in. Vincenzo said, "Great work, Joe. I'll see you get a commendation for this."

"I don't deserve one, Lieutenant. I wasn't able to save the girl."

Vincenzo put his arm around Joe's shoulder and led him away from the scene. "Look, you and I both know we can't save everybody, no matter how hard we try. Shit happens, that's all there is to it. She put herself out there and made herself vulnerable. That's not your fault. So, stop blaming yourself. You did your best, that's all anyone can ask of you."

"I think because I kept disrupting his plans in bars, he became desperate and started preying on hookers. I didn't expect that."

"Look at it this way. He won't be killing any more women. You made sure of that. You did good."

Not long after, Margaret Kummeyer showed up. She interviewed Joe along with anyone else who would answer her questions. She left to write her story before other members of the media arrived on the scene.

When Medical Examiner Kendra Solitsky arrived, she looked at Joe and said, "I suppose you're the one responsible for this?"

"No. Someone I arrested was."

"You look like shit if you don't mind me saying so. Why don't you go home?"

"When I can, I will."

Michael Fleming was taken to the district police headquarters, finger-printed, booked, and placed in a cell under suicide watch. He refused to answer any questions and asked for an attorney.

Joe got to Destiny's apartment at 2:30 am. She had a glass of wine waiting for him and they talked for an hour. In between, he was staring off into space. When she saw he was beginning to fade, they went to bed. Joe was asleep as soon as his head hit the pillow. Destiny cuddled up next to him, and they slept. But after about an hour, Joe suddenly awoke, sitting up in bed and startling Destiny.

"What's the matter?"

"Nightmare, again. Frightening."

She put her hand on his arm. "Well, I'm here. Try going back to sleep."

He laid back down and looked at the ceiling. "I don't know if I can. I'm wide awake."

She spoke softly into his ear, "I have a cure for that if you're interested."

Chapter Forty-Seven

Destiny let Joe sleep and had breakfast ready for him. He didn't seem to have any trouble falling back to sleep after they made love, and he slept the remainder of the night and into the morning.

When she woke him, he was annoyed she had let him sleep. "You should have gotten me up. Now, I'm going to be late for work."

"You're kidding! You're going to work? After last night?"

"Of course. There's going to be all sorts of shit to do."

"Call in sick. Take a vacation day. Reports can wait."

"Will you just back off?"

"All right. Have it your way."

He pretty much ignored her while they ate breakfast. Joe checked his email and saw there was a task force meeting scheduled for 10:00 am. He sent Vincenzo a message saying he would be there but would be in late. Joe drove home, cleaned up, and made the short trip to work.

Joe walked into the conference room, still looking ragged around the edges from stress and lack of sleep.

His fellow detectives congratulated him on the arrest, but to him, last night was both a win and a loss. Sam handed him a copy of the Chicago Tribune with Margaret Kummeyer's front-page story on the murder and the arrest.

When Vincenzo walked into the room, everyone took their seats.

"First, I want to say this task force has done a great job. The work you've put into this investigation has been exemplary, and I'm sure Superintendent Tennyson and the mayor, as well as the citizens of our city, will be relieved to know this maniac is now off the street and behind bars."

Vincenzo went on to explain the circumstances of Joe's surveillance and arrest of Michael Fleming. The victim was identified as Jamie Chambers, seventeen, a runaway from Mendota.

"Now, for the interesting part," said Vincenzo. "When Fleming was brought in last night, he was printed, and they found they were already in the system. Anyone want to hazard a guess who they belonged to?" There were no takers, so Vincenzo continued. "Joe, you didn't arrest Michael James Fleming. You arrested David Eugene Burton."

For a few seconds, the room was silent, and then there was a cacophony of responses from the detectives.

Sam leaned over to Joe and said, "Way to go, Sherlock! You were right."

"I don't know how the hell Burton pulled off this identity change," said Vincenzo. "We're going to let California figure that out. Looks to me like they cremated the wrong guy. That's their problem. But we not only have Burton for the Jamie Chambers murder, but I'm sure his DNA will be a match to the DNA taken from the body of Deanna Frost. So, we can charge him with that one, too.

"So, where does that leave the task force?" asked Nelson.

"We're done," said Vincenzo. "It's not official yet. But I think with everything we've already learned, we've got our man. I'll let you know when it's official and you can go back to your regular assignments."

"What about Fleming's...I mean Burton's home?" asked Cardona.

"A search warrant was issued and a search is being conducted as we speak. So, we're done here."

Everyone was glad to see this intense investigation come to an end. Joe was in a daze and found himself sitting, staring at his computer screen for a long time, doing absolutely nothing. Flashbacks of the alley played like an endless video loop in his mind. What he could have done differently. Preventing the killing. Walking Jamie out of the alley unharmed with Fleming in cuffs. What could have been but wasn't.

At noon, he and Sam were called to Burton's house. The detectives and the forensic team found something they would want to see.

Joe and Sam drove to the Bryn Mawr Avenue address. When they pulled up, they saw an officer leaning against the corner of the house puking his guts out.

"What the hell is that about?" asked Sam.

"Got me," said Joe.

They were met at the front door by Detective Kelly Radisson.

"Hey," said Sam. "Looks like you got a sick man out there."

"Yeah. Twenty-three years on the job, and he couldn't handle this one."

"What do you have ?"

"Follow me."

Detective Radisson took them down into the basement, opened a bookcase, revealing a carpeted room behind it. Inside was a love seat positioned so it faced a wall containing rows of frames.

"Check out the frames on the wall in there," said Radisson. "That's what made Hostler lose his lunch."

Joe and Sam walked inside and saw nineteen matching aluminum frames on the wall. A closer look revealed behind each glass was the perfectly preserved trophies Burton had taken from his victims. Each was displayed against a black velvet background and had a small engraved plaque with a woman's first name.

"Oh, my god," uttered Sam.

"Sick," whispered Joe.

"He even labeled them."

"Unbelievable."

"They look like they've been tanned, like animal hides."

"We know of eight. There are two, possibly from Mesa. But...nineteen?"

"Who are all these women?"

"I don't know. At least he's provided us with first names."

"You think they can get DNA from these?" asked Sam.

"I dunno."

Sam turned away. "Seen enough?"

"I'll never be able to un-see this. Let's go," said Joe.

As they passed a basement workbench, Sam noticed bags labeled alum, soda ash, and salt. "What the hell are those?" he asked.

"Tanning chemicals," said Joe. "He was preparing for one more."

They walked upstairs and Joe approached one of the evidence techs and asked, "What have you done with the cat?"

"What cat?"

"Burton has a rare cat, a Havana Brown. If you haven't seen it, it's probably hiding. Most likely scared to death with all the commotion going on in here. The cat is evidence, so don't let it run out the door. The cat hair you collect is important evidence, but we need the cat, too.

Joe called Evelyn Stewart-Bruce. After explaining the situation to her, she agreed to come to the scene, locate the cat, and keep it so forensics could get a sample of hair for DNA comparison.

"What will they do with it afterwards?" she asked.

"I have no idea."

"Well, I will take it upon myself to find a special home for it, if that's all right. I would not want to see it sent to a shelter."

"I'm sure that can be arranged. I don't think our murder suspect will have any objections."

"Murder suspect, indeed! I'll be there in half an hour. If anyone sees the cat, leave it alone. The poor thing is probably frightened out of its wits."

"Thank you, Evelyn."

As they passed Radisson on their way out of the house, he asked, "So, what do you think?"

Joe said, "I think I should have killed him."

Evelyn Steward-Bruce successfully retrieved Fidel from under the bed in Burton's bedroom. When questioned with his attorney present the next day, the only thing Burton was concerned about was the welfare of his feline friend, and he wouldn't cooperate until he knew his cat was safe and in good hands. Evelyn Stewart-Bruce agreed to Skype with the police to show Burton she had his beloved Havana Brown in her care. Not only that, she assured him that she "absolutely adored" his cat, and Fidel would have a special place in her own home along with her two Russian Blues. Burton bid farewell to Fidel and then broke down into tears saying Fidel was the only thing he ever loved.

Two days later, Joe went to Police Headquarters to meet with Commander Charles Reese, Area 3 Deputy Chief, and Police Superintendent William Tennyson. The brass congratulated both Vincenzo and Joe on the arrest of Burton, and after a few minutes, they were escorted into a room filled with members of the press. Joe was introduced as the arresting officer and Lieutenant Vincenzo as the Head of the Serial Killer Task Force.

"I want to commend Detective Joe Erickson of Area 3, not only for making the arrest of the suspect in this case. But it is also Detective Erickson, through his investigative skills, who uncovered the vital facts that linked six murders over the past two years. Without his diligence and research, this serial killer may not have been discovered."

Superintendent Tennyson motioned Joe forward for a photo-op moment and shook Joe's hand while camera strobes flashed over applause. Joe hated the recognition and preferred to keep a low profile. But like Destiny told him, "You need to take credit when you deserve it. And you deserve this."

Then Tennyson had Lieutenant Vincenzo step forward and said, "I also want to commend Detective Commander Lieutenant Sal Vincenzo. He and his detectives spent countless hours sifting through mountains of evidence and investigating the crimes committed by the person who has been terrorizing our city for the past two years. Lieutenant Vincenzo, the City of Chicago thanks you and your team."

But two days later, Joe was having problems. He was sitting at his desk, staring at his computer screen, unable to function. He was haunted by the face of Jamie Chambers. He couldn't get her image out of his mind. And then there was Burton's perverted smile and the frames on his wall, appearing again and again.

Joe felt a hand on his shoulder. "What's wrong, man?" Sam asked. "You seem to be in la-la-land." Sam had been Joe's partner, his best partner, his most trusted partner for a little over a year. In that time, they'd grown to know and trust one another. And Sam could sense something was going on.

"I don't know. I…I can't seem to let go, you know? There's something about this Burton case that's like...I don't know...wiped me out or something."

"What do you mean?"

"I can't focus. I get nightmares that wake me up, and I can't get back to sleep. I pick fights with Destiny. I just sit here and stare at the computer like a damned zombie. I don't know what's happened to me. I just feel pissed off all the time."

"Maybe you need to take some time off. You pushed yourself awfully hard on this case, you know what I mean? Go see Vincenzo. Take a couple of weeks. Hell, you deserve it."

"Yeah, maybe I should."

"Take some time with Destiny, and you'll be the old Joe before you know it."

Joe turned to his computer screen and began reading his email. He opened a message from Margaret Kummeyer which asked if she could interview him. *I think I've given you enough already, Margaret.*

Then his cell phone rang. He didn't look to see who the caller was before he answered it.

"Hello."

"Joe?"

"Yes?"

"This is Maude." Her voice was shaky and filled with emotion.

"Yes, Maude."

"I've got..." He could hear her break down. She quickly regained her composure and said, "I've got some bad news for you, Joe. Your...Your dad passed away..."

"Oh, no..." was all he could get out.

"After lunch, I rang the doorbell and didn't get an answer and thought he might be taking a nap. I tried again later and nothing...so I went in. He was sitting in his recliner, but he was gone. The coroner's here. He thinks it was a heart attack."

"Ohhhh..." Joe's voice trailed off into silence.

"I'm so sorry. I thought you'd want to hear it from me rather than...you know."

Joe's mind practically imploded, and all he could say was, "Thank you." Then he ended the call. Tears welled up in his eyes, and he slipped off his chair and somehow his body crawled under his desk where it curled up in a fetal position and started rocking back and forth. His cries alerted Sam who wasn't far away.

"Jesus Christ, Joe! What's going on?"

Joe didn't respond. He couldn't do anything but rock back and forth and cry.

Sam yelled out, "Need some help here!"

Cardona and several other detectives came running.

Sam said to Cardona, "Go get Vincenzo," and to another, "Call 9-1-1." Vincenzo was shocked. He crawled under the desk and tried to talk to Joe, but it was no help. Joe wasn't hearing him.

Sam reached into Joe's desk and retrieved his Glock and placed it in his own desk. "What the hell happened?" asked Vincenzo.

"I don't know," said Sam.

Vincenzo picked up Joe's phone and checked the last call Joe had received. He called it. When he connected with Maude, he found out about the death of Joe's dad, and he suspected it may have thrown Joe over the edge.

Vincenzo told the others. " It looks like Joe's had a breakdown. He needs medical attention."

Vincenzo had never seen anything like this happen to one of his detectives and he was at a loss. He tapped Sam on the arm and said, "Try talking to him. See if you can reach him, Sam."

Sam crawled under the desk and spoke softly. "Joe, whatever it is, it'll be all right, okay?"

"In a barely audible voice, Joe whispered, "My dad…" And then he started rocking back and forth again.

"You're going to be okay, buddy. You're going to be okay."

Vincenzo shooed everyone away except Sam, and within ten minutes the EMTs arrived and coaxed Joe out from under the desk, put him on a gurney, and wheeled him out of the building and into the waiting ambulance.

Vincenzo and Sam followed them to the hospital, and once there, Vincenzo made a call to Destiny. She arrived fifteen minutes later.

They waited for almost an hour before a doctor approached them.

"I'm Dr. Bellingham. Are you here about Joe Erickson?"

"Yes, we are," replied Vincenzo.

"He's resting comfortably right now."

"Can I see him?" asked Destiny.

"He's been given a sedative so he's sleeping. We're going to monitor him all night, and tomorrow, if he's up to it, we'll conduct a psychiatric evaluation. But from what I can tell, it appears he's suffered an event related to acute stress disorder. Has he been exposed to trauma recently?"

"Yes," said Destiny.

"He's a police detective, and he's pushed himself very hard conducting a murder investigation," said Vincenzo.

"And what he's seen recently is traumatic, to say the least, and he blames himself for not preventing another murder," added Sam. "Even though there's nothing he could have done."

"And what may have pushed him over the edge is a phone call he just got telling him his father died," said Vincenzo.

"Sounds like a lot," said the doctor. "I'm sure the psychiatrist in charge will want to know as many details as possible."

"Will he be all right?" asked Destiny, wiping tears from her face.

"We'll have to wait and see. We'll know more tomorrow. And now, if you'll excuse me, I have patients waiting." And with that, she turned and started to walk away.

"Can I see him, at least?" Destiny pleaded. "I'm the closest thing to family he has left."

Dr. Bellingham turned and said, "I suppose. Come with me."

Destiny followed the doctor down the hall and into a room where Joe slept.

Destiny walked up to Joe's bedside and looked down at him lying there. He was breathing normally, looking peaceful. She picked up his hand and held it in hers. It was warm. Such a strong hand but capable of so much tenderness. She didn't know how long she had been standing there, but suddenly she heard a voice.

"Excuse me, but it's time to go now." A nurse stood at the door.

Destiny leaned over and kissed Joe on the forehead. Whispering in his ear, she said, "I love you." Then she left the room.

Chapter Forty-Eight

D estiny went to the hospital each day but was not allowed to see Joe. Dr. Harold Bunsch, the psychiatrist in charge of Joe's case, had given orders that he was not to have visitors. She was finally able to schedule a meeting with the doctor.

"Doctor, I'd like to know why Joe can't have any visitors. "

"Ms. Alexander, Mr. Erickson is in no condition to see anyone. His treatment involves a combination of medication, intense therapy, and counseling. He cannot have any outside influences upsetting the balance of his therapy regimen at the present time."

"I doubt I would upset his therapy. I think seeing me would help him."

"Until he's well into his therapy, and I find out what factors contributed to his condition, I cannot assume anything. And that includes you, I'm afraid."

"Do you have any idea how long this therapy regimen may take?"

"That all depends on the patient's response. It's difficult to predict because every patient responds differently.

Destiny wasn't getting anywhere and decided to pursue another angle with him.

"Can you tell me what Joe's condition is? Did he have a nervous breakdown?"

"I can't discuss that with you," said Dr. Bunsch.

"Why not?"

"Privacy issues, of course."

"Doctor, Joe is the only child of an only child. His parents are both deceased. He has no living relatives. We're not married, but I've been his significant—"

Growing impatient, Dr. Bunsch interrupted her. "You have to understand I'm bound by the law. HIPAA. You've heard of it, I assume. If he wants you to have access to his medical information, he'll have to sign a waiver. And right now, he's not of sound mind and body to—"

At this point, Destiny had had enough. She stood up, and cut him off saying, "Dr. Bunsch, I hope you're a better shrink than you are a person." Then she walked out.

To compound matters, a week later Destiny received a phone call from Miles Beckley, a former FBI colleague, who was on the faculty at the University of California at Santa Barbara. He was one of the good guys she had worked with during her tenure with the Bureau.

"Miles. This is a surprise. Nice to hear from you."

"How are you?"

"I'm doing well, thank you. Last I heard you were teaching on the West Coast."

"UC Santa Barbara. Yeah, I'm still here."

"Great. What can I do for you?"

"Well, it might be more like what you can do for us."

"Oh?"

"We have a bit of an emergency here. Dr. Woodson, one of our senior faculty members, suffered a stroke two days ago, and it sounds like he'll have a long recovery."

"That's too bad."

"It is. He's a wonderful teacher and a great colleague. I thought of you because he's presently teaching an introductory course in forensic psychology, among others. I know your Master's is in forensic psych. We have visiting professor funds available if you'd be interested in coming out and taking over his class. If you're available, of course."

"Oh, my...I don't know what to say."

"Are you available?"

"Maybe. I'll have to check. When do you need to know?"

"As soon as possible."

"I was afraid you were going to say that. Let me give you a call tomorrow if that's all right."

"That would be great. I think you'll find Santa Barbara an agreeable place to spend some time."

Destiny took his phone number and plopped down on her couch. *What to do?* She didn't have any freelance work lined up at the moment, and while she had plenty of money in the bank, the salary from a teaching job would be welcome. But how would she keep tabs on Joe? She would need to speak with Dr. Bunsch to see if he could give her any indication as to Joe's prognosis.

When Destiny checked in again with the main desk at the hospital, she found Joe was still not receiving visitors. She asked to speak with Dr. Bunsch. After their last meeting, she was surprised he agreed to see her.

"I want to apologize for what I said the last time I was here. I was upset and should have monitored myself ."

"Apology accepted."

"The reason I'm here, Doctor, is because I find myself in a dilemma. I've been offered a teaching position effective immediately. It's at UC Santa Barbara. They've lost a faculty member, and I've been asked to step in. I need to know if I should accept it or not. I want to be here for Joe during his recovery but—you understand?"

"I do." Dr. Bunsch paused and made a church steeple with his hands. "Well, if I were you, I would accept it. First, I can't predict how long it will be before he can be released from the hospital. It's too early to tell. And secondly, I think it would be best for him to avoid any stressful situations once he's been released from our care. Sometimes a relationship can prove detrimental to a patient's recovery."

Destiny thanked Dr. Bunsch and left his office. She couldn't understand how her love for Joe could prove detrimental to his recovery. Wouldn't someone's love and support help a person recover rather than hinder it? She didn't understand the doctor's reasoning. *I guess this seals the deal. I'll call Miles and tell him I'll accept the position.*

When she got back to her apartment, she sat down with a glass of wine and thought things through one more time. Her consultancy business always ran hot and cold, and right now she wasn't receiving calls. What if Joe had to be hospitalized for months? Waiting for him to be released when she couldn't even see him didn't make any sense. So, she called Miles and told him she accepted his offer. After making a plane reservation, she packed her bags and tossed the contents of her refrigerator. Then she sat down at her desk and wrote Joe a long letter. When he arrived home from the hospital, it would be waiting for him. She hoped he would understand.

The next day, she was on a plane bound for Santa Barbara. She emailed Lieutenant Vincenzo and let him know what was going on. He said he understood and would keep her informed about Joe's condition.

* * *

Joe was released from the hospital three weeks later. A considerable amount of mail had accumulated while he was away, and he was surprised to see a letter from Destiny. She hadn't tried to email or text him, and he was curious why. His cellphone was confiscated by Dr. Bunsch anyway so it wasn't like he could have responded.

The letter was long and explained why she decided to take the temporary teaching position in California. Her thoughts about leaving him were bittersweet and her words betrayed feelings of guilt about not doing more to intervene on his behalf. She said she wished she could go back and do some things over again. She ended by giving him her love and said she looked forward to seeing him when she returned to Chicago. Logically, he understood, but not emotionally. Her absence left a wound, and that wouldn't heal easily. He read the letter again and then slipped it back into the envelope.

Joe called his dad's old friend and attorney, Foster Simmons, to find out about his dad's funeral. Foster was pleased to hear Joe's voice.

"Oh, Joe, I'm so glad you called. I was hoping I would hear from you," he said. "How are you doing?"

"Much better, thanks. Can you tell me about Dad's funeral arrangements?

I'm afraid I was in no shape to get back there."

"Well, your father left detailed instructions with me in the event of his death. I received word from Lieutenant Vincenzo telling me you were hospitalized, so I went ahead and carried out his wishes."

"What were they? He never told me anything about it."

"He wanted to be immediately cremated and interred next to your mother. He asked that in lieu of a funeral, a memorial service be held at a later date at the church followed by a reception at the Community Center where people could be served the wine he'd been collecting."

"That sounds like him."

"I have his will here, and I'll go over it with you when you return to Marathon at some point in the near future."

"That sounds fine. Thank you, Foster. You've been a good friend to Mom and Dad over the years, and I appreciate your help with everything."

"You're welcome, Joe. Take care, now."

Joe ended the call and hit Maude's number. She had a key to the house, and there needed to be some things done like emptying the refrigerator and disposing of dirty clothes. He was hoping that maybe some of the church ladies could take care of that. Doing thoughtful things for the bereaved wasn't unusual for people living in small towns. She picked up right away.

"Maude? It's Joe Erickson."

"Joe! How are you?"

"Getting better."

"Oh, I'm so glad to hear that. It sounded like you had quite a time."

"I guess that's one way to put it."

"Have you talked with Foster, yet?"

"Yes, I did. I was wondering if you could contact some of the ladies from the church and if they could come and clean out Dad's refrigerator and see if there is any laundry that needs to be done. I'm not going to be able to get there for a while."

"Oh, that's already been done," said Maude. "The house is all buttoned up."

"Really. Who did that?"

"Well, I did."

"You did?"

"Of course. It was the least I could do for you and your dad."

"Maude, you're wonderful. Anybody ever tell you that?"

"Both of my boyfriends do all the time!" said Maude, giving a long laugh that Joe knew all too well.

"Oh, Maude. You're too much."

"They say that sometimes, too!" And she cackled again.

"I'd appreciate it if you'd keep an eye on the house, and feel free to help yourself to a bottle of wine or two downstairs. I think Dad would approve."

* * *

Joe went on medical leave from the Chicago Police Department and attended counseling twice a week. He couldn't work, and he had to find things to keep himself busy because sitting around doing nothing was not an option.

He got in touch with Dennis Scott, a fellow detective who had retired a couple of years back. Dennis was a fellow gearhead, and Joe had heard Dennis had started working for a high-performance car shop. Joe had always wanted to modify his Camaro, but apartment living in Chicago made that difficult. He swung by Dennis' shop one day and reconnected with him. They discussed Joe's car. A month later, they were busy adding a supercharger and new exhaust system, as well as upgrading the suspension and adding better brakes. The result was one mean machine that was a blast to drive.

Joe took cooking classes and turned into a first-rate cook. He attended film festivals, went to an occasional play or concert, even tried the opera. He was feeling better, and his therapy sessions were cut back to once a week.

Through a couple of unfortunate incidents, Destiny and Joe failed to communicate with one another. Joe sent Destiny a Christmas card figuring he would hear from her once she received it. She sent him a card but he didn't receive it. He called her after the first of the year and left a voicemail message. After not getting a return call, he thought, *Maybe she lost interest or gave up on me. Doesn't want to be associated with a crazy person.*

Destiny was asked to stay on and teach another class the following semester. Dr. Woodson had recovered enough to teach a partial load, but they needed someone to pick up the slack. Two weeks into the semester, Destiny was driving home one Saturday evening after attending a university function when her car was t-boned by a drunk driver who ran a red light. The car slammed into Destiny's driver's side door. The impact set off the Mercedes' side airbag which probably saved her life. She was taken to the hospital, unconscious, where she was diagnosed with a concussion, a broken fibula in her left leg, several broken ribs, and a fractured humerus in her left arm. Fortunately, none of her injuries required surgery, but she was hospitalized for two weeks. Her mother flew out to be with her. Eight weeks later she was back to what she considered normal, but it would take many weeks of working out to get back in top physical condition again. Her cell phone had been destroyed in the crash, and as a result, she never received Joe's voicemail message. She wanted to phone him during her recovery, but she was afraid news of her car accident might cause him undue stress, so she decided to put it off.

In May, she left Santa Barbara for a two-week consulting job in Atlanta. She decided that when she went back home to Chicago, she could make contact with Joe again. She thought seeing each other face-to-face would be better than a phone call.

When spring rolled around, Joe was feeling well enough to return to work, but he knew he would have to secure a release signed by his shrink, and he didn't think Dr. Bunsch would give it to him. He was still bothered by occasional nightmares, but other than that, he felt good. His counseling had been reduced to once every two weeks, and he was taking only one prescription medication for depression, his "happy pills" as he referred to them.

He stayed in touch with Lieutenant Vincenzo and his fellow detectives at Area 3, sometimes putting in an appearance on the floor. They were always glad to see him, and he noticed they were keeping his desk open and ready for him the day he could return to work.

Since being released from the hospital, Joe made it a point to get up every morning at 5:30 and jog three miles. It seemed to clear his mind and give him time to think. He was convinced this physical regimen contributed to his recovery. Returning to The Fitness Center was not possible. Too many bad memories, and when he went to check out another gym, the exercise machines brought back memories of Anita and their workouts together. The horrific flashbacks were too much. He didn't know when he might feel comfortable working out in a gym again. Maybe never.

In late May, Joe decided to give Foster Simmons a call. He needed to get back to Marathon to settle his dad's estate. He was feeling antsy and thought a trip might be just the thing to blow out the cobwebs.

"Well, Joe! Good to hear your voice."

"How are things in Marathon?"

"Oh, you know Marathon. Nothing ever changes but the time of day."

"Something to be said about predictability, huh?"

"Indeed, indeed. What can I do for you?"

"I thought I would drive to Marathon and take care of dad's estate. Six months have passed, and I figured it's time to tie up loose ends."

"Of course. When were you thinking about coming?"

"First week of June. Does that work for you?"

"Sure. I'll be here. Why don't you give me a call or stop in when you get into town and we'll set up an appointment to go through the will and take care of everything."

"That works for me. It'll be nice to see you again, Foster."

"I'll be looking forward to it. You take care, now."

Joe had two weeks to prepare for the trip. He'd have to call Maude and let her know he was coming. Dr. Bunsch needed to know that he'd be out of town. His counseling sessions were voluntary now, and Joe continued with them so Dr. Bunsch would sign off on Joe's paperwork so he could go back to work. And wouldn't it be just his luck to draw a shrink who was a stickler for details.

* * *

On June 2nd, Joe packed his Camaro, locked his apartment, and headed for Iowa. Not that long ago, he was making the same trip when he found out his dad had suffered a heart attack. He wished he could have made it back one more time to see him before he passed, but things got in the way, mainly his obsession with catching David Eugene Burton. All water under the bridge now.

For the first time in his life, Joe had nothing to come home to. Time had taken it away, and he was left with only a house. He walked through the rooms and looked around. Everything still in its place. Things. Things accumulated over a lifetime.

He stood in the living room for a long time. After a few minutes had passed, he realized he had better go next door and say hello to Maude. Tomorrow would begin the process of breaking ties with Marathon and giving up a house full of memories. Then he would travel back to the Windy City, his adopted home, and get back to doing what he was destined to do: apprehend the people who snuff out the lives of others.

Acknowledgements

Jerry Fess for his cover design; Joyce Johanson, my first reader and editor; Bill Johnson, Chicago Police Department (retired); Patricia Whitaker Granstra and Jane Chalstrom Jensen; and especially Harriette Sackler, Shawn Reilly Simmons, Verena Rose, and the staff of Level Best Books.

About the Author

Lynn-Steven Johanson is an award-winning playwright whose plays have been produced on four continents. Born and raised in Northwest Iowa, Lynn holds a Master of Fine Arts degree from the University of Nebraska-Lincoln. He lives in Illinois with his wife and has three adult children.

CPSIA information can be obtained
at www.ICGtesting.com
Printed in the USA
JSHW030744130721
16853JS00001B/7

9 781953 789587